MW01135200

THE LAST DAYS
VOLUME 4

End
of the
World

Books by Kenneth Tarr

The Last Days Series
Gathering Storm
Pioneer One
Promised Land
End of the World

Middle Grade
Birdlegs (coming in October 2014)

THE LAST DAYS
VOLUME 4

End of the World

Kenneth R. Tarr

This is a work of fiction, and the views expressed herein are the sole responsibility of the author. Likewise, certain characters, places, and incidents are the product of the author's imagination, and any resemblance to actual persons, living or dead, or actual events or locales, is entirely coincidental.

End of the World (Last Days Series #4)

Published by Truebekon Books

Copyright © 2014 by Kenneth R. Tarr
Photo copyright © Tumarkin Igor
Cover design copyright © 2013 by ePubMasters
Ebook design by ePubMasters

All rights reserved. No part of this book may be scanned, uploaded, reproduced, distributed, or transmitted in any form or by any means whatsoever without written permission from the author, except in the case of brief quotations embodied in critical articles and reviews. Thank you for supporting the author's rights.

ISBN: 978-1-500866-52-5

Printed in the United States of America
Year of first electronic printing: 2014

To my dear wife, Kathy, who kept me alive long enough to write this novel, and to my daughter Rachel whose help and encouragement made the book possible.

Israel and Its Neighbors

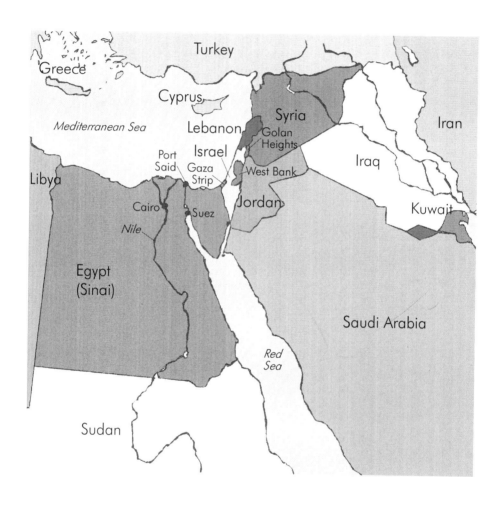

Close-up of Israel

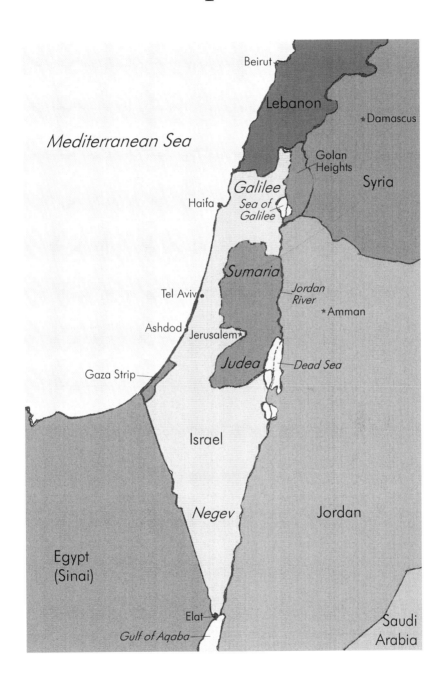

Cast of Characters in *End of the World*

Adelstein, Elazar: Major general, chief of the Israeli air force.

Adler, Lewis: Head genealogist for a London firm of twenty researchers.

al-Boutros, Ibn 'abbas: President of Syria.

Aldridge, Colton: UGOT's lead false prophet.

al Kadir, Abd: Jordanian lieutenant general, second-in-command to King Hussein.

Babcock, Jarrad: Paul's best friend. A lieutenant in Zion's army. Killed in Israel.

Baranski, Lucius: Israeli colonel.

Benson, Randolph: UGOT's associate to the Middle East.

Benson, Wilford: President and prophet of the Church.

Berg, Izaak: Israeli brigadier general.

Cartwright, Douglas: President of the republic of Zion.

Chorney, Yeshaya: Lieutenant general, chief of the General Staff of the IDF.

Christopher, Steven: Central story hero, now age fifty-eight.

Christopher, Mary: Central story heroine, now age fifty-three.

Christopher, William: Oldest son of Steven and Mary, age thirty-five.

Christopher, Andrew: Steven and Mary's son, killed in *Promised Land*, resurrected in *End of the World*.

Christopher, Daniel: Steven and Mary's youngest son, falls in love with Rachel Salant.

Christopher, John: Steven's younger brother, age fifty-four.

Christopher, Paul: Steven's younger brother, age forty-five.

Cohen, Abir: One of David Omert's five war ministers.

Danziger, Phineas: Israeli major general of Russian ancestry. Also a war minister.

Delisle, Lucienne: Galloway's French mistress and associate to North America, age fifty-one.

Drescher, Konrad: One of the two generals chosen by Galloway to lead his private army.

Eidelman, Ruben: Israeli colonel who greets John on his return from the southern Negev.

Fatemah: Iranian colonel serving under Major General JahAngir Massoud.

Fischer, Danny: Israeli brigadier general.

Galloway, Gerald O.: English billionaire, world leader of UGOT, age 72.

Hadad, Zaahir: Leader of the abortive Syrian attack on Israel from the Golan Heights.

Hirsch, Binyamin: Israeli colonel serving under Brigadier General Hugo Tandler.

Hussein bin Abdullah: King of Jordan.

Isaacs, Ephrem: Youngest and shortest of Israel's two prophets.

Jamison, Michael: Mormon general in charge of Zion's forces in Israel.

Jamshad: Iranian lieutenant colonel serving with Commander JahAngir Massoud.

Johnston, Ruther (Ford): Old mountain man who journeys to Zion with Pioneer One and later to Israel. Made a colonel by President Cartwright.

Kassis, Da'iyat: President of Egypt. Resembles Gamal Nasser.

Khoury, Aali: Prime minister of Lebanon.

Krupin, Anatoli: The Russian colonel who informs Galloway that no Americans have landed recently at Ashdod.

Laurent, Pascal: One of the two generals chosen by Galloway to lead his private army.

Lazar, Mosheh: Chief of the first contingent of the Ten Tribes. Chosen to be a colonel in Zion's forces heading for Israel.

Levin, Jacan: Oldest and tallest of Israel's two prophets.

Mahmoud al-Mamoun: Egyptian President.

Massoud, JahAngir: Commander of the Iranian army that makes the first attack of the UGOT coalition armies east of Jerusalem.

Metzger, Chagai: One of David Omert's five war ministers.

Moskal, Beth: Israeli colonel, originally stationed in Galilee.

Mustafa, Wadi: Egyptian lieutenant under Colonel Sarkis at the Straits of Tiran.

Nahas, Taban: Traitorous leader of Hezbollah forces stationed in southern Lebanon.

Nigel, Lucas: Flattering earth name chosen by Lucifer.

Omert, David: Second David and king of Israel. Holds off UGOT's forces by brilliant strategies, age fifty-one.

Parmet, Ronen: Jewish colonel who leads a unit west across the northern Sinai.

Radzik, Aaron: Prime minister of Israel, in power just before Omert is made ruler.

Raphan, Yaakov: A leader of the Ten Tribes, later chosen to be a lieutenant colonel in Zion's forces heading for Israel.

Reuben, Varda: Israeli colonel.

Ribicoff, Seth: Israeli lieutenant colonel.

Rieckel, Raanan: Israeli chief of Camp Ashdod. Welcomes second group from Zion.

Sarkis, Qaasim: Egyptian colonel who closes off the Straits of Tiran with artillery.

Shamon, Faruq: Palestinian president.

Stoller, Ofek: President of the Chief Rabbinate of Israel.

Sun, Deshi: Chinese general, commanding officer of the great Chinese army.

Tandler, Hugo: Israeli brigadier general in charge of the First Division.

Urbach, Heru: tIsraeli major general commanding the Fifth Division fighting in Gaza.

Vorhaus, Elkan & Mical: A young Jewish couple killed in Tel Aviv by a Hamas rocket.

Walmann, Herschel: Jewish major serving under Colonel Parmet in the Sinai.

Whitman, Marcus: UGOT's associate in charge of Western Europe.

Widtsoe, Jason: Senior LDS apostle.

Yankel, Efren: One of David Omert's five war ministers.

Yehoshua, Chaim: Israeli war minister, best friend of David Omert.

Zadok, Harrod: One of David Omert's five war ministers.

Prologue

The terrible tribulations predicted in prophecies of the last days began in the Lord's house in the Rocky Mountains. From there, natural disasters, diseases, and civil disruptions spread across the United States like a virulent plague. These events made governments at all levels reel to and fro like a drunken man, and the total collapse of the federal government was hastened by a wicked, worldwide conspiracy. Soon the same tribulations were visited upon the nations of the entire planet.

During these extremities, the LDS prophet sent the first contingent of saints, called Pioneer One, across the barren, mob-infested plains to establish a new nation in the land promised as the center stake of Zion, and these faithful modern pioneers answered the call and did the work, followed by later companies of hardy saints. Eventually, they built the New Jerusalem with its marvelous new temple, and they created the greatest and freest nation the world has ever seen, a nation prospered by the power of God and destined to fill the earth.

It was in Daviess County, Missouri, that Adam, the father of the human race, came and presided over the great conference of Adam-ondi-Ahman, at which Christ himself appeared to declare himself to be the king over all the nations of the earth, according to the will of the Father, and to receive all the priesthood keys of past dispensations. In addition, the Lost Ten Tribes came forth from the lands of the north, after enduring many trials and great suffering, bringing with them the words of the Lord that were given to their prophets of ancient times, and soon they united with the saints as one people.

As New Zion grew, it welcomed millions of poverty-stricken immigrants from every country in the world, people who sought nothing more than peace and the freedom to worship as they pleased. The new nation quickly began to spread across the American continent and increased in power and splendor, striving to live by celestial laws.

Yet soon they learned of a new threat. The same secret combination of evil that had helped to topple the American government declared open war on the tiny nation of Israel, another branch—though a wayward one—of the covenant people of the Lord. In view of the overwhelming forces arrayed against Israel, how could it survive, and what could New Zion do to help?

PART ONE

Armageddon

Chapter 1

In a grove of trees near the commune of Nanterre, a suburb of Paris, Gerald Galloway sat on a shaded bench in early spring. A soft morning breeze whispered among the trees and made their bright green leaves shimmer. He was there to contemplate what he should say to his collaborators at the meeting soon to take place in his private compound located nearby. As the supreme leader of UGOT, the Universal Government of the Twelve, Galloway was determined to motivate them with powerful, inspiring words.

He looked up at the sound of movement not far away. A tall, dark-haired man was walking slowly toward him. Gerald cursed under his breath, for he hated to be interrupted just when he needed to think.

"Good morning, my friend," said the tall man.

"Yes, isn't it?" Gerald replied, his voice heavy with irritation.

"Am I disturbing you?" the man said with a smile.

"As a matter of fact, you are."

"I'm sorry, Gerald."

"How do you know my name? Who in the blazes are you?"

The newcomer's eyes flashed, and he smiled even wider. "I know all about you. Don't you recognize me? My name is Lucas Nigel. You and I have talked many times."

"I have never seen you before and I don't recognize your name. You must be insane."

Lucas laughed. "Well, I *can* get a bit crazy sometimes, when the situation requires it, but usually I'm fairly calm and rational. Perhaps I can help you remember."

Suddenly a bright light burst from the stranger's body, and he rose several feet in the air. "Do you recognize me now?" he said, his voice slicing through the brilliance.

Gerald put one hand to his mouth, and his eyes bulged. "Why, you're the angel who visited me many times in my private chamber."

The "angel" glided to the earth as he returned to his former state. "No, you're wrong. I'm not an angel. I am the god of this world, and as its ruler, I have power over everything and everyone on it."

"I'm sorry, Master," Gerald said, standing suddenly. He thought about kneeling but quickly rejected the idea. He would kneel to no one, no matter how powerful that being might be. "This is your natural appearance?"

"No, my natural form is one of great glory. I use this image from time to time so men can feel more comfortable when they communicate with me."

"Do you have further instructions for me?"

"Yes, but first I want to say I am pleased with you. You have done everything I asked, and now you are ready to take the final steps."

"And mighty steps they will be. As you instructed, I will soon order our allies around the world to move against our enemies in open warfare, and I know they will succeed as long as they follow the plans I have given them."

"Good. Now I will give you one further instruction at this time. I require you to take personal command of your impending invasion of Israel, at the head of a great army."

Gerald's chest tightened. "But, Master, isn't that foolhardy? Wouldn't it be wiser for me to direct operations from a safe distance like any other general should? What if a stray bullet happened to injure or kill me? Besides, I'm seventy-two years old and my health—"

"You will do as I say or I will find someone else to replace you. The success of your campaign depends on it."

Gerald seethed inside. He was the only person on earth who could have devised UGOT's ingenious plans and manipulated and tamed the disparate powers of the earth. Those strategies were his creation and his alone. Certainly none of his stupid associates could have accomplished it. Not even this immortal could have done it by himself, and in reality this god had made only one or two genuinely useful suggestions. "I will do as you ask. But may I pose a question or two, my divine guide?"

"Inquire as you wish."

"Why were we not able to destroy the Mormon empire? We procured a great army from Mexico and sent them to the Rocky Mountains to destroy the Mormons located there, and that army was defeated. We sent another mighty army to wipe out the fledgling Mormon republic in the American Midwest, and that second army not only failed but completely disappeared. To this day, I don't know what happened to it. Later, we sent four modern warplanes to both Mormon kingdoms, and they too mysteriously vanished without even delivering their nuclear warheads."

Lucas smiled sardonically. "I was there and saw it all. For your instruction, I will answer your questions. You did not fail, at least not completely. In the first war you killed thousands of the religious fanatics, and in the Missouri campaign you succeeded in slaughtering a hundred thousand young idolaters. You did not win the war, and your bombers failed, in part because warriors on the other side interfered."

"Warriors on the other side?"

"You know, our holy opposition. Michael, for example."

"Michael?"

Lucas scowled. "You need to become better acquainted with your opponents. Michael, the warrior god, otherwise known as Adam. The same character who gave us so many problems in the preexistence."

Suddenly Gerald felt foolish. "You said we failed in part because of interference. How could we have done better?"

"In two ways. I have already mentioned one. You allowed others, an associate and your incompetent War Office, to plan and execute the missions. You should have personally checked all the details of each operation and then led your troops into battle, so to speak. The second reason you failed is because you did not call upon me to show you the way. However, besides all that, when you engage in military operations, or in any other type of difficult campaign, sometimes you win and sometimes you lose."

"I understand," Gerald replied. "I assure you that I will not make the same mistakes when we invade Israel."

"Good. That is one crusade we cannot afford to lose. As for the Mormon kingdom, we'll get back to them as soon as we finish with the Jews. We will even have the pleasure of killing thousands of young Mormon soldiers during our campaign in Israel.

"There are also some other things you must remember when you attack Israel and its allies. Give no quarter, execute prisoners in public demonstrations, torture captives for information, assassinate their leaders when possible, and spread lies and propaganda to achieve your goals."

Those words pleased Gerald immensely. "Yes, I already planned to do those things and much more. Now may I ask you one more question, divine Master?" Lucas nodded. "Are you the same being who appeared to our prophet, Colton Aldridge, and gave him power to do his miracles?"

"I am the inspiration and the power behind Colton and all your miracle workers. Now go to your meeting with your associates and other collaborators. Set them on fire and plan very carefully. I intend to show the opposition that they will not win in the end. Oh, one more thing. When you invade the so-called Holy Land, take special precautions with the water supplies of your armies."

At those words, the god of this world disappeared as quickly as he had come.

What? Gerald thought. *I've already instructed our allies to bring tankers full of water, so what is he talking about? Um, okay, I'll arrange to have regular overland shipments brought into the war zone, just in case, and even special trucks carrying millions of bottles of water.*

Gerald heard the rumble of thunder and saw bolts of lightning streak to earth miles away to the north. Soon the wind picked up and gusts of rain struck his face. As he hurried toward his compound a few hundred yards away, he cursed and said to himself, "Blasted weather! Nice and sunny one minute and a violent storm the next."

Soon after his interview with Lucas Nigel, Galloway met with his associates, war ministers, and key collaborators sent by his most important allies, at his headquarters in a large compound near Nanterre. His favorite spiritual adviser and miracle worker, Colton Aldridge, was also there. The purpose of the meeting was to discuss their plans regarding the massive offensive that UGOT was about to initiate. When Gerald entered the conference room, his confederates had already taken seats around a massive oak table covered with trays of hors d'oeuvres and bottles of French wine.

Gerald smiled at the people he considered his puppets and sat down at the head of the table. "Dear friends and fellow liberators, let me get right to the point. In a few hours from now, I will issue an order to our coalition forces around the planet to commence their great mission of freeing mankind of all the religious fanatics whose primary goal is to enslave the world with their doctrines, rites, and customs.

"More specifically, our task is to destroy the nations and peoples who have refused to join our righteous cause. We have many enemies, but the worst of these is the Jewish race. When we accomplish these wonderful goals, we will enthrone rationalism, empiricism, and secular humanism as the guiding philosophies for all mankind. At that time, man will no longer be governed by superstition but by reason and pure science.

"I myself will lead a great army to Palestine to make sure the work of annihilation is accomplished quickly and effectively. In the past, I have allowed others to plan and conduct important campaigns in faraway lands, and the results have not always been good." He looked at Lucienne Delisle, his associate in charge of North America, but she did not return his gaze. "However, this time, I assure you the outcome will be different."

Galloway spent the next three hours pointing out on a huge world map the location and size of their forces and their military capabilities. He also noted where those forces would probably find the largest pockets of resistance from Jewish, Christian, and Mormon communities throughout the world. Dozens of red arrows described the general pathways their coalition armies would take, and all of the arrows ended up in the land of the Jews.

"Now I will have my assistants give you a carefully researched list indicating the location of over five hundred Jewish settlements spread out across the world. As our armies move toward Israel, they will make frequent stops and even minor detours to attack and destroy these communities." Several assistants circulated among the "world liberators" to distribute the lists.

Next, Gerald praised his confederates, glorified the nobility of their souls, recognized all their hard work, and told them they could not fail. He encouraged them to utterly destroy the targeted peoples they would encounter, show them no mercy, take no prisoners, plunder their wealth, and ravish their women. In the end, they would receive even greater rewards when they sacked the cities of Israel, enjoyed the enemy's riches, and became the saviors of mankind.

Lucienne Delisle raised her hand, and Gerald gave her a nod. "Gerald, why do we need to bring all those armies to Palestine? It's so time-consuming and expensive. Why don't we simply drop a few nuclear bombs on Israel and be done with it?"

Gerald smirked at her obvious ignorance. Lucienne had been one of his lovers for many years, but now the flame between them was becoming dimmer. "For several reasons, my dear," he said, his voice laced with acid. "Nuclear weapons are immensely messy and would pollute the land for decades to come. I have warned our coalition forces who possess nuclear weapons that if they utilize those bombs, we ourselves will retaliate against them in like manner. Since we want to defeat the Jews in war and take advantage of all their wealth and technological advances, we'll only use conventional weapons in our conquest. Many of those weapons are very sophisticated and can achieve spectacular victories without resulting in widespread contamination."

"President Galloway," Randolph Benson said, "isn't it true that today's conventional weapons are also very devastating in their effects and can wipe out a country's infrastructure almost as completely as nuclear bombs?" Benson was Gerald's associate in the Middle East.

"You would be right if we were going to employ such weapons indiscriminately. But if we use them on Israeli troops and military installations, and avoid using them on cities and towns, we can minimize damage to the infrastructure. Remember, the Jews are not like the Arabs, who often hide their troops and weapons among the civilian population. Moreover, conventional weapons will not pollute the environment."

The walls of the compound began to shudder and rattle as if some great behemoth was assailing it, and the sound of violent winds filled the conference room. The participants held on to the table before them and looked around in great fear. After a minute of such terror, there was a deafening blast as a bolt of lightning struck the building directly. The computers in front of Galloway's accomplices shorted out with sudden bursts of flame.

"Don't worry, my friends," Galloway shouted above the roar of the storm. "This building is built to withstand just about anything. The reinforced concrete walls are three feet thick, and we installed lightning rods on the roof and high-capacity lightning arrestors. I'm sure it'll be over in no time. You know how it is these days."

"Well," Lucienne Delisle called out, "apparently your lightning protectors didn't do squat. Our computers just went down."

Gerald glared at her. Only Lucienne would dare criticize him. "Yes, but at least we still have lights. I assure you we can replace the computers, and by the time you leave today the storm will be over. Now let's get back to business."

Despite Gerald's haste, they waited about ten minutes until there seemed to be a lull in the turbulence outside. Then Janet Griffin, UGOT's associate for East Asia, said in a loud voice, "President Galloway, back to your statements about conventional weapons. You make it seem certain that they'll be sufficient to bring success in our campaign, and I wish it were that easy, but aren't you forgetting all the natural impediments to our great invasion? Things like the storm hitting us right now.

"The armies we've procured in East Asia will be in grave danger if they try to travel by sea to the Middle East because of all the violent typhoons these days. This early in the season there have already been six of them. The storm surges on the coasts of Korea, Japan, the Philippines, and even China have inundated coastal cities and killed thousands of people. In addition, China has been experiencing unusual rainstorms inland for several months, and many areas near the great rivers are flooded. As a result, troop movements are very difficult. I understand that many other regions of the world are also dealing with similar problems."

"Yes, ocean travel is always precarious these days," Gerald replied, "and you're right that there are extreme weather conditions in many parts of the world. Do any of you want to add to what Janet has said?"

"Yes, I do," said Juliska Ferenci, the associate in charge of Eastern Europe. "In southeastern Europe, we've had several late-season blizzards of unbelievable ferocity. They've hit the entire region around the Black Sea, including southern Russia, Ukraine, Romania, Bulgaria, Georgia, and even northern Turkey."

Gerald was not surprised. "That's what I understand from the reports I've been getting. It's very unusual to have blizzards in early April."

"The blizzards and the cold have caused hundreds of roads to be impassable," Janet Griffin added, "and the shores of the Black Sea are frozen over for ten miles out. Before the blizzards struck, people reported extremely heavy rainstorms with hailstones weighing twenty pounds or more."

"As most of you know," Coleen Addison said, "I'm in charge of Australia and Oceania. On the east coast of Australia, there have been incessant rainstorms, resulting in dozens of flash floods and mudslides. I'd say nearly one tenth of Australia is covered with water. By contrast, the western half of the continent is going through a deadly drought, with hot, dry winds sweeping the region. The people there are very close to starvation."

"That may be to our benefit," Gerald said. "Australia has been one of the countries that has shown reluctance to support our cause. They only committed one small army of five thousand, and I'm not sure they'll follow through with that. Later, we may have to teach them a lesson."

Julian Kennedy, the associate for Central and South America, spoke up. "We've had a lot of bad luck in my area too. There have been three earthquakes in Central America and four in South America in the last four months. They've all been over 7.0 on the Richter Scale. And there have been rainstorms and flooding in Ecuador and Columbia. These events have resulted in the death of about nine million people, with an estimated eighteen million made homeless."

Gerald didn't want to hear more. "Yes, I can see the problem," he said angrily. "However, we must go ahead with our plans in spite of these little inconveniences. So how do you people suggest we move troops?"

"Well, since it's extremely dangerous to move troops by sea, I propose we convey most of them in trucks by land or use air transport," said Ernest Hopkins, the associate for Southeast Asia. "I don't see any other way."

"Why don't we leave it up to our allies to decide how they want to transport their forces to Palestine?" said Associate Randolph Benson. "They alone are most familiar with the ways and means they have of moving their armies. For example, I don't see how Indonesia and the Philippines can transport troops other than by sea."

"In the long run," Gerald replied, "that's what we'll have to do. Still, I believe we need to encourage them to avoid travel by sea if at all possible." Gerald took another sip of wine. "The main thing is, I want them to arrive in the vicinity of Palestine by the beginning of August. That gives them four months, which is plenty of time, even if they have to make their ground forces walk all the way across Eurasia. So I want those of you who are here as representatives of our allies to communicate these ideas to your national leaders. Okay, is there anything else?"

They continued to discuss problems and plans for another eight hours, with several breaks to enjoy Galloway's catered meals and refreshments. After the meeting, Gerald directed his lieutenants to open worldwide communications with all his allies. They needed to deliver one single message: begin to mobilize your troops.

When they left the compound in the early evening, the storm drenched them as they rushed to their waiting vehicles. They drove away slowly and carefully, their wheels creating small waves in the inches of water covering the road.

"It's started, Steve," declared John Christopher, after bursting into Steven's office in Independence, Missouri. It was the second week in April and the weather was superb, with a soft, warm breeze that caressed the cheek as if the elements promised a bright new future for Zion.

"What's started?" Steven said, his brow raised with concern.

"UGOT's move against Israel." John was still trying to catch his breath after running up the stairway.

"UGOT's move—where did you get this information?"

"My friends and I have been monitoring world events for about a year now. In the last three months, we've been intercepting wireless communications from UGOT to governments all over the planet. UGOT has been targeting Jews and Christians for decades, gaining influence, establishing coalitions, and building armies all over the earth. Well apparently, their timetable has run out and Gerald Galloway has commanded his allies to mobilize." John and several of his friends had organized a club of ham radio buffs to communicate with people from other nations by a network of relay stations.

"When did this timetable run out?"

"I think it happened a few days ago. It's hard to tell because their communications are encoded, but this morning I deciphered the final part of their code, and the message is clear."

"The president and the prophet know about this?"

"I don't know how they could, unless they got the message through the newly reactivated transatlantic cable. Even then, I don't know who would dare to inform on UGOT. Of course, our leaders might have communications experts who are monitoring the world scene just like I am."

For about a year, Galloway had backed away from corrupting the world's nations and from persecuting those he perceived as threats, but recently he had resumed his plans with renewed energy.

"I suppose they don't know yet or they would have informed me," Steven said.

At that moment, the phone rang and Steven answered. John waited patiently while his brother talked for nearly fifteen minutes.

"That was the president," Steven said, when he had finished the call. "This morning the prophet received a revelation telling him that Gog and Magog were now marshaling forth their armies with the intent of annihilating Israel, and he immediately called President Cartwright."

John's face blanched. "So it's Armageddon, right?" Steven and John both knew that the scriptures used the words "Gog and Magog" to describe two worldwide conspiracies. Both secret combinations would be inspired by Satan. The first would be formed shortly before the Second Coming of Christ and perpetrate the great war called Armageddon. The second would appear at the end of the Millennium and initiate the second war of Gog and Magog, also called the Battle of the Great God.

"Well, we knew it was coming someday," Steven said sadly. "I just hoped we'd have more time to prepare. I believe the prophet knew this was about to happen, even before his revelation. No doubt that's why he issued a memorandum two months ago recalling all missionaries from Gentile lands."

"So you think it wasn't because the people were beginning to reject the missionaries and to even attack them openly?"

Steven stood and went to the window. "No, I figure the prophet had already sensed that UGOT was ready to move and that the nations controlled by them would reestablish their programs to murder and incarcerate Mormons wherever they could find them."

"You know what this means, don't you?" John said with a frown.

"It means a lot of things, but what do you have in mind?"

"It means the Second Coming of Christ will occur soon, probably within the next few years."

Steven paused, thinking. "Hmm, I guess you're right." The very thought of such a great and terrible event sent shivers down his spine. As the Church taught, the Second Coming would be great for the righteous but terrible for the wicked.

"When do we leave?" John asked.

"Leave? Where are we going?"

"To Israel, obviously."

"Israel! What for?"

"To fight UGOT's coalition armies, what else?" John said with exasperation.

Steven swallowed hard, and his stomach churned. "You want to leave our nice, comfortable home, travel across dangerous, storm-tossed seas, and fight in the most terrible, bloody war in the history of mankind?"

"Why not? It's our duty."

Steven remembered what Douglas Cartwright, the president of New Zion, had just said on the phone: the Lord had told the prophet that he required his people in Zion to raise a mighty army and hasten to Israel to help defend the remnant of his chosen people against Satan's armies. "Hey, brother, I'm way too old. I'm fifty-eight now. Let's leave the fighting to the young guys."

"So? I'm old too, but they'll need leaders who have military experience. That includes us."

"I'm the governor of Missouri, and the people here need me. Besides, Mary would never hear of it."

"Excuses, excuses. Where's your dedication? Where's the commitment? The people can take care of themselves. That's the kind of government we helped to create for this nation. As for Mary, who wears the pants in your family?"

"Mary does, believe me."

"Baloney. You know our sons will volunteer for the army. Do you want them to go alone without the benefit of our wise guidance and protection?"

"You make a good point. Look, I'll talk to Mary about it later today."

"Good. Besides, you already know how the great war will turn out in the end."

"Uh, yeah, but I believe the scriptures say that a huge number of the good guys will die also."

Acting as if he hadn't heard Steven's comment, John started for the door. "I'm going to inform Tania that we'll leave shortly and be gone for quite some time."

"Quite some time! Like how long?"

"Years maybe. I don't know."

Steven studied John's face to see how serious he was. "Why so long?"

"Well, the scriptures talk about the war of Armageddon lasting at least three and a half years. We'll have to stay until the end, which should be spectacular."

"Um, I always thought that scripture was figurative, but even if the war does last for years, that doesn't mean we have to stay there all that time. We could—"

"Oh, and I need to tell Paul too," John said, still not paying attention. "I know he'll be excited to go. By the way, did the prophet say when UGOT's armies would reach Israel?"

"In about three or four months."

John scratched his head. "Why so long?"

"Because travel is difficult these days, especially on water. Also, I understand those armies will be doing some fighting along the way, but the prophet didn't say what that was all about."

John nodded, charged out the door, and headed for the stairs.

With a lump in his throat, Steven watched him leave. *Mary is going to kill me*, he thought.

Just as John closed the door, the phone rang. Steven picked up the receiver and heard a familiar voice—it was the prophet, President Wilford Benson. "Oh, hello, President Benson. How are you?" Steven listened for a while and said, "You want to see me today? When should I come?" A short pause. "Okay, I'll be right over, within ten minutes. Yes, thank you. See you soon."

Steven rushed out of his office and headed for his car. It took him no more than three minutes to make the trip to the prophet's office, a short distance from the temple. He knocked on the prophet's office door, not knowing what to expect.

"Come in," the prophet said. Steven entered and saw the haggard church leader sitting behind his oak desk. President Benson was now eighty-two years old and looked as though he hadn't slept in a week. In spite of that, he smiled when he saw Steven and gestured toward a chair in front of his desk.

"Sit down, my friend," the prophet said. He quickly reviewed all the information that President Cartwright had communicated to Steven earlier on the phone. Then he added, "Steven, last night the Lord revealed to me that he needed you to perform another great mission, this time in Israel."

"Mission? What kind of mission?"

"The Lord wants you to travel to Israel as the spiritual leader of the young soldiers he sends to help Israel in their time of need. He also wants you to baptize and ordain Israel's principal leaders, David Omert and Chaim

Yehoshua. David Omert is the leader God has raised up to be the Second David, who is to rule Israel just before the Second Coming of the Lord."

"But those leaders are Jews and are no doubt faithful to the Jewish religion. How can I convert them to Christianity much less the gospel? Won't they reject me outright?"

"Don't worry about that. The Lord has already prepared the way."

"Whew! That's a relief. Okay—"

"Wait. Before you accept this mission, there is more you need to know."

"More?" Steven felt his heart skip a beat.

"Yes, the Lord also wants you to baptize and ordain the two Jewish prophets that God will soon call. As the Book of Revelation says, those prophets will act as witnesses of the Messiah and as defenders of Israel against Gog's evil hosts."

Steven swallowed hard and his stomach began to burn. "The Lord wants me to do that too?"

"Of course. You're the man of the hour. We will ordain you with power and the blessings of inspiration from God. You were chosen before to accomplish several great missions and you always fulfilled your duties in a manner pleasing to God. So, will you accept this call?"

"You don't think one of the apostles would be a better choice?"

"Perhaps, but obviously the Lord doesn't think so. Do you accept the call?"

"Absolutely."

"Good. I knew you would. I want you to be a spiritual leader for our troops. Remind your men on every occasion that our people and the people of Israel are actually of the same lineage and are one chosen nation under the covenant of the Lord with Abraham, and when we fight for them, we are really fighting for our brothers and sisters."

"I'll do my best to fulfill this sacred calling," Steven said with determination.

"I know you will. Before you leave today, I want to give you a few basic facts you need to know before you travel to Israel. Most people believe the State of Israel is much larger than it really is, but in reality it is only slightly larger than New Jersey, our fifth smallest state. The state of Missouri, ranked number twenty-one in square miles among our states, is over eight times as large as Israel. By contrast, the Arab world comprises over five million square miles and is larger than Europe, Canada, China, Brazil, and the United States combined. So you can see why it is crucial for Israel to hold on to as much land area as possible—land that rightly belongs to it.

"As for population, I understand there are about eight million two hundred thousand people living in Israel, including the so-called West Bank. Seventy-five percent of them are Jews, about twenty-one percent are Arabs, and about four percent are non-Arab Christians and other small communities. That means only six million one hundred thousand Jews live in Israel. Compare that to the Arab world in general, which now has a population of over four hundred million people, and nearly all of them seek the destruction of Israel and every Jew living there. By this you can begin to get an idea of the perilous situation Israel finds itself in."

Steven said nothing because he was stunned, but deep inside he ached to do his part to defend the tiny nation inhabited by another branch of the Lord's chosen people.

The prophet remained silent for a couple of minutes and then summoned his two counselors and three apostles, and they laid their hands on Steven's head and gave him his special call and ordination.

"You're not going!" Mary said with flashing eyes.

"Why not?" Steven was shocked to see her standing there with her fists on her hips and her eyes staring him down.

"For a dozen reasons."

"Like what?"

"You're too old. You're the governor with lots of duties. You're not thinking of me or the children. It's too dangerous and you'll get killed." Then her eyes suddenly welled with tears.

Steven realized that her last reason was the real one. "The lieutenant governor can take over in my absence, and I *am* thinking of you and the children. William will want to join our army, and since Daniel's twenty-two, he'll want to go also. I need to be there to guide and protect them."

"What about me?"

Steven swallowed hard, knowing that leaving her alone for so long would nearly tear his heart out. "I must be there when it all goes down. We've got to stop UGOT's forces in Palestine. If we don't, they'll come here when they've finished with Israel."

"No, that's not right. The prophecies say Gog's armies will be destroyed during the war of Armageddon, so they won't be able to attack our republic. But I'm afraid you'll be killed or seriously injured in Israel, all of you."

"That's giving the worst case scenario. I'm sure God will protect us." Steven decided to play his trump card. "Mary, I especially need to go because the prophet gave me a special calling to fulfill in Israel."

Mary's eyes widened in surprise. "He did? When?"

"About half an hour ago." Steven rehearsed his visit with the prophet.

Mary looked down without saying anything for a long moment. Finally tears came to her eyes and she looked up. "You should have told me that right from the beginning. All right then. I'm going with you. I also want to watch over my sons and witness the marvelous events you've been talking about."

"You can't go. No women have been called to go to Israel."

"Why not? I know for a fact that the Israeli government conscripts its female citizens as well as the men."

"Young women. You're fifty-three now."

Mary's mouth formed a pout. "Well, I don't think it's fair. I'm very strong and I know how to use a rifle. And if that isn't good enough, I'm a nurse and I could help on the battlefield or in one of the hospitals."

"But our leaders haven't called any of our women to go to Israel."

"Why not? It doesn't seem fair to me."

"It's because there'll be death and suffering and years of violent fighting."

Mary burst into tears, and Steven knew he'd gone too far. In a gentler voice he added, "Besides, the president has specifically declined to allow women to join the army. It would be much harder for me if I had to add you and Gabrielle to the people I would have to look out for. Listen, sweetheart, what if I promise you here and now that the boys and I will return safely?"

Mary's face showed a hint of resignation. "Does Daniel have to go? He's so young and inexperienced."

"I'll let you try to talk him out of it."

At this, Mary covered her eyes and shook her head.

❧

Within a few days, the news spread like wildfire throughout the Republic of Zion. At the word "Armageddon," people reacted in different ways. Some cried and went to bed, locking themselves in their rooms. Many who had been a bit lax in saying their prayers began to pray in earnest. Others became excited and wanted to know all the details.

When it was announced that the prophet and the president were asking for volunteers to fight in the great war, tens of thousands of young men, and many not so young, flocked to the designated recruitment centers to offer their services. They responded with such great enthusiasm because the prophet of God told them the Lord needed them to defend the freedom of all decent people on the earth against the tyranny of the worldwide evil conspiracy and also because their brothers and sisters of the House of Israel desperately need their help. At the recruitment centers, most of the volunteers were accepted quickly and returned to their homes to gather the things required by the authorities. They were especially careful to clean their weapons and gather all the ammunition they could find.

And thus the nation mobilized for war with one heart and one mind.

Chapter 2

⚜

David Omert had been elected prime minister of Israel twenty-two years ago and had served for eight years. His government was so effective that the country had peace, stability, and unparalleled prosperity during his tenure and for years afterward. With the help of his friend, Chaim Yehoshua, and other conservatives, the government had encouraged progress in science, education, manufacturing, health care, and public works. Israel had become a wealthy nation and a veritable Garden of Eden.

However, the greatest accomplishment of Omert's terms as prime minister, at least in his eyes, was the beginning of the construction of the Third Temple on the Temple Mount in Jerusalem. He had authorized the construction during his second year in office and expected the work would take between twenty to twenty-five years to complete.

Omert had also procured vast sums of money for the reconstruction of Jerusalem, which had suffered many attacks from rockets and missiles fired by Palestinians and other Arabs from the West Bank. In many places the city was in ruins, and it had become a dangerous place to live in. The strange thing was that many of the bombs had also destroyed the homes and businesses of many Palestinians living in the city, but that fact had not stopped the attacks.

In order to prevent further damage to the holy city, David had authorized the development of several types of defense systems, such as the Arrow anti-missile interceptor system, with batteries installed completely around the city. These systems were extremely effective in destroying incoming missiles and bombs, but of course they could do nothing against suicide bombers, who walked around the city blowing up people and buildings with no concern for their own lives or the lives of the innocent people they murdered.

Since the Israelis could no longer buy arms from the United States or the other countries they had previously depended on, it became necessary for them to design and manufacture their own weapons. David Omert had sought out the best and brightest of Israel's scientists, engineers, and inventors to pursue this goal, and they had been extremely successful, producing dozens of sophisticated new weapons.

Israel had accomplished all this in spite of the continuous opposition of the Palestinians and other Arabs and the influence of UGOT, which used its worldwide propaganda machine to blame Israel for all the problems of the Middle East. One of UGOT's primary goals was to delegitimize Israel in the eyes of the world. Gerald Galloway, the so-called president of UGOT, had managed to convince most of the world's nations that the great Jewish conspiracy was the cause of their civil strife and the intractable insolvency of their economies, and he blamed Israel and the Jews living outside of Palestine, or the diaspora, for the world's suffering and growing poverty.

He had also convinced his allies and friends in other nations that the only way they could be whole again was to murder Jews wherever they found them and to annihilate the State of Israel.

Israel's Arab enemies were well aware of this, but even the boldest of them still hesitated to initiate armed conflict with the small nation that had beaten them so soundly in every major past engagement, battles that Israel had won because of its military prowess, its highly advanced technology, and the courage of its people.

Yet recently things had changed, and the Arabs had gained a new hope of destroying their ancient enemy once and for all when UGOT entered the picture, providing them with training in military tactics and supplying them with vast amounts of war matériel.

Toward the end of David's time as prime minister, the influence of left-wing parties in the Knesset had grown steadily until they finally gained control of the government. The new leaders cut expenditures to the military and provided fifty percent of the nation's young men and women with legal exemptions from the draft. Especially onerous were the continued exemptions and subsidies given to thousands of young ultra-Orthodox Jews, who now made up twenty-five percent of the population.

The ultra-Orthodox Jews had always resisted the draft, using their numbers and influence to avoid it. Any time the public suggested they should share in safeguarding the nation from rabid enemies bent on their destruction, the religious Jews marched in the streets, chanting loudly and waving poignant placards, demanding their God-given right to study the scriptures and the commentaries relating to them. So, in the name of God they were perfectly happy to let the secular Jews risk their lives defending the nation, while they spent most of their time studying the holy texts and debating doctrine. They even claimed they were making more meaningful contributions to the glory and salvation of the nation than the secular Jews by providing the land with firmer and more righteous foundations.

Hundreds of informed citizens, including many who had fought in Arab-Israeli wars, warned the leaders that if the Arabs defeated Israel, there would be a universal bloodbath, and every Jew would be executed outright. However, the popular darlings of the left-wing movement refused to believe that the average Arab, the ones they called "moderates," would permit such carnage. They were either ignorant of history, which was most often the case, or they closed their eyes to the clear lessons of the past. In the final analysis, the liberal leaders had seriously endangered the country by depriving the Israel Defense Forces, or the IDF, of the means necessary for defending the nation.

The liberals made endless concessions to the Palestinians, employing the failed strategy of exchanging land for promises of peace. The Palestinians rejoiced at Israeli gullibility and took everything they could obtain and gave nothing in return, while continuing—and even accelerating—their vicious attacks on innocent Israeli citizens.

First the liberals focused on the territory west of the Jordan River, called the West Bank by the Arabs and the media, but Judea and Samaria by Israelis. In spite of the fact that the Palestinians had no historical basis for claiming that the West Bank belonged to them and that the Jews were "occupiers" of their lands, the Israeli leaders ordered Jewish settlements in the West Bank to vacate the region. Many Israelis violently protested this action, fearing that the Arabs would use the West Bank as a convenient base for firing upon Israeli communities, just as the terrorist organization Hamas had used Gaza—after it had been turned over to the Arabs in 2005—as a vantage point from which to fire thousands of rockets into Israel.

Next the liberals ordered the demolition of the four-hundred-mile

Security Fence, constructed on the borders between the West Bank and Israel. The propaganda machine of the liberal media called the barrier a monument to exclusion and intolerance, but in reality it had been built to protect Israeli communities from frequent Palestinian terrorist attacks and to prevent this region from becoming a convenient pathway of invasion against Israel from Jordan, Iraq, and Iran.

The left-wing radicals then turned their attention to the Golan Heights, a small region—ten miles wide and forty miles long—on the northeastern border of Israel, east of the Sea of Galilee. Israel had captured this region in the 1967 war. The radical liberals agreed to give the Golan Heights back to Syria, on the condition that the Syrians would never again use that land as a base for shelling northern Israeli towns, as they had regularly done in the past. This concession was made in spite of the fact that Syria had never had any real claim to this land and had exhibited a long history of global terrorism, trafficking in narcotics, and demanding the annihilation of the Jews.

Israeli citizens became especially incensed when news leaked out that their leaders were considering giving control of east Jerusalem to the Arabs, but due to public outcry, Israelis leaders finally backed away from that policy. When the Palestinians saw the Knesset reject the leftist proposition, they were outraged and increased their secretive terrorist attacks because they had planned on making east Jerusalem the capital of the new Palestinian nation.

As a result, after fourteen years of liberal rule, Israel was in an extremely precarious position. Despite all their concessions to Jordan, Syria, and the Palestinians, the terrorist attacks continued and accelerated to the point that over one hundred thousand assaults occurred since David Omert had been prime minister. Even Egypt began to ignore their treaties with Israel and sent hundreds of suicide bombers into southern Israeli communities.

Israel had created high-tech early warning systems, including satellites, but these proved inadequate to prevent continuous incursions, and thousands of innocent Israelis died. What Israel really needed was the physical and topographical buffers they had won during the 1967 war, such as the Gaza Strip, the high ground of the Golan Heights, which was a natural barrier to Syrian tanks, and the heights and depressions of the Jordan Rift Valley they had once possessed in Judea and Samaria. Israel also needed to rebuild the Security Fence in the West Bank.

Before long, Israel's national intelligence agency, Mossad, and many other sources discovered that Syria, Lebanon, Jordan, and Egypt, and other Arab nations farther away, were amassing their military might and moving their forces into position to make a united assault against the hated Jews. All this was similar to what had happened in 1967, but this time things would be much worse. Meanwhile, the Israeli government was frantically making belated preparations to meet the approaching onslaught.

Because of the stupidity, inadequacy, and complacency of the liberal Israeli government and the legislature, there was a national uproar, fueled by anger and the fear of a coming genocide. Tens of thousands of furious citizens, normally patient and peace-loving, stormed government offices and overcame their leaders, throwing them into makeshift prisons.

Then the voices of millions of Israelis united and called for the return of David Omert as the supreme leader of Israel. In this dire situation, they needed one good man to rule with absolute power, without the interference of divided factions. Many referred to him as the Second David, in memory of King David, the second ruler of ancient Israel. Only such a man could save Israel from annihilation.

⚜

David Omert was sitting on the ground with his back against the trunk of an olive tree in the Garden of Gethsemane. It was a beautiful spring day in early April. The sun was bright, and a soft breeze flowed down from the Mount of Olives. He looked up when he heard the sound of footsteps coming toward him. It was his best friend, Chaim Yehoshua.

"I thought I might find you here," Chaim said in Hebrew. "I've been looking for you. What are you doing?" He knew that David often sought solace in this garden at the foot of the Mount of Olives, especially when he was deeply concerned about something.

"Just thinking. I'm glad you came."

"Thinking about what? Wait. Don't tell me. I already know." Chaim sat down on the grass next to David.

David smiled. "I'm sure you do."

"It's about what the people want you to do. Have you made a decision yet?"

David turned and looked Chaim in the eyes. "I have no choice. I have to answer the nation's call. Most of the leaders we have today are incompetent, especially the former prime minister. And our situation is so desperate that if we don't act now, Israel will soon no longer exist."

"You can't really believe that, David. You know that Israel has a great destiny to fulfill, not only for our people but for the whole world. Do you want my honest opinion?"

"Yes, of course."

"You are the man of the hour. The man Israel needs at this perilous juncture. This is the reason you were born a Jew. But now I see you here in Gethsemane, pondering how to handle the situation. Personally, I think you're having a crisis of self-confidence. I say get over it. You know what to do and how to do it. No man in Israel is better qualified, including me, to be the ruler of Israel."

"But an absolute ruler? Israel has been a democratic republic ever since the birth of the nation in 1948."

"I know, but the people want you to be the chief executive officer only for the time necessary to get us out of our current dilemma. When we're able to reestablish our security and stability, and be rid of the Arab threat, you can call for new elections to fill the seats in the Knesset and the government. In other words, you'll be the ruler *pro tempore.*"

"Sorry, I've forgotten most of my Latin. What does *pro tempore* mean?"

"It means for the present time."

"How do you know the people want me to be a temporary ruler? How do you know these things?"

"Well, since you left the cabinet as minister of defense six years ago, you've kind of been in seclusion, and you don't pay enough attention to the news reports."

"That's not entirely true. I sometimes watch European news, but I get fed up with their biased reporting. I'm tired of seeing all those sickening stories on the plight of the poor suffering Palestinians at the hands of us ruthless Israelis."

"Yeah, that infuriates me too. If the Palestinians don't want to see their families die and suffer, they shouldn't teach their children to glorify suicidal terrorists and to hate Jews, and they should stop making unprovoked attacks on innocent Israeli families. They alone are responsible for the torments of their people. At any rate, we're straying from the main point."

"Yes, we are. In any case, I see the Messiah himself as the King of Israel, and the only king."

"That's not what you really believe."

David gaped. "I don't?"

"No, the truth is, you believe the Messiah is Jesus Christ, the Son of God. So that means he would be the King of Kings, not just a king."

"You're right. That *is* what I believe."

"Well, thanks to all your preaching years ago, I believe it too," Chaim admitted, looking around furtively to see if anyone was within earshot.

"Unfortunately, we don't dare admit this to the public or even to our friends. The people, especially the religious Jews, would brand us as traitors and apostates. From that moment on, they wouldn't listen to anything we said, and they would certainly reject me as the most powerful man in the nation." David had complete confidence in Chaim, knowing he would never reveal their Christian beliefs to anyone.

"You're right, of course. When I think about our strict laws against proselyting in Israel by other religions, I can see your point. The supreme Israeli leader can't believe in Jesus and Judaism at the same time."

Most faithful believers in Judaism believed that Jesus was a bold man who stood up to the Romans, but that he was also a false messiah because he did not fulfill the requirements of the prophecies in Isaiah and Ezekiel and tried to change the teachings of Jehovah by claiming that the Law of Moses was done away in him. They rejected Jesus's claim that he was the Son of God because God had no son, for there was only one God and he was a single, unchanging being throughout all eternity. They even denied that Jesus was a prophet.

At the same time, the Jews believed that the real Messiah would be a great prophet, second only to Moses, but would still be a normal man, not a divine being with miraculous powers. He would save the Jews from their enemies, build the Third Temple, establish the Messianic Age, and rule as King of Israel. He had not yet come, but every Jew loyal to the religious traditions looked anxiously for his arrival.

Neither David or Chaim said anything for a full minute. Finally Chaim said, "That reminds me. Why are you sitting here in this garden?"

David looked over at him in surprise. "What? Why am I here? To think about the future, as I said before."

"You know, of course, that this is a sacred Christian site. If any religious

Jews, or even secular ones, see you here, they'll get suspicious and start rumors."

"You're right. Let's get out of here."

Mary Christopher and six of her lady friends approached the office of President Douglas Cartwright at the capitol building in Independence, Missouri. The president's secretary looked up as they approached her desk, a shocked look on her face.

"May I help you?" she said.

"We want to see the president," Mary said with a firm voice.

"Well, you'll need to see the head of his office staff, Mr. Jeffreys. Do you have an appointment with Mr. Jeffreys?"

"Certainly not." Mary turned toward her friends and said, "Come on, girls, I know where his office is." She proceeded to march down the hall toward the president's office, her companions jouncing along behind her, their hips swinging dangerously wide.

"Wait!" the secretary yelled. "You can't just walk— Security! Security!" she called in her loudest voice.

Within moments, two armed security guards appeared from nowhere. They pointed their weapons at Mary, and one of them shouted, "Cease and desist or we'll be forced to shoot."

Mary threw him her most withering scowl. "Shoot away, big boy, if you think you need to, but I don't have time for your shenanigans. I'm the governor's wife and a good friend of the president. If you shoot me, you'll live to regret it."

The guards were nonplussed and followed the women down the hall, still brandishing their weapons but clearly fearful of taking further action. The secretary continued to yell her head off near her desk some distance away.

Mary and the others bounced into Douglas's office without knocking, and the president, sitting alone at his desk, looked up in surprise. The guards followed the women into the office, remaining on alert.

"Douglas, I need to talk to you," Mary said. "Do you have a moment?"

Recognizing Mary in the crowd of women, Douglas relaxed visibly and gave her a big grin. "It's good to see you, Mary. To what do I owe this honor?"

"We want to give you a bit of trouble if you don't mind."

With a hand he dismissed the guards. "Sit down, all of you." As they found seats, he added, "A bit of trouble? I can't imagine you ever bringing me trouble. What's this all about?"

Mary took a deep breath and looked at her friends for support. Then she said, "It's about that dumb rule you made about not allowing women to travel to Israel with the men."

Suddenly Douglas's face turned a little green. "But, Mary, it's for their own safety. We don't want our women injured in a dangerous war zone."

Mary shook her head in disgust. "It's very kind of you to worry about us weak females and want to protect us. But you're forgetting we did a lot of fighting, right alongside the men, against all kinds of marauders and even UGOT's great army. You weren't nearly so worried about us then."

"But this is different."

"Different? How? Fighting is fighting, no matter where it takes place."

"But your husband . . . husbands."

"Doug, I'm sick of hearing about what our husbands think. Sometimes they go overboard trying to protect us. Haven't you ever heard of nurses on battlefields giving medical treatment to the wounded? All the women here, and hundreds of others, have nursing experience, and we'll be desperately needed in Israel. Without us, hundreds of soldiers will die from their wounds, many of them men from this nation."

"But giving emergency treatment is the job of male medics. The nurses serve behind the lines in field hospitals."

"Okay then. That's what we'll do."

"But we're sending doctors, and Israel has a nursing corps."

"Doctors smockters. Most of them can't even insert an IV properly, much less install a catheter or change a bandage. And I happen to know that the Israeli nursing corps is seriously lacking in the number of nurses. Think about it. They'll need us desperately over there. I expect you to give us permission to go to Israel, and if you don't, we'll visit you every day for a year until you do."

"But the prophet said—"

"The prophet got the idea from you. He'll go along if you ask him."

With that, the women huffed out of the president's office and glared at the two guards still waiting outside the door, one of the ladies hiking up a disgusted shoulder as they walked by.

Douglas shook his head wearily and used a handkerchief to wipe the beads of sweat from his forehead and neck.

The next day it was publicly announced that qualified nurses would be recruited to accompany the troops to Israel, and Steven Christopher resigned himself to the fact that Mary would make the trip with him.

⚜

The only power that the former Israeli prime minister, Aaron Radzik, retained was to arrange for the installation of a new leader. Four days after David and Chaim's discussion in Gethsemane, Radzik called for a special national referendum, and the sole proposal on the ballot was whether or not David Omert should be chosen president pro tempore of the nation. A few days later, the results were in: eighty-five percent of the voters approved the new leader. However, in this case, the president would not be a figurehead as all past Israeli presidents had been but would be given the powers of an absolute ruler.

Since David Omert would soon become a ruler with total power, similar to that possessed by Israel's ancient kings—Saul, David, and Solomon— Radzik asked the president of the Chief Rabbinate of Israel to anoint the new leader with oil in a solemn assembly before thousands of witnesses. The ceremony was followed by a national celebration and a new birth of hope in the hearts of the people.

⚜

Alexi Glinka, UGOT's associate in charge of Russia, put in a special call to Gerald

Galloway while the dictator was having lunch on the patio behind his country manor in Hampshire County, England. "Yes, Alexi, what is on your mind?" Galloway asked.

"President Galloway, sorry to disturb you. It's probably nothing important, but it has been bothering me a great deal. I understand the Jews have recently revolted and thrown out all their current leaders. Now they have elected one of their former prime ministers, David Omert, to take over the reins of government as their king, with absolute power in Israel. Do you think he'll be a problem for us?"

Gerald frowned with displeasure. "I'm aware of those changes in Israel. Apparently, he's one of the most capable leaders Israel has ever had. And he's really a hardcase. It's an unfortunate turn of events, but I assure you that no leader, however effective he may be, can help Israel now.""Thank you for that reassurance, sir. That gives me peace of mind."

Gerald hung up and continued eating his lunch. A few minutes later, Elenore, Gerald's stately wife, approached him and said, "There's someone to see you, dear."

"Who?"

"That genealogist you wanted to talk to. He's at the door to the patio."

Gerald looked toward the house and saw a short man in a business suit, holding a hat in his hands and wearing spectacles far too large for his face. "Tell him to come."

She walked over to the man, said something quickly, and disappeared into the mansion as the man headed toward Gerald.

"Good day, sir," Gerald said in a friendly voice as the man extended a hand.

"Good day to you, Mr. Galloway. You called my office?"

"Yes, my secretary did. Yesterday morning, I believe."

"My name is Lewis Adler. I'm the owner of Genealogical Researchers."

"I've heard you people are the best in the world at what you do. Is that right?"

"There's no reason for me to be modest. Yes, I believe we are the best."

Gerald smiled as the little man straighten to his full height of five feet four inches. "I've also heard you do something with DNA."

"We do. We combine records research with genetic genealogy."

"How does that work, exactly?"

"Well, we take a sample of the client's saliva and send it to a lab in London that has the largest DNA database in the world. Fifty million samples at present. Meanwhile, we search computerized genealogical records in order to reproduce the client's family tree. These days we often go back over five hundred years, sometimes farther depending on circumstances. From our staff of twenty-three, we assign three separate experts to verify the research on every individual. I myself am the third expert to check the work of the others."

"Sounds thorough."

"It's very thorough. When we have established the family tree, we compare the client's lineage with the report from the DNA lab. Nearly always their report supports our findings."

"What's the possibility of error?"

"About one chance in a thousand."

"That's unbelievable! Just off the top of your head, how would you describe my lineage?"

The genealogist cleared his throat. "The name Galloway is of Scottish origin. It probably comes from Gaelic 'gall,' which means stranger or foreigner, and Old English 'weg,' which means road. So the name Galloway might mean a stranger traveling on a road."

"Interesting. I suppose in a sense I truly am a stranger on a road. When can I receive your report?"

"Usually, it requires about four months, but in your case I'm sure we can do it sooner. I'll need your birth records and any family documents you might have. And also a sample of your DNA."

"How do you get that? A blood test?"

"No, it's a lot easier than that. I can do it right now." He opened a small satchel, removed some plastic bags, a comb, a cotton swab, and plastic gloves. After putting on the gloves, he ran the fine-toothed comb through Gerald's gray hair several times and, leaving the strands of hair in the comb, dropped the comb into one of the smaller bags. Next, he rubbed the cotton swab against the inside of Gerald's cheek and put the swab into a second bag. He labeled a larger plastic bag and put the two smaller bags into it. "Okay, we're done."

"Thank you. Please go into the house and ask my wife for my records. I travel around a lot, but you can reach me by first contacting my wife at the number you already have. Send me your bill with the results."

The prim little man gave a crisp bow and retreated into the house.

As Gerald watched him go, he thought about what the research might show. Surely he was the descendant of some great lord or king. Even his divine guide, who visited him from time to time, assured him of this. In his heart of hearts, Gerald felt he must be a descendant of Charlemagne, the mighty ruler of the Holy Roman Empire. He couldn't wait to receive the genealogical report to verify his speculations.

Major General Dimitri Petrov led his tank battalion into the Russian city of Tambov around noon. He was a tall, bold man with silver hair and a strong, jutting jaw. They had traveled southeast nearly three hundred miles from a military installation on the outskirts of Moscow. For the first two hundred miles he had moved his T-90 MS main battle tanks on huge tank transporters because the paved highway was relatively intact for that distance. However, the remainder of the highway had been seriously damaged by earthquakes and floods and especially by militant Muslim terrorists intent on destroying the roads—and the entire infrastructure, for that matter—of this nation of infidels, who had slaughtered so many of Islam's faithful, especially in the lands surrounding the Black Sea.

Tens of thousands of Islamic terrorists were doing the same thing all over Europe, Asia, Africa, and South America.

So Petrov was forced to disembark the tanks from the trucks and travel the remaining distance on dirt and gravel roads. His corps of sixty tanks was accompanied by fifteen thousand soldiers, most of them transported in small trucks and various kinds of armored personnel carriers, or APCs.

Following a book of maps and a kill list, Petrov had stopped at Tambov to hunt down the local Jewish community not far from the city. His orders were to exterminate every member of the village, including men, women, and children.

This would be his first of many such liquidations on the long and difficult journey to the Holy Land.

The general left his main unit a few miles outside the city limits and proceeded in his own tank southwest along the bank of the Tsna River. He was accompanied by another tank, three armored fighting vehicles, and a troop of foot soldiers. According to the map, his target was not far from the river.

This assignment was insufferable for Petrov. Why had his stupid superiors commanded him to destroy peaceful Jewish settlements? These people had never harmed anyone. Better to have sought out the Muslim terrorists who were bent on destroying the motherland. But as usual, those masked cowards were always in hiding, revealing themselves only briefly to wreak havoc. And to think that his final destination was the Holy Land where he would be forced to help other hate-filled terrorists of the same race as they strove to annihilate the home of the Jews. It was a bitter pill to swallow.

A young Jewish couple, named Abel and Karmia Golding, bounced along the country road in their old Ford pickup truck, laughing happily at the shenanigans of their three small children in the truck's bed. Fortunately, the kids were all secured with straps improvised by Abel. As they rounded the last hill before reaching their village, Abel suddenly hit the brakes hard. Karmia's head almost slammed into the dashboard.

"What are you doing, Abel? Are you crazy? I almost—"

"Tanks and soldiers!"

Karmia looked up and followed his gaze. What she saw stunned her into silence. Abel poked his head out the window and shouted for his children to be quiet. He put the truck into reverse and backed down the road and out of sight of the soldiers.

Stopping his vehicle a hundred feet down the gravel road, he said to Karmia, "Stay here. I'm going to climb the hill and check it out."

"Nuts to that! I'm going with you."

Abel knew better than to argue. He ordered the children to stay in the truck, promised to return in a few minutes, and hurried up the hill with Karmia. When they reached the top, they lay down on their stomachs and watched as the tanks swung their turrets toward the village and the soldiers hurried to get into formation. People in the village, who had been talking to each other or doing some type of work, looked up and stared at the newcomers, clearly stunned by the fearful sight. Their beautiful new synagogue stood bright and shiny in the middle of the town.

"What are those soldiers doing?" Karmia asked. "Why are they here?"

Abel ignored her. "Why are the idiots just standing there like sheep waiting for the slaughter?"

"The slaughter!"

Before she could say more, the two big tank guns boomed and spit flames fifteen feet out from their muzzles, and the shells exploded into the synagogue, obliterating the sacred building. At the same time, the machine guns on each tank opened fire, mowing down people and animals and shattering buildings and vehicles. The carnage lasted only about a minute and was followed by a deathly silence. At that point, forty soldiers, brandishing AK-47 rifles, rushed forward to finish off any survivors.

"Let's get out of here!" Abel exclaimed. Karmia's pale face was wet with tears, and she seemed paralyzed. Abel grabbed her arm and began to pull her down the hill. "We've got to warn our friends and get the children to a safe place."

They reached the pickup and drove into the nearby countryside to warn as many of their fellow Jews as possible. They managed to save dozens of people by their timely warnings, and the hapless victims of terror hastened to predetermined places where they had set up secret refuges after enduring years of persecution from the Russian government.

Abel and Karmia had also built a shack in a remote wooded area, and they rushed to get there when they had warned everyone they could. Fortunately, they had supplied the shack with enough food and water to last several weeks.

After they had settled in, Abel walked outside to use his cell phone. His brother, who lived with his family in Kimry, Russia, which was almost four hundred miles away, answered the call after several rings.

"Vitali, is that you? This is Abel."

His brother said several things, but the reception was intermittent and Abel had trouble understanding. Finally, Vitali's voice came in clear. "Yes, it's good to hear from you, little brother."

"I have important news to tell you!" Abel blurted out in desperation.

"What is it?" Vitali replied. "What's happened? You sound terrible."

Abel described in detail what had happened to his local Jewish community in the last two hours. He ended by telling Vitali that he and Karmia were in hiding.

"Are you sure it was a contingent of the regular Russian army?" Vitali asked.

"Absolutely certain."

"Then it must represent a new policy of the Kremlin. What does it mean for us, Abel?"

"I believe we're facing the Second Holocaust. Do whatever you can to save your family and friends."

Another community of Jews, citizens of Turkey, had decided to leave their homeland in great haste and migrate to Israel, which was about two hundred and twenty miles to the south. After leaving Turkey, they would have to walk along the eastern Mediterranean coast through the dangerous land of Syria for fifty-six miles, and then continue down the length of Lebanon, another hundred and forty miles. They had very few supplies, but fortunately they had remembered to bring whatever guns and ammunition they had been able to secretly acquire. These forbidden items were carefully hidden from view.

The first contingent had left Osmaniye—a city of about two hundred thousand people—in southern Turkey several days ago. There had been only seventy refugees at the beginning, but as they traveled along, nearly a hundred of their brothers and sisters—fellow citizens—had joined them with the same destination in mind. At first they had possessed a dozen or so vehicles, but soon their gas tanks had run dry, and they had been forced to abandon them, one at a time.

Bella and Yannic Kleinberg and their five children had left their home precipitously after hearing, in media reports and in personal communications, that the new policy of the Turkish government was to apprehend and incarcerate all people of Jewish ancestry. They were not fooled and knew those detainees would never be seen again.

The young family trudged along the road, all of them carrying bundles. The sun was high in the sky, the heat oppressive, and they were weary and drenched with sweat. The blisters on their feet and the strained muscles of their aching legs made walking sheer torture. It became even more difficult when Bella and Yannic had to carry the two younger children.

The refugees were ten miles from the Syrian border when shots rang out, coming from an area east of the road. Several of the refugees collapsed to the ground, and the others looked around confused, not understanding what was going on. As Yannic spotted a group of men moving in the bushes about fifty yards distance, a Jewish man kneeling close by drew a pistol from his pack and began to return fire. Soon others followed suit, and before long, a full-scale battle was in progress. By that time, most of the travelers had dropped to the road or sought safety in the ravines on the sides of the highway. From time to time, the louder booms of powerful hunting rifles were heard from the enemy position, and more refugees toppled to the ground with gaping wounds.

"Who are they, Yannic?" Bella cried, lying next to him on the hard gravel.

"I don't know." Yannic fired several rounds with his illegal handgun and then slipped in another clip.

He saw the man who had first defended the column rise and rush toward the attackers, calling for others to join him. Yannic jumped to his feet, and he and twenty other men charged across the field toward the partially hidden enemy. All these men were armed and determined to fight for their families. When the cowardly assailants saw the defenders almost upon them, they broke and ran for their lives, scrambling through the bushes to reach safety on the other side of a ridge not far away. As the sixteen ambushers climbed the low ridge, the Jewish fighters shot all but two of them. These two slid over the crest, and their pursuers decided not to follow.

The refugees buried their dead and gave assistance to the wounded, using their meager supply of bandages and medicines. Since it was still mid-afternoon, they continued their journey, with heads hung low and tears bathing the eyes of most because of the loss of family and newfound friends.

"Do you know who they were?" Bella asked her husband.

"No, but I know they were civilians speaking Turkish."

Bella said nothing for a full minute, clearly stunned. "Why would regular people, citizens of Turkey like us, want to do us harm?"

Yannic shook his head sadly. "Most likely because of the government's statements on the news that we are now enemies of the state. When that kind of thing happens, the worst comes out in some people, and they feel justified in committing horrible acts, all in the name of protecting their homeland."

"Maybe they thought we were helpless and just wanted to steal our belongings," Bella added.

"I suppose that's possible, but they chose a violent way to do it."

Holding onto Yannic's arm, she continued to plod along without saying another word.

In the late afternoon, Bella stopped suddenly. "What's that roaring sound, Yannic?"

He stopped and listened, and the travelers near them halted also, asking each other questions. The noise became louder, and Yannic searched the skies to the north. After a few tense moments, he screamed, "It's a plane, coming right for us, flying low and fast. Run for cover, everybody!" In spite of his heavy pack, he scooped up his little ones and ran for the ditch adjoining the road. Bella and the other children followed close behind.

The F-16 C fighter jet came in low at two hundred miles an hour, and when it reached the rear of the refugee column, its powerful gun began to strafe them at one hundred rounds a second. In four seconds it had torn up the road for a quarter of a mile and killed nearly every person still on it. Yannic could tell it was a Turkish warplane from the distinctive insignia on its fin.

After the jet had flown over, Yannic rose and looked to see what had happened. He felt dizzy and sick when he beheld the terrible sight of the mangled and bloody bodies covering the road. Seeing that the fighter was circling for a second run, he rushed his family to the protection of some trees fifty yards away and made everyone fall to the ground behind any cover they could find.

The warplane made another run but fired no rounds. Apparently, the pilot figured he had done a good job the first time. Yannic waited ten minutes to make sure the attacker was gone, and then he and Bella ran to the road to check for survivors. When they arrived, they saw a dozen of their fellow countrymen examining the bodies in hopes of finding anyone still alive. The scene was heart-wrenching, but Yannic knew that whoever had survived the attack and could travel would continue the journey to their ancient home in the Holy Land, even if they died in the attempt.

They had no other choice.

Chapter 3

⌘

Most of the nations of the earth, with the exception of Canada, Australia, the United Kingdom, the Republic of Zion, and a few smaller nations, had committed themselves to join the great crusade against Israel. UGOT had given them some absolute commands: bring all the firepower in their possession, be ready to fight to the death, and make sure they were in Palestine by the first part of August. It was up to each nation how they transported their armies to the battle zone.

The leaders of several nations in Southeast Asia, including Vietnam, Cambodia, Thailand, Laos, and Myanmar, decided to send their armies westward by land, fearing the growing violence of the waters of the Bay of Bengal, the Arabian Sea, and especially the Indian Ocean. Needless to say, those armies did not travel together because of the many disputes and hatreds that remained from the past.

Their brigades of artillery, tanks, and infantry moved up Indochina on reasonably good roads, but when they reached the relatively narrow neck of land south of the Himalayas through Myanmar, also called Burma, the few roads available quickly became narrow and treacherous. Their progress was slowed, but their generals were confident they would reach Palestine in plenty of time to enjoy the destruction and plunder of Israel. After they exited Myanmar, they would have to travel across Bangladesh, India, Pakistan, Iran, Iraq, and Jordan, or the northern tip of Saudi Arabia, depending on the route they chose. The long trip would be gruesome, but at least they would have the pleasure of obliterating thousands of Jewish idolaters along the way.

⌘

Forty-two members of the Tangail Evangelical Holiness Church were worshiping in their newly constructed little church just outside Tangail, Bangladesh, when their services were interrupted by an unusual noise. As a group, they rushed outside to see what was going on. Was it the local Muslims who for months had been threatening them with death and beating them for daring to believe in Christianity instead of Islam, which was by far the predominant religion in the country?

To their surprise, it wasn't the intolerant neighbors at all, but some bizarre strangers dressed in forest green uniforms. The Christian peasants saw rifles, tanks, cannons on trailers, all types of armored cars, and hundreds—maybe thousands!—of soldiers.

"Have these men come to free us from the persecution of the townspeople?" asked an old Bengali to those standing near him. They shook their heads in confusion, their blank looks showing that they had no answer to the question.

Lokesh Khanna put his arm around his new wife of three months and tried to guide her away from the gaping community of believers, but she was just as mesmerized as the others. "Let's get out of here, Indra. This doesn't look good."

"But maybe our Christian brothers and sisters from the west have sent these men to protect us."

"No, these soldiers have an eastern look and are wearing ugly green uniforms."

Lokesh, normally a gentle man, used more force than he ever had before to lead his wife back into the crowd and then off to the side, sliding quickly into the dense forest thirty yards away. Fully concealed, they peeked out of the foliage to see what would happen.

The commander of the military unit gave the signal, and a hundred or more soldiers dropped to one knee and began to fire upon the helpless, unarmed Christians. Within fifteen seconds, all of them lay on the ground dead or nearly dead from multiple wounds. Then the commander walked forward slowly and deliberately, pulled out his service revolver, and began to finish off the victims who showed any signs of life, shooting them point-blank in the head.

As one of the commander's lieutenants came forward, the leader said in Vietnamese, "Check each of these filthy Jews to make sure they're dead."

The lieutenant caught sight of something unusual attached to the bullet-riddled wall of the church. "My illustrious General, I don't think they're Jews."

"What do you mean? Sure they are. The map shows a Jewish community located right here."

"The map must be wrong, sir. I believe they're Christians."

The commander glared at his subordinate. "Nonsense! How do you know that?" he growled.

The lieutenant pointed to the church wall. "Because that's a Christian cross on the church."

After eyeing the cross for a few seconds, the general said with indifference, "Well, who cares whether they are Jews or Christians? It's all the same, isn't it?"

Lokesh and Indra couldn't hear what the commander said, but they saw what he did. They slipped away quietly into the forest, hoping to find refuge in another village and determined to keep their religious beliefs a secret from that moment on.

David Omert began immediately to make radical changes in Israel, knowing that the nation had very little time to prepare for the dreadful crisis looming over them. After careful consideration and research, he summoned thirty-two of the most brilliant and experienced people in the nation. They would function as his cabinet of advisers. Most of them were given power over the various departments of civil life, but five were assigned to be ministers of defense. One of these was Chaim Yehoshua, David's trusted friend. The defense ministers were given two days to suggest the names of the people they believed to be the most qualified military leaders that Israel had to offer to lead the army. He also instructed them to come up with effective overall strategies for protecting the nation.

The day after he first met with his new advisers, he appeared on national TV with a special announcement. He began his speech by introducing his new counselors, one by one. Then he presented some shocking new decisions.

"My fellow citizens, I assure you that these new advisers are well-qualified and dedicated people. Now I wish to inform you of a number of important determinations I have made in your behalf. My advisers fully concur with all of them. As of today, the Defense Service Law, which has authorized military conscription since the founding of this nation, is revoked. In other words, we will no longer require military service from our people. From this time forward we will ask our citizens to *volunteer* for military service.

"Many in this nation will be astonished at this decision. They will say the nation is doomed without the draft. They will say I am wrong to think that our people will volunteer. They will affirm—in their fear—that the Israel Defense Forces will no longer have sufficient troops to adequately defend our nation. And they will declare that the imminent destruction of Israel will rest fully upon my shoulders.

"But I say to you that they underestimate the courage and patriotism of our people. I believe more people will come forward than when the draft was in force, happy and willing to offer their services to their country. I know that those volunteers will make us much stronger in the face of the innumerable hosts of an enemy with vast resources.

"At the same time, we will no longer provide funds for students to go to school, especially since most of those students have been exempt from the draft. Some have even enrolled in school for the purpose of avoiding military service. The payments that once funded the schooling of students will now be used to increase the wages of military personnel. I have also annulled the law that requires military service as a prerequisite for obtaining employment.

"Let me make a few things absolutely clear. Our sworn enemies will succeed in destroying our precious homeland. They will make good their threat to slaughter every single individual of this great nation. They will achieve their goal to plunder Israel of all its wealth, resources, and technology. *Your* wealth, resources, and technology. And they will prosper by using their victories here to help them enslave or destroy all other nations and peoples who refuse to accept their dominion.

"And how will they achieve those victories? Only if you do nothing. So that is why I ask you, our young people, to volunteer for our armed forces. Without you, we are lost.

"We will also increase the size and effectiveness of our reserve forces, providing them with better equipment and training. As most of you know, the reserve forces have saved this nation from annihilation many times in the past. Many of you who volunteer will be asked to become part of that crucial force.

"In addition, we will no longer adhere to the failed doctrine of trading land for peace, no matter what the media says, no matter how much the United Nations General Assembly condemns us, and in spite of all the uninformed criticism brought against us by the so-called world community. You realize, of course, that the General Assembly is controlled by the Arab nations, and other anti-Semitic countries, and automatically accuses and condemns us for nearly every problem in the world.

"But back to my point. The policy of land for peace has never worked in the past and will not work in the future. In the course of our history as a nation, we have given in to our enemies over and over again in the naive hope that by giving them concessions, they would accept our right to exist as nation and cease engaging in violent attacks against our people. But our enemies have never kept their promises. Instead, they have used our weakness and desire for peace against us.

"Now to address the problem of the Palestinians. The leaders of the Palestinians demand that we must recognize the doctrine of the two-state solution to the Palestinian problem. They say we are guilty of preventing them from forming their own nation by our incursions into their territory. However, the Palestinians are no more than disparate Arabs tribes left stranded in Israel by the Arab nations at large so that those Arab nations might exploit the plight of the Palestinians as a means of destroying Israel.

"The Palestinians have never been a nation and have no historical right whatever to the territory they claim belongs to them. So I encourage you to reject the propaganda from Arab nations and their sympathizers on the world stage, propaganda that claims the Palestinians are entitled to our God-given land to form a nation—a nation we know they are not entitled to.

"Furthermore, in the event that any nation or terrorist organization within a nation fires rockets or missiles into our communities, or makes violent incursions into our boundaries, we will respond with proportionate force, and any territory we take in battle will be considered an integral part of Israel.

"In the near future I will institute many other strong measures to ensure our survival as a nation and our prosperity. I hope and pray that you will support me and my counselors in our endeavors. Everything we strive to do will be for your welfare. Good day and God bless."

After three weeks, the Republic of Zion had recruited more than seventy thousand volunteers. The majority had already fought in battles to defend Zion against large armies, or in skirmishes to protect their communities from roving bands of marauders, who occasionally attacked towns, especially on the borders of the land. Since Zion had grown rapidly in the last four and a half years, those borders were almost as far apart as those of Old America.

Many of the military commanders who had been in charge of Zion's forces in the campaign against UGOT's invading army were called to serve. Again, Michael Jamison was selected as the commanding general. The president of the republic, Douglas Cartwright, also chose Mosheh Lazar and Yaakov Raphan, chiefs of the first company of Ten Tribes to arrive in Zion, to be colonels, assigned to lead their own people under the command of General Jamison.

The Ten Tribes segment of Zion's troops comprised about eleven thousand soldiers, and Jewish Americans contributed nearly five thousand men. Several thousand recruits were not members of the Church but believed in the cause of Israel.

Though nearly all the volunteers had some military experience, their commanders put them through a two-week crash course of training. As a crucial part of that program, they learned a great deal about Israel, including the topography of Palestine, the customs of the Israelis, and about Israel's military training and equipment.

The first companies were scheduled to leave during the third week of May, and the leaders expected that they would arrive on the east coast of the Republic of Zion in five or six days, traveling in caravans of trucks. Fortunately, there were now four firms that ran transatlantic cruise ships from many ports in the Old World to the new republic. This was the result of the millions of migrants who wanted to travel from many nations to the safe haven of Zion. The cruise ships carried an average of four thousand passengers.

The cruise ships were the only way a nation could transport large armies, because the old troopships and ocean liners used during World War II and later were obsolete and had been purposely sunk, had been preserved as museums or floating hotels, or sat rusting away in isolated ports.

At this time, it was extremely dangerous to cross the Atlantic Ocean—or journey on any sea for that matter—because of the many violent storms encountered, and the great cruise ships were always in danger of being sunk by colossal waves. Yet the profit was so lucrative that the companies were willing to accept the risks, especially since their owners never ventured upon the waters themselves. However, the leaders of New Zion and the Church assured the troops that the Lord would bless them and give them safe passage.

The generals of Zion surmised that the sea voyage would take about ten to twelve days, barring unforeseen impediments, and they hoped to disembark the troops at Ashdod Port on the western coast of Israel.

Two weeks after instructing his five defense ministers to give him the names of the most qualified military leaders in Israel, David Omert met with his war ministers and the military personnel they had proposed in a closed meeting at the Knesset building. Twenty of the selected people were men and three were women.

"I welcome all of you to this meeting," David said. "As you know, we find ourselves as a nation in dire circumstances. Not only has UGOT commanded its coalition of governments to mobilize their forces for a united attack on Israel, but the Arab nations that surround us have stepped up their terrorist attacks, and there are signs that they are assembling their troops to attack Israel before the UGOT coalition armies arrive on the borders of Palestine."

"When do you expect those armies to arrive?" asked Abir Cohen, one of the defense ministers.

"From the reports we've intercepted, they should arrive in less than three months, in early August."

There was general consternation in the room, and everyone turned to his or her neighbor and engaged in animated discussions. David gave them a minute to talk before he called for order.

"If you have questions, please ask them one at a time by raising your hand. I'll try to answer every question I can."

"Three months gives us little time to prepare," Danny Fischer said. Fischer had served as a brigadier general in dozens of past engagements against Hezbollah and Hamas terrorists. He was a short, plump man with a round, red face, lit by large blue eyes.

"Time to prepare!" exclaimed Beth Moskal, a colonel currently in charge of a Jewish brigade on the west bank of the Sea of Galilee. She was a tall brunette of thirty-five with a surprisingly muscular body, wide blue eyes, and a narrow face. "How in the world do we prepare for armies numbering in the hundreds of thousands?"

"Probably millions," David corrected.

Brigadier General Izaak Berg, an old war veteran who was short and had a square face and a body like a tank, declared, "Well, our only hope is to use the bomb. Before they even get close to Israel. What else can we do?"

"Yes, General Berg is right," said Lieutenant Colonel Seth Ribicoff. "What choice do we have?"

David noticed that no one was raising his hand as he had asked, but he decided not to scold them because he wanted them to express themselves as freely as possible.

"That's crazy," replied Chaim Yehoshua, his face red and angry. "If we use the bomb, they'll do the same. Some of those nations have atomic arsenals."

"That's right," Beth Moskal agreed. "And we know who they are. China, North Korea, India, Pakistan, Iran, France, Germany, and the United Kingdom. All UGOT would have to do is give them the go-ahead, and they could hit us with enough nuclear power to destroy every inch of Israel."

Colonel Lucius Baranski, who had become a national hero because of his courage on the battlefield, looked perplexed. "What I don't understand is why UGOT hasn't used the bomb against us in the first place. It would be cheaper, quicker, and more effective. Why mobilize the armies of so many nations? Since they have their nuclear arsenals spread widely across the planet, they can't really be afraid we'd use nukes against them. Even with the world's most effective intel, we haven't been able to locate all the sites. They could hit us with a preemptive nuclear strike, and we'd never have a chance." Baranski was a tall, bold man with bright green eyes and a slender but powerful body. He was quickly recognizable from his bald head. Many compared him to the great Moshe Dayan, minus the eyepatch.

No one said a word. Clearly they had no idea why UGOT had taken their present course of action.

David decided to give them his opinion on the matter. "I have no proof, but I believe there are several possible explanations as to why Galloway has commanded his allies to transport their troops to Palestine, instead of employing nuclear weapons."

"Wait!" declared Colonel Varda Reuben. "I seem to be out of the loop. What do you mean transport troops? And millions of them! President Omert, when you spoke of UGOT mobilizing forces, I thought you meant their coalition partners would gather their fighting forces and put them on alert. Then at the appointed time, dispatch warplanes and paratrooper air transports to this region for an attack against Israel. But move millions of troops here by ground transport!" Reuben was a short woman of immense will and energy, with a profound knowledge of military tactics.

"I know," David replied. "It's perfectly crazy. But as I said, Galloway must have personal reasons for that plan of action."

"What reasons?" asked Colonel Baranski.

"I can only guess. I've expended a great deal of energy trying to learn everything I could about Galloway, but there's still a lot of mystery surrounding him."

"I think he's just a nut job," Chaim Yehoshua said angrily. "Kind of like Hitler."

David grinned at his friend's bluntness. "I think he's insane too, but there seems to be a method to his madness. He wants to destroy Israel as a nation without destroying our wealth and technology because he promised to give that wealth to his allies as an enticement to gain their support. Also, he wants to use his ground invasion forces as a means of annihilating hundreds of Jewish, Mormon, and Christian communities in the countries they pass through as they proceed to Palestine."

"But doesn't Galloway already have enough power and wealth?" said Phineas Danziger, an Israeli major general who was born in Russia but migrated to Israel fifteen years ago. David had chosen Danziger as a war minister because of his credentials. He had been a lieutenant colonel in the Eight-Day War, had fought in many Arab incursions, and was an expert on military strategy and tactics. His famous book on the subject was read by nearly every Israeli officer in the Israel Defense Forces. "The guy's seventy-two now and doesn't have many years left to enjoy all his wealth and power."

David gazed somberly at the table in front of him, slowly shaking his head. "No doubt he figures he can leave his empire to his children or grandchildren when he dies. Yet there's some other secret motivation I can't put my finger on. Something sinister."

"Okay, Mr. President," said Beth Moskal. "What are we going to do about the invasion forces and our Arab neighbors?" The primary Arab nations involved in the struggle included Lebanon, Syria, Jordan, Iraq, Egypt, and Iran.

"We are going to strike the Arabs in the next few days," David replied. "I have publicly warned them that we will no longer respect the territory of nations which allow terrorists to operater on their land, and we will no longer tolerate troop movements near our borders. Apparently, they thought I wasn't serious."

"I don't understand why they would suddenly become so unusually bellicose," said Phineas Danziger. "They're directly ignoring the instructions of Galloway and his associates."

"Well, by special intel leaks, I have disseminated some juicy propaganda claiming that UGOT is actually exploiting his Arab confederates."

"Great strategy!" said General Izaak Berg. "More details, please."

"I encouraged Arab leaders to believe that UGOT wanted them to delay attacking us until the coalition armies arrived so that those forces might receive the glory for conquering Israel and obtain most of its riches. In other words, I wanted the Arabs to believe that UGOT despised them as much as the Jews and would turn on them after defeating Israel."

"And you think they bought it?" Danny Fischer asked.

"It seems so, from what the Arabs are doing."

"Still, aren't we asking for trouble?" Izaak Berg said.

David laughed and said, "We already have trouble coming our way—big trouble. The purpose of this is to divide and conquer. We defeat the Arabs before the foreign armies arrive, and then we concentrate on UGOT's coalition."

Colonel Varda Reuben frowned and said, "However, that might not be as easy as you seem to imply. The Arabs have four times the troops we have, with better weapons and training than ever before. Besides, thanks to our former liberal leaders, they now control the Golan Heights, the Gaza Strip, and the West Bank. I seriously doubt we can defeat them in six days or even six months."

The fact that Arab battalions controlled the Golan Heights, the West Bank, and Gaza meant that they had platforms in very close proximity to Israel's borders from which to launch missiles into Israel, and their armies could invade by traveling no more than a few miles.

David looked at Varda with confidence, showing no sign of worry or fear. "I didn't say it would be easy, but we'll succeed, and it won't take as long as you might think. It's true that Israel is in a precarious situation, but we still have the finest army and the most sophisticated military technology in the world. Most of all, our soldiers, and the people in general, know they are fighting for their very existence and for their homeland. We have leaked another rumor that will soon reach the ears of certain Arab leaders."

"What rumor?" asked Lieutenant General Yeshaya Chorney, chief of the General Staff of the IDF, or the Israel Defense Forces. Chorney was a handsome, likeable man in his forties, with a short beard and long black hair. His competence as a strategist had been proven in many past encounters.

"Well, I made sure that a special communiqué to one of our majors serving near the Syrian border was intercepted by Syrian authorities. In that report we indicated that we had irrefutable evidence that if a war was initiated with Israel, King Hussein bin Abdullah of Jordan planned to send a strike force directly into Jerusalem to capture our capital, and thus put himself in a position to control the holy sites and annex the city to Jordan. He would do this while we were occupied fighting the other Arab nations on our boundaries."

"Whew!" Chorney said. "I'll bet Ibn 'abbas went wild when he heard that." Ibn 'abbas al-Boutros was the president of Syria and had ambitions of being the top Arab leader in the Middle East. He also considered himself to be the hero of Syria because he had quelled the decades-long civil war in that country by defeating local insurgents and driving out foreign terrorists like al-Qaeda.

"Obviously," David continued, "our purpose was to profit from the traditional bickering and mistrust between Arab nations. When they're fighting with each other, they can't be as effective in fighting us."

They talked for another half hour, discussing upcoming battles, before the meeting came to a close. All but David and his five war ministers drifted out of the room, and David started the next meeting.

"Okay, gentlemen," David said, "you heard the little trap I've laid for Ibn 'abbas al-Boutros. Now how can we exploit it?"

Phineas Danziger laughed. "By setting another one."

"Please explain?" David said.

Danziger gave a review of a plan based on deception, and after an hour of discussion on the details of the plan, David and the other war ministers accepted it enthusiastically. It was a plan that would take place against Syria only and unfold near the Sea of Galilee and the Golan Heights. Its goal was to gain control of the strategic Golan Heights.

Thousands of people came to the large field ten miles east of Independence near Interstate 70 in the third week of May. Today was the time scheduled for the first contingent of Zion's army to depart for the Holy Land. Hundreds of vehicles had been procured to transport the four thousand soldiers, seventy-three nurses, twenty-one doctors, and dozens of support personnel.

There were conveyances of all kinds, including military trucks, box trucks, panel trucks, large vans, and even pickup trucks. Just about anything that could carry eight or more passengers. Most of them were powered by batteries or solar panels, a few by regular gasoline engines.

As the young warriors waited to board their means of transport, a great crowd of family members and friends swarmed around them, most with sad countenances and tears streaming down their faces. There seemed to be endless hugs, kisses, last-minute words of advice from family members and especially from sweethearts. One young woman was heard to warn her fiancé to be faithful and not get too friendly with any of the beautiful, dark-eyed Jewish girls.

General Jamison, the commanding officer, was pacing up and down impatiently, for it was seven thirty and they were scheduled to leave at eight o'clock. Not all his men had arrived yet, but soon he would have to blow his whistle, the signal for the departure.

Steven Christopher and his family stood near a five-ton truck whose bed was loaded with supplies and covered with a thick tarp of canvas. Those who would travel in that truck included Steven Christopher and Mary and their sons, William and Daniel; John Christopher and his sons, Cory and

Michael; Paul Christopher and his son, Matthew; and Jarrad Babcock. The leaders of the Ten Tribes, Mosheh Lazar and Yaakov Raphan, would ride in a different truck a short distance behind.

As the Christophers were saying good-bye to their family and friends, including Douglas and Elizabeth Cartwright and Andrea and Preston Moore, a strange sight worked its way through the crowd. Steven was amazed to see that it was none other than Ruther Johnston, dressed in mountain man clothes and packing his big Sharps rifle.

"Ruther!" Steven exclaimed with pleasure. "You're back from your excursion. How long has it been? Six months, right? How was the Canadian wilderness? You're certainly a sight for sore eyes. I bet you've come to see us off. How did you know today was the day?" Everyone began to hug Ruther, who was very popular with those present and even with most of the people living in the region around Independence. As Steven embraced the old man, he noticed that his clothes were rough but surprising clean, and he smelled good, as if he had actually taken a bath.

Ruther put down his heavy pack. "Well, yuh see, I had ta make certain yuh poor, inexperienced Mormons didn't git yerselves lost on the trail to that Israeli land over thar."

Not understanding the import of Ruther's words, Mary declared brightly, "It's so nice of you to go to so much trouble to say good-bye and wish us well." The others nodded in agreement.

"You won't have to give us directions, Ruther," Steven said. "For the most part, we'll simply head east on I-70. And then the boat trip . . . Hard to get lost."

"I don't think he's here to give you directions," said Jarrad. "He plans on going with us." Jarrad had been a second lieutenant in Zion's army, but had been promoted to lieutenant recently because of his service record in the skirmishes with the bandits.

"With us!" cried John Christopher. "But, Ruther, aren't you getting a bit long in the tooth to travel thousands of miles and fight in a great war?"

"Little John, yuh always was kinda persnickety about insignificant little details. I may look a mite elderly, but actually I'm bearin' down on the full prime of life. I'd like ta see you survive for six months in that Canadian bush country."

"How old are you now?" Paul Christopher asked.

"I'm a young seventy-six."

"I'm worried about you, though," Andrea said. "What if you get hurt in Israel? You'll arrive in the terrible heat of summer. There'll be months and months of gruesome fighting. The men will have to march hundreds of miles over dusty terrain and spend weeks or longer in dirty trenches. Many of our men will die, and the rest may not be able to come home for months, maybe years."

"Jist my cup of tea," Ruther exclaimed with a toothless grin. "Lookee here, folks. You're all forgettin' the forty or fifty times I done bailed yuh all out of death's jaws. With this here long gun, I'll teach them Arabs a thing or two." Ruther lengthened the first vowel of the word Arabs.

Steven had to admit that Ruther had a point. "What do you think, Douglas?"

"Well, we've focused on recruiting young men to go over there, but I suppose we could make an exception for an unusual warrior. Ruther, in view of your experience in battle, I, the president of the Republic of Zion, hereby give you a commission as colonel in our army."

"Thanks, Doug. I loves yer highfalutin words. I'll admit I'm probably worthy of the honor you done bestowed on me. Now, let's git this here show on the road. We gots some fightin' ta do."

Shortly before the troops left for the East Coast, the prophet, Wilford Benson, and several apostles arrived to bless them on their journey. President Benson offered a five-minute prayer, promising the brave soldiers that they would have a safe journey to the Holy Land. Next, the senior apostle, Jason Widtsoe, also gave a prayer in which he promised them that they would play a significant role in the defense of their Israeli brethren and that many of them would see the face of the Savior.

After Jason's prayer, the prophet stood again and said, "I want to communicate one more important matter to you, especially those who are traveling to Israel. In accordance with the will of the Lord, the First Presidency has called and ordained Brother Steven Christopher to a very special mission, and he has willingly accepted the responsibilities that mission entails. We have called him to be the spiritual leader of all the troops traveling to Israel. Moreover, he has been given the authority to baptize and ordain the principal leaders of Israel and the two Jewish prophets the Lord will soon raise up in that land, as described in the eleventh chapter of the Book of Revelation. We enjoin you to support Steven in his great calling. May God bless all of you in your more general mission of supporting the cause of the Lord in Israel."

Ten minutes later, the new warriors solemnly said farewell to their homeland and climbed into their trucks. Other contingents would follow them every three or four weeks, as circumstances permitted.

Chapter 4

❧

In late May, the great Chinese army of three million troops snaked laboriously over the never-ending gravel roads, around hundreds of sharp turns, and past dangerous precipices, with drops hundreds of feet to the valleys below. They were following the great highway through the Pamir Mountains of Tajikistan, often referred to as "the roof of the world." The Chinese Politboro had decided not to send troops through India for fear that Indian forces would attack them or block their progress because of past border disputes in the south.

This army included almost twenty thousand light tanks, four thousand Type 99 main battle tanks, twenty-six thousand armored personnel carriers, several hundred artillery tractors and transporters, over fifteen thousand transport trucks to carry troops and supplies, about six hundred fuel tankers, and a thousand water tankers. The tankers were relatively small to allow them to negotiate the twists and turns of the Pamir Highway.

Earlier, when the Japanese had asked permission to travel through China on their journey to Palestine, the Chinese had refused outright because they didn't want their traditional enemy to transport a large army into their country. The result had been several battles between Japanese and Chinese fleets on the Sea of Japan, in which both countries had suffered defeats. Now the Japanese had no choice but to move their armies by sea, a very perilous enterprise.

The Chinese commanding officer, General Deshi Sun, a young prince from one of the richest families in China, was very proud of his army and the glorious things it had already done. It had wiped out sixty Jewish communities, slaughtering every inhabitant by cutting their throats with swords. They had also murdered the citizens of twenty-one Christian settlements because the general had trouble distinguishing between them and Jews.

And that was not all. The Chinese army had already been attacked numerous times by guerillas armed with AK-47s and grenade launchers. One of the favorite tactics of the guerillas was to slip into the Chinese camps before sunrise and slit the throats of sleeping soldiers. More than six hundred soldiers had been killed that way, many of them junior officers. General Sun never found out who the guerillas were, but he surmised that they must be Jews seeking revenge or mercenaries hired by Jews.

These problems didn't diminish the great pride of the commander because his troops had been fairly successful at defending themselves during the attacks and usually succeeded in killing most of the black-hooded assailants before they could escape. General Sun swore an oath that he would exact full vengeance on the Jews when he reached Palestine.

The Syrian army attacked at three o'clock in the morning. Three infantry brigades, comprising about ten thousand men, entered Israel from the Golan Heights, supported by two armored brigades, an artillery barrage, and air cover. After the guns had blasted eleven Israeli towns in the vicinity of the Sea of Galilee, the infantry swept down to finish the job. But when they rushed into the communities, bent on murder and mayhem, they received an unbelievable shock.

The towns were completed deserted, and not one Jew was found dead.

The Syrians forces were confused and in disarray. The soldiers and their leaders had no idea what to do because such an unforeseen turn of events was not in their battle plans. They didn't know whether to proceed forward to attack other Jewish towns farther south or to retreat back to their bases in the Golan Heights. Their junior officers showed, as usual, a surprising lack of flexibility, and the commander himself, colonel Zaahir Hadad, had a paralysis of thought and did no more than vent his fury, making angry accusations against Syrian intelligence.

But then the Syrians received an even greater shock. Eight F-35 Israeli warplanes swooped down on them, strafing the troops with machine guns and firing Delilah cruise missiles at tanks and armored vehicles. Some of the jets carried AIM-7 Sparrow missiles for aerial combat. After a battle of twenty minutes, ten Syrian warplanes were shot down and the surviving Syrian jets escaped to the north.

Shortly after the aerial attack, Israeli infantry and armored battalions appeared as if from nowhere, and within an hour the Syrian forces were surrounded. Their supply lines were cut and they could not retreat to their bases on the Golan Heights. The entire battle was over in less than five hours. Most of the Syrian forces had been wiped out, but the survivors raised white flags in surrender, and the Israelis quickly took them as prisoners of war.

As a result of this battle, the Israelis gained control of the Golan Heights, which could now be used as a crucial buffer against incursions from enemies in the northeast. When news of the victory became known to the people of Israel, the psychological effect was immense. They suddenly gained a renewed confidence in their leadership and a greater hope of surviving as a nation.

When the leaders of the Arab nations surrounding Israel learned of the Syrian defeat, they went crazy and condemned Israel's aggression in the most violent terms. They demanded that the world implement the old Palestinian doctrine of BDS, or boycott, divestment, and sanctions. They called for a meeting of all Arab leaders to plan strategies against their common enemy. And finally, they asked all decent peoples everywhere to accelerate their preparations for taking military action against the Jews in a second Holocaust.

Most nations outside the Middle East made fun of these threats and rants, knowing Syria had disobeyed UGOT's instructions, had jumped the gun, and therefore deserved the beating it had received.

But eighteen other Arab nations took this call to arms seriously and threatened to hold recalcitrant nations responsible by depriving them of oil shipments from oil-rich nations like Saudi Arabia, Iran, and Kuwait.

⊰⧈⊱

The truck caravan transporting the troops of Zion was scheduled to reach the American East Coast in six days. The highway near their home in New Jerusalem was in good repair, but as they approached the coast, the roads became progressively worse. There were a few incidents involving attacks from small gangs of bandits, firing upon the army from a great distance, but only a few soldiers were wounded. Even though General Jamison sent out patrols to track the bandits down, they were seldom able to engage their enemies in a firefight. Still, it was enough to make their attackers think twice and the patrols greatly increased the security of the army. When they reached the coast, it took only one day to load the supplies and to board the troops.

Their cruise ship was named *Glory of the Seas* and could easy carry five thousand passengers plus a crew, but the leaders of Zion's forces had decided to limit the number of each group to four thousand men. Even then the ship seemed crowded, no doubt because of all the military gear and weapons they had brought with them. There was no such thing as luxurious accommodations and fancy amenities on these cruise ships, since their purpose was to transport masses of people, not provide them with the trappings of a pleasurable holiday.

As the ship set out to sea, the captain ordered his radioman to contact Jerusalem to tell Israeli leaders they were coming with an army of four thousand men from New America. They had to do this on special, predetermined frequencies so that the message would not be intercepted by UGOT. After an hour of trying to make the connection, the radioman finally reached someone on the other end. The communications expert in Jerusalem made arrangements to connect the captain directly with David Omert himself. David received the news with gratitude and said he and others would meet the Americans when they arrived at Ashdod Port.

During the land trip to the East Coast, Steven had spent a great deal of time counseling and encouraging the troops, and he continued to do so whenever possible on the ship. He praised the men for their courage and sacrifice in obeying the Lord and promised they would reach Israel safely and make a great contribution to the war effort.

The cruise ship was about halfway across the Atlantic Ocean, six hundred miles west of the Azores, when the terrible storm struck around noon. The seasickness that had afflicted hundreds of passengers during the first few days, and then had gradually faded away, returned with a vengeance. Once again, the medical staff had to distribute medicines to ease their suffering from vomiting and nausea.

Shortly after the storm began, Steven took refuge in his cabin with Mary, Ruther, and his brothers, John and Paul. Their sons inhabited another cabinet on the same deck, and Jarrad Babcock was also bunking with the boys.

"Steve, how long do you think the storm will last?" Paul asked as he held on tight to the desk at one side of the cabin.

Steven was at the large cabin window, but he couldn't see anything except regular sheets of rain splashing against the thick pane. "Who knows?" he called back. "I understand a storm can last a day or two or as long as a week."

Suddenly the ship lurched violently to starboard and in seconds swung almost as far to port. Immediately the cabin lights flicked out, and Steven heard Mary scream. Something heavy slammed against the window, and Steven thought for sure it would break, but it didn't. He fumbled his way in the dark, calling Mary's name, and in the roar of the storm he could barely hear her voice.

When he finally found her, he grabbed her and carried her to the bed, where they lay down together, holding each other tightly as they were rocked to and fro. After a few minutes, the light came back on, and Steven guessed that the ship's generators had kicked in.

"Steven," Mary cried, "are we going to drown?"

"No, no, we're not going to drown. This is the way it always is on these big ships during a storm. I've never heard of one sinking." He was trying hard to reassure Mary, but he was just about scared to death himself. As he wondered if the ship had enough life boats for all the passengers, frightening images of the movie Titanic flashed through his mind. He struggled to regain his composure, and he felt better when he remembered that the ship's captain had told him during dinner two days earlier that the *Glory* was one of the safest, best equipped, and most stable cruise liners in the world.

After eight hours the storm finally let up and the ship began to rock less. Everyone seemed less worried and started conversing more freely. None of those who gathered in the cabin at the onset of the storm had wanted to leave. They had done a lot of praying and now felt their prayers had been answered.

Around eight thirty, there was a knock at the cabin door. John opened it and let a ship steward enter. "Sorry we've neglected you all," the steward said. "The storm has caused us a great deal of trouble preparing food. We have only been able to make some potato soup with bread and butter." He lost his balance and fell against the cabin wall. "Oops, sorry. I usually have my sea legs, but the storm has had everybody flustered. I know many have been sick, so the head galley chef told us to check on how many people wanted something to eat. You can eat it here or come down . . . oops . . . to one of the dining rooms."

Steven looked around at the others and understood their wishes. "We'll have it here, if that's okay. How many of you want soup?" Everyone except Paul raised a hand. "I guess we'll have soup for four, please."

"I'll have one of the waiters bring you a pot of soup and the necessary dishes and utensils."

"Thank you," Steven said. "Also, do you think you could find a package of chips for my brother here for when he feels better?"

"Certainly," said the steward as he left the cabin.

After eating, they discussed a number of subjects, and Steven noticed the mournful look on Paul's face. "What's wrong, little brother? You don't look happy. The ship's still wobbling back and forth quite a bit, but I believe the worst is over."

"Oh, it's not that. I was wondering if this war we're heading for will really last three and a half years like the Book of Revelation seems to say. That's a terribly long time."

"So you really miss Jane a lot, don't you?" Steven replied.

"Yes, more than I ever thought I could. I've never been away from her for more than a few days. So what about my question?"

"I don't know for sure, but I do know that many of the numbers given in Revelation are symbolic. You'll probably be back in your wife's arms much sooner than you think."

Paul smiled and gave Steven a hug.

David Omert, Chaim Yehoshua, and Ofek Stoller, the president of the Chief Rabbinate of Israel, stood on the Temple Mount in Jerusalem and gazed at the beautiful new temple which had recently been finished by the dedicated labor of thousands of skilled workmen. It had taken almost twenty-one years to complete. The religious segment of the Jewish population called it the Third Temple, but those of a more secular inclination called it the Fourth Temple because they considered King Herod's extensive renovations just before the birth of Christ to be a different temple from the original.

The construction of the new temple would never have been possible if it had not been for a surprising and fortuitous event that occurred almost twenty-three years earlier during the Eight-Day War between the Arabs and the Israelis. During that war, the Iraquis had fired dozens of Scud missiles into Israel, hoping to weaken that nation and achieve a definitive Arab victory over their hated enemies. But when they used Scuds to destroy Jewish homes and garrisons in the western part of Jerusalem, they miscalculated and shot several Scuds into the Old City, making a direct hit on the Temple Mount, thus completely demolishing two of the most sacred Islamic shrines in the world, the Dome of the Rock and the Al-Aqsa monastery.

In order to deflect the responsibility away from themselves, the Iraquis had blamed the Jews for the destruction, and the other Arab nations and the international community believed their false accusations, in spite of the fact that the Israelis had always shown the utmost respect for all Islamic holy places. The first result was that the Arabs grew even more bitter and inflamed in their hatred of Jews. The second consequence was that the Temple Mount was razed of Arab edifices, thus clearing the way for the construction of the Jewish Third Temple. Most Jews praised God for making this miracle possible.

Solomon, the son of King David, had spent about six years building the First Temple, from 970 BC to 964 BC. When the Babylonians conquered the Kingdom of Judah, King Nebuchadnezzer destroyed the temple in 586 BC and took thousands of Jews into exile in Babylon.

Sixty-five years later, Zerubabel was one of the men who led the first wave of Jews back to their home. After King Darius I of Persia appointed Zerubabel governor of the Province of Judah, the new governor began to rebuild the holy temple, which was completed around 516 BC. This was called the Second Temple.

However, in the days of Herod the Great, the king decided to rebuild and embellish the Second Temple. He made it broader and wider and doubled the total area of the Temple Mount. He also built four gigantic retaining walls around the Temple Mount. The work began around 19 BC and was not completely done until AD 63. In reality, it was almost a completely new temple but was still considered to be the Second Temple by the Jewish people.

This was the temple where Christ chased out the money changers with a whip.

Unfortunately, this beautiful temple, whose gleaming white stone could be seen from a great distance away, was destroyed by the Romans in AD 70. Only a portion of one wall, the Wailing Wall, remained standing and became for centuries the most holy spot on earth for Jews.

But now the Second David had finally arrived and built the Third Temple, which was even more exquisite than Herod's temple.

"When do you want me to dedicate this glorious temple, King Omert?" said Ofek Stoller, head of Israel's Chief Rabbinate.

"Please don't call me king. Call me president." Stoller nodded his obedience. "I'm sorry, my friend, but you will not dedicate the temple." Stoller's eyes grew wide, and he looked at David in shock. "And not just you, but no man. Only the Messiah himself will dedicate the temple."

"But that may not be for a long, long time," Stoller declared, his voice betraying a touch of anger. "Perhaps not even in our lifetime."

"No, it will be sooner than you think. I don't know when for sure, but it will be soon."

After gazing at the temple for another five minutes, Stoller looked toward the west section of the Temple Mount and was surprised by what he saw. "Why do you have those big telescopes set up over there at each corner?"

David smiled and said, "They aren't telescopes. They're laser guns, part of our THEL laser defense system."

"Lasers? But why?"

"To protect the temple from incoming enemy projectiles. They can intercept and destroy artillery shells, mortar bombs, rockets, missiles, drones, and even warplanes. We have two more installed on the Mount of Olives to perform the same task. You can't actually see the laser beams, but they travel at nearly the speed of light and can hit targets twenty to thirty miles away, depending on atmospheric conditions."

"And this was your idea?"

"Well, mine and my advisers'."

"President Omert, it seems we've chosen the right man to lead Israel."

Gerald Galloway, the supreme ruler of UGOT, was furious. He had just finished reading reports from his private news service regarding the Syrian attack on Israel and their subsequent ignominious defeat in battle. Then the outrage of the Arab world, condemning the Jewish infidels and calling for war, provoked his anger even more.

After he had read the reports in his luxurious apartment in Paris, he listened to the news reports on public television, cuddled up on a couch with his French mistress, Lucienne Delisle. Their relationship had cooled somewhat recently, but Lucienne had used every artifice at her command to revitalize his interest, even supplying him with some special pills to help him along. After all, Gerald was seventy-two, and one never knew how long he might be around. By currying his favor, she hoped to be named his successor as the leader of UGOT. Of course, she might have to first arrange for the murder of his children and grandchildren, which should be fairly easy since he had not trusted any of them enough to bring them into his inner circle.

"How dare they!" Gerald fumed. "Making an attack before the appointed time. They were supposed to increase their capacity to wage war and wait until our allies arrived. I told them we would begin in the first part of August and not before. Believe me, I'll make them pay."

Lucienne stroked his leg and looked at him with eyes as tranquil as a limpid pool of water. "But why, Gerald darling? This might be a good thing if we looked at it differently."

"A good thing? In what way?"

"Do you like Arabs?"

"No, you know I despise them. They are probably the most entrenched religious fanatics on earth, and they are as disgusting as the Jews. I've told you this before."

"I know, I know. Well then, let them kill themselves now, so we won't have to do it ourselves later."

"Kill themselves?"

Lucienne thought that Gerald could be extremely dense sometimes. She puckered her red lips and gave him a passionate kiss on the mouth before drawing back to say, "Yes, my dear. Let them gather their armies and attack Israel all they want. That will keep Israel busy defending itself instead of having more time to prepare for the real war. No doubt the Arabs will lose as they've always lost when they've made all-out war on Israel. Especially now since Israel has a dynamic new leader."

"You make an interesting point, my love," Gerald said reluctantly.

"Of course I do. Let the Arabs and Jews kill each other and waste their economic and military resources. That way, the Jews will be all the weaker when we arrive in August. By the way, Gerald, this really isn't *my* idea."

Gerald was confused. "Not your idea? Whose is it then?"

"Yours."

"Mine! What do you mean?"

"You know, for the future master of the universe, you sure can forget easily. I remember almost twenty-three years ago that you planned to use the warlike tendencies of the Arabs to weaken Israel. However, we had not yet gained sufficient control over our coalition forces to profit from the Arab-Israeli conflicts."

"The Arab-Israeli conflicts?" Gerald hated that he was showing more and more signs of memory loss.

"Yes. One of them was the Eight-Day War twenty-three years ago. Problem was, Israel handily defeated the Arabs by employing admittedly brilliant strategies without suffering many casualties or loss of matériel."

"Oh, yes. I remember now. It *was* my idea. That's why I thought your—my—idea was so interesting. Actually, it's a brilliant strategy, worthy of a genius. You're right. We'll use the same methods again, and this time we'll be ready to profit from them."

"I'm sure you won't regret it."

"I surely hope not. Do you think David Omert will give us trouble when we lead our armies against him?" Gerald became angry as he so often did at the very thought of the new Israeli ruler.

Lucienne smiled. "Oh, I'm sure he'll do his best. He might even make things a bit interesting. But, in the long run, the final result is a foregone conclusion, isn't it?"

"Yes, it is."

"Have you talked to your prophet, Colton Aldridge, lately?"

"We're always in close contact."

"Has he said anything about this recent Arab proclamation of war against Israel?"

Gerald caressed her hand on his leg. "Not really. We haven't even discussed it, and that's okay. However, I told him he needs to plan on being in Palestine for the real war, to do some spectacular miracles against the Jews. Actually, we probably won't need his help, or that of our other miracle-working prophets, but some of them will be there as a little extra insurance."

At that moment the apartment shook violently, knocking over their glasses and bottles of wine, hurtling several painting masterpieces from the walls, and splintering an expensive glass coffee table. The earthquake lasted a full thirty seconds.

"Seems like we're getting these quakes once a week now," Lucienne said with fear in her eyes. "When is it going to end?"

Gerald put his arm around her shoulders. "When we finish the mission we have before us."

The *Glory of the Seas* docked at Ashdod Port at mid-afternoon on the west coast of Israel, after voyaging twelve days on the Atlantic Ocean and the Mediterranean Sea. The water at the piers of this exceptional port were deep enough to handle the huge cruise ship without problems.

Steven Christopher descended the gangplank with his brothers, their sons, Ruther, and Jarrad, before the main body of troops began to disembark. He looked around and was surprised to see no one on the pier except a number of dock hands. At first he wondered if the Israelis had gotten the message that they were coming, but then he realized that the host country would probably want to keep their arrival as quiet as possible. Shortly after he reached the wharf, he noticed that General Michael Jamison and several high-ranking officers were following them down the plank.

He waited until Jamison caught up to him, and together they set out to find accommodations in the suburbs of Ashdod not far away. Before they reached the end of the pier, Steven saw a group of men heading toward them. The obvious leader of the group was a tall, good-looking man who appeared to be in his early fifties. He had short black hair, a husky build, and wore a blue dress shirt without a tie and light-colored suit trousers. The man walking next to him on his right was almost as tall as the leader but was slender and had an angular face and reddish brown hair. He and the other men were dressed like their leader. Because of the heat, they had removed their ties, and some carried suit coats draped over one arm.

"Good afternoon," the tall man said as he approached Jamison and shook his hand. His smile was open and friendly. "You must be General Michael Jamison, commander of this army from America."

Jamison looked somewhat perplexed as he shook hands with the newcomer. "Well, actually from New America, or the Republic of Zion as we call it. Yes, I'm General Jamison. How did you know? I don't think we've ever met before."

"Well, your radioman gave us a description of you."

"Oh, I see. And who would you be, sir?" Jamison asked.

"My name is David Omert, the president of Israel."

"I'm certainly glad to meet you, Mr. President."

Jamison introduced the people he was with, and Omert did the same, explaining especially that the Israeli with the reddish hair was Chaim Yehoshua, one of his ministers of war.

"I've heard about all the remarkable things you're doing here in Israel," Jamison said.

Omert chuckled a bit. "I guess people can accomplish a lot of surprising things when they're pushed to the brink."

"Yes, indeed," Jamison agreed. "We've experienced the same thing in New America. I'm impressed that all of you speak such excellent English."

"Thank you," Omert replied. "Here in Israel we require our children to learn not only Hebrew but also English and Arabic."

"May I ask you a question, Mr. President?" Steven said.

"Please call me David. Here in Israel we are usually much more informal than what you'll find in other societies, even in government meetings. The same is true of our military, which scorns all the ridiculous traditions and the pomp and circumstance you find in most military establishments. We usually address each other by first names. So what is your question, Steven?"

Steven realized David was probably referring indirectly to pompous Old American and British military conventions and protocols. "The thing is, I expected to see some warships as we approached the European continent, especially when we entered the Mediterranean and came close to the Israeli coast. But we saw nothing except a few merchant vessels and fishing boats. No one challenged us or even came near us."

David gave him a boyish grin. "You didn't even see warplanes?"

"Well, come to think of it, I did spot some aircraft far away to the north through my binoculars when we approached the Straits of Gibraltar and when we were in the Mediterranean."

"That was us, keeping an eye out for your safety."

"Oh, I didn't realize."

Omert winked at him. "We kept an eye on you ever since you ran into that great storm in the Atlantic. You had us worried there for a while. Especially since you're the only nation that has offered to help us against our enemies—at least so far. I thank God that he guided you here safely."

"I admit that I was also concerned you might mistake us for the enemy, because you didn't send any ships to escort us in," Steven said.

"Do you see those hills over there, a few miles north of the port?"

Everyone turned to look. "Yes," Jamison said.

"Well, on those hills are several artillery emplacements. They are there to protect the port and this section of the coastline. They can fire shells twenty miles out to sea. If you had been an enemy, we would have used them and squadrons of warplanes against you. But we knew you were friendly allies." Then David laughed out loud. "The enemy doesn't usually travel on cruise ships."

As the troops began to file past them, David said, "General Jamison, please tell your officers to instruct your men to continue down the road you see off to our right. A mile down that road, you can load them into trucks waiting there. We'll transport them to a military base five miles to the east where we've constructed barracks to house them. Do your troops have any experience in war, general?"

"Absolutely. Most of them are veterans from wars against invading armies and from many skirmishes with bandits. They all have experience with hunting rifles and other small firearms, and some have served in artillery battalions. However, in America we have very few tanks, armored personnel carriers, or anti-tank weapons. And no warplanes or warships."

"But still, they have battle experience. We'll give them a bit more training in Israeli battle tactics, and we may employ some of them in armor and artillery."

Right then, Ruther Johnston, Mosheh Lazar, and Yaakov Raphan strolled by, Ruther carrying his Sharps rifle with the thirty-four inch barrel.

"Who's the mountain man with the cannon?" David said. "And the two giant Indians?"

Steven gave a short summary of his relations with the three men. When he mentioned that the two "Indians" were members of the Lost Ten Tribes, David was fascinated because he realized they were his brethren of Israelite lineage, and he promised to get to know them better.

"We can always use such fighting men," David affirmed. "Thanks for bringing them." He looked at General Jamison. "You mentioned you had no late-model warplanes." The general shook his head. "Well then, I guess you didn't bring any aircraft with you on the ship, did you?"

Jamison chuckled. "No, I'm afraid not. However, if you had let me know, we'd have brought a few solar airplanes. I don't know where we'd have put them on the ship, but I'm sure we could have stuffed them in somewhere." Both men laughed at that.

David suddenly became serious. "I want to tell you people how grateful and blessed we feel to have your support. I know it's a great sacrifice."

"You may not know it," Steven said, "but we also have another sixty thousand troops on their way to help, maybe more."

David's eyes filled with tears. "You never know, it may be the difference we need to survive."

Chapter 5

In their terrible anger, five Arab nations—Egypt, Lebanon, Syria, Jordan, and Iraq—began to mobilize their armies. When the embedded media stationed in the various Arab countries questioned the leaders about the troop movements, the Arab leaders told them that all they were doing was engaging in military exercises in view of the intelligence they had gathered showing that multiple hostile armies from many infidel nations were now bearing down on them from all parts of the globe.

They also fed the same story to the so-called "peace-keeping" forces of the United Nations. The Arabs tried to embellish their answer by declaring that their preparations were also justified because in these turbulent times there was always a grave danger of their nations being attacked by domestic terrorists and insurgents. After all, they had a right to defend their liberty and the safety of their helpless populations, didn't they?

But the Arabs called Palestinians offered no excuses whatsoever. After all, for over seventy years they had been zealously shooting thousands of rockets into Israeli communities and deploying hundreds of guerilla bands and suicide bombers. The bombers were especially considered blessed, for by killing themselves and as many of the reviled Jews as possible, they assured themselves a blissful place in heaven on the right hand of Allah for their sacrifices in the great cause of Islam. So the Palestinians immediately multiplied tenfold their threats and their attacks.

The Arabs were now much more confident of victory than they had ever been since the 1948 War against Israel. They felt that they were even in a better position at this time than they had been during the Eight-Day War twenty-three years ago. At that time, Israel had complete control of Gaza, the Golan Heights, and the West Bank. But since liberal Israeli leaders had made unwise concessions to the Arabs, Israel had lost control of those regions and the buffer zones they represented. Even though Israel had regained six miles of the western part of the Golan Heights during their battle with Syria eleven days ago, the Arabs still felt confident of victory.

Qaasim Sarkis, a colonel in the Egyptian army, stood on one of the gun emplacements just outside the city of Ras Nasrani, studying the scene through binoculars. He examined the sea to the south for five minutes but saw no Egyptian warships. Maybe they wouldn't arrive after all, and that was fine with him. He felt that he already had sufficient firepower to maintain the blockade and didn't need the help of the Egyptian navy. He looked to the east and saw the Straits of Tiran and beyond, Saudi Arabia. Next he turned toward the west and viewed the Sinai Peninsula and Egypt farther away. Finally, he rested the binoculars on his chest and turned to his subordinate, Lieutenant Wadi Mustafa, who had just arrived with a troop of reinforcements.

"Nothing yet, my friend. But our warships could still show up any time now."

"Do you mean the decision has already been made?"

"Yes, it was made yesterday morning, twenty-nine hours ago."

Mustafa didn't look happy. "Sorry for my ignorance, my Colonel, but I've spent the last eight hours traveling to this post and didn't receive any communications concerning new developments. So can we expect an Israeli attack soon because of our blockade?"

"No doubt, and I welcome it! We're ready for them. As you can see, we have twelve artillery guns right here, and we've already prevented a dozen merchant vessels from passing through the straits. However, these guns can do a lot more than that! They've been equipped with the latest computerized aiming technology and can easily destroy incoming aircraft or warships descending the Gulf of Aqaba. In addition, we have a dozen warplanes ready to go ten miles west of here. I promise you that if the Israelis attack our position, we'll give them a very unpleasant welcome."

In effect, the Egyptians were blocking all shipping through the Straits of Tiran, and the Israelis had always considered the closing of the straits to be the same as a declaration of war. All shipping to and from the southern Israeli port of Eilat on the Gulf of Aqaba came through the Straits of Tiran, which connected the Gulf of Aqaba with the Red Sea and the Indian Ocean. Blocking the straits would constitute an economic stranglehold on Israel.

Sarkis looked to the south again through his binoculars and examined the sea horizon. "I think that's them, lieutenant." He handed Mustafa the glasses. "Tell me if I'm right."

"Yes, sir. I can barely see three Egyptian ships heading this way."

"I told headquarters we didn't need a naval blockade," Sarkis snarled. "Our guns can do the job just as well and a lot cheaper, but of course they never listen to me."

Mustafa's face was growing increasingly sour. "Sir, when the Israelis finally attack, we may need the guns, the warplanes, and the ships."

David Omert called an emergency meeting in Jerusalem with his war ministers. He had extended a special invitation to some of his visitors from America, including General Michael Jamison, Colonel Steven Christopher, Colonel Mosheh Lazar, and Lieutenant Colonel Yaakov Raphan. They met early in the morning in a conference room near Omert's office at the Knesset building.

After he had introduced the newcomers to his ministers, David read a detailed report produced by Mossad, the premier Israeli intelligence service, on recent Arab movements. "Well, gentlemen, that finishes the report. What do you think we should do?"

"I think it's all bluster," said Chagai Metzger. "We certainly need to put our forces on alert, but I doubt the Arabs will attack. Surely they remember what went down in the past when they attacked us. I also base my opinion on the fact that they've made no effort to employ any diversionary strategies whatsoever." Metzger was a short, chubby man with a bald head and red face. His opinion usually held a great deal of weight because he was an experienced military man who had won many battles.

"I disagree," Chaim said. "David has made our position quite clear. Remember what he said on national television. He openly warned the Arabs that we would interpret any buildup of forces or military maneuvers near our borders as acts of war."

"Well, we can consider such behavior as acts of war," said Harrod Zadok, "but I'm wondering if we shouldn't wait until the enemy opens hostilities? If we attack first, we'll be condemned as aggressors by the international community." Zadok was the youngest man in the room. He was of medium height and build, had immigrated to Israel from Russia eight years ago, and had distinguished himself as a leader in the IDF.

"I don't care what the so-called international community thinks," said Efren Yankel. "Most of those suckers blame us no matter what we do. If we don't act aggressively now, the Arabs will consider it weakness and take advantage of it." Yankel was a white-haired man who had spent the first part of his adult life in the military and the second part as a legislator in the Knesset.

"Well," David said, "it looks as though we're divided on whether we should act now or wait and see. I wonder what our guests from America think." He nodded toward General Jamison.

"I believe it's very dangerous for you to wait and see," Jamison said. "You're really between a rock and a hard place. You should use the same strategy your leaders did in 1967. Since your enemies are obviously threatening you, I believe you should make preemptive strikes while you still can."

Steven, Mosheh, and Yaakov indicated their agreement with that proposal.

"I appreciate your input," David said. "I'm also of the opinion that we need to act now and aggressively."

At that point, one of David's office staff entered the room. "Sorry to interrupt your meeting, Mr. President, but we just received a special communiqué. I think you should read it." He handed a piece of paper to David.

David read it quickly and said, "It seems the Egyptians have blockaded the Straits of Tiran. Three hours ago."

"Well, that cinches it," Chaim said. "We have no choice but to deliver a military response."

Everyone in the room agreed enthusiastically.

"Okay, gentlemen," David said, "what we need to do now is to devise a coordinated plan to make preemptive strikes before it's too late, and we don't have much time to do it."

They spent the next six hours formulating their plans, and finally decided to send a token force to Egypt to make it look like that was were the primary invasion would take place. At the same time, they would send most of their forces toward the north and east to capture the capitals of Jordan, Syria, and Lebanon. In other words, their entire strategy was based on deception and diversion. At the end of the long session, David asked each of his ministers to depart that same day by helicopter to visit their forces in the five main regions under their supervision. Their task was to explain in person the battle plan to the troop commanders.

David Omert had arranged accommodations for each of the Americans at his personal bunker-compound near the center of the city, a few hundred yards west of the Knesset building. Mary and Steven had been given lodging in a small room with basic facilities and walls of reinforced concrete.

They ate a spartan meal in the compound mess hall, enjoying the conversation of their hosts and their fellow Americans. David Omert's wife, Edra, was a tiny, quiet woman with blond hair, blue eyes, and a slim body. They had three grown children. Chaim's wife, Heisa, was an exuberant woman of average height with black hair and a quick smile. They hadn't been able to conceive children but had adopted a boy and a girl, who were now in their thirties.

David Omert was impressed with Mosheh and Yaakov as they related the story of their former homeland, Shee Lo, and their long, perilous journey to Zion. The Jewish hosts were especially amazed and intrigued about the special kind of Hebrew Mosheh and Yaakov spoke. They also asked many questions concerning the location of Shee Lo, and how the Ten Tribe travelers had moved from their world into the present one.

After the meal, Steven and Mary retired to their room, feeling immensely tired. As they lay on the queen-size bed, Mary was full of questions. "What are they going to do about the Arabs?"

"David Omert has asked us to be very discreet talking about it, so all I can tell you is that things are going down very quickly."

"What things?"

"I can't tell you."

Mary frowned and pouted a little. "Oh, come on. You know I can keep a secret."

"No way. I promised."

Mary leaned over and caressed his cheek. "Pretty please."

"I'm sorry, sweetheart. I can't tell you."

"What about our sons, Daniel and William? Will they be involved?"

"I doubt it. They're going through special training. They're not ready."

Mary sighed with relief, but soon she put on a worried look. "I hope they don't get hurt doing all that training." She was silent for a while and then said, "You know, Steve, as a mother I have a right to know what our sons might be facing."

"As I said before it's a military secret."

The next morning, the mess hall was noisy as forty-five people, anxious to eat breakfast, stood in a long line at a serving counter and dished up their own selection of food. Steven was surprised to see that men and women of all ranks mixed together in the line and at the tables, without any concern whatever for protocol. There were also several members of Omert's government there.

David Omert, Chaim Yehoshua, and their wives entered a little late, standing at the door briefly to peruse the diners. David caught sight of Steven and Mary, said something to those with him, and led his group in their direction.

As they sat down, David said, "I'm glad there's room for us at this table. I'm anxious to hear all about your New America. We've received several thousand immigrants from there already."

"Haven't you been getting immigrants from all over the world?" Mary asked.

"Yes, indeed," David said. "Thousands of them from every country on earth. Fleeing the tyranny of UGOT and the intolerant governments of their own countries. Of course, they come from America only because they are of Jewish ancestry, not because they are persecuted." David's face took on a grim look. "Right now you people are relatively safe so far away across the ocean, but some day UGOT will seek to invade your shores."

"They already have," Steven replied. "At least twice. But with the help of God we survived."

"Yes, I know God has a powerful hand in all of this."

During the meal and after they had finished, they talked about the destruction of Old America, the birth of the new nation, the return of the Ten Tribes, and the voracious designs of UGOT and its leader, Gerald Galloway.

When nearly all of the other diners had left the mess hall, David lowered his voice and said to Steven and Mary, "The Lord spoke to me one night in a dream. He showed me your faces, told me your names, and assured me I could depend on you in every way. For that reason, I believe I can trust you with a secret known only to my friend, Chaim, and our wives. My secret is also Chaim's secret, and Chaim has given me permission to reveal it at this time. We have kept it for many, many years and we desperately need to share it with someone."

Steven was intrigued but also worried, because some secrets could be dangerous. "I'm willing to hear your secret, but I can't speak for Mary."

"I'd like to hear it also," Mary said.

"You're Christians, aren't you?" David asked.

"We certainly are," Mary said.

"Well, so are we. Our wives also."

Steven and Mary looked at each other in disbelief. "I'm amazed to hear that," Steven said. "The most powerful men in Israel, the leaders of the Jewish nation, are Christians?"

"Sshh. Not so loud," David said, in spite of the fact that there were only two people left in the hall, and they were sitting in a far corner. "If the people knew it, they would reject us as leaders."

"And probably stone us," Chaim added.

"How long have you been Christians?" Mary asked in almost a whisper.

"Over two decades," David said.

"Were you converted by Christian missionaries?" Steven asked. "I know there are many Christians living in Israel."

"No," David replied. "It's illegal for missionaries to proselyte in Israel. Church schools of any denomination can teach classes in religious history and doctrine, but they can't proselyte."

"We weren't aware of that," Mary said.

David paused, wondering how to express himself. "Well, I suppose you might say we converted ourselves. By reading the Bible."

"The truth is, David converted both of us," Chaim said. "One day long ago he admitted to me that he had been studying the Christian Bible, looking for answers to save Israel. Eventually he received a witness that the Jewish Messiah prophesied in the Old Testament was none other than Jesus Christ. The life of Jesus as depicted in the New Testament was a very close parallel to the words of the Old Testament. I too started reading the Bible and became convinced of the same thing. So we've been closet Christians ever since."

Steven thought, *So this is what the prophet meant when he said the Lord had already prepared the way for the conversion of David Omert and his friend to Christianity and the gospel.* He felt a sudden increase in joy and self-confidence in his ability to fulfill the mission the Lord had given him. "We appreciate your trust in us," Steven said with sincerity, "and we promise we won't reveal your secret to anyone."

"Not even your closest friends or your sons," David added. "The more people who know, the better the chance that the truth will leak out. But now I'd like to mention one more thing."

"Yes?"

"I want both of you to serve in the same unit as Chaim and I."

Steven hesitated a long moment. "We'd be glad to, right, Mary?"

"Of course, but what do you mean by the same unit?"

"Let me explain," David said. "In the Israeli military, we have a tradition that the leaders lead. In other words, our officers guide their men into battle, especially if it involves an infantry assault. They don't just sit in the background and give commands by radio. If we aren't willing to go to the front lines, then we shouldn't order our troops to do so."

"So we may find ourselves on the front lines?" Mary said with a touch of fear in her eyes.

"It's possible. However, I promise you that I won't expose you to really dangerous situations. You especially, Mary, will be behind the lines doctoring the wounded."

Steven gave David a serious look. "But isn't that a little foolhardy and dangerous to you, to lead your men into the fray? After all, you're the hope of Israel right now."

"I know God will protect me until my mission is completed."

Jacan Levin and Ephrem Isaacs were sitting on a grassy knoll watching their herds of sheep in the narrow valley below, a few miles from Bethlehem. Jacan owned forty sheep and Ephrem forty-six, but they grazed their sheep together, and as close friends, they didn't care if their herds got mixed up. The sheep grazed on the lush green grass and drank from a shallow stream not far away. They had just finished anointing each sheep, on the eyes and nostrils, with a few drops of olive oil that they poured from a ram's horn, just like shepherds had done in Biblical times. The oil healed the animals and protected them from flying pests, so they were grazing more peacefully now than before.

These men were a dying breed, for sheep herding was a thing of the past and provided no more than a pittance, barely enough to feed their families. Their wives had to supplement the family budget by washing clothes for neighbors and by selling knitted shawls. Soon they would have to sell their sheep and find other means of survival. Only eight other shepherds owned sheep in the vicinity, six Palestinians and two Christians. Jacan and Ephrem were Jews and proud of their heritage. However, they didn't care about politics, and the squabbles between the various ethnic groups completely confounded them.

Jacan was forty-five years old, and Ephrem was his junior at forty-two. While Jacan was over six feet tall, thin but wiry, with blondish hair that always seemed to be in his eyes, Ephrem was short and stocky and had close-cropped black hair. Both were completely ordinary-looking Jews.

They were dressed almost alike: sneakers, jeans, flannel shirts, and baseball caps. As they watched their herds by night, they protected themselves from the chill by donning knitted sweaters and by wrapping woolen scarves around their necks. Later, they took turns guarding the sheep from neighborhood dogs and other predators. After guard duty, they would roll up in woolen blankets, using backpacks as pillows.

During daylight hours, they took turns visiting their families in nearby Bethlehem, a town now inhabited mostly by Palestinians. The only intellectual pursuit they had engaged in was to take free classes in English twice a week in Bethlehem. They had been doing this for years and had finally learned to participate in simple conversations with people fluent in English. Other people in the neighborhood took the same classes at different hours, and they all shared the responsibility of watching one another's flocks.

Everything was quiet and peaceful as the sun dropped below the horizon. They talked about mundane things, mostly about the sheep and what they might do in the future. Before long, the sheep were nothing but white, blurry shapes in the distance, and they had to depend mostly on hearing for signs of danger. They kept their heavy staffs close by as the main weapons for protecting their flocks. As they talked, they gazed into the magnificent heavens filled with millions of pinpoints of light. A half moon kept the stars company.

All at once Jacan became aware of something unusual. He looked behind and saw a light descending from the sky, becoming brighter as it neared the earth. He roused his friend, who had started to nod off. "Look, Ephrem. There's a weird beam of light up there."

"Huh? A light? Where?" Ephrem turned and looked skyward, his eyes bulging at the sight.

"What is it? A comet? A falling star?"

But the light didn't move away into the distance like Jacan expected. Instead, it drew closer and seemed to be descending right on top of them. Soon the light became so bright it began to hurt their eyes, and they ducked their heads into their laps, afraid to look any longer. Jacan kept his head down and refused to look up, but he couldn't help but notice that the entire hillside around them was lit almost as if it were daylight. He steeled himself and chanced a glance, and what he saw astounded him.

The brightest part of the light was only twenty feet away and about ten feet in the air. In the center of the light was a man, smiling down on him in a kindly manner.

"Look up, Ephrem," Jacan said. "There's an angel in the light."

Ephrem looked up gingerly, his eyes still partly covered with his hands. "An angel, you say. I don't—oh yeah, I see him. Who is he?"

"How am I supposed to know? Let's ask him."

As they gazed on the angel, their eyes adjusted to the brightness and no longer burned. In fact, the light seemed to caress their eyes.

"Who are you?" asked Jacan tentatively.

The angel smiled even more broadly and said, "I am a servant of God. My name is not important, but my message is, for it comes from the Almighty."

"Please, glorious angel, what is your message?"

"The Lord has chosen you to deliver his words to this people, words of great hope but also of warning."

"Oh, God has chosen you, Jacan. Whew! I'm off the hook!"

The angel gave a small laugh. "No, he has chosen both of you."

"That's what I was afraid of," Ephrem murmured.

"Don't try to dodge your responsibilities, brother," Jacan replied. "We need to stick together."

"Yes, you do," the angel said. "Always. God's words are established in the mouth of two witnesses."

"What is the message we're supposed to deliver?" Jacan asked.

"The Lord gives you two commissions. First, you are to go among this people, the Jews, and declare repentance unto them. Because of their wickedness, the anger of God is kindled against them, and their enemies have power over them. And then when the Spirit commands, you must announce to them that the coming of the great Messiah must shortly come to pass.

Jacan's mouth dropped open. "The Lord wants us poor, ignorant shepherds to bring such a glorious message to this nation?"

"Yes."

"But why would they listen to us?" Ephrem exclaimed. "Many mighty, learned rabbis live in Israel. Most of the people honor them, and surely they will heed the proclamations of those great men."

"They will not listen to the rabbis, but only to the humble and meek who have been chosen by God."

Jacan was so afraid he thought his heart would stop, and he wasn't at all convinced by the angel's words. "I'm sure the people will laugh at us and maybe throw us into prison."

"The people will have no power over you. It is you who will have power over them. Many of them will listen to your voices and will repent."

"How can we have such power?" Ephrem asked, his voice trembling.

"You will be endowed with power from on high. I see that you are troubled in your hearts. Go home now, tell your families about this vision, ponder these things in your minds, and return here tomorrow evening at this time for further instructions."

"But our sheep?" Jacan said.

"The Lord will send another angel tonight to watch over your sheep."

Then the angel and the light ascended to heaven and disappeared. The two shepherds left the fields and returned home, their minds marveling over the miraculous revelation.

The following evening, Jacan and Ephrem sat on the same knoll, waiting for the divine visitor. Their minds were full of questions, most of which their wives had insisted they ask. The main concern the women had was how their husbands would support their families—and even themselves—while they were off preaching to the people. A short time later, the smiling angel descended in the same manner as the previous night.

"The Lord blesses you and forgives your sins," the heavenly being said in greeting. "Ask me the questions that concern you."

"My wife wondered how we will support ourselves and our families as we fulfill the commission you have given us," Jacan said.

"You will sell your flocks and thereby obtain the means to live for a few months. After that, the Lord will inspire the people who hear you to give you and your families food and raiment for your needs, and that in abundance, and they will also meet all your other obligations."

"You said we would have power over the people," Ephrem said. "How can that be, holy angel?"

"By that expression I mean the Lord will give you power to stay the hand of the many enemies who seek to destroy your nation."

"Are you saying we'll be able to perform miracles that will defeat their armies?" Jacan asked in amazement.

"In part, yes. But you will not perform the miracles yourself. The prophet Elijah did not call down fire from heaven by his own power. Moses did not part the Red Sea by his own power. They called on God to do those mighty works, and the Lord performed those miracles at their request because of their faithfulness. And so it has been with all the great miracles of the past."

"So all we need to do is obey God and ask him to fight our enemies," Jacan said, feeling strangely more confident now.

"Yes."

"When do you want us to begin this sacred mission, and how long will it last?" Ephrem asked. It was his wife who had reminded him three times to ask those questions.

"You will begin your mission on the morrow, and it will last almost until the coming of the Messiah."

"And when will the Messiah come?" Ephrem said.

Nice try, Ephrem, Jacan thought.

The angel turned to Jacan with an even wider smile and then back to Ephrem. "It is not for you to know the exact time of the coming of the Messiah, but it shall come to pass in a little season. Now bow your heads, both of you, and I will give you authority to perform this very special commission for the Lord."

They bowed their heads and the angel came closer, laying his hands on their heads. He blessed them, charged them to be faithful and diligent, encouraged them to fear no earthly influence, and endowed them with power. He also explained that sometimes they would receive directions from another voice, the voice of the Holy Spirit.

When he first saw her, Daniel Christopher couldn't keep his eyes off her. Her hair was long and dark, and her body was slender, shapely, and toned. She was only five feet five inches tall compared to Daniel's six feet. Her eyes were dark brown, the same color as her wavy hair, and her teeth were gleaming white and perfectly spaced. She was simply spectacular, even in her military uniform. Daniel suddenly believed in love at first sight, and from that point on, he could only see perfection in the woman he adored.

She was housed in the women's barracks on the other side of Camp Ashdod. The male and female troops had separate quarters, but they exercised, trained, had classes, and ate mess together. Daniel tried hard to position himself close to her whenever he had the chance. For the first week, she didn't appear to notice he existed, but at the beginning of the second week she caught him staring at her from twenty feet away. Since the young man couldn't seem to turn away his eyes, she gave him a sly little smile.

Later that day, he sat next to her in a class on military tactics, and their interaction really began—in a way at least. Daniel could only speak English, and the young woman's native language was Hebrew. However, she had learned a smattering of English in several English language classes.

"What's your name?" Daniel asked. He knew it would be a magical name, and he wasn't disappointed.

"I call me Rachel Salant," she said, her beautiful eyes gazing deep into his in such a way that he felt his heart melting.

"I'm Daniel Christopher."

She whispered his name several times as if trying to memorize it. "You come America, yes?"

"Yes. You're Jewish, aren't you?"

She giggled at that. Struggling to find the right words, she said, "I think I am looking pretty Jewish. I was borned in Israel. Sorry, many Jewish womans speak very good English, but I am always getting bad grades in that."

"Oh no! You speak perfect English. I understand everything you say."

Her mouth formed a subtle smile as she looked at him from the corners of her eyes, as if she didn't believe a word of it. "We grateful you Americans coming help us in this terrible times."

"It's nothing really. I'm grateful I came, especially now. But you look much too young to be in the military. Don't you have to be at least nineteen?"

"I being twenty-one now."

"Wow! You look a lot younger than that, like maybe eighteen."

"No. Twenty-one."

"What's that v-stripe on your sleeve?"

"It shows I be, how do you say . . . sergeant first class? I in charge of a platoon of thirty or more soldiers."

Daniel's eyes grew large. "Wow! Sergeant first class! Too bad you won't be my sergeant. I guess you'll lead a platoon of women."

"No, it is possible you be in my platoon. In our army today, they mix womans and mans in some units."

"So you might be my boss?" Daniel said without even trying to hide his delight.

"Maybe, if you being assigned that way," she said with a coy smile.

At that point, the teacher entered the room and began his fifth lesson on Israeli military maneuvers. After the lesson, Daniel was disappointed when Rachel told him that she had to hurry away to do a three-mile jog in full military gear. As he watched her leave the classroom, he wondered if there was any way he could arrange to be assigned to her platoon and maybe the same post of operations.

Chapter 6

On the first day of their errand for the Lord, the shepherds, Jacan Levin and Ephrem Isaacs, put on their best clothes: jeans and shirts that were clean but had spots and tears in many places and ratty sneakers with pieces of newspaper lining the bottoms to cover the holes worn through the soles. They walked the streets of Jerusalem aimlessly, without a clue as to how they should begin. After an hour of such uncertainty, they both heard a voice speak to their minds. *"Stand on those stairs to your left and declare repentance to this people. Fear not, for I am with you."* It was a soft, deep voice, unlike the angel's, which had a lighter, tenor timbre. They figured it must be the voice of the Holy Spirit.

"Did you hear that voice?" Jacan asked his friend.

"Yes, someone told me to not be afraid, but to go over to those stairs and start preaching."

"That's also what I heard. Let's do as the Lord asks."

They walked up a dozen steps and turned to face the people walking upwards toward them.

"You go first!" Ephrem whispered, obviously frightened out of his wits. Surely these rich, well-dressed people would laugh at them or maybe worse. Jacan was older and wiser than he and could bear the embarrassment better.

"I knew you were a coward deep down," Jacan said out of the side of his mouth. "Always wanting me to do the hard stuff. Okay then. I'm not the slightest bit afraid." He girded up his loins and in his loudest voice declared, "Repent ye, oh sinful nation, for the judgments of God are upon you. The Lord has seen your evil deeds and lest ye repent, he will send the enemy against you, to your complete destruction."

"Man, that's pretty good," Ephrem murmured, looking at his friend with envy. "You sound like one of them prophets in ancient times." Both of the shepherds had heard many readings from the Hebrew scriptures in their synagogue.

Many of the people ascending the stairs stopped at stared with wide eyes and open mouths at the two peasants in tattered clothes. This was something new in Israel. Two old-time prophets—or crazies thinking they were prophets?

"It's your turn now," Jacan muttered.

"Me? What should I say?"

The crowd of curious people was growing larger and larger, many asking each other who were the idiots blocking the concrete stairway.

"Whatever you feel is right. Listen to the Spirit."

Ephrem paused and listened and then looked at the crowd. Finally, he raised his voice and said, "The Lord commands all of you to repent of your worldly ways and your unbelief. You have turned away from God's righteous paths in order to satisfy your lusts. If you don't repent, the judgments of God will soon fall upon you."

A short, brown-haired woman close by in the throng called out, "What lusts are you talking about? I'm a good person. I'm a mother. I never harm anyone."

Ephrem was stymied, not knowing how to answer. He looked again at Jacan for help.

"We speak to all of Israel, not just to individuals," Jacan declared. "Search the scriptures and your hearts, and you will know what your sins are."

After hearing his friend, Ephrem felt he too might be getting the hang of things. "That's right. If you do that, you'll soon recognize your faithlessness, your adulteries, your murders, your abortions, your incests, your—"

"That's enough," Jacan hissed. "Don't overdo it."

"Oh, sorry," Ephrem returned, a bit sheepish. He looked at the angry faces in front of him and decided he had better change the subject.

"These guys are false prophets," a tall woman shouted. "All they do is make false accusations." She was about six feet tall, had flaming red hair, weighed over two hundred pounds, and looked as though she could mangle both shepherds with her bare hands.

The short, brown-haired woman turned to the crowd and raised her right hand high. "Wait. Let's hear them out." She turned toward Jacan and Ephrem with another question. "How do you know these things? You speak as if the Lord has given you a revelation, but what proof do you have? Also, I'd like to know what authority you have. Are you ordained rabbis?"

Ephrem nudged Jacan, encouraging him to field those difficult questions. Jacan leaned over and whispered into Ephrem's ear. "It's your turn now. You need to get some guts. Just tell them the whole story, starting with us sitting on the knoll watching our sheep and ending with the angel's commands."

So Ephrem told the whole story in a loud, sincere voice, while the audience of over fifty people listened attentively. When he was done, Jacan added one point. "My good friend here forgot to say that the angel laid his hands on our heads and gave us the power to do this work."

Many in the crowd seemed impressed, but the giant redhead was madder than ever. "Like I said, they're false prophets. Show us a sign if God has called you to go about preaching his word."

Now the two shepherds were really scared and didn't know what to do. At that point, the secret voice said, *The Lord allows you to show them a sign. This will be the first of many, for this is a day of miracles. Ask if there are any sick among them.*

"Are there any sick among you?" Jacan said.

A smallish Jewish women with light brown hair pushed through the throng, pulling her twelve-year-old daughter behind her. "Yes, here is my daughter. She is blind from an illness she had three years ago. If you are truly prophets, you should be able to heal her."

Both Jacan and Ephrem felt a knot form in their stomachs. *Be not afraid, my sons,* said the deep, soft voice. *Place your hands on the child's eyes, and she shall be healed.*

Jacan walked down four steps until the girl was within his reach. He extended his hands and touched the girl's sightless eyes. Then he declared, "O Lord, I, thy servant ask thee to heal this child from her affliction." He said it three times and stepped away.

The girl blinked her eyes rapidly and looked around. The mob stared at her with expectation, many with scowling faces. After about half a minute the girl exclaimed, "I can see! Mom, I can see!"

The people were astonished and crowded around her, most trying to verify that she could indeed see. Jacan and Ephrem turned and walked up the stairway and disappeared, now full of confidence in their power to accomplish their mission in a way pleasing to God.

The noise of the miracle spread rapidly throughout the city. Many of the citizens rejoiced, but others scoffed or were filled with terror because of the prophet's words of warning.

⚜

Colonel Ronen Parmet of the Israel Defense Forces rode in his jeep at the front of his motorized infantry, amused at the shocked looks on the faces of the Egyptian citizens of Arish as he traveled through the city, which was on the main highway near the Mediterranean coast. They were heading west across the northern part of the Sinai Peninsula, an area that was mostly desert with towns few and far apart. Sitting in the back seat next to him was Major Herschel Walmann, who acted as if he were sightseeing on the French Riviera. Parmet was in charge of a caravan of one hundred trucks transporting nearly two thousand troops.

The unit also included fifteen tank transporters carrying twelve light tanks and fourteen armored personnel carriers, or APCs, and six flatbeds loaded with big guns. They were traveling to the Suez Canal, about a hundred miles to the west. The reason they were not transporting main battle tanks was so they could move fast— very fast—especially when they needed to retreat. At present they were moving along leisurely at twenty-five miles an hour between towns.

"You seem to be enjoying yourself, major," Parmet said.

"Well, it's nice to be doing one's duty without being fried to death by the desert heat. This breeze is wonderful. I'm glad they assigned us to the northern route. Right now, I'll bet those guys in the south are dying from the heat." The second Israeli unit was almost identical in the number of troops and vehicles. It was forty-seven miles to the south, traveling west on the highway that ran through Mitla Pass on the way to the city of Suez. "Still, I don't understand why we're going so slow. At this speed we'll never get there."

"Omert told me it has something to do with timing. He even ordered me to stop at dusk and camp out."

"But aren't you the slightest bit worried about some Arab sniper putting a hole through your head? This jeep is completely open and unprotected."

"Yes, I know. At least that's a quick way to go. However, there's little chance of snipers being way out here. The land is relatively flat and there are few trees of any size."

"Colonel, I know what our basic job is, but I don't know how close we're going to need to get to the enemy."

"I don't know either. We'll stop when I receive the word from headquarters."

The colonel's aide sitting next to the driver in the front turned around with a perplexed look on his face. "Colonel, may I ask you a question?"

"Certainly."

"Why are we spread out so far apart? There must be a hundred yards or more between each vehicle. Sometimes two or three hundred yards. Wouldn't it be safer to travel closer together?"

"There's a good reason for it. This way, it takes us a lot longer to move by any given point. As a result, any Arabs seeing us pass will think our unit is much larger than it really is. Perhaps even ten times as large, and that will affect them psychologically and emotionally. So when they report our presence to the Egyptian authorities, their emotional state of mind will cause them to grossly exaggerate our strength."

"Whose idea was that, sir?" Walmann said.

"President Omert's."

"Well, it's brilliant. So do you think this entire mission will be a success?"

At that moment, three Rafale warplanes roared overhead, flying west.

"All right!" Parmet yelled. "Those guys are part of the plan. My guess is there'll be fifteen to twenty such flights all over the Sinai."

"They don't fly right over Egypt, do they?" Walmann asked.

"No, they'll drop a few bombs just west of the canal and then turn back."

"Do you think the Egyptians will try to intercept?"

"Of course, but they'll have to fly most of the way across the Sinai to do it. And if they get lucky and overtake our boys, they'll probably get shot down. They have good planes, but our pilots have better training."

"I know," Walmann said with open pride.

The goal of David Omert in dispatching troops and warplanes toward Egypt was to make the Arabs believe that was where Israel would make the

primary offensive against their enemies. In reality, it was in the north that
Omert intended to carry out the major operations.

Ibn 'abbas al-Boutros, the president of Syria, was rabid with anger. He
slammed the intelligence reports, which he had just received, on his desk and
glared at his military chief of staff, in spite of the fact that the chief was not
responsible for the problem. The six other commanders and one admiral
in the room had read the reports and had supposedly made every effort to
verify the information before the chief passed them on to the president.

"These reports seem to say the Israelis are mobilizing their forces in the
Sinai," Boutros said.

"Yes, my President, that is correct," the chief replied.

"So that means they're making a preemptive attack on Egypt," Boutros
concluded.

"Unfortunately, that seems to be the case, Mr. President," said a tall man
who had a short white beard and was second-in-command to the chief.

"And when they're done with Egypt, they'll turn on the rest of us, one
at a time," said another general, who was short, fat, irascible, and unbelievably ugly.

"You don't think this is just a limited attack against the Egyptians?"
Boutros asked. "Maybe it's no more than a diversionary maneuver to make
us think their main offensive is against Egypt."

All the generals shook their heads forcefully.

"No, sir, we've checked into the matter thoroughly. Residents in the area
have told us the invading armies are transporting tanks and artillery. That
means a full-scale operation," said the tall general.

"Residents? Don't we have trained personnel in the area to confirm
this?" Boutros said angrily.

"Well, yes," said the chief. "Some of those residents have served in the
military."

"The reports say *brigade* strength. How many brigades?"

"From what we've learned," replied the ugly officer, "there are seven or
eight brigades heading for Egypt. Also, witnesses say they've seen a dozen
squadrons of warplanes flying west in the Sinai, some of them dropping
bombs on cities near the Suez Canal."

"In the name of Allah!" cried Boutros. "That means total war!"

"Mr. President, we must act immediately before it's too late," said the chief of staff. "If the Israelis defeat the Egyptian army, our combined forces may not be enough to stem the tide of Israeli aggression."

"You're absolutely right," Boutros said, his eyes wild. "We must mobilize our forces at once and rush to fight beside our brothers, the Egyptians." *Think of the glory the Arab world would pour upon me if I saved Egypt from destruction. I would be the great hero of Islam.* "My excellent generals, how do you suggest we transport our troops to Egypt? Obviously, we can't take the direct route straight through Israel."

"The best way would be to move our troops to the coast of the Mediterranean and transport them by sea," said the ugly general.

The other commanders expressed their agreement.

"You are right, of course. I authorize all of you to act on this as soon as you leave my office. Chief, how long will it take us to move our army to Port Said?" Port Said was a large city and harbor in northeast Egypt.

The chief of staff replied, "We could transport about ten thousand troops by cargo planes in one day. The remaining troops would have to travel to the Mediterranean coast and embark on ships at either Beirut, Latakia, or Tartus, depending on their current location. I estimate we could move two hundred thousand men to Port Said in three or four days. Of course, the Lebanese will join us in this operation. They have approximately fifty thousand regular troops, not counting their reserves."

"But where in Allah's name would we procure enough boats to transport two hundred and fifty thousand troops? Admiral?"

"Well, we now have seventy-one naval boats of various sizes and the Lebanese have somewhere around fifty. There are also hundreds of fishing boats in the ports mentioned by the chief. If we appropriate the use of the larger ones, we should easily have sufficient space to transport the troops."

Boutros was pleased with that report. "I'll call Prime Minister Aali Khoury and King Hussein and review our plans. I will especially plead with them to join us in this great crusade against the Jewish infidels. Aali will of course transport his troops by sea also, but as for Hussein, he'll have to make that decision himself."

Daniel Christopher and Rachel Salant were sitting on a bench in the shade, trying to catch their breath after a hard workout. Now that Rachel was his platoon sergeant, she made him do more pushups than anyone else because he spent more time gawking at her than paying attention to the drills. Rachel opened her lunch sack and gave him an egg sandwich, and he shared an apple. Nearly every day, they walked to the far side of the base—so none of their platoon members would know they were fraternizing—and ate lunch together. They did not realize that most of the platoon knew they were getting romantically involved. She usually gave him lessons in Hebrew and he tried to teach her English.

Suddenly, they heard a siren calling the troops to line up on the main field fifty yards away. In such an emergency call, the troops were not required to line up by platoons or squads, so Daniel made sure he was next to Rachel.

Five minutes after the soldiers had assembled, the camp commander exited his office and took a position in front of them. His aide handed him a microphone, and he began his announcement immediately. "People, we have been advised by general headquarters that we will be transported to the front. Get your gear and weapons together as soon as possible. You'll receive your orders concerning where you'll be stationed from your company commanders. We'll move out at 1400 hours."

Since Camp Ashdod included over a thousand Americans, he repeated the message in English. The other three thousand American volunteers had been assigned to different training camps shortly after Zion's troops had disembarked from the cruise ship.

From the captain in charge of their company, Daniel and Rachel learned that they would be on active duty in northwestern Israel, near the Lebanese border. Daniel's older brother, William, was assigned to the Golan Heights area. John's sons, Cory and Michael, were stationed in the southwest, near the Gaza Strip, and Paul's son, Matthew, was posted in the vicinity of Tel Aviv.

"Rachel, how will they transport us?" Daniel asked.

"In troop trucks most of the way. Then in armored personnel carriers, infantry fighting vehicles, half-tracks, and jeeps. Most of us will eventually have to walk."

"I'm sure that's what I'll end up doing."

Rachel smirked at him. "Walking is good for you."

Six hours after David Omert issued the order for the "invasion" of Egypt, he also ordered his First Division, located in southern Galilee, to maintain their position and prepare to march northward toward Lebanon at his command. The Second Division, stationed in central Israel, was ordered to move immediately eastward across the West Bank to the Palestinian city of Nablus, thirty miles north of Jerusalem and the largest city in the West Bank. They captured this city easily and then began to march east toward Amman, the capital of Jordan, a distance of about forty-five miles. The Third Division, which David led himself, left the vicinity of Jerusalem and, crossing the West Bank at its narrowest point, headed northeast toward Amman, forty-four miles away. Eventually, they would join forces with the Second Division just outside Amman.

The key to all this was speed and precise timing.

All three divisions traveled in jeeps, armored personnel carriers, and small trucks. They also transported light tanks, Merkava main battle tanks, and artillery. The troops themselves wielded machine guns, mortars, hand grenades, M16 rifles, IMI Tavor assault rifles, sniper rifles with scopes, and anti-tank RPGs, or rocket propelled grenade launchers. The troops were supported by squadrons of Rafale and F-35 fighter jets.

Their commanders had received general instructions to engage any foreign forces they encountered as they hurried toward the enemy capitals: Jordan's capital, Amman, to the east; Syria's capital, Damascus, to the northeast; and Lebanon's capital, Beirut, to the north.

As Steven and Mary Christopher bounced along in an armored personnel carrier with David Omert and Chaim Yehoshua, they discussed many subjects. David had brought along two well-armed lieutenants, both members of the special forces and trained in radio communications. They also carried cell phones because the phones sometimes worked when the radios didn't. It was crucial that David be able to communicate with his commanders to receive reports and give instructions. All of them, including Mary, were dressed in olive green military uniforms. Mary kept her medical supplies close by in a large black bag.

For short distances they were able to drive on paved roads, but more often they traveled on gravel roads or across wild country. The going became especially rough when they had to cross ravines or ground covered with boulders or sand. Fortunately, their vehicle, which had room for eight passengers and two drivers in the front, seemed unstoppable.

David turned toward Steven and Mary, who were sitting in the second row of seats. "I know you're worried about your family members, and I don't blame you. War is always uncertain. However, we normally have an extremely low casualty rate in these engagements. Our leaders, and that includes me, have always had the primary goal of protecting the lives of our troops as much as possible. If our plan works out, and I'm sure it will, we'll probably meet very little resistance during this campaign."

"I know my brothers, John and Paul, are a part of this division," Steven said, "but I don't know where my sons, William and Daniel, are."

"I checked on your sons myself," Chaim said. "William is serving with the Fourth Division in the Golan Heights. As for Daniel, he's been assigned to the First Division operating near the Lebanese border. Both of them are fine and taking things in stride. The captain of Daniel's company informed me that Daniel is wild over one of our female sergeants."

"Daniel's always in love with some girl," Mary said. "He'll get over it as soon as they're
separated. And then it will be another girl."

One of the lieutenants moved forward and talked to David for a minute in a low voice. Afterwards, David leaned over to the driver and said, "Slow it down a bit."

"How fast?" the driver asked.

"Oh, down to about twenty miles an hour." He turned to the others and said, "We're a little ahead of the Second Division, despite our terrain being rougher, so we're slowing down somewhat. It's vital that we arrive at the same time."

Both divisions heading east met with resistance from isolated bands of Palestinian military groups, but after short skirmishes, the enemies were destroyed or routed. A few times, the commanders ordered patrols to leave the main body to scour the nearby countryside for contingents of Palestinian guerillas. All this David and Chaim had expected, but they knew they wouldn't run into any serious resistance until they approached the Jordanian capital.

Fifteen miles from Amman, both armies were hit by incoming Jordanian F-16 warplanes, but the Israeli air force engaged them almost immediately, before the enemy jets were able to do more than destroy several of the advance trucks. David told the others that the hostile planes had come from an airbase in Amman. Since the Israeli pilots were much better trained and had superior numbers, most of the Arab F-16s were shot down within half an hour.

Both divisions arrived in the vicinity of Amman at the same time and were met with intense shelling from areas inside the city and from its outskirts. David kept his forces just far enough away from the city that the shelling was largely ineffective. He grabbed the radio and ordered the Rafale and F-35 squadrons to make a direct attack on the Jordanian artillery batteries. They watched from their secure location until the artillery was silenced after twenty minutes. Only one Rafale was hit by aircraft fire. Then David ordered his forces to move forward to mop up any resistance that might remain in the capital.

Steven took part in several clashes on the outskirts, alongside David and Chaim, but David ordered him not to proceed into the city to participate in the extremely dangerous action of street-to-street and house-to-house fire-fights. As David led a patrol in trying to clear a street in downtown Amman, he was delighted when a squad of special forces captured and brought in Lieutenant General Abd al Kadir, who was the second highest-ranking officer in the Jordanian army. Only the commander-in-chief, King Hussein himself, had more authority. However, David knew that the king had already left the country with an army to offer assistance to Egypt because the monarch had bought the false reports circulated by the Israelis that their primary objective was to defeat Egypt first.

General Kadir expressed great fear that the Jewish ruler would simply execute him, but David laughed and promptly made him a prisoner of war.

Steven and Mary were sad that they had not caught sight of John or Paul during the engagement. At least then they would know they were still alive. Mary spent most of her time behind the lines caring for wounded Israeli and Jordanian soldiers. Since night had fallen before the battle was over, the fighting continued into the nighttime hours. At around three in the morning, David ordered half his troops to get a few hours sleep because he knew they needed to be fresh in order to obtain a decisive victory.

At daybreak, the surviving defenders surrendered, and David shipped hundreds of them off in trucks to prisoner-of-war camps a few miles north of Jerusalem. He left a small detail at Amman and then ordered his forces to proceed west until they reached Ramallah, six miles north of Jerusalem. Ramallah was the Palestinian administrative capital of the West Bank. At that point the two armies divided, with the Second Division heading south, traveling through the lower portion of the West Bank until they reached Israeli territory.

The Third Division, still commanded by Omert himself, proceeded north through the upper portion of the West Bank, heading for the Syrian capital of Damascus. The purpose of traveling through the center of the West Bank was to engage and defeat known Palestinian military bases as the Israelis continued on to their ultimate destinations. Once again, the essential thing was coordination, speed, and timing.

As they journeyed north, David radioed the commander of the Israeli navy and instructed him to dispatch warships from the ports of Ashdod and Tel Aviv. The Israeli navy had only a limited number of small warships, submarines, and patrol boats and could not engage in a full-fledged naval operation, but they could harass and delay the Syrian and Lebanese fleet with hit-and-run maneuvers while it sailed toward Egypt and during its return voyage to home ports. At the same time, David contacted his Fifth Division, located twenty miles east of Gaza, and put them on alert.

The mighty Arab fleet had just reached Port Said in northeast Egypt when the Syrian dictator, Ibn 'abbas al-Boutros, got the bad news. It had taken nearly four days for him to receive the message because his communications experts in Damascus were confused as to what the Israelis were doing. After all, there were troops moving toward Egypt, and other forces racing all over Israel, heading east, west, north, and south. Finally, the "experts" had belatedly decided that the enemy was coming directly toward Damascus. Learning this, Boutros was suddenly desperate to return to his country as soon as possible.

"Those stupid idiots!" Boutros ranted. "The incompetent, bungling fools! I'll have their heads when I get back. It's bad enough that Jordan beat us here to Egypt. Flying in twenty thousand paratroopers. I didn't even know King Hussein had that many transport planes."

He contacted Aali Khoury, the Lebanese prime minister, who had just disembarked at Port Said, accompanied by his elite personal guard. Khoury also was furious because his specialists in Lebanon hadn't contacted him at all and seemed unaware of any threat. Khoury vacillated, unable to decide what to do. After all, it might only be Syria that was threatened, for the relations between Israel and Lebanon were not nearly so lethal as those between Israel and Syria. Lebanon was often considered the pussycat of the Arab world.

At the angry insistence of Boutros, demanding he make up his mind, Prime Minister Khoury finally decided to disembark fifteen thousand troops with their equipment to succor Egypt in its day of trial and then return to Lebanon immediately with the rest of his forces. The return trip of the combined fleets should have taken only two days at most, but this time it was Boutros who couldn't make up his mind. The terrible thought had suddenly hit him that if he missed out on defeating Israel on the plains of the Sinai, he would also lose the glory of such a marvelous victory. So he waited at Port Said for two extra days, finally deciding to return to Syria only when he realized the action in the Sinai was clearly stalled.

When President Da'iyat Kassis of Egypt learned that there were Israeli armies speeding west across the Sinai, supported by warplanes, he grilled his chief of intelligence, Kadeem Abadi, in an effort to comprehend the magnitude of the threat. Several of his most important generals were there, after being called for the emergency meeting. Kassis resembled Gamal Nasser, the president of Egypt who had been defeated by the Israelis in 1956 and 1967. He was tall, good-looking, and husky, with close-cropped hair and a mustache. Unlike Nasser, he had a small goatee.

"Kadeem, how large are these Israeli forces and what kind of equipment do they have?"

"From the reports I've received, they are division strength. They are transporting light and heavy tanks and artillery. Also, they have air support."

"How many divisions?"

"Some reports say three, others say four."

"That *is* a major offensive. Have you sent out reconnaissance planes to verify it?"

"My President, we have sent out many, but Israeli warplanes shoot them down as soon as we approach their forces."

"What about ground observers?"

"We've received several communiqués from scattered military posts, but most of the observers are citizens."

"Umm. Citizens are not always reliable. Still, it does sound bad, and we cannot take chances. Generals, I want you to mobilize our ground forces and the air force. Send them out in a front just east of the Suez Canal. The Israelis are creatures of habit and will no doubt follow their old invasion routes, but Kadeem, I want you to verify the roads they'll take at this time. We must drive them out of the Sinai with a direct frontal attack."

"Mr. President, can we depend on help from our allies?" asked the commander of Egypt's armor brigades.

"Fortunately, yes. The Jordanians have already flown in twenty thousand paratroopers and seventy medium-size tanks, and the Syrians and Lebanese have just arrived at Port Said with a huge army. I don't know the real extent of their strength, but President Boutros hinted that I would be impressed with their sacrifice." He looked over at the general in command of his ground forces. "General Nazari, I want you to make sure the Jordanians are placed first on the front lines."

Chapter 7

Once the Third Division exited the northern West Bank, it turned northeast and traveled around the southern tip of the Sea of Galilee and into the Golan Heights, where it met with the Fourth Division that had been stationed there shortly after Israel had captured the western portion of Golan in a recent engagement. From there, both divisions continued northeast toward Damascus.

Three hours before he left the West Bank, David Omert had ordered the First Division, waiting in southern Galilee, to proceed north to capture Beirut, the capital of Lebanon.

The Israeli forces moving into Syria met little resistance until they reached the vicinity of Damascus, when suddenly they were struck by a ferocious barrage of Syrian artillery. David stopped the forward progress of his army and had a quick consultation with half a dozen of his top military commanders. On their advice, he turned the forward units of his army and withdrew out of the effective range of the enemy guns.

At that point, Syrian warplanes zoomed out of the heavens, firing missiles at his forces, destroying a dozen trucks, five armored transport vehicles, and several tanks. Some of the enemy pilots seemed to take delight in strafing his men as they dropped out of their trucks and ran for cover in nearby rock formations. Finally, Israeli air support arrived and engaged the enemy warplanes. Within fifteen minutes, the Rafale and F-35 fighters destroyed most of the enemy aircraft, and the few survivors turned and flew north to save themselves. David was very upset that his air force had not properly timed their arrival as he had ordered.

When the Israeli warplanes had finished their aerial dogfights, they attacked the Syrian gun emplacements and troop concentrations with missiles and bombs, doing everything possible to avoid civilian communities. Soon the enemy guns fell silent.

David then ordered his army to proceed toward the city. He was grim when he thought that once more they would have to engage in the perilous task of street-to-street fighting.

"David, may I ask you a question?" Steven said as their APC sped along the road toward the city.

"Yes, of course."

"Is your ultimate goal to conquer and hold all of Syria and Lebanon?"

"Certainly not. My purpose is to recover all the land we need as buffers against future incursions and attacks from our Arab neighbors, and to show them—by capturing their capitals—that they place their nations in grave danger when they continue to threaten Israel."

"So you want to repossess the Golan Heights, the West Bank, and possibly the Gaza Strip?"

"Exactly. Not only repossess but annex those territories."

"Then do you think it's really necessary to ferret out all enemy resistance in the city? We lost a lot of good men in the house-to-house fighting in Amman."

David considered that for a minute. It was hard for him, but he finally had to admit to himself that what he had done in Amman was not really necessary. He had wanted not only to defeat the enemy but also to destroy the morale of the people and their leaders, hoping that would perhaps deter them from future hostilities. But it was difficult to say these things to Steven.

"However, I can understand," Steven continued, "that you might want to teach your enemies a lesson." Steven knew the history of Israel, and he seemed to realize that David was probably justified, to some degree at least, in seeking revenge against his implacable enemies, who had slaughtered so many of his people. "But I believe you'll instill fear and caution in their hearts by the simple fact that you've overcome the military forces defending their capitals."

"You're right. We won't engage in street fighting. Instead, we'll mop up from a distance, reorganize our forces, and set out immediately for Beirut."

At that moment, a forward observer ran back to the commander's APC, his binoculars bouncing against his chest. "Commander Omert, I just saw a line of tanks issuing from the city, followed by troops."

"What kind of tanks and how many?"

"I counted about sixty of them before I broke off to report. But I believe there are more behind them. Most look like T-62s but there are quite a few T-80 main battle tanks."

Chaim whistled and said, "T-80s! I heard they had a fleet of upgraded T-80s, but I didn't believe it."

"How many troops?" David asked.

"Hard to tell, but I saw what looked like a platoon behind each tank."

David, Chaim, and several commanders hurried forward to check the enemy forces bearing down on them. "Now it looks like eighty or ninety tanks with still more coming," David said.

"And massed in one central place!" Chaim complained.

"I thought they took most of their fighting vehicles with them to Egypt," a colonel said.

"That's what Mossad reported to me," David noted, "but it seems Boutros hid these armor-supported troops in the capital as insurance." After pondering the problem for a while, he issued orders to his commanders, and he and Chaim walked back to his APC where Steven and Mary were waiting.

"Okay, let's mount up," David said.

"Are we going to retreat?" Mary asked.

David laughed. "Heavens no! We're going to try a clever little maneuver."

The Israeli army withdrew about eight miles and then split into two parts, one heading off to the right for a half mile and the other to the left for the same distance. Next, both wings advanced slowly in the direction of Damascus. David tried to describe to the others what they were doing as they did it, but all the occupants of the APC still looked puzzled, even Chaim.

"I don't understand what you're doing," Mary said, her eyes wide with concern.

David grinned and said, "Well, a great military thinker once said that all warfare is based on deception. Another more recent strategist said that the key to victory was to use indirect methods and surprising tactics to overcome an enemy, and by contrast, the sure way to meet defeat and waste human life is to engage in direct confrontations."

"Sounds interesting," Mary said, "but I still don't know what you're doing."

David looked into Mary's eyes, intrigued at her boldness and intelligence. "Well, first we withdrew our army for quite a distance. That probably gave the enemy the impression we were weak, frightened, and even intimidated by their show of force. It also greatly extended their line of support from the capital. Now we're moving forward to their right and left. Soon we'll be able to fire on their tanks and troops from two positions, with everything we've got. In other words, we'll have them surrounded, more or less."

David's plan worked surprisingly well. The firepower thrown at the enemy decimated troops and war machines at a surprising rate. Two hours after the engagement began, the enemy forces were annihilated, and the few remaining survivors fled into the countryside. As a result, the Syrian capital was now controlled by the IDF. The Israelis also took casualties, losing nearly four hundred soldiers, seven tanks, and a dozen other vehicles, but compared to what they had accomplished, they knew it had been a necessary sacrifice.

Jacan Levin and Ephrem Isaacs went throughout the city of Jerusalem, always traveling together, bearing witness to the power of God and the judgments that would fall upon the Jewish nation if they didn't repent and ask forgiveness of the Lord. After testifying for a few days in Jerusalem, they walked to nearby towns and cities and preached the same message. At first, most of the people scoffed at them because they viewed these unrefined peasants as dolts and fools who were falsely accusing them, ignoring the fact that they were the chosen people of God, the righteous ones who were innocent of serious sins. The orthodox Jews ridiculed them even more because they had not been ordained by the traditional religious leaders.

From time to time, religious Jews would pick up stones to throw at the men they considered blasphemers and false prophets, or they would attack the peasant preachers with rods and sticks as the two "accusers" passed by. However, the shepherds seemed impervious to all physical attacks, for the rocks usually missed their mark and the rods bounced off, causing only minor harm. At this point, the shepherds didn't show any sign of retaliation. They blessed those who wanted blessings, comforted the forlorn, and healed the sick and handicapped. On those occasions, none dared revile them or attack them.

Then early one morning during the second week, they added a new dimension to their message.

Jacan stood on a low wall skirting a fountain in the center of Jerusalem and gazed at the people passing by. Most had heard of these strange men and stopped to hear what they had to say. Jacan raised his voice and declared, "Oh people of Israel, the Lord has commanded us to give you a very special message today. It refers to the hope our people have had for thousands of years, but which is seldom preached in your synagogues anymore. Behold, I declare unto you a great mystery."

"What mystery, preacher?" said an impatient man standing close by. "Why don't you get to the point? What can you tell us that we haven't heard a thousand times before?"

Jacan was so filled with the Spirit that he couldn't resist using language he had only experienced in the Tanakh, or Written Torah. "Behold, the Almighty has revealed to us that the coming of the great Messiah is upon us."

Many of the spectators laughed, and a short, fat woman called out, "That's hilarious, preacher. We've been hearing that for as long as I can remember, and my grandparents heard it, and my great-grandparents."

"That's right," said a tall man in a business suit. "Dozens of men have risen in the history of Israel and claimed to be the Messiah, but they all turned out to be liars and fakes." By this time, nearly a hundred people had gathered around the shepherds.

Ephrem climbed on the wall and stood next to Jacan. "Neither of us claims to be the Messiah," he shouted back, much more sure of himself than he had been at the beginning. "We are no more than two of his forerunners."

Most of the crowd laughed, but a few stared at the preachers intently. The short, fat woman yelled even louder, "What proof do you have? Are you great scholars or wise men or miracle workers?"

At that instant, several gigantic explosions illuminated the eastern sky, and the crowd fell to the ground in terror. Most kept their heads down, but a few raised them, searching the heavens. There was crying and fearful mumbling. After a minute passed, the crowd began to scramble to their feet, dusting off their clothes and rubbing painful knees. One man said, "It's nothing but more Palestinian missiles. Looks like our defense system took them out."

"Not all of them," Jacan said. He put his hands together and raised them to the level of his face. "Dear God, please defend this people from the approaching menace." At those words, a bolt of lightning fell from the cloudless sky a few miles to the east and struck a flying object, producing a tremendous explosion that lighted the heavens and shook the earth. Once again the crowd fell to the ground and remained there for several minutes until the tiny fragments of a disintegrated missile stopped raining down on them. Slowly, they began to get to their feet.

"How did you do that?" exclaimed a pudgy, bald-headed man, brushing debris from his clothes. "You destroyed a missile and saved a lot of lives."

"I didn't do it, God did," Jacan declared. "The Spirit told me what to do, and I asked the Lord for help."

From that moment on, the reputation of the humble witnesses spread throughout the land, not only in the vicinity of Jerusalem, but all over the nation of Israel, and even beyond. Those who had seen this miracle and their many healings spread the word. Some of the people rejoiced, but many feared that the Messiah's coming might truly be near and they were not ready to receive him.

"Do you think I could that?" Ephrem said as they walked down a crowded street a short time later.

"Do what?"

"What you did. Zap evil things with lightning."

"No, you can't control the elements any more than I can. I've told you a dozen times: if we do our duty, we ask God, and he does the miracle."

Daniel and fifty of his comrades, both women and men, were dug in a mile from enemy lines. Rachel Salant was their sergeant, and she crawled from one point to another, keeping her troops informed of changing circumstances. Daniel followed her with his eyes every time she passed by. Daniel and Rachel had tried to keep their growing relationship a secret, but the others in their platoon, and even most of their company, knew what was going on. Who could miss the signals in their eyes? Nobody objected because they saw that Rachel played no favorites and was harder on Daniel than on anyone else. Daniel loved all the attention he received from Rachel, even though it usually consisted of him being required to do hundreds of extra push-ups and scores of gruesome assignments that none of the others had to endure.

Their platoon had been assigned to the First Division, and that force had been ordered to move to the northern border of Israel. Brigadier General Hugo Tandler was the commander of the division, and he sat in his APC with Colonel Binyamin Hirsch a thousand yards behind their front line, waiting for instructions from headquarters. They had halted a few miles from the border between Israel and Lebanon because they had run into determined resistance from Hezbollah battalions spread out along a twenty-mile perimeter. Like Hamas, Hezbollah was an Arab terrorist organization, but Hamas worked mostly in the Gaza Strip while Hezbollah was stationed in southern Lebanon.

Fifteen minutes earlier, Hugo Tandler had informed David Omert of the situation. No one in Israeli intelligence had dreamed that the Lebanese forces stationed in Beirut would leave the city and set up a perimeter seventy-five miles to the south.

"What does Omert plan to do?" Hirsch asked.

"I don't know," Tandler replied. "He wanted to consult with his staff. I sure don't want to make a head-on assault. They've got tanks and artillery over there. We could lose a lot of troops."

They waited another ten minutes until the general's cell phone rang. "Hello, Tandler here." He listened for a few minutes and then hung up.

"Omert says we're to do nothing right away. He's going to drop paratroops behind enemy forces to cut off their lines of supplies and communication. Meanwhile, he's going to continue northwest to Beirut, but he'll change course and head southwest to reinforce us if we need further help. If he maintains his current heading, he expects to reach the outskirts of Beirut in about two and a half hours."

"Whew! That's a relief."

"The president said he can't believe the Lebanese would leave their capital virtually unguarded, and he chuckled when I told him how thinly their commander had spread his troops out on the border. You know, I respect Omert for many reasons, but the main one is that he's always concerned with avoiding Israeli casualties."

A half hour later, they saw a squadron of transport aircraft fly by, heading north.

"There they are," Colonel Hirsch said. "It won't be long now."

Rachel Salant's platoon saw the transport planes overhead, and she radioed her superior to find out what was happening. When she heard the good news, she made sure her people got the word. They received it with grins and shouts of joy.

Two hours later, Rachel ordered her platoon to move forward. In Hebrew she said, "Okay, the party's over, boys and girls. Let's show them what real soldiers look like."

Daniel turned to one of the men he knew could speak English. "What did she say?"

"She said we're going to attack the enemy. The paratroops have dropped behind their lines, and we have them in a trap."

When they reached the enemy line, they saw thousands of troops and vehicles rushing away to the north. Tandler and Hirsch surmised that the enemy commander had decided to make an all-out attack on the Israeli forces that had just dropped behind them, because those forces had fewer troops and less firepower. But Tandler knew what Omert would do next, and he didn't even need to call in to find out. The president would tell the paratrooper squadrons to withdraw toward Beirut and avoid engaging the Lebanese and Hezbollah forces directly. Meanwhile, Omert would turn the combined Third and Fourth Divisions southwest in order to reinforce the paratroopers, and the enemy would be caught between two superior forces.

Within a few hours, their guesses proved to be right. When the commander of the enemy army found himself in a vise, he surrendered, and his army and the capital were taken without hardly firing a shot. Now the Israelis must prepare for the return of the great naval fleet from Egypt.

Fifteen miles before Colonel Parmet's brigade reached the Suez Canal, the colonel received a call from President Omert to stop his advance and spread out his forces to create a front. Omert gave the same instructions to the southern brigade. He told his officers that he wanted to give the Egyptians the impression that these Israeli forces were about to launch a full-scale campaign. Two days after Parmet had stopped his advance, in the early afternoon, he and Colonel Walmann discussed the situation.

"Well, we've been sitting here under this canopy for two days, doing nothing but twiddling our thumbs and frying in the heat!" Major Herschel Walmann complained to Parmet. "Meanwhile the Egyptians have been massing troops and organizing what looks like a major offensive."

"I know," Parmet replied, "and our forward scouts tell me the Jordanians have joined the Egyptians with a large army."

"So you were right when you said the transports that flew over two days ago were carrying paratroops and equipment from Jordan."

"I'm afraid so."

"Colonel, we know we're not going to attack an army a hundred times our size, so why are we still here? I say let's get the devil out of this place." Right then, Parmet's aides and driver returned from visiting some female soldiers in a nearby APC and plopped down on camp chairs.

"It's not for us to decide. I'm not sure what Omert is thinking, unless he hopes to confuse our enemies and keep them guessing."

Walmann looked toward the west with a worried expression on his face. "It's a dangerous game to play. What amazes me most is that the Egyptians didn't attack us days ago."

"Maybe it's because they don't know our strength. Egyptian intelligence is notorious for being indecisive or just dead wrong." The radio chirped, and Parmet answered. "Hello. Yes, Mr. President. This is Colonel Parmet." After listening for a while, he hung up and eyed his friend with a grin. "Time to move out."

"Move out? You mean attack?"

"Nope. Head for home as fast as we can go."

"Whew! It's about time. I'm bored to death and dying in this desert heat. Where to exactly?"

"Gaza. That's where we'll make an attack. The southern brigade has gotten the same instructions." After Parmet had informed his subordinate officers down the line, he ordered several aides to pack their bedding and gear and throw them into the small truck that had followed them all the way across the Sinai. Then Parmet and Walmann jumped into their jeep, and the colonel ordered the driver to swing around and go east on the same road. As they sped along, much faster than before, he laughed and said to his friend, "This should drive the Egyptians nuts."

❦

The second contingent of Zion's volunteer soldiers arrived at Ashdod Port shortly before noon. There were over four thousand of them, and they had made the ocean crossing in a cruise ship without any problems, except for some seasickness from the movement of an active sea and from the terrible food they were forced to eat. In Zion there was almost no junk food. As the troops streamed off the boat, carrying big packs and hunting rifles, Raanan Rieckel, the commander of Camp Ashdod, stood on the wharf and watched them go by.

The camp commander turned to an officer standing close by. "Good day, sir. Are you General Michael Jamison, the officer from America?" Jamison nodded and they shook hands. The commander also noticed an old man dressed in skins and a coonskin cap standing not far away, carrying a long rifle. "We're grateful for the great sacrifice you people are making in our behalf."

"You're entirely welcome. We couldn't stop these men from coming even if we tried. We all consider the Israelis as our brethren."

"Thank you for that. It's wonderful to have friends who are willing to support us in our time of need." He swallowed hard and wiped his eyes with his sleeve. "I understand President Omert has asked you to be one of the officers in charge of the action against Hamas?"

"Yes he has. Colonel Ruther Johnston and I have just arrived from Jerusalem."

"Okay, let's load your men into trucks and head for our base not far away. We need to give them special training."

"What kind of training?"

"It's training in street-to-street and door-to-door combat. It's a type of guerilla warfare and is very dangerous. Hamas fighters are experts in it. By the time we've finished instructing your men, our guys from the Sinai and the Fifth Division located just east of Gaza will be ready for the operation. We call it Operation Cloudburst."

"Seems appropriate."

"Can your men use those long rifles they're carrying?" asked the camp commander."

General Jamison expected that question and he knew other questions would follow. He had fielded similar questions from David Omert when the first contingent of Zion's troops had arrived weeks ago. "Most of them have fighting experience, and some are excellent shots."

The commander didn't look convinced. "Have your guys ever done any street fighting?"

"Quite a bit, as a matter of fact. Back home we've had hundreds of skirmishes with gangs and violent mobs."

"That's a terrible situation, but at least it'll serve them well here."

At that moment, Ruther Johnston sauntered up. "General, when are we hittin' the road? I'm gettin' kinda itchy ta show them terrorizers a thing or two."

Jamison introduced the two men, and the commander said, "That's a big gun, Mr. Johnston."

"Call me Ruther."

"Ruther. I've never seen a rifle that big. Is it effective?"

"Yep. I kin shoot the tail off a skunk six hundred yards away."

"Wow! At your—"

"Don't say it, brother. Old age is jist a figurement of the imagination."

"I meant to say it'll come in handy shooting holes in the enemy's water tanks and barrels. And also enemy snipers."

"You betcha. Dryin' up their water supply is a dern good way to make 'em skedaddle or throw their paws in the air."

After leading the new troops to trucks a short distance away, Commander Rieckel transported them to the military training camp a few miles to the east. The men received a good lunch and broke up into many small units to receive instruction on the attitudes and strategies of all Arab militants, especially Hamas and Hezbollah. They learned why Arab terrorists hid their weapons deep within civilian populations. Whereas the Israelis used their weapons to protect their people, the Arabs used their people to protect their weapons. In other words, the Israelis were motivated by love and respect for their citizens, but the Arabs were motivated by their hatred of Jews and their contempt for the lives of their people.

Soon they would leave for the Gaza Strip, about twenty-four miles to the south. There they would join up with Israeli forces in the area and with others coming up from the Sinai.

Meanwhile, David Omert brought all his forces to the eastern shores of the Mediterranean, concentrating them around the three main ports of

Beirut, Tartus, and Latakia. He also set up batteries of big guns near the beaches and alerted his air force. The enemy flotilla would soon arrive, and he intended to prevent them from landing. If they insisted on fighting, he planned to destroy their ability to do so. Now all they had to do was wait.

Chapter 8

That night after dinner, Steven and Mary cuddled together in an oversize sleeping bag. Their tent was lit by one lantern powered by batteries.

"Aren't you ever afraid, Steven?" Mary said.

"Pretty much all the time, but I try to not let it get to me."

"Me too. But then I tell myself this is probably the best thing I could be doing to serve my Father in Heaven, and he'll give me—us—protection. That makes me feel better. I pray for you every day."

"Funny. I do the same. Pray for us, I mean."

"By the way, I've been listening to the radio every day during this campaign, and I've heard reports about two strange men walking the streets of Jerusalem calling people to repentance."

"Oh? I'll bet that's going over big."

"Well, a lot of people don't like it. Some have attacked them, but others seem to listen. And that's not all. They're also claiming that the Messiah will appear any day now."

"There have been hundreds of people throughout history who've claimed to receive revelation that the Messiah would come soon, and they were always wrong. Yet, the guys you mention may be different. We know from the scriptures that two prophets will be raised in the last days to act as forerunners to the coming of Jesus Christ, just as John the Baptist was a forerunner when Jesus appeared to start his mission on earth."

"But these men have never mentioned Jesus Christ, only the Messiah."

"Well, the Messiah is Jesus Christ, but maybe they're wise enough to say 'Messiah' and not 'Jesus Christ' because they know the Jews can't bear to hear the name Jesus used in that context. That may be how they avoid getting shot, stabbed, or stoned."

"Some people claim they've seen them perform miracles."

"What kind of miracles?"

"They heal the sick, and once they brought lightning down from the sky to explode what was probably a Palestinian missile."

"Umm. This is getting more and more interesting all the time. Maybe they are the prophets that the scriptures talk about."

"There's one thing that bothers me though."

"What's that?"

"Well, I heard somewhere that the two prophets who preach in Jerusalem in the last days will be apostles or others high up in the Church."

"I've heard that too, but John and I have discussed this numerous times and we've found no evidence whatsoever to back it up. Do you have your triple combination here in the tent?" Mary looked around in her bags for a while and then handed him her scriptures.

Steven made a quick search and said, "Ah. Here it is. In the Book of Mormon, 2 Nephi 8:17–20, the Lord is talking to the city of Jerusalem, and in verses nineteen and twenty he calls the two prophets the 'sons of Jerusalem.'" He turned the pages again until he reached Doctrine and Covenants 77:15. "In this verse, Joseph Smith answers the question concerning the identity of the two witnesses or prophets mentioned in the eleventh chapter of Revelation. Joseph says, 'They are to be raised up to the Jewish nation in the last days.' This seems to indicate that they won't be two Mormon leaders traveling to Israel to testify of Jesus Christ. Besides, Mormon apostles are called to lead church members, not the Jewish nation."

"That's interesting. I never thought of it that way. The reports I've heard say that these two Jewish preachers are poor, obscure, uneducated shepherds, pretty much the opposite of Mormon apostles."

"That doesn't surprise me. Can you imagine what would happen if two Christian leaders came from a land far away and tried to convince the Jews that Jesus was their Messiah?"

"They'd reject them outright, or worse."

"Right. The Jews will only be convinced that Jesus is their Messiah, and the Son of God, when Christ descends to the Mount of Olives, identifies himself, and saves them from the armies of Gog."

"You know, Steven, I already felt that, but hearing you go through it eases my mind and comforts my heart."

Steven took her face in his hands and kissed her on the lips. "Good. Now we can get some sleep."

The young couple, Elkan and Mical Vorhaus, stood at a big window in their apartment on the fifth floor of a high-rise building in Tel Aviv. The view of the city, looking west toward the Mediterranean, was spectacular. But even more wonderful was their baby boy, Asa, born a month earlier, who stared at his mother's face with what they felt was rapt attention. In spite of all the turmoil and war in Israel, they gave thanks to God for the many blessings he had given them.

Soon Elkan would graduate from medical school and start his internship at the Tel Aviv Medical Center a few blocks from their apartment. After that, he would serve in the Israel Defense Forces wherever they decided to send him. He prayed it would be in Jerusalem. Mical had been a nurse at the medical center for almost a year and also hoped to offer her skills to the military. She prayed they wouldn't separate her from her husband.

Their happy contemplation of the glorious view was suddenly interrupted by a huge explosion that hurled them across the room and engulfed them in flames. All three died instantly, and their dreams died with them.

Later it was determined that their apartment had been struck by a new long-range Hamas missile fired from the Gaza Strip. Seven other missiles struck various areas in Tel Aviv with a similar devastating effect.

When David Omert, waiting on the outskirts of Beirut, received news of the vicious attack, he was outraged. This wicked action confirmed his determination to call for the capture and occupation of the Gaza Strip. He was furious at Hamas, the terrorist faction that controlled the Gaza Strip, and also at the Palestinian leaders who had formed a coalition government with Hamas.

In the past few years, the liberal Israeli leaders, listening to the "humanitarian" appeals of the international community, had relaxed the tight Israeli blockade established all around the Gaza Strip. It had been put in place to prevent Hamas from receiving weapons and the means for making them.

The same leaders, in an effort to show good will, had also inactivated the ten batteries of Iron Dome, placed in strategic locations in southern Israel, especially near Gaza.

One of the first things David did as the new ruler of Israel was to reactivate Iron Dome. Those anti-missile systems had been expensive but a complete success. When the radar unit of a battery detected a rocket or missile fired from enemy territory, the sophisticated system could track the projectile and destroy it with interceptor missiles. Each battery could fire up to twenty interceptors in seconds. The result was a ninety percent reduction in rockets and missiles hitting Israeli communities.

After the new rocket attack on Tel Aviv, Omert ordered all his forces in the Gaza area to commence a ground invasion of the Gaza Strip. This included the Israeli Fifth Division located near Gaza, his forces coming from the Sinai, and the new American troops that had just landed. Next, he commanded the chief of the air force to carpet bomb a five-mile band of territory south of Gaza in order to destroy the tunnels dug by Hamas for moving arms and munitions from Egypt to Gaza.

He had already warned Hamas several times that if they continued attacks on Israel, he would move against them in force. However, this operation would begin by dropping thousands of leaflets over Gaza, as had been done in past operations, warning non-combatant civilians to take shelter and keep clear of Hamas militants.

Two days after the new troops from America had arrived at Ashdod Camp, they were transported by trucks to the vicinity of Gaza. Close to noon that same day, General Michael Jamison and Ruther Johnston walked slowly across an open field toward the safety barrier the Israelis had built completely around the Gaza Strip. They were followed by over four thousand troops from Zion, who wore no uniforms but carried hunting rifles, many with scopes. They halted a mile from the wire fencing of the barrier, hidden from view by some low ridges covered with bushes.

"Okay. We'll wait here until the Israeli forces arrive," said General Jamison. "It shouldn't be long."

Twenty-five minutes later, a troop of Israeli infantry appeared, coming in from the northeast. A major general of the Israeli Fifth Army climbed out of his APC and approached. "You would be General Jamison, I assume," he said, extending his hand in a friendly manner.

"Yes. And who do I have the pleasure of meeting?" Jamison said, shaking his hand.

"I'm Major General Herut Urbach." He looked at the American troops. "You seem to have some capable men. Are they ready to fight?" Jamison nodded. "All right, please summon your unit officers so they can listen to what I'm going to say. They'll need to relay that information accurately to their troops."

Jamison sent some officers to round up every unit leader in his army—over forty men. When they arrived and gathered around, Urbach acknowledged their presence and began his speech.

"Gentlemen, we'll proceed to the security fence slowly, pretty much side by side. When we're about two hundred yards away, I'll demolish a section of the barrier with our tank cannons. Then we'll proceed and enter the Gaza Strip. Our job will be to engage anyone who offers resistance. We'll enter every house and building and clear them of enemy militants. We also have troops that just arrived from the Sinai who will enter the area through tunnels dug by Hamas, clearing the tunnels as they proceed.

"Your men must be extremely wary of people who seem to be innocent civilians. Even women and children. Make every individual drop to the ground with their hands in sight." He gave them the Arabic words to express this and certain unmistakable gestures. "If they don't fall down, shoot them. Search every person, every room, and every building for weapons, bombs, grenades, and ammo. Tell your men not to turn their backs on anyone. We have troops on all three sides of the Strip, about sixty thousand men, including your guys.

"We estimate that Hamas has around thirty-eight thousand armed militants. I believe that at least half of them will surrender immediately when they see our numbers. My men will take charge of those who surrender and herd them into several central locations. I hope your men will not hesitate to shoot those who resist. These terrorists are cold-blooded and have no qualms about killing anyone, not even babies. Do I make myself clear?"

The American officers said yes and returned to instruct their men. The American troops had already received instructions similar to Urbach's during the two days they had spent at Camp Ashdod, so they had no trouble absorbing the information. Urbach gave the unit leaders half an hour and then ordered all the troops to advance on the enemy.

The fighting was gruesome and continued all day, but by four the following morning the Gaza Strip had been taken. Approximately ten thousand Palestinian fighters died and fifteen thousand were wounded. The Israelis lost nearly seven hundred men with twelve hundred wounded. In general, the Americans performed courageously, experiencing about three hundred casualties with almost five hundred wounded.

After two days of struggling to return home, the Arab fleet finally arrived in the vicinity of Beirut, Lebanon on the same day as the Israeli capture of Gaza. The delay was due to the continual harassment heaped upon the fleet by the tiny Israeli navy. The navy didn't have the ships or the firepower to destroy the fleet, but it did an excellent job of making a pest of itself.

David Omert was ready. He had assembled twenty batteries of artillery near the shore and had massed over a hundred thousand troops in the area. He had also sent several brigades northward to the ports of Latakia and Tartus, in case some of the flotilla fled north. As the largest Syrian ship led the others toward the dock at Beirut, David figured it was the vessel commanded by President Boutros. When the ship was about six miles out, he gave a prearranged signal, and two batteries fired a warning salvo over the incoming vessel. He knew the ship was just a big boat and not a genuine warship with batteries of powerful guns.

Still, the ship kept coming.

"He's either stupid or really stubborn," Chaim said as he watched the vessel through a small telescope.

"Maybe both," David replied.

"I guess you'll have to be more convincing."

David watched the ship through binoculars and confirmed that it was not stopping. He signaled again and six batteries fired salvos, three exploding in front of the ship and three exploding behind it. At that point, the ship slowed and then stopped.

"Finally," David said. He turned to his communications officer. "Get Boutros on the radio. If that doesn't work, try the satellite phone."

A few minutes later, he heard Boutros's voice on the receiver. "You are President Omert? Why are you calling me?" Boutros said in Arabic.

David was fluent in Arabic and answered him in the same language. "I'm sure you know by now, but I'll give you a summary." He quickly described the size and power of his army, explained that he had effective control of Jordan, Syria, Lebanon, and their capitals, and demanded that Boutros and Khoury surrender immediately. He assured him that if they signed peace treaties with Israel, agreed to never attack Israel again, and recognized the Jewish state, their countries would be returned to them. But if they did not accept these terms, Israel would occupy their nations permanently.

Boutros ranted and raged for ten minutes, claiming that Omert was an evil tyrant and a mass murderer. Finally, he calmed down a little and demanded time to think it over and consult with Prime Minister Khoury. Two hours later, he returned to the radio and said that he and Khoury, after serious consideration, had decided to sign the treaty. Omert told him they needed to come to shore in a small boat for the signing. An hour later, when the signing was finished, Boutros and Khoury angrily returned to their ships. The question for all Israelis was, would they honor the treaties in the future?

❧

The next day, David ordered all his forces in Syria and Lebanon to return to Israel as quickly as possible. His communications expert finally contacted King Hussein, the ruler of Jordan, who had left Jordan and now commanded his troops in Egypt. Hussein was impatiently waiting to attack Israeli forces in the Sinai. He was shocked when David told him that his country was essentially under the control of the IDF, for in his haste to mobilize an army and leave Jordan to help defend the Egyptians, he had left his country vulnerable to Israeli occupation. David made him the same offer as he had Boutros and Khoury, and Hussein accepted with only a little hesitation.

The final result of the campaigns of the previous week was to return to Israel complete control over the lands the liberals had surrendered during their tenure: the Golan Heights, the West Bank, and the Gaza Strip. And now they had also gained more authority in east Jerusalem.

Soon Israel would desperately need these territories as buffers in the approaching conflict—the war of Armageddon against UGOT's combined forces.

⟨✦⟩

Lucienne Delisle, Gerald Galloway's French mistress, sat on the luxurious divan and put her slim, tanned legs on Gerald's lap. He could never resist her when she enticed him, and he caressed her legs sensually. She was still exquisite, even at age fifty-one. Once again they were spending a few days together in their private suite at Le Bristol Hotel, located in the heart of Paris. Gerald had acquired complete possession of the entire fourth floor of the sumptuous hotel.

"Gerald, I'm so glad we've renewed our relationship," Lucienne said. "I was starting to think you didn't care for me anymore."

"Of course I care. I've just been busy trying to coordinate the many elements of our project. Besides, I'm probably getting too old for romance." Gerald was seventy-two but still vigorous and active. He had often been in awe that so many great world leaders, like Castro, Stalin, and Mao Tse-tung, had been able to live to a ripe old age. Those giants of history proved that a long life was certainly possible when regrettable events didn't interfere.

"Oh, you're not old. Just look at you. Most people think you're in your fifties. And everyone I know is envious of all you have accomplished. But you seem a little depressed today. I know we've had somewhat of a setback in the Middle East, right? We thought a preliminary war between the Arabs and the Jews would decimate Israeli forces and waste their resources, but it seems we were wrong, if I understand the recent news reports."

"Well, not entirely. Israel lost several thousand troops and consumed much of their stockpile of munitions. At the same time, the Arabs lost even more troops and were exposed as fools. We'll use up hordes of the Islamic fanatics in the coming war, making it easier to eradicate them after Israel is destroyed."

"Still, my darling, David Omert, the ruler of Israel, showed some remarkable military acumen, didn't he?"

"He did indeed. I analyzed his strategies carefully and will be better able to deal with him five weeks from now when our armies begin to arrive. He was lucky to face enemies that have terrible intelligence capabilities, cannot work together, and vacillate like the waves of the sea."

"Perhaps you're right, but he still makes me nervous."

"Don't worry about him, my dear. I'll handle him when the time comes. He won't have it so easy when he's surrounded by fifty million trained warriors."

The drought started at the beginning of June and continued plaguing Israel for weeks. Fortunately, Chaim Yehoshua had convinced Knesset members, before David Omert had been anointed ruler of Israel, to pass a bill providing for the storage of large amounts of water. Most of the water was stored in underground drums, in covered reservoirs, and in one-liter, plastic bottles. As the troops battled the enemy in the various theaters of the recent war, they carried millions of these bottles with them.

The four Arab nations involved in the war had a better supply of water because they could find sources in the Euphrates and Nile rivers, although the level of those rivers was running low due to overuse. Since Turkey was friendly to their cause, it had promised the Arabs to ship in hundreds of drums of water from its own sources in the event that their friends ran short. At the beginning of the war, the Lebanese had attempted to block and divert the sources of the Jordan River to inhibit Israel's ability to support armies, and they had partially succeeded. But after overcoming Syria and Lebanon, David Omert had restored the normal flow to the Sea of Galilee.

Israel had invested billions of shekels in building two desalination facilities just offshore in the Mediterranean Sea, but they were not scheduled to be operational for several months. When they went on line, they would be able to provide one fifth of Israel's water needs. There were also four smaller desalination plants located throughout Israel that currently supplied over a third of Israel's water. The Israeli government had promoted these and other water projects for decades because their meager natural resources of water had been a grave problem for Israel ever since the founding of the nation. Unfortunately, UGOT warplanes had succeeded in bombing three of those vital water desalination plants.

So as the drought persisted into the third week of June, the situation became extremely serious. The stores of water were running dry, and the people had barely enough to drink, much less bathe or wash clothing. That's when Jacan Levin and Ephrem Isaacs decided to take action.

"Do you think we can do it, Jacan?" Ephrem asked as they walked up a narrow street in east Jerusalem near the Temple Mount.

"No! How many times do I have to tell you? We can't do it, but God can."

"Oh yeah. I forgot. Go ahead and ask him."

"You depend too much on me. The Lord chose you too, so you ask."

"But you're the one who gets the results. You ask."

"If I get results, it's because you always insist I do the work. Today it's your turn. Have confidence. I promise you the Lord will listen."

"Okay, I'll try." Ephrem looked around, waiting for a break in the swarming crowd, but there was no break. He noticed the haggard and desperate look on the faces of the people he loved and decided to do his best. He knelt on the street and began to pray. "Dear God, as thy humble servant I ask thee to give an abundance of rain to your people right away because—believe me, dear Lord—they really need it."

Some of those walking by scowled, but others seemed curious and slackened their pace. A few stopped to listen. Ephrem continued his prayer, reviewing the suffering of the people from the drought and several of the miracles God had done in ancient times. His prayer was so sincere that many of those who had stopped looked up at the sky.

They weren't disappointed. Huge masses of dark clouds began to move in from the Mediterranean and darkened the heavens above. Then the deluge hit, causing everyone to run to the nearest cover, but the downpour quickly turned into a gentle, consistent rain. The people laughed with delight and the children stuck out their tongues to feel the blessed moisture. The rain fell all day across the entire country, slowly soaking into the soil and filling the reservoirs, and it would continue off and on during the month of July. However, very little rain reached Arab lands.

Those who had heard the prayer and seen the miracle spread the word throughout Jerusalem, and many of the people began to believe that these two shepherds were indeed prophets. And if they were true witnesses, the Messiah would soon come and judge them for their works. It was a hard idea to bear. Only the righteous Jews, or those who thought they were righteous, rejoiced at the thought of the coming of the long-awaited Blessed One.

Chapter 9

A month later, near the end of July, UGOT's coalition armies began to arrive on the borders of Palestine, a few million troops at first with more coming all the time. They came from all parts of the planet except Canada, Australia, the United Kingdom, a few smaller countries, and of course New America—all those who had refused to join the coalition invasion. The enemy hovered on the boundaries of the land, thirty to forty miles from Israel, like a lion stalking fat, unwary zebras grazing peacefully under shaded trees. Their leaders hoped to expose the Holy Land as being unholy. Yes, they knew the Jews had suffered indescribably for over twenty-seven hundred years, their misery culminating in the Nazi Holocaust, but they intended to make that suffering nothing in comparison to what they had planned for the Jews.

Hundreds of warships from Turkey, Greece, Italy, France, and Spain plied the eastern Mediterranean, closing off the sea as a possible escape route for any Israeli citizens trying to flee clandestinely to the west.

The only ships getting through this naval blockade were those from Zion, for nearly every week, small American boats sneaked through the maritime barrier by night, bringing troops, food, water, weapons, and hope to the tiny beleaguered nation. No longer did they dare come in cruise ships because those giant boats were easily seen, but they came in spite of the risk of death on the high seas or obliteration from UGOT forces if they were detected. By this time, America had supplied over eighty thousand troops.

By the first week of August, the UGOT coalition armies numbered over forty million, the largest army ever assembled in any war in world history. And more troops were on the way.

In an emergency meeting held in his private compound near the commune of Nanterre, Gerald Galloway had assembled UGOT's associates, war ministers, representatives of confederate nations, and miracle-working prophets, all of them anxious to learn how to proceed.

"Well, ladies and gentlemen, here we are at last," Gerald said, his eyes flashing. "We have reached the moment of decision. The moment when truth, science, and righteousness will engage in the ultimate combat with fanatical belief and sanctimonious religion." Gerald dared to say this even to the leaders of nations who still held some belief in pagan religions, but whose faith had waned radically in the growing worldliness and secularism of the world.

"I assure you all that we will win the great prize, which is complete control over the destiny of this planet. Our coalition armies have already wreaked havoc against hundreds of pockets of Christian and Jewish communities as they struggled against impossible odds to fulfill their great mission to reach the vile land of the Jews."

There was applause and a buzz of enthusiasm from the assembly of fifty-five people, who were sitting in six rows of comfortable chairs.

Randolph Benson, UGOT's associate for the Middle East, raised his hand in the first row, and Gerald acknowledged him. "Unfortunately, we've had a few setbacks also, Mr. President."

"You must be referring to the recent war in Israel. Yes, you're right, Randy. But it wasn't really our doing. The foolish Arabs took action without the permission of UGOT, and they got what they deserved. To extricate themselves from their dilemma, they all signed peace treaties. Since that time, their leaders have asked me what they should do, and I told them the solution was easy—just tear up the treaties, and I understand they did so. Even Kassis Da'iyat, the president of Egypt, has destroyed the peace treaty his country has had with Israel since 1979. You might be surprised to learn that the recent war has also had numerous other benefits, too many to review at this time."

"But Israel also recovered some strategic territory," said Marcus Whitman, the associate in charge of Western Europe.

"That's true," Gerald said with a frown. "Still, it's a small thing. It won't help them when they face millions of troops with the best equipment in the world today." He hesitated, then said, "Permit me to let you in on something I haven't reported to you before in our communications. One of our initial strategies was to deprive Israel of water. We've already bombed some of their water desalination plants, and soon we'll cut off their main source of water—the Jordan River."

"However, it's been raining for a month in Israel, so they'll have plenty of water for the foreseeable future," said Lucienne Delisle. Everyone in the room knew that Lucienne was Gerald's "secret" mistress and had known it for years.

"I know. I know. It's no big deal. The rain is a fluke and won't last much longer. Israel has always had fewer water resources than just about any nation on earth. It's a serious weakness I plan to exploit."

Colton Aldridge, UGOT's foremost prophet and a worker of great miracles, waved his hand vigorously in the third row. Gerald recognized him immediately. "Apparently, you haven't heard the news, Mr. President," Colton said.

"What news?" Gerald growled.

"Well, it seems Israel has two new prophets."

"So? Israel's had hundreds of prophets over the years," Gerald said impatiently.

"I know, but these men appeared only recently, and the reports say they can work miracles. Many Israelis believe they produced the recent rains with divine power."

Gerald was astounded and struggled to control his anger. *What now?* he thought. *New impediments? Why didn't my informant, who claims to be the god of this world, tell me about this?* "Where did you learn these things, Colton? Do you have some crystal ball?"

"No, Mr. President. I just read news reports about Israel on the Internet."

"Thank you for that information," Gerald said, his eyes glaring in spite of himself. "That's why we have you and our other miracle workers. To counter and overcome those of the enemy. I suggest you consult with your source of inspiration on how to do that.

"Now let's turn to the main subject—our current initiative against Israel. Soon we'll move against Israel, and I myself will travel to the region to personally take charge of operations. The Jews have been successful at defeating the Arabs in their locality, but we'll see how they handle our overwhelming superiority."

Steven Christopher went alone to the Garden of Gethsemane, just east of the walls of Jerusalem, wanting to pray and be alone with his thoughts. Just being in this sacred place brought him a feeling of awe and serenity. This was where the Lord had taken upon himself the sins of the world, a redemption completed by his sacrifice on the cross and his resurrection.

As Steven knelt, he heard someone enter the olive orchard. He glanced up and saw a familiar face—Lucas Nigel, who looked just as he had many years ago on the plains of Wyoming. He was young, handsome, tall and slender, with light brown hair, piercing blue eyes, and that perpetual, maddening smile. He was dressed casually in sneakers, a blue sport shirt, and gray cotton trousers.

"Good day, Steven. How are you?" he asked, his smile widening.

"Lucas Nigel! I thought I told you not to bug me again."

"Bug you? What a quaint expression. Well, I don't always do what I'm told, do I?"

Steven clenched his fists. "No, you never follow rules."

"Oh, it's not that I don't follow rules. I'm very obedient to some rules, especially my own." He laughed at his own wit. "And, Steven, what have you always said about anger? Since you feel it's inherently evil, you shouldn't give in to it. But right now you look like you want to punch me out. You don't want to promote evil, do you?

"How do you dare come to this holy place?"

"Oh. It's holy? I didn't realize. I'm just keeping a promise I made you long ago. Remember? I told you I would see you someday again in a foreign land."

"Yes, I remember, but that's not what I mean. How can you, the incarnation of evil, enter the place where Christ atoned for the sins of the world?"

"You don't say. Is that what Jehovah did here?" Lucas said with a tiny smirk. "Steven, Steven, I'm surprised at you, a learned man who forgets his history—biblical history, that is. Let me refresh your memory. In the past I visited many so-called holy places. I appeared in the Garden of Eden and gave Eve a choice. I was with Jesus himself when he was in the wilderness for forty days. And later, I carried him up to a pinnacle of the temple in Jerusalem. Yes, he and I were that close. I'm really his brother, aren't I?

"Also, I was near Jesus in this very garden just after the angel consoled him and he sweated great drops of blood. It was a terrible moment for me and it hurt to see him suffer so much. But remember, I offered to do the job in the preexistence. I was with Joseph Smith in the Sacred Grove, just before the main man appeared. I could go on and on, but I don't want to bore you, except to say that I've been an important actor in all the crucial events in history."

"But always for evil."

"Not always. It depends on how you feel about my role."

Steven struggled to control his anger and impatience. "Why are you here today?"

"I decided to try one more time to get you to listen to reason."

"Reason? You'll have to explain that one to me."

"Don't you realize that most of your people, the ones you brought from America, will die in the great war soon to be visited upon Israel? I would really hate to see that because I have a special feeling in my heart for you, whether you believe it or not. It's not your fight, so no one could blame you if you refused to join in."

"We knew that was a possibility when we came here, but we came anyway. I'm sure you're exaggerating. Some will die, of course, but not most."

"So you refuse to believe me—again. Remember when I told you that your people would suffer terribly if you insisted on going to Missouri and building New Zion? You didn't believe me then either, and a hundred thousand of your young men died in the war against UGOT, including your son, Andrew."

"That's true, but at least we obeyed God."

"And you're obeying him again, right?"

"Yes."

"What if the dead were to include your lovely wife, Mary, your two brothers, your sons, your nephews, or you yourself? Are you ready for that?"

Steven swallowed hard at the thought. "It's a sacrifice I'm willing to make if the Lord requires it."

"Oh, he'll require it, I assure you. Well, you're certainly a hardcase. I hoped you'd let me protect your people during the war. The truth is, I have the power to do that."

"I won't make deals with the devil."

"Devil! Strange how much that name always offends me. It's not fair. I'm a son of God and the Bringer of Light."

"Not anymore."

"Steven, David Omert has not even tried to get along with Gerald Galloway. He should at least consider listening to him. This world has always suffered terribly from cruel wars, and all Gerald wants is to bring peace and make it a better world for all people everywhere."

"All Galloway wants is to annihilate the Jews, Christians, Mormons, religious people everywhere, and to rule the world with an iron fist. There's no way David or anyone else can reason with him."

"I'm sad to see you won't budge, as usual. I was so wanting to teach you the Adamic language."

"That's the most ridiculous thing I've ever heard! Like I'm going to take lessons from you."

"Oh, not me directly. I've written a wonderful little book on it, and I thought you might like a copy. The structure of the Adamic language is incredibly simple despite it being the most beautiful, expressive language in the universe. It's the language spoken by the Gods throughout eternity." Steven rolled his eyes and thought, *He's really getting desperate now, trying to appeal to one of my weaknesses.* "I have a question for you, Lucas."

"Oh, good! I love questions."

"Surely you're smart enough to know that in the end you can't win this war of good and evil against the Almighty Father. You don't have the power. Remember, the Father had no trouble casting you out of heaven. All he had to do was to give the job to Michael."

"So where is your question in that little tirade?"

"My question is, why do you persist in fighting him?"

"Well, some of you Mormons seem to think that I realize I'll lose in the end, and that I persist in the war to obtain as much company as possible in the eternal worlds so I won't be all alone in my terrible suffering. But I assure you, that's not true. The truth is, I genuinely believe I'll win the war this time."

"That's all bluff. I think you have three reasons for continuing this losing battle. First, you really do fear being alone in eternity. Second, you want to ease your misery by having as many people as possible suffer the same agony that you will suffer. Like they say, misery loves company. And third, you want to win over as many suckers as you can to your cause so you can govern a host of slaves in outer darkness. That's important because you have a desperate need to control and dominate."

"Hah! Outer darkness! There's no such thing as outer darkness. But back to the point. None of those reasons are true. The truth is, I really plan to win."

"How?"

"I'll tell you, but first let's consider the hypothetical possibility of me losing the war."

"All right, consider it."

"Even if I did lose the war, don't you think God should reward me for making his plan of salvation possible? Without my opposition, the faith and character of man could not be tested and man would not be worthy of the promised reward. Personally, I think I deserve some credit for all my hard work."

"Yes, opposition is necessary, but you don't oppose God in order to further his plan. You only resist because antagonism and disruption are integral components of your basic nature. In other words, you do it from weakness. You simply can't help yourself."

"Clever argument, Steven. But do you want to understand why I know I can win?"

"Why?"

"By the creative use of six wonderful principles: freedom, diversity, tolerance, equality, cooperation, and respect. All these qualities are inter-related and mutually supporting. The truth is, as we speak I'm winning the war by implanting these great notions deep in the heart of mankind. In fact, these days, most people have come to accept these virtues as highly desirable, thanks to me. In the mass media, in classrooms, in boardrooms, in private conversations—everywhere—you see people embracing those marvelous principles, promulgating them, and fervently condemning all those who do not practice them.

"At the same time, the only ideals people get from the other side is slavery to rules, uniformity in belief and behavior, intolerance to alternate life styles, inequality in status and opportunity, discord and dissension in decision making, and the lack of respect for unconventional opinions."

Steven gazed intently into Lucas's mesmerizing eyes. "It's true you're winning most men and women to your cause by popularizing those princi-ples, but you gave yourself away when you said you used them in a 'creative' way. What you actually do is push those ideals too far, and thus you corrupt and debase qualities that are normally good if used wisely. And you pervert not only those qualities but nearly every noble ideal by distorting them and pushing them to extremes.

"For example, your brand of freedom is nothing but license to disregard the normal standards of human decency. In your value system, diversity and tolerance mean people should be willing to accept immoral and degrading behaviors even if they break God's laws or the standards of decent society.

"To you, equality means that government should have the power to make rules redistributing wealth. In other words, you want government to steal from those who work hard in order to give handouts to those who think the world owes them a living simply because they exist.

"In your belief system, cooperation in decision making means that every member of a committee should follow the opinions of the majority in order to keep the peace and to accomplish the goals established by those with the most influence, whether or not those goals might hurt people in the long run.

"And finally, you believe people should show respect for any and every opinion, no matter how foolish that opinion might be. In that way, you hope to give more credence to fools who promote immoral, wasteful, or disruptive ideas and programs. By contrast, I don't feel obligated in any degree to automatically respect the opinions of others. I honor their right to have an independent opinion and to express it as they desire, but I don't have to respect the opinion itself, because most opinions aren't worth a straw. Only opinions that are based in reason and supported by factual evidence are worth considering seriously."

"Hmm, I see you have answers for everything. But you won't get people to understand them. Most people just go with the flow of popular opinion and don't think too deeply."

"You're probably right about that, but you still won't be able to defeat the Father because he'll raise up people of goodness, integrity, and honor who will comprehend and resist your tactics and your propaganda. Enough people to accomplish the ultimate designs of the Father."

Lucas's eyes blazed in frustrated anger. "Well, Steven, you can believe and act as you wish, but I assure you that I'll make you and your noble people pay dearly." At that, Lucas turned and stomped away, not grinning at all now.

The day after Steven's interview with Lucas Nigel, David Omert met with his five war advisers at his compound in the heart of Jerusalem. He had also invited General Michael Jamison, Ruther Johnston, Steven Christopher, and six of his generals.

"Well, gentlemen," David said, "you know the predicament we're in. The enemy is all around us. Millions of them. Do you have any suggestions?"

The men looked around at each other without saying a word.

"I can understand your silence. It's a hard problem to solve. Still, we've been in what seemed like impossible circumstances before. That's where we were in the War for Independence in 1948, but our predecessors survived and created this nation."

Ruther raised his hand, and David recognized him with a nod. "I ain't a military man by trade, but I say we should ferret out their weaknesses."

"Thank you, Ruther, I've been thinking the same thing. What are their weaknesses?"

"Sometimes their strengths are their weaknesses," Jamison said.

"What do you mean, General?"

"Well, when you've got an army or armies as large as theirs, it presents some special problems. Like supplying their needs."

"That's a good point," Chaim Yehoshua said. "It's going to be a serious problem for them to come up with food and water for such vast numbers, especially if the war goes on any length of time."

"They'll also need an enormous amount of fuel for their vehicles and warplanes," said one of the war ministers.

David frowned and paused a moment. "I understand that UGOT ordered every ally to bring huge supplies of all those things, and Mossad's recent reports show they did. Still, as Chaim just said, it won't do them any good if the war continues six months or more. Unless they can be resupplied by nations close by, such as their European allies."

"In my opinion," Steven said, "we should focus on the thing they need the most."

"Which is?" David asked.

"Water. Because of the selfish water policies of Syria and Turkey, and the misuse of water resources by the Iraquis, the Euphrates River is drying up. The same is true of many small streams in the Middle East. Of course, there's very little rainfall in the region in the summer months, especially in Palestine. For the last two years, drought conditions have prevailed in many countries. So, to make a long story short, I think we should first try to deprive them of the water they brought with them."

David liked the idea and smiled. "What do the rest of you think?"

There was a general murmur of approval.

"Good. UGOT seems to be stalling, probably until the remainder of their forces arrive. So perhaps we should make the first move before they begin their invasion. Most of their water seems to be stored in water tankers or trucks loaded with jerricans or water bottles. We could attack those supplies first and then concentrate later on their lines of communication. We also need to attack the trucks bringing in water shipments overland from Europe. All right, people, what do you think of these proposals?"

"I think I can speak for all of us by saying it's an effective strategy," Chaim said.

David looked around and saw that the others agreed with Chaim. He turned to his air force chief of staff, Major General Adelstein. "Elazar, let's get together with your staff right after this meeting to plan some air raids. We need to begin them immediately." Adelstein nodded with a smile, clearly pleased to be asked to take the first steps against the enemy. "One last thing, gentlemen, we must always present a confident and positive attitude before our troops. I believe God is on our side and won't let us down, no matter how impossible our situation seems to be."

"Yeah," Chaim said. "Just tell your men that the bigger they are, the harder they fall." Everyone laughed at that and exited the room in a lighter mood.

From a hill fifteen miles from the Israeli border, Major General JahAngir Massoud, commander-in-chief of the Iranian army, studied Jerusalem and its suburbs through a powerful telescope. He was frustrated with all the waiting. He commanded over two hundred thousand well-trained troops that were ready for action, including units from the elite Revolutionary Guards, but he couldn't move them forward without the permission of UGOT. If it hadn't been for all UGOT's stupid rules, Iran would not have needed to mobilize such a large army. They could have attacked Israel months ago with nuclear weapons. All it would have taken was four or five bombs dropped at strategic locations, and Israel would have been paralyzed before it could have retaliated.

Massoud felt that it was nerve-racking to have other forces, millions of them, all around him, each army hoping to be the first to attack and claim the prize. When he expressed these feelings to two of his subordinates standing nearby, they supported him and echoed his sentiments.

"I know how you feel, General," said Colonel Fatemah. "We could have easily conquered Israel by ourselves without the help of all these infidels. Nuclear bombs certainly would have been enough, as you say. Or we could have made an all-out attack using conventional weapons, if the Supreme Leader had approved it." The Supreme Leader was the head of state and the highest ranking political and religious authority in the Islamic Republic of Iran.

"Exactly," agreed Lieutenant Colonel Jamshad. "If it had been me, I would have started off by firing the twenty-six Ghadr-110 missiles we have in Tehran to key spots in Israel. At the same time, I would have dispatched a hundred Fateh-110 missiles from Jordan, followed by squadrons of E14 Tomcat warplanes. Then I would have mobilized our entire army of five hundred thousand troops that I would have already positioned a few miles from Israel. In two days they could have swept the entire nation, killed every Jew in the country, and liberated the Palestinians."

"My, my, aren't we ambitious," Massoud said, glaring now at his subordinate. "That's why you're just a lieutenant colonel and I'm a general. What do you think the Israelis would be doing while you're sending in those forces? Playing chess in their synagogues and throwing Frisbees in local parks? And if you were to mobilize our entire forces, who would protect Iran from our enemies?"

"Sorry, sir, I was out of place in my comments," Jamshad said, his eyes cast down.

"Yes, you were. Still, I admire your enthusiasm—but just do what you're told."

"Absolutely, sir."

At that moment, Massoud's communications man approached and handed him the satphone. "Call just came in from Tehran, sir."

"Thank you." Putting the handset to his ear, he said. "Yes, this is Massoud." As he listened, his smile broadened, and a few minutes later he returned the handset to the radioman. "Good news. We have permission to attack Israel, approved by UGOT and authorized by our Supreme Leader. It seems UGOT thinks we deserve the right to begin the war."

"Where and when are we supposed to attack?" asked Colonel Fatemah.

"Jerusalem in one hour."

Suddenly Colonel Jamshad shouted and pointed to the western sky. High above, there were a half dozen specks rapidly growing larger. Massoud finally realized what they were—F-16s! The jets swooped down like hawks chasing prey at two hundred and fifty miles an hour, leveled out at five hundred feet, and flew straight toward them.

The three astonished soldiers watched bug-eyed, their mouths agape, as the jets swooshed overhead and released twelve Maverick guided missiles into their transport caravan. The explosions shook the ground as the jets rose steeply and made a tight turn toward the west.

Massoud wondered how much damage they'd caused and why they'd made just one raid. Ten minutes later, several officers rushed up and reported that the Israeli jets had destroyed about three quarters of their water supply.

Massoud turned to his colonels and said with a flat voice, "Prepare the troops now for a march on Jerusalem. How many Fateh-110 missiles do we actually have with us, Colonel Jamshad?"

"Twenty-three."

"Good. They are the most accurate missiles in the world. Begin firing them at east Jerusalem as soon as possible. I want to destroy the new Jewish temple and soften up the city's defenses."

"Did you hear that?" Ephrem asked Jacan as they looked up at the bright new temple.

"Yes, I did. A soft, persistent voice in my mind."

They ceased movement and listened carefully.

"The voice is telling me to go to the Mount of Olives and to ask God to protect the city and the holy temple," said Ephrem.

"That's the message I'm getting too. Come. We must hurry."

They exited the Temple Mount, walked east across the Valley of Kidron, passed Gethsemane, and climbed the Mount of Olives. Waiting there anxiously, they wondered what would happen next. A few minutes later, the gentle voice spoke to both of them. *"Ask the Father to protect the city and to visit the storm upon the evil army approaching from the east."* The humble, ragged prophets didn't fully understand what they were doing or what would happen, but they knelt and began to pray fervently. After their prayers, they stood and looked eastward with dread in their hearts. Did they show enough faith in their prayers? Would God answer them? Would he protect them and the city from the coming onslaught? Ephrem trembled as he thought of the scriptures that told how some ancient prophets died during their missions for the Lord.

Nothing happened. They knelt again and repeated the same prayers. After they had finished, they studied the sky and finally saw several tiny, round spots heading toward them. Silent killers bearing terrible destruction. As they watched, they were shocked when each of the spots exploded in blazing flashes of light. Soon more appeared, and they too exploded before they reached the Mount of Olives. That same scene continued for ten minutes with identical results. The prophets had no idea whether the flying things were destroyed by the Arrow anti-missile interceptors located around Jerusalem or by the THEL laser guns installed near the Temple Mount. But deep in their hearts they felt that it was the work of the Lord.

As they continued to regard the land to the east, they began to see movement on the ground. After watching another half hour, they could make out discernable images: tanks, trucks, and marching troops.

"It's an army!" Ephrem said, looking at Jacan with terror in his eyes.

"I see it. Don't get so worked up. I'm sure our defense systems will attack any minute—or the Lord himself."

"I certainly hope so." *This job of being a prophet sure has its drawbacks,* Ephrem thought. "Maybe we should get out of here and find some army barracks, or an underground cave." He turned to retreat, but Jacan grabbed him so firmly that he couldn't move.

"No. The Lord will stop them with great power."

Ephrem wondered how Jacan could be so sure, but then he remembered the deep, gentle voice talking about a storm.

"Look, Ephrem," Jacan said.

"What? I don't see anything. Except the enemy army."

"Behind the army. That cloud."

"Oh, yeah, I see it now. What is it?"

"I can't be sure, but I think it's a dust storm. You know how dry it's been this season, especially in Jordan."

To see better, Ephrem put his hand above his eyes to block out some of the sunlight. "Hey, it's really boiling up. It's sure going to give that army a good dusting."

"Dusting my eye! My guess is it'll be a lot worse than that."

They could feel the wind pick up and swirl in wild eddies all around them, even this far away from the enemy. They watched breathlessly as the dust storm grew dark and rose thousands of feet, and as it hit the army, it began to rotate as violently as a tornado, picking up tanks and other heavy vehicles and carrying them into the sky. The gigantic whirlwind swept over the entire army, engulfing them in its fury.

"That's for sure not caused by the Israel Defense Forces," said Ephrem, gaping in awe at the power of the storm.

"Nope. That's an act of God."

After twenty minutes, the storm dissipated, and all that was left was the mangled and devastated remains of what had once been an army.

"I guess we won't have to worry about them," said Jacan. "Now we understand the third job the Lord has given us."

"Third job? What third job?"

"Ephrem, I love you, but you sure can be dense sometimes. This is what I mean . . ."

Gerald Galloway, Lucienne Delisle, and Colton Aldridge were sitting in a conference room of the hotel complex Gerald owned in Damascus. Gerald had promised his associates and his confederates that he would come to the Middle East and take charge of the war against Israel in person, and here he was, keeping his promise and obeying the demands of his "master."

He had also ordered UGOT's private army of one hundred and fifty thousand men to assemble ten miles north of Damascus. Most of them had been stationed at bases in Europe and Eurasia, but he wanted them close by to spearhead the move against Israel. They were the best trained and the most experienced warriors in the world, and also the highest paid, and they were furnished with the finest, most technologically advanced weapons known on earth. The only army close to their equal was the Israel Defense Forces.

Gerald had selected two experienced generals to lead this army. The first was General Konrad Drescher, a tall, thin German of sixty. He had narrow lips and hard blue eyes. He wore a mustache and was always impeccably dressed in uniforms that looked like they had been made during World War I. Gerald's second choice was 49-year-old Major General Pascal Laurent, who was a Parisian born in an elite family that owned a chain of French drugstores. He was of medium height and had a tanned, muscular body and a wide, square face. He was immediately recognized by the red scarf he often wore. Both generals were currently with the army, training subordinates at their temporary base.

After going through a dozen intelligence reports and reading the main sections to the others, Gerald scowled and angrily slammed the papers on the coffee table in front of him. "That David Omert must have the biggest crystal ball in the world. How did he know our coalition armies carried their water in tankers? They look just like fuel tankers. And how did he know we were transporting more water from Europe in convoys of trucks? He's made dozens of air raids on nearly every coalition army, blasting their water trucks and tankers. What I don't understand is why he goes after our water. Why not strike our artillery or our armor or the troops themselves? We can always replenish our water supplies." In saying this, Gerald seemed to forget the earliest warnings of his master to take special precautions with his water supply. "The jets appear from nowhere, hit fast, and then fly away before we can do a thing. We don't even seem to be able to detect their incoming warplanes on radar."

Lucienne was used to Gerald's sudden outbursts and answered him dispassionately. "I've received unconfirmed reports that the Israelis have developed new cloaking technology, which can be installed on both old and new planes."

"That must be it," Gerald replied. "There doesn't seem to be any other explanation. I need to get with my aviation engineers to see if they can duplicate it or defeat it."

"Sooner or later we'll capture one of those planes intact," Lucienne assured him, "and when we do, your engineers can reproduce the technology by reverse engineering."

"Yes, you're right. I'll notify our allies to do everything possible to seize an Israeli warplane during our invasion." He paused, trying hard to control himself as he addressed another problem. "These reports don't mention another situation our observers in Jordan just reported to me before this meeting began."

"What's that, Mr. Galloway?" Colton asked with trepidation. Every time he admitted that he wasn't aware of something, Gerald criticized his prophetic powers.

"I'm surprised you don't know," Gerald replied impatiently. "It's what happened to the Iranian army I ordered to move westward to capture Jerusalem."

Lucienne's exotic eyes widened in surprise. "What happened?"

"They were completely wiped out by some crazy, freak sandstorm. But it wasn't your typical sandstorm. It was monstrous and hit them like a gigantic whirling tornado." Gerald was so angry, he put his head between his hands to help him gain self-control.

Colton gave a sly smile and thought, *He wants to rule the world and yet he can't control himself. He seems to get less stable as he ages. Sometimes he's cold and calculating like he used to be and at other times he cries like a baby.* He waited a few minutes until Gerald seemed to recover and then said, "Like you said, Mr. Galloway, it was a freak accident and will probably never happen again. May I change the subject?"

"Of course. Go ahead, Colton."

"Well, you asked earlier why Omert goes after our water supplies."

"Yes."

"I believe he is taking advantage of our weaknesses."

"What weaknesses!" Gerald roared.

"Our need for water. We have over fifty million troops, and an army that size drinks an unbelievable amount of water. I think it's a mistake to believe it will be easy for us to replenish our water supplies. The Middle East has suffered from a drought for two years and the Euphrates has nearly slowed to a trickle. Also, it's summer, and normally there's very little rain at that time."

Lucienne laughed with a hint of mockery. "That's not entirely true. It has been raining steadily in Israel—and only Israel—for a month now. A nice, gentle, ground-soaking rain."

"I've heard about that," Gerald snarled. "Just our rotten luck."

"Well, anyway, I figure that's why Omert is attacking our water storage," Colton added.

Gerald looked at Colton with new respect. "I think you're right. Do any of you have suggestions?"

Lucienne smiled and patted Gerald's hand. "Don't worry, my dear, we can solve this little problem easily with a bit of effort. I think we should tell our allies to do their best to hide and protect the water supplies they have left. Try to put as much of it as possible in small bottles and distribute them among the troops. Also, we could organize a half dozen or more convoys to import water, rather than only one convoy at a time."

"Those are interesting ideas. If we used small bottles, the supply would be harder to destroy. And you, Colton?"

"I believe we should start a total offensive against Israel immediately. There's a lot of water there and plenty of Jews to slaughter."

"Okay, thank you. I'll pass your ideas by Generals Drescher and Laurent to get their input."

Chapter 10

❧

Shortly after his meeting with Lucienne and Colton, Galloway consulted with Drescher and Laurent, who agreed with the recommendations of the others. Immediately, he contacted his coalition partners and warned them that the signal for the armies to begin hostilities would be given within forty-eight hours. Several weeks earlier, he had planned the exact disposition of each invading army, indicating precisely where they would enter Israeli territory. In all, there were thirty-five large armies and a dozen smaller ones, totaling over fifty million troops. There were also armies from every Arab nation in the Middle East and Africa. These nations were bitter over the defeat of their brethren living near Israel and they called for the final annihilation of the Jews.

Galloway had decided to lead his own private army of one hundred and fifty thousand into Israel along the coast of Lebanon, and he moved his headquarters and his army from Damascus to an area south of Beirut. He insisted that both Lucienne and Colton accompany him at all times. He had come to a conclusion about the sandstorm that had destroyed the Iranian army in Jordan: it must have come about by some freakish local weather pattern that UGOT's meteorologists had not detected. He scoffed when Colton suggested that the disaster had been created by the two Jewish sorcerers who were defending Israel against the Iranian attackers.

After installing his operation in his new headquarters, Galloway gathered some key people, including Lucienne Delisle, Colton Aldridge, Alexi Glinka, and two other trusted associates, for an emergency planning session at one o'clock in the afternoon.

"Okay, people. In about seventeen hours we'll give the signal for the attack. As we agreed in Damascus, I contacted the Palestinian president, Faruq Shamon, and told him what we wanted to do. He enthusiastically agreed to do his part, which is to make sure the Palestinian people living in Israeli territory are alerted to the impending invasion and are prepared to start an open revolt just before the invasion takes place." He looked at his watch. "So in a few minutes, we can expect a universal uprising of the Palestinian people. This will be the first phase of our operation."

Alexi Glinka opened his fourth bottle of Almaza beer. "But do the Palestinians have enough weapons to give the Israelis serious trouble?"

"They have more than you might expect. The terrorist groups, Hamas and Hezbollah, have been sneaking weapons and ammo to them for years. Another terrorist organization named ISIS, or the Islamic State of Iraq and Syria, made up of ferocious Sunni militants, has also supplied the Palestinians with weapons and expertise. So I'd say twenty to thirty percent of the Palestinians are armed. As for the others, Shamon has asked them to use stones, knives, tools, Molotov cocktails, or any other weapon they can devise. He has assured them that their insurgency will be vital in helping to defeat Israel. I also encouraged Shamon to promise his people that all of Palestine will be theirs for their new Palestinian nation."

Lucienne smiled at Alexi's obvious infatuation with the famous Lebanese beer. "Gerald, tell our associates here what you plan to do with the Arabs that were defeated in the recent war. They weren't at our meeting in Damascus."

"Oh, yes. The Arabs still have most of their military capability. Egypt was untouched by the war. Lebanon, Syria, and Jordan have about two thirds of their troop strength. As for their role in the future, I've commanded their leaders to dispose their armies on the front lines, all around Israel. To those forces I have added other Arab troops from Saudi Arabia, Iraq, Iran, Pakistan, Yemen, and Qatar. When our coalition attacks, the Arabs will take the brunt of the defensive fire."

"That's brilliant," said Randolph Benson, UGOT's associate for the Middle East. "That way, we'll kill two birds with one stone."

Gerald flashed them a broad smile. At that moment, Lucienne recognized the old, unscrupulous dictator she had been so attracted to in earlier years. It was his idea to exhaust and destroy the foolish Palestinians by a futile uprising and then decimate the armies of the other Arab nations by putting them on the front lines in the coming attack. Gerald had always considered the Arabs to be almost as detestable as the Jews.

David Omert met with his thirty-two advisers and a dozen military leaders in an emergency meeting at the Knesset building. Present also were some of the leaders of the American army, including General Michael Jamison, Colonel Mosheh Lazar, Lieutenant Colonel Yaakov Raphan, Colonel Steven Christopher, and Colonel Ruther Johnston.

"Well, ladies and gentlemen, we now face the might of UGOT's armies. Over fifty million against our two hundred and twenty thousand regulars and six hundred thousand reservists. Things look bleak but not hopeless. The reports I've received indicate they will begin their invasion within six hours. I have, of course, stationed our troops in about twenty locations around our borders, with orders to prevent the enemy from entering Israel at all costs. To make matters worse, there has been an uprising of Palestinians living within our borders. At this time, the Israeli police are doing a good job of controlling it, but it seems to be spreading rapidly, and we may need to use the military to control it. Do you have any questions or suggestions?"

"Are the Israeli Arabs joining the rebellion?" asked Chaim Yehoshua.

"Apparently most of them are not. They seem to prefer Israeli citizenship to being citizens of an Arab nation. However, that may change if they feel we are losing the war."

One of the advisers raised his hand, and David acknowledged him. "Are we still bombing their water supplies?"

"Absolutely. We've had great success doing it. Still, I don't believe that strategy will fully bear fruit until after a month or so."

Mosheh Lazar raised his hand, and David nodded. "I know things look bleak, but on a positive note, we do have certain advantages over the enemy."

"Please explain, Mosheh."

"Well, the Arabs nations hate each other and are seldom capable of working together. Besides, they are terrible fighters. Also, UGOT will have a lot of trouble controlling so many different armies with different weapons and battle tactics, and their sheer numbers will make it extremely difficult for them to maneuver effectively. They'll have to move over a much larger territory while we can send detachments very rapidly within the close boundaries of Israel in order to reinforce weak spots. And probably most important, such massive armies will have serious challenges replenishing their arms and supplies."

"Thank you, Mosheh," said David. "I trust that gives the rest of you a little more hope. I would like to mention, however, that our resources are limited too, and it might be even harder for us to replenish them."

"I'd like to add to Mosheh's comments," said General Jamison. "Military history shows that sometimes forces with vastly superior numbers can be defeated by a small army when the larger army makes a direct frontal attack on the homeland of the smaller army."

Steven knew that Mosheh and Michael were doing their best to give the Israeli leaders reassurance in a hopeless situation.

"Here they come!" someone shouted down the line, over the din of machine-gun fire and the nearby explosions of grenades and bombs.

Without warning, Sergeant Rachel Salant jumped into the trench next to Daniel Christopher. "How's it going, soldier?" she yelled. She hunkered down farther into the ditch. "For the sake of Pete, keep your head down. Are you wanting to get it blowed off?"

"No, thanks," he replied, moving closer to her as she crouched next to him.

"Not too close, Danny. The others! I'm still your platoon leader, you know." She pushed her M16 to the top edge of the ditch and fired a short burst and then another. "I think I hit a couple. They are Arabs! Are you believing it?"

"Yeah, Arabs everywhere. I thought we defeated them weeks ago."

"We did, but there are millions of them. Always around, either glaring at you or trying to kill you."

An Israeli captain quickly slid by them in the trench, shouting, "Hold the line, people, no matter what!" This contingent of the Israeli army was dug in just south of the border with Lebanon, a few miles from the Mediterranean coast.

"Reminds me of the trench warfare I've read about in World War I,"

Daniel said. Several warplanes swooped by, flying low, their jet engines whining loudly. "Heading north. Must be our guys."

"I know," Rachel said. "The trench warfare, I mean. I was thinking the same thing."

Suddenly, a cloth-hooded figure appeared at the top of the trench and quickly dropped next to Rachel, stabbing her in the back with a long blade. Daniel turned and slammed the man in the head with the butt of his rifle, knocking him to the other side of the ditch, stunned and unable to defend himself. Daniel aimed and shot him three times in the torso.

Then he grabbed Rachel and cried, "Rachel, Rachel. Talk to me."

"Can't . . . can't. Got me. I'm . . . dying."

"No! You're not dying! Stay with me. I'm getting you out of here. Find a medic." To the others fighting close by, he called out, "Cover me, guys. I'm taking Salant for help."

As he scrambled out of the trench, carrying Rachel, his comrades opened a barrage of fire upon the enemy.

Leaving the trench, Daniel sloshed his way through the mud as fast as possible, shouting, "Medic, medic!"

Jacan and Ephrem stepped out of the rickety little car at a crossing of three roads a few miles from the northern shore of the Sea of Galilee. The kindly old Israeli who had driven them there refused any payment because he was proud to transport the two new prophets of Israel, even to this dangerous region during a great war. He had promised them that he was ready to drive them anywhere in Israel as long as his money held out and his car didn't fall apart. The prophets had no idea why the Spirit had directed them to go to this area.

Rushing past the three men were hundreds of Israeli trucks, tanks, APCs, and thousands of troops, retreating to new positions on the western side of the fresh water "sea." They had been driven from Golan by a coalition of foreign armies, including Syrians, Russians, Germans, and Vietnamese. The prophets watched in fascination, their hearts heavy at the terrible scene, but they didn't know what to do.

So they went to the side of the road, knelt, and began to pray as their driver watched from the side of his car. The passing soldiers eyed the two shabby peasants in threadbare clothes as they prayed out loud to God. Tired and discouraged after seeing so many of their comrades killed that day, the warriors scowled as they tramped by, and one of them said, "You idiots! You need guns not prayers." Another exclaimed, "What good are you to Israel, you fools?"

When they had finished their prayer, they looked to the northeast and saw a terrible sight: enemy armies traveling down three roads directly toward them. They walked back to the dilapidated car and asked the driver if he could use his binoculars to identify this new thing. After studying the approaching armies for a few minutes, the old man said, "I recognize the troops on the left road and I can see their flags clearly. They are Syrians. As for the army on the middle road, I can make out their tanks and uniforms, but I don't recognize them. Their flag has three bands—black, white, green—connected by a red arrow. I think it's the Palestinian flag."

"What about the army on the right?" asked Jacan.

"Their flag looks the same except there's a white star on the red arrow. I'm not sure—"

"It's the Jordanian flag," said Ephrem.

All at once they noticed objects coming over the eastern hills and dropping toward them, moving fast. The sky seemed to be full of them. The prophets and the driver slid under the car, apparently hoping they would be safer there. However, they couldn't help but peek out to see what was happening. Abruptly the warplanes began to spit bullets, tearing up the roads and the ground for hundreds of yards around them and moving on toward the retreating troops, blasting soldiers and vehicles. After the first squadron had flown over the Sea of Galilee, they separated into two groups and peeled off sideways, and then a second squadron roared in from the heavens, firing bullets and missiles, wreaking even more havoc. A few warplanes were blasted out of the sky by defensive cannons, but most of them eluded destruction.

Jacan didn't know if Israeli missiles had destroyed those planes or if it was an act of God.

But suddenly he realized that a miraculous thing had occurred. Neither he, Ephrem, or the old driver had been hit by the machine-gun fire, and the old vehicle had only a few new holes in it.

"Maybe we'd better get out of here," the driver said.

"Please wait. We need to pray again," Jacan said.

The prophets knelt beside the car and offered the same prayer as before. As they prayed, they heard the voice. *"Your prayers have been answered. Look up and behold the power of God."*

The ground began to tremble, growing stronger by the second. Jacan and Ephrem couldn't maintain their balance, and they fell to the earth while the old man held on to his car. The shaking continued, increasing in intensity. The ground began to open in giant fissures, and trees, bushes, and sections of the roads were swallowed, and still the quaking continued. Jacan raised his head and looked eastward toward the Golan Heights. What he saw was a nightmarish scene: thousands of troops falling into crevasses or being buried under great masses of earth hurtled toward them by some tremendous force.

Finally, the earthquake stopped as quickly as it had begun. Miraculously, the quake had jolted the Golan Heights far more than it had the region around the Sea of Galilee. The prophets and the old driver drove away toward the south, avoiding the fissures as they went. The Spirit was speaking to the witnesses again, telling them to hasten to another place in Israel.

The battles raged for over a month on all fronts along the borders of Israel, with Muslim and Israeli armies facing one another in deadly direct confrontations. The Lebanese, Syrian, Jordanian, and Palestinian regulars were soon joined by the armies of other Muslim nations: Saudi Arabia, Kuwait, Iraq, Afghanistan, Iran, and Pakistan. In the south, Israel battled the forces of Egypt, Qatar, the United Arab Emirates, Yemen, Oman, Algeria, Nigeria, Tunisia, and Libya. Many other Islamic nations also sent troops to the various war theaters.

Among the Muslim nations, a shocking thing took place—a small miracle—because the various branches of Islam, including Sunni and Shiite Islam, temporary ignored their differences and fought side by side. However, they suffered from several serious problems: there were simply too many of them, their troops were far less competent than their opponents, and their weapons were technologically inferior to those of the Israelis.

During that first month, about two million Muslim soldiers died in battle, while Israel lost over two hundred thousand. The tremendous losses incurred by Muslim forces were extremely demoralizing to them, but Israel's losses were even more disastrous because they amounted to almost one-fourth of the nation's armed forces.

And still the war continued. Bullets, bombs, grenades, missiles, and laser beams shot back and forth night and day, with only occasional lulls. Warplanes and attack helicopters swooped down regularly on the troops of the opposing forces, and it was often confusing to the soldiers on the front lines to know if the machine-gun fire that ripped into them came from friends or foes.

Thousands of tanks attacked on both sides of the battle lines, blasting enemy vehicles and troops with their deadly machine guns and cannons, and frequently rolling over entire squads trapped beneath their relentlessly rolling tracks. Dead bodies and body parts strewed the ground everywhere, and the wounded had little hope of finding medical assistance; most bled to death right where they were hit.

Inside Israel, the Palestinian uprising took the form of guerilla warfare. Small groups of armed fighters hid in houses, barns, fields, trees, dugouts, or any other place of concealment. Formerly, these Palestinians had been neighbors if not friends—the same men who fixed appliances, clerked at local markets, sold merchandise on street corners, or made deliveries. At every opportunity, these armed assassins sprang from their hiding places, wielding guns, knives, or other weapons. Many were women and children. They attacked Israeli police, soldiers, and unarmed civilians, massacring men, women, and children indiscriminately. Muslim snipers made assaults from high places, focusing especially on soldiers in transit.

It wasn't long before average Israeli citizens began to fight back using the same tactics as the rebels.However, during the sixth week of the great war, both inside Israel and on the front lines, the tide began to turn in favor of the Israelis. Their troops succeeded in overrunning enemy lines in many places, and when that happened, the Muslim fighters deserted their positions and fled in terror.

At times this didn't result from superior Israeli firepower but seemed to happen when the Israelis were on the verge of defeat. Word quickly spread among Muslim forces that two strange men turned up at those times, standing boldly in full view of the enemy, and when they appeared, terrible things occurred—earthquakes, tornadoes, flash floods, poisoned food, and sudden, deadly illnesses that struck entire Arab companies.

Sometimes, just as a great victory seemed close, the Muslim hoard was struck by fire and lightning from the heavens, and many cried out that Allah had abandoned them.

Mary and Steven Christopher were exhausted and welcomed the protection of David Omert's reinforced compound near the center of Jerusalem. Steven had recently commanded an infantry brigade a few miles east of the city. Mary was there too, a few hundred yards behind the front line, caring for the wounded. At times, she inadvertently exposed herself to danger by rising too high, calling for the assistance of medics. Many of the medics, when they reached her side, chastised her for not keeping down.

About one-third of Steven's brigade were soldiers from America, and he was proud of their bravery and competence. Ruther was his second-in-command and seemed tireless in spite of his age. His greatest accomplishment during most battles was his uncanny accuracy with his Sharps long gun. Over and over again, from hundreds of yards away, he blasted giant holes in the base of water barrels the enemy had brought to the front, making sure he did so before the opposing troops filled their canteens from the new supply.

But his supreme achievement during one encounter was to fire a .50 caliber bullet directly into the muzzle of the big gun on a Jordanian tank that was about to crush a squad of American soldiers hiding behind a low wall. After the bullet went in cleanly, there was a violent explosion, and the tank jerked to a stop in a cloud of black smoke. All those who saw it were astonished that a seventy-six-year-old man could even see the muzzle of a cannon at two hundred yards.

David Omert and his friend, Chaim Yehoshua, entered the dining room where Steven and Mary were eating dinner. Their clothes were dirty and ragged, their faces pale and haggard, because they too had been fighting the Arabs attacking from an area south of the city.

"Good evening," David said as he and Chaim plopped down at the same table.

"Good evening," said both Steven and Mary.

"You two look as bad as we do," Chaim joked.

"We're mostly just tired," Mary replied, wiping her mouth with a napkin.

"Steven's worse off than me. I have a few bruises, but he's got a dozen cuts. Took me half an hour to fix him up."

An Israeli private approached them and gave David and Chaim plates of potatoes and beans, the fare for the day. They dug in hungrily because they hadn't had anything to eat since that morning.

"Your brigade was fighting a few miles east of the Mount of Olives, right?" Chaim asked.

David answered for Steven. "Yes, that's where I assigned him. It's a crucial position, and we can't afford to have it breached. From the report I received today, Steven and his guys did a tremendous job. Is the enemy still out there, Steven?"

"Actually, they suddenly abandoned the area around four o'clock."

"Suddenly?" Chaim asked.

"Yes, for no reason I can see. We had inflicted some damage on them, but their army was still intact. I figured they must have received a report about another Israeli force approaching. Or maybe they were called away to another position by their leaders." He looked at David. "I intended to ask you about it."

"No, we didn't dispatch additional forces. We don't have them available."

"Steven, did you see anything unusual, like two peasants hanging around?" Chaim asked. "Two guys in their thirties wearing beat-up clothes? Always together? Standing on walls or hills, looking like they're just asking the enemy to shoot them?"

"No, I don't remember—"

"Yes, you do, Steven," Mary said. "Remember the two men I pointed out? The ones walking on the ridge toward the Arab line. I asked you if you thought they had a death wish."

Steven's eyes became more alert. "Oh, yeah. Now I remember. So what?"

"Well, they're probably the reason the Palestinians took off," Chaim enthused. "There's no other explanation. The Arabs were afraid the two prophets would curse them or something."

"I've heard about two miracle workers traveling around Israel making life miserable for our enemies, but I didn't know if it was true. So you think the guys we saw were those two prophets?"

"I'm sure of it," Chaim said.

"I'm sure of it too," David said. "Chaim and I believe they're the two witnesses talked about in the eleventh chapter of Revelation."

"The ones who hinder Gog's armies and are finally killed on the streets of Jerusalem?" Mary asked.

"Exactly," Chaim said. "Then they are resurrected after three and a half days and taken up to heaven."

"It doesn't actually say they were resurrected," David corrected. "Verse twelve of the same chapter says a great voice calls from heaven and commands them to 'come hither,' and they ascend to heaven in a cloud. In the scriptures, the word 'heaven' can have several meanings. It can mean God's realm, or the expanse around the earth, as in the 'heavens,' or simply any place above the earth. The voice that calls is not necessarily that of God nor is it certain that it comes from God's abode. There's a special problem when we assume that people are resurrected before Christ's Second Coming because that's when the first resurrection is to occur. It's only by tradition that people suppose the two prophets will be resurrected. Remember that Lazarus was brought back from the dead but wasn't resurrected."

"You've really been studying the Bible," Steven said, remembering that David had told him so when he'd confessed his conversion to Christianity. Steven decided that David's knowledge of the Bible and his belief in Christ might help him fulfill the calling given to him by the prophet back in New Zion. "So let me ask you a question."

"Please do," David said.

"Do you have a Bible available?"

David looked around to make sure no one else was in the dining room and then walked over to a drawer and extracted a worn copy of the Bible. He handed it to Steven.

Steven turned to the end of the Book of Revelation and read verses eighteen and nineteen. "So it says that if any man should add things or subtract things from the words of this book, that person would receive God's condemnations."

"Basically that's right," David said.

"Well then, what do you think these two verses mean?"

"It seems clear enough," David replied. "No one has a right to alter the Bible by adding to it or taking away from it."

"But let's look at the matter a bit more carefully. Note how specific the prophet John is. In verse eighteen he says, 'The words of the prophecy of *this* book,' and '*these* things,' and 'the plagues that are written in *this* book.'

In verse nineteen he says, '*this* prophecy,' and 'written in *this* book.' So again, what prophecy and what book is he talking about?"

"The Bible obviously."

"But the Book of Revelation is the only book in the Bible that is written entirely as apocalyptic prophecy. Other books, such as Daniel, Isaiah, Jeremiah, Ezekiel, and others, have portions containing apocalyptic prophecies, but most books of the Bible present other subjects, such as history, commandments, doctrine, and teachings."

"So you're saying John was referring only to the Book of Revelation, not to the Bible as a whole?"

"Exactly. Among the early Christians, the Greek words *ta biblia* meant 'the books,' and in Latin *biblia* also meant the same. So the scriptures were seen as many separate books, not just one. Later, the Latin *biblia* evolved into a feminine singular word meaning 'bible.' In other words, the original idea of many different sacred books came to mean one book. We have to remember that both the Old Testament and the New Testament began as oral traditions among the faithful and were not gathered together into one book until much later.

"Many biblical scholars believe Revelation was written by John around AD 77 when he was in exile on the island of Patmos. At that time, the books of the New Testament had not yet been compiled into one collection. Later, John wrote his gospel and three epistles at Ephesus between AD 80 and 90. In other words, he added to the New Testament after Revelation was written.

"Also, before the year AD 150, the early Christians saw no need to write down the actual words of the original authors of the books of the New Testament, but afterwards that need became apparent. It wasn't until AD 397 that the Church of Rome, or the Catholic Church, finally settled on the canon of the New Testament in its present form, and the oldest complete manuscript of the whole Bible belongs to the eleventh century AD."

"I see your point," David said. "John the Revelator was saying he didn't want anyone messing around with his prophecy called Revelation."

"Yes, I believe that was his meaning. In our church, we have another book that we consider to be scripture. It's called the Book of Mormon. It tells of God's dealings with ancient peoples in the western hemisphere between 600 BC and AD 421. It teaches the same gospel as the New Testament, but since it didn't receive the same abuse as the Bible from careless scribes and biased translators, it clarifies many of the ambiguous or controversial readings in the New Testament."

"I didn't realize the New Testament was all that ambiguous," David objected. "Basically, it seems fairly clear to me."

Steven chuckled. "Well, maybe that's because you possess a special gift of inspiration. But the best evidence of the Bible's lack of completeness and clarity is probably the huge number of different Christian denominations. I understand there are more than forty thousand of them, and they all use essentially the same Bible. In spite of that, they still argue over the meaning of thousands of passages, and often these disagreements lead to hatred and even bloodshed."

"Well, I consider myself to be an honest and open-minded person," David said, "and I don't want to reject a book—and certainly not condemn it—until I've given it a fair test by reading the entire book. I admit that when I read the Bible, I sometimes find myself confused on some important points. I would like to read your Book of Mormon."

"I'll give you a copy later tonight."

David and Chaim started to leave the table but were stopped by Mary. "Oh, I wanted to ask how we're doing in general against the enemy."

David gave her a grim smile. "We've lost about half the Golan and a third of the West Bank, but we still hold Gaza. As for casualties, we've lost a great number of good men and women, and we estimate the enemy losses to be over two million. The best news is that the Arabs seem on the verge of breaking and retreating en masse. Obviously, when they do, we'll still have to deal with UGOT's main coalition forces."

Steven felt a sense of overwhelming sadness when he realized that Israel's casualties no doubt included thousands of American soldiers. But he was grateful that so far his own family and his brothers were okay. Just before he and Mary went to bed to catch a few hours of sleep, Steven made sure he gave David a copy of the Book of Mormon and an extra one for Chaim.

"There's something I don't understand," Mary said as she lay next to her husband in the darkened room.

Steven was half asleep and mumbled, "Wha . . . what's that . . . dear?"

"Well, the Book of Revelation says Gog's armies will number two hundred million, but Galloway has only about fifty million. Does that mean his coalition armies are not the armies of Gog?"

Steven paused for a half minute, trying to clear his mind of the cobwebs. "Uh, let's see. Oh, yeah. We talked about this before. Don't you remember? While we were at Adam-ondi-Ahman?"

"I vaguely recall a discussion about that, but I don't remember what you said."

"The pertinent passage is in verse sixteen of the ninth chapter of Revelation. In that verse, John the Revelator says Gog's armies would amount to two hundred million soldiers. I told you before that I believe many of John's numbers are figurative or symbolic."

"I know. You mentioned that to Paul on the cruise ship, but I was so tired I didn't really understand your point. Please explain what you meant."

"Well, actually, John uses images constantly in Revelation, especially in the ninth chapter, and most of those figures are in the form of metaphors and similes."

"You're saying Gog won't really have two hundred million soldiers."

Steven was finally getting his mind back. "That's right. All the armies of the world today, even including reserve forces, don't add up to seventy million troops."

"You're probably right. It must be symbolic. There's no way on earth that an army of two hundred million could work together well or get enough water and other supplies to wage a war for very long."

"Hah! There wouldn't even be room enough for them in all Palestine."

"So then, John's prophecy saying Armageddon will last three and a half years, and the two prophets being resurrected—I mean, brought back to life—after three and a half days might also be symbolic?"

"It's possible. Especially the length of the war. I can't imagine Galloway keeping his forces here that long. It would be impossible to supply fifty million troops in one small region for three and a half years."

"So what does John mean by two hundred million and three and a half years?"

"He's probably trying to convince future readers that Gog's army will be truly terrible and invincible. That way, when Christ saves the Jews and destroys Gog's armies, the world will see and know that Christ is an all-powerful God. As for the three and a half years, that's an incomplete number. The digits three, seven, twelve, and twenty-four are symbolic numbers, meaning something that is holy and complete, but three and a half goes beyond what is holy and thus is faulty and unrighteous. That's exactly what Gog's war is because it's waged against the chosen people of the Lord."

"So you're saying the war won't last three and a half years?"

"I think it's unlikely. I can't imagine Israel resisting such a great army for so long. As for the mention of three and a half *days*, that may or may not be symbolic. At least that number depicts an event that could actually take place."

There was silence for ten minutes while Mary stared at the changing reflections of light on the ceiling. Finally, she said quietly, "Steven, I have another question." When he didn't answer, she rolled over and heard him breathing softly, sound asleep.

Chapter 11

At his center of operations in Beirut, Galloway called an emergency meeting of his associates and the leaders of his coalition armies. There were about fifty of them. Conspicuously absent were the Arab leaders, for they had already fled Palestine to hide themselves in any safe places they could find.

After he had served his confederates some finger foods, Galloway stood and welcomed them with a smile of confidence. "Since every minute counts under the present circumstances, let me get right to the point. Our Arab allies have essentially been defeated but have served their purpose: they have significantly depleted Israel's resources and its troop strength. A few days ago, Arab national leaders and high-ranking officers took an abrupt holiday to parts unknown, and when what's left of their armies learn this, it will only be a matter of hours before they abandon the battlefields."

"So we'll launch our primary offensive at that time?" asked Randy Benson, UGOT's associate for the Middle East.

"Exactly. First we'll spend some time, perhaps a week or so, softening them up with a steady barrage of missiles and bombs, followed by regular flights of attack helicopters and fighters. When that period is over, I don't expect the Israelis will be able to offer much resistance. We'll probably be able to walk into Tel Aviv and Jerusalem as if we were on vacation. Are there any questions?"

"I have one," said Colton Aldridge. "What about Israel's two prophets?"

"Prophets?" Gerald said with impatience. "What two prophets?"

"I told you about them before. Twice. Remember when I said Israel has two sorcerers performing miracles against us?"

"Vaguely."

Colton's lips grew tight. "Well, it's my job to know these things. I've been keeping track of them for a month, and I believe they created the whirlwind that destroyed Iran's elite army in Jordan. I also believe they're the cause of the destructive earthquake in the Golan Heights, which destroyed three Arab armies. Apparently, they have also thwarted us in many other ways. They even travel around Israel encouraging and inspiring the people by healing the sick and declaring that the Jewish Messiah will come soon to destroy their enemies."

Gerald's eyes flashed with anger. "Blast it! Do any of the rest of you know about these prophets?" There was silence in the room as the participants eyed each other with puzzled looks. Finally, a Russian general raised his hand and said, "Yes, I've received several intelligence reports of stories told by fleeing Palestinians. Essentially, they substantiate what Aldridge has said." At that point a German officer admitted that he too had received the same type of reports.

"Such men can be very dangerous," Gerald grumbled. "We must do everything possible to eliminate them. Colton, I want you to use your special talents to locate these so-called prophets. As quickly as possible. And give me a full report on their activities. You should have told me about them sooner!"

"But I —"

"No buts! Find them!" He ground his teeth and clenched his fists but fought to control his fury. After a long moment of silence, he said, "Okay, people I want you to meet a friend of mine." He looked to his right and waved a man forward. The man was very tall and had the body of a wrestler, obviously an Arab, but was dressed in casual western clothes. "This is Taban Nahas, a leader in Hezbollah forces stationed in southern Lebanon. He's a man of many talents. One of which is—how should I say?—nullifying undesirable people."

Nahas grinned wickedly as if he would be delighted to display his talents against anyone in the room. A chill went up the spine of Lucienne Delisle, who was sitting in the front row, and a sudden image leaped into her mind of this assassin raping her and then slitting her throat.

"Taban," Gerald said, "do you think you and your buddies can deal appropriately with the two prophets in question? If we find we need your expertise, that is."

"Certainly, President Galloway, we'd be happy to. We all speak Hebrew like natives and will have no trouble operating in Israel."

John and Paul Christopher had been sent to the extreme southern portion of Israel to serve with an Israeli brigade near the port of Eilat in the Negev desert. This port was located at the northern tip of the Red Sea on the Gulf of Aqaba. John had been made a major and Paul a captain. Paul limped badly because he had taken a piece of shrapnel in his right leg and had recently been operated on in a hospital in Eilat.

Although Arab troops had charged their positions nearly every day, they had protected themselves behind strong defensive barriers and had always taken a heavy toll on the enemy, and when the enemy had fired rockets and missiles, or dispatched warplanes, the defenders had hunkered down in trenches and concrete bunkers and were very hard to hit. Then under the cover of darkness, the Israelis had sent out dozens of small, rapid-moving contingents to make surprise raids on enemy positions. This tactic was perhaps the most damaging to the morale of their opponents.

Thirty-five thousand Israeli troops had been holding the Arabs back for over a month, protecting their homeland from a southern invasion.

Today, John and Paul were on a rise, studying enemy troop movements through a long-range telescope mounted on a steel frame.

"Something really weird is going on over there in Jordan," Paul said.

"What?"

"Don't know for sure. Take a look."

John got up from a concrete bench and strode over to the telescope. He spend several minutes looking to the east and then rotated the telescope toward the west. "Same thing happening over here."

"What do you make of it?"

"Looks to me like they're pulling out."

Paul looked through the scope again. "Holy cow! I think you're right. We've whipped their bu—tails for sure! Woo-hoo!"

They watched the Arabs leave all day long, and by nightfall, the deserts were empty of enemy forces. But the next day, they got another shock. British and Canadian transport planes began to enter the area from the east, flying over Jordanian territory. They landed every ten minutes for several hours, disembarking a total of twenty thousand troops and hundreds of military vehicles. Israeli troops watched them with shouts of joy, and many ran forward to embrace the newcomers.

Yet later they received an even bigger surprise. A half dozen huge transport ships appeared in the Gulf of Aqaba, sailed into the port one at a time, and began to disembark troops. The brothers didn't recognize their flag and had no idea where they came from, but they knew they were friendlies. Filled with curiosity, they walked up to three men, two soldiers and a sailor, standing on a dock after coming ashore.

"Hey, guys," Paul called, "where are you from?"

"Down Under, mate," said a husky, muscle-bound soldier with a cigarette dangling from his lips. "And you?"

"We're from America."

"That's ace! Yanks in the flesh!" said a skinny soldier wearing a hat far too big for him. "I've been hearing a lot about you blokes and your new country. So you're here fighting UGOT, just like us?"

"Definitely," Paul replied. "There's about ninety thousand of us here now."

"Good onya," said the sailor. "That Galloway's a first-class ratbag."

"He sure is," Paul replied. "Say, where'd you blokes get those transport ships? I thought they were relics of the past."

The cigarette guy threw his weed on the dock and crushed it with the toe of his boot. "Government bought a lot of 'em from the States and the old country when they put 'em in mothballs after the big wars. Didn't cost us a lot of moolah neither. Meanwhiles, we fixed 'em up in case we might need 'em like in the present difficulties."

"But ocean travel is so dangerous these days," John said. "How did you manage it?"

"Well now, Australia's an island continent," said the sailor, spitting on the dock. "We couldn't just drive here in trucks! So we hopped into these floaters and skirted coastlines all the way here. That's what took us so long."

"Hah, my friends here sure do yabber a lot," said big hat. "Say, Yanks, would yuh like to grab some coldies with us?"

"Coldies?" John said. "What's that?"

"What you blokes call beer."

"No, but we'll grab some soda, if that's okay."

As the five men started off for an outdoor restaurant a half mile away, the husky soldier said, "Tell me something, Yanks, how di'yuh get your guys over here?"

"Lots of cruise ships," Paul replied.

"Cruise ships!" exclaimed muscles. "Yuh hear that, boys? They came on cruise ships!" All three Aussies burst into uncontrollable laughter.

On the same day that the new troops arrived from abroad, David Omert finally got an interview with the two peasant prophets. The Jerusalem police had just located them that morning and immediately escorted them to the president's compound.

As they entered David's office, he and Chaim rose and embraced them warmly. "Welcome, my friends," David said. "I've been wanting to talk to you ever since I heard about you."

The shepherds looked at David with unusual curiosity. Several times in the past, the angel had given them a vision of the face of the great Jewish leader, called the Second David. Each time, the divine being had told them that this man would have a special relationship with the Savior.

"It's him," Ephrem declared.

"Yes, I know," Jacan said.

"Do you know me?" David asked. "Have we met before?"

"In a way," Jacan replied. "The angel showed us your face and said you would be the one to greet the Messiah in behalf of all Israel."

David was so filled with a miraculous burning that he was unable to speak. Finally, he said, "Thank you for that. It tells me a great deal about the future."

Ephrem smiled and embraced David again. "The angel said that when we meet you, we should be sure to give you that message. We have simply done his bidding." He turned to Chaim. "The angel also told us that you would stand by your friend, David, through every trial to the very end. God has a role for you too."

With tears in his eyes, Chaim hugged both the prophets even harder than before.

"Well, it's getting late and you two must be hungry," David said. "Can I get you something?"

There was a brief silence, and then Ephrem licked his lips and said, "Do you, uh, happen to have any peach cobbler pie?"

Jacan scowled and jabbed his friend in the ribs. "He means no. We had a good meal this afternoon."

"But they didn't have any pie at all," Ephrem protested. He looked hopefully at David. "You know, all the shortages these days."

A warm smile filled David's face. "I don't believe we have peach cobbler, but we might have apple." He pushed the button for the kitchen on the intercom module attached to his desk.

"Do you think you might have a little ice cream to put on top of it?" Ephrem asked. That earned him another poke from Jacan.

Speaking into the module, David said, "Send up two pieces of apple pie . . . with ice cream topping if you have it. Wait!" He looked at Chaim, who smiled and nodded. "Make that four pieces," David said. "Yes, thanks." He noticed Jacan's irritated look. "It's no problem at all, I assure you. It's the least I can do for all the things you've done for Israel, endangering yourselves constantly."

He waved them to chairs and sat nearby. "Please tell us your story, all of it if you don't mind."

Jacan began their story, starting with the appearance of the angel in the fields and reviewing every important thing the Lord had done at their request. As he told their story, an orderly entered with pie and ice cream.

"How do you manage to reach so many places in Israel? Do you have a car?" Chaim asked.

"No," Ephrem said, balancing a huge forkful of pie and chocolate ice cream close to his mouth. "A little old guy drives us around in his rattletrap car and doesn't charge us a cent. Not that we could pay him anyhow."

"I see," David replied. "Would you like me to provide you with better transportation? I have a driver who used to be a professional chauffeur, and I could also give you an officer from the special forces who is highly trained in all—"

"Oh, I think we'll stick with our old guy," Jacan said. "We love and trust him. Still, you could give him a better car to take us places. Especially one whose brakes work properly. As for protection, we have the Lord on our side."

David decided not to get into the ultimate destiny of the two prophets as described in the Book of Revelation. He was sure the Lord had already revealed it to these two faithful men, and they had willingly accepted it. What they needed to do was concentrate on their great mission as the protectors of Israel and the forerunners of the Messiah.

At that moment, a soldier entered with special dispatches from the front. After reading all the reports quickly, he said, "Well, it seems our Arab enemies have retreated on all fronts." Chaim picked up the last report that David had missed and started to read it.

"You mean they're running for their lives, don't you?" Ephrem said.

"Yes," David said happily. "Now we can concentrate on our worst enemy."

"You missed this report," Chaim said, waving a paper in his hand.

David was surprised at his own carelessness. "What does it say?"

"It says that the armies of several foreign nations have just arrived at Eilat. From Canada, the United Kingdom, and Australia. About thirty-five thousand of them. They've also brought a significant amount of modern weaponry with them, including some advanced warplanes that are capable of firing laser cannons."

"So we have more friends in the world than we thought," David said with a grin.

The two prophets excused themselves, explaining that the Spirit was calling them to Gaza.

Two days after the Arab armies pulled out, Gerald Galloway ordered a massive invasion of Israel on all fronts. UGOT's armies totaled over fifty million troops from most of the nations of the earth and outnumbered Israel's army, including the American troops and those who had just arrived from abroad, by about fifty-five to one. Gerald placed himself at the head of his own private army of a hundred and fifty thousand, assisted by Generals Drescher and Laurent. He also consulted his most trusted associates, especially Lucienne Delisle and Randolph Benson, and frequently received "spiritual" counsel from Colton Aldridge, his favorite miracle worker. Traveling south from Beirut along the Mediterranean coast, it took them only one day to cover the seventy miles from their base to the Israeli front lines.

Meanwhile, Daniel Christopher and his buddies had relaxed a little after seeing the Arab army running away. Of course, sentries watched enemy territory carefully for any sign of movement. Most of the soldiers wrote letters to loved ones, celebrated, and even played baseball. But Daniel himself was depressed and worried, not knowing the status of Rachel Salant. He had managed to carry her to a station set up by the Israeli medical corps, and they had given her life-support treatment and had shipped her off immediately to Haifa in northern Israel for professional care. Daniel was especially sad that he had not been able to give Rachel a blessing because a delay of even a few seconds might have cost her life. After the medics had rushed her away, he had said many prayers in her behalf and had inquired concerning her status often, but he had not yet received a response.

Daniel was lying on his back under the sun, enjoying a break in the stormy weather, when he heard a loud siren. He jumped to his feet, grabbed his gear and rifle, and rushed with hundreds of fellow soldiers to the trenches on the front line. They filled the trenches in seconds and gazed northward, trying to catch sight of the enemy. Every young face was contorted with anxiety.

Finally, they saw them a half mile away. Hundreds of tanks rumbling across the ground toward them in a line that seemed to have no end. Protecting themselves behind the tanks came thousands of enemy troops, wearing many different uniforms. The main thing was, they weren't Israeli uniforms.

Then within ten minutes, everything turned into a mind-boggling world of confusion and chaos. The deafening roar of thousands of bullets, shells, concussion grenades, and bombs tearing into the Israeli line was unbearable. The defenders fought with determination and courage, but whenever they ventured up to the ridge of the trenches, they were invariably slammed backward, their bodies ripped to pieces by enemy fire.

In the midst of the din, Daniel heard warplanes tearing by overhead, but he couldn't tell if they were friend or foe. Yet when machine guns raked them from above, mowing down dozens of troops in one pass, and lasers disintegrated bodies in an instant, he knew that most of them were enemy planes.

In spite of the danger, Daniel rose a dozen times and shot bursts of gunfire toward the enemy, cutting down several foes each time. After twenty minutes of this nightmare, Daniel heard a siren sound a quarter of a mile to the south, calling for retreat.

As one body, the defenders scrambled up the near side of their trenches and ran away from the line as fast as possible. Rushing southward, they passed dead soldiers and motionless tanks, trucks, jeeps, downed warplanes, and APCs that were twisted, smoldering wrecks, sprouting torn, burned corpses. Daniel hurried along for hundreds of yards, sickened by what he saw. Then he stumbled upon an unusual aircraft and quickly examined it. He had seen several of them during the retreat and wondered what they were. Upon examination, he recognized it as an enemy drone, but what shocked him most was the laser cannon it carried. Wasting no more time, he continued on, hoping the enemy would not overtake him.

A few minutes later, he heard moaning and saw a wounded Israeli soldier not far away, so small that he didn't even see him at first. When he reached the soldier, he bent over, picked him up, and threw him over his shoulder. It was difficult because he still wore his backpack. As he stumbled along through the rubble, the man groaned at nearly every step, but then voiced an abrupt expression of gratitude in a soft, feminine voice. That's when Daniel realized that the soldier was a woman.

At last, after a half mile of staggering forward with his burden, he reached a stand of trees that appeared to be safe for the moment. He lowered her to the grass and put a tourniquet on her upper leg and a compress on the wound to stop the bleeding below her knee. Then he continued on as before, and the farther he went, the fewer soldiers he saw. Occasionally he stopped briefly to give them both a break and to release the tourniquet, but neither felt like talking. Just before nightfall, he stopped at a barn miles from the front, laid the girl on the hay, and removed his backpack.

"Are you okay?" Daniel asked her. The girl was in her early twenties and had blonde hair and a narrow face. Daniel thought she was very pretty.

"I think so, thanks to you. The bleeding seems to have stopped, but my leg really hurts."

"I imagine it does. And you've got a dozen cuts elsewhere. I'm Daniel Christopher. What's your name?"

"I'm Ruth Tishler."

"That's a nice name."

Daniel examined the wound carefully. "Looks like a piece of shrapnel went right through your calf. I see entry and exit wounds. What happened to your backpack?"

"Some guy took it. He said he wanted to help me, but as soon as he removed my pack, he took off with it."

Shaking his head in disgust, Daniel removed a small first aid kit from his pack. He found a plastic bag, extracted a pill, and handed it to her. "Here, take this for the pain." The Israeli army had supplied every soldier with a half dozen Percocet tablets in case of emergencies.

"Thank you," she said, swallowing the pill with water.

"Now let's dress that wound and your other cuts and scrapes."

When he had finished, he leaned back into the hay. "That was some battle, wasn't it?"

"Horrible. I never dreamed it could get that bad. All that screaming and crying. People torn to pieces, body parts and blood everywhere. We didn't have a chance." She was silent for a full minute. "Do you think the same thing is happening everywhere?"

"Maybe. I don't know . . . Yeah, probably." He paused, willing his heart to slow down. "Still, I know God will save Israel in the end."

She looked at him hopefully, waiting for him to explain, but he said nothing more.

After overpowering the Israeli defenders guarding the Lebanese border, Galloway's army spent the remainder of the day executing the wounded and hunting down survivors, for he had firmly established the general policy for all UGOT's forces of taking no prisoners. They especially delighted in nailing Israeli officers to crosses in full view of the troops, after great quantities of food and wine had been consumed by all, so that the drunken soldiers could enjoy watching the terrible scene, mocking the agony of the crucified as they died a slow death. Galloway himself drank so much alcohol that his aides had to carry him to his tent for the night.

The next morning, Galloway was ecstatic. At his temporary headquarters near the abandoned city of Maalot-Tarshiha, six miles south of the Lebanon border, he showered Lucienne with kisses and even hugged Colton Aldridge. "Well, it worked just as we planned! A marvelous victory! A shining achievement! My army overpowered Israeli defenses on the Lebanon front, and if my dispatches are accurate, our coalition armies did the same on all fronts. All we have to do now is march toward the center of the country from all positions, compressing their forces, like a fist crushing a bug. Soon I'll capture Jerusalem and crucify David Omert and his friends on Golgotha just like the Jews crucified Christ."

Lucienne glowered at his excessive exuberance. "I hate to burst your bubble," she said, her voice flat, "but we haven't won on all fronts. It's certainly too early to claim a victory. The defenders of Jerusalem fought our armies to a standstill, and they still have complete control of the capital and its environs. And that's not all. We haven't prevailed in the southern half of the Negev. Foreign armies just arrived and are helping the Israelis."

"How do you know this?"

"Our radioman intercepted an Israeli communication half an hour ago."

"Why didn't you tell me right away?"

"I tried, but you were nowhere to be found."

"I was congratulating my commanders on our victory. Anyway, how many troops have the foreigners brought in?"

"About forty thousand, the same number as the Israeli troops already stationed in the Negev."

"Eighty thousand," Gerald mumbled. He felt a sudden surge of anger, followed quickly by another rush of enthusiasm. "Not to worry. I'll lead our forces into Jerusalem from the west. And who do we have in the Negev?"

"You should know," Lucienne said, glaring at him. "You stationed them there."

"Yes, yes, I realize that, of course. Just remind me. I can't think straight right now."

"Russians, Germans, and Spanish."

"That's right. Don't worry. They have a combined force five times as strong as our enemies. Give them a little time. If they can't do the job, we'll go south to help them when we're done with Jerusalem."

The attack on Jerusalem was the most violent and intense of all. It began in the second week of September on the same day that Galloway's units overran Israeli defenses in the north. A great army of two million, comprising the forces of France, Italy, Greece, Portugal, China, and Vietnam moved toward the capital in a wide semicircle, assailing its defenses with all the firepower modern machines could produce. The battle started early in the morning and raged all day without a break, but the hundred and twenty thousand defenders held their ground in spite of the onslaught.

When night fell, the invaders ceased their attack, except to maintain a continuous barrage of rockets and missiles. One of their primary targets was the new temple, but the defenses around the Temple Mount were so effective that not one bomb succeeded in striking it.

The following morning, the two peasant prophets arrived from Gaza where they had helped to prevent UGOT's armies on the Egyptian border from capturing the Gaza Strip. The moment they arrived, David Omert summoned them to an emergency meeting at his compound with his war advisers, several senior officers, and his American leaders serving in the vicinity of Jerusalem.

When David introduced the prophets to Steven and Mary, the shepherds gazed at Steven curiously, just as they had David when they first met him. After everyone had taken a seat, David began the meeting immediately.

"Ladies and gentlemen, I'm sure you've heard the news by now," David said. "The enemy has succeeded in invading our country and have begun to tighten the noose around our necks. Fortunately, we maintain control of Jerusalem and its environs, the Gaza Strip, and the southern Negev."

He picked up a paper from the table in front of him and consulted it as he spoke. "Early this morning I received a dispatch from our lookouts near the enemy lines east of Jerusalem. It says our adversaries have just brought in ten vehicles carrying high-powered laser batteries. We already heard they had recently developed this technology, but these new weapons are solid-state lasers rated at over a hundred thousand watts, similar to the Skyguard system we installed around the Temple Mount. The only real difference is their laser beams are green."

"How do they make them green?" Chaim asked. "Laser beams are invisible to the naked eye."

"I don't know," David replied. "I assume they've developed new technology."

"But what's the purpose of giving color to the beams?" asked one of the war ministers.

"The information I have on it says the color has no effect on the laser's power. Personally, I think UGOT wants to profit from the psychological effect it will have on our troops when they see hundreds of green rays flashing by."

"Sort of like the colored rays of the Star Wars movies," Chaim added.

"Exactly." David said, grinning in spite of himself. He saw Steven's hand raised and nodded to him.

"In view of this new laser threat, we can be grateful for all the drizzle we've been getting."

"You're right, Steven. The lasers are not nearly as effective when the atmosphere is full of rain, fog, or dust particles. However, those same conditions will also diminish the effectiveness of our lasers around the Temple Mount. Okay, let's move on. For the moment, we need to focus on protecting the capital. What we need now are ideas—good ones."

"Well, yuh gots the best defense weapons right here amongst us," Ruther said, looking at Jacan and Ephrem. "They done saved Gaza fer us."

David had planned on asking the prophets for help, but Ruther had beat him to it. He looked at them and said, "How can you help us now, brethren?"

"The angel—I mean the Lord—will help us if we ask him," Jacan replied. "First of all, I think we need to ask God to destroy the enemy lasers."

"Then there's a lot of other things we can ask the Lord to do, when we see what's needed," Ephrem said with surprising self-confidence.

"God's help," David said enthusiastically. "That's something we have that UGOT doesn't. Still, the Lord expects us to do all we can as mortals to help ourselves. At present we have only a hundred and twenty thousand troops protecting the city. Our other forces are pretty much scattered and disorganized throughout the nation. In spite of that, I wanted to inform you that I've issued a general call to all surviving units to come to the defense of Jerusalem as quickly as possible. As long as we hold the capital, Israel can never be defeated."

"Some units may not be able to reach Jerusalem," Chaim noted. "UGOT forces may prevent them from doing so."

"I realize that," David said. "In that case they'll just have to dig in and resist as best they can."

"Mr. President," Mary said as she raised her hand. "I'm just an ordinary woman, ignorant in all military matters, but a minute ago you said something that got me thinking. You said UGOT wanted to use green laser beams to destroy the confidence of our fighting men. So I say, why don't we pull the same trick on them? Why don't we undermine the morale of their men?"

"Great idea!" David said. "I appreciate your courage in speaking up. What do you have in mind?"

"Well, do you have ways of getting information into the hands of the enemy?"

"Of course. Lots of ways—infiltrators whispering into the ears of enemy leaders, intercepted dispatches, overheard radio communications, notes left on desks, and many others. Do you have something specific in mind?"

"I sure do. Why don't we lead UGOT into believing that we already have four or five hundred thousand troops here to defend Jerusalem? And at the same time, it wouldn't hurt to let them learn that a half million new troops arrived from America at our western ports during the middle of the night when they were celebrating their great victories and neglecting to monitor our coastline."

David laughed out loud. "Yes! I like it! Mary Christopher, you have a devious mind. Steven, where did you find this woman? We'll do both things right away. It might just give us some precious time."

"I doubt that Galloway will buy that," said a second war minister. "It's too fantastic to believe."

Mary frowned a little at the minister's excessive assurance that he was right. "I think Galloway will buy it. And why? Because that type of man is governed mostly by hatred, fear, and doubt. His imagination will conjure up the worst scenarios possible, and he'll act accordingly."

"I agree," David said. "Galloway will believe it."

Chapter 12

❧

Daniel Christopher jerked awake, feeling as if he were being attacked by someone wielding a knife. But soon he realized where he was: in a barn ten miles from the front. He lay there without moving, listening intently. He heard nothing except the chirping of birds and the soft breathing of Ruth Tishler, who was still asleep not far away. He was grateful he had found her on the battlefield and rescued her because if he had not, she would surely have been tortured and shot by the enemy. He wondered if his parents were safe and if they were worried about him. He also asked himself how the rest of his relatives were faring. Were any of them still alive?

His reverie was suddenly interrupted by the sound of cautious foot-steps slowly moving around the building. That must have been what had awakened him. He picked up his rifle and walked quietly to the barn door, waiting for the intruder to enter. The door swung open slowly and the barrel of a rifle appeared. Fearing the worst, Daniel raised his gun and started to pull the trigger, but then a familiar face popped into view—Jarrad Babcock.

"I almost shot you, Jarrad," Daniel said.

"Nah! I would have shot you first for sure. My lightning reflexes, you know. But seeing as you're Steven's little kid, I held back just in time." Jarrad had been Paul Christopher's best friend for decades and was now forty-six years old. The Israeli army had recognized his rank as lieutenant in the army of Zion. At that moment, Ruth Tishler limped toward them and appeared near Daniel's shoulder.

"Who's the little beauty, Daniel? I thought you were madly in love with your platoon sergeant, Rachel . . . what's-her-name. Remember, I was at

Camp Ashdod with you after we arrived, and I saw you ogling her all the time."

"Rachel Salant. Rachel was stabbed almost six weeks ago, and they took her to the hospital. This is Ruth Tishler. She was fighting on the same front as me."

"He saved my life," Ruth said. "Carried me here and treated my wounds."

"I always knew you Christophers were born heroes," Jarrad quipped.

"I don't feel like a hero. So what are you doing here? I haven't seen you since Ashdod."

"I was serving in the same brigade as you, but in a different battalion. I'm on the run too. Tell me, where are you two headed? This whole region is unsafe. Overrun with UGOT's troops, and I understand from what other fugitives have told me that they'll execute you on sight if they catch you."

"I have no doubt. Ruth and I haven't decided where to go, but I'd really like to find Rachel."

"Do you know which hospital they took her to?"

"The biggest one in Haifa, I think."

Jarrad leaned his rifle against the barn door and wiped his forehead with his sleeve. "Whew! I figure that's about thirty-five miles from here. Hopefully UGOT hasn't captured that city yet. There are about seven hundred thousand people living in the Haifa area, and they should have some pretty good defenses. The problem is, how do we get there, especially since we've got to look out for Ruth?"

"I'm not leaving Ruth here. We could both support her until we find some means of transportation. I wish we had crutches."

"Oh, I'm not suggesting we leave her. In any case, we need to get moving right away. Do you have any food?"

"Just K rations."

"Same here. Well, they'll have to do until we reach Haifa."

They set out slowly, supporting Ruth on both sides. Since the region was crawling with UGOT troops, they were forced to travel on back roads and hide in gullies and coverts whenever they spotted any sign of the enemy. After six laborious hours, they began to see Israeli civilians and soldiers rushing southward. Since they were helping a wounded Israeli soldier, a friendly young couple stopped and offered them a ride to Haifa in their pickup truck.

※

In the land of Jerusalem, the gruesome battle continued, beginning at sunrise and quickly becoming a nightmarish scene of tumult, commotion, explosions, and human agony. Every hour, hundreds of warriors on both sides died with terrible wounds, some rapidly, some slowly. Not only were there few to attend the wounded, but medical supplies were often lacking to help repair their bodies or ease their suffering. But then, shortly past noon, the fighting stopped abruptly.

When David Omert first took charge as president, he designed a defense system for Jerusalem. He had ordered work crews to dig a deep trench all around the city, located about a quarter of a mile beyond the city boundaries. On the outside rim of this ditch he had installed coils of barbed wire that were three feet wide and rose six feet high. Defenders could easily shoot through the wire, but the treacherous barrier would be immensely difficult to penetrate by enemy soldiers. This was the first line of defense.

Fifty yards inside the first trench, he had excavated a second trench that also encircled the city. This was the second line of defense. Between the two lines he had installed several additional rows of barbed wire. It was clearly a defensive setup because the defenders would have great difficulty passing through the barriers in offensive charges against the enemy.

Inside these two great circles, he had constructed a formidable row of elevated concrete bunkers sixty to seventy feet apart. They also encompassed the city. Every tenth bunker was a smaller observation post that was furnished with .50 caliber machine guns to be used only in emergencies. This was the third defensive line.

And finally, two hundred feet inside the second trench, there was a third one dug—but only on the eastern perimeter of the city.

Steven, Mary, and Ruther welcomed the lull in the fighting but couldn't rest. They watched enemy movements beyond the front line, protected in an observation bunker.

"Here they come," Steven cried, looking through his binoculars. He handed the glasses to Mary. "Look just to the left of the center position, on the winding road."

"Yes, I see them. One laser per truck. They're so huge. And terrifying!"

As Mary said that, one of David Omert's orderlies escorted Jacan and Ephrem into the same bunker. "What's huge and terrifying?" Ephrem said.

"Those laser batteries."

"May I use your binoculars?" Jacan asked, and Mary passed them to him.

After Jacan had studied the scene for a minute, he handed the glasses to Ephrem.

A few moments later, Ephrem said, "They're lining them up on an elevated frontage road about half a mile from here. Looks like they're getting ready to fire. Yeah, you're right. They *are* scary."

"I think it's time we asked for help," Jacan said.

The two prophets knelt on the hard floor of the bunker and offered a silent prayer. Almost immediately they both heard the same voice and the same short message. *"I have heard your prayers, my sons. Fear not, for their weapons will not fire."*

Jacan and Ephrem got up quickly and stood next to Ruther. "Soon you'll see a miracle, my friend," Ephrem assured the mountain man. "And you won't even need your big gun."

"Steven!" Mary cried. "The rain has stopped. I don't know when."

"You're right. That's not good news. It's up to the Lord now."

"Do we need to find better cover?" she asked.

"No, I can't think of any place that would be safer. They'll probably aim over our heads, trying to destroy the temple."

After ten minutes, the enemy had not resumed their attack, and Steven continued to check their movements. "They have the laser batteries in place and it looks like they'll start their next attack by firing them first. Any second now."

Instead of ducking down into the bunker, everyone looked out the viewing port. The wide glass-like screen of the first laser on the left lit up, the immediate prelude to producing the beam, and in a fraction of a second the entire gun was covered in vivid streams of electrical energy. The same thing happened to the other nine lasers almost instantaneously. Apparently, the enemy had decided to fire all the lasers in rapid sequence, with only a second or two between each firing. The result was that all ten lasers were destroyed within less than fifteen seconds, and none of them had fired beams. Fifteen billion dollars wasted in seconds. The electrical shorts had also electrocuted the teams handling them.

All at once, a great cheer arose from the voices of thousands of Israeli troops who were anxiously watching the scene. Not only cheers, but laughter and jeering. Hearing the derision, the hostile forces maintained an angry and sullen silence.

Steven turned to the prophets and said, "We're so grateful you're here. I know the Lord has sent you to defend Israel in this time of great crisis."

Jacan nodded toward Ephrem, inviting him to answer. "Thank you, Steven Christopher," Ephrem said.

"Oh, you remembered my name from the meeting in David's compound."

"Yes, certainly, but the Spirit had already revealed your countenance to us, told us your name, and said you had to the authority to endow us with the final power we need. By us, I mean David Omert, Chaim Yehoshua, Jacan, and me." Steven said nothing because he already knew what Ephrem was talking about.

Then the prophets froze and lowered their heads, listening to something the others could not hear. A few seconds later, Jacan raised his head and said earnestly, "The Spirit has given us a warning. We must abandon this bunker immediately, all of us. Right now."

Jacan and Ephrem exited the bunker as fast as they could, with the others following. They raced toward the third trench and flung themselves inside, crouching low. They had no sooner done so when they heard a deafening explosion, and instantly, fragments of wood, metal, and concrete were propelled violently over their heads and into the far side of the trench.

After the battering had ceased, they pushed themselves up and looked over the edge of the ditch, trying to discover what had happened. Steven was astonished to see that the bunker they had just left was no longer there, but had been demolished by an explosion, probably from a guided missile. He slipped to the bottom of the trench when he heard a voice on his radio. After talking a moment, he released the transmit button and said to Mary and Ruther, "David wants us to meet him at his compound."

As they left the combat zone, the fighting resumed in earnest.

Seven ranks of enemy soldiers slowly took shape through the smoke of exploding rockets and mortar bombs, the lines extending as far as the eye could see. They were making their third massive offensive that day against Israeli defenses. Behind them came two rows of battle tanks, their turrets rotating back and forth as if looking for kills. In response, the defenders on the front line laid down an intense fusillade of gunfire with their M16 and Tavor assault rifles. The bullets slammed against countless bodies but—surprisingly—bounced off, causing no apparent damage. Here and there a soldier was struck in exactly the right place and crumpled to the ground, but most kept right on coming.

The defenders were terrified and disheartened at the ineffectiveness of their guns. Some cried out that the advancing forces were not men, but demons, while others declared that their foes must have been supplied with a new type of body armor. Also dismaying was the fact that dozens of enemy soldiers carried flamethrowers, and Israeli commanders feared they were UGOT's dreaded new model that could shoot a stream of flame outward for over a hundred feet.

There seemed no way to stop them—until the Israeli army opened fire with their .50 caliber machine guns. At that point, enemy troops began to collapse by the hundreds. Soon a squadron of Israeli warplanes appeared overhead and fired incendiary bombs, engulfing entire enemy platoons in great fireballs. At the same time, invisible beams of Israeli laser guns raked enemy lines, incinerating anyone or anything they touched. This scene of complete devastation and chaos seemed to go on forever.

Watching the devastation, Steven felt sick. These were cruel ways to die, but this vicious enemy had always resorted to every type of brutality, short of nuclear weapons. If Israel hesitated to defend itself with these extreme measures, it would soon be utterly destroyed, and every man, woman, and child would be slaughtered without mercy or consideration.

Later in the day, the enemy regrouped and made two more attacks on Jerusalem, and each assault was as violent as the others. But each time the brave defenders beat back their assailants. The result of this great battle was that Israel still held firm in defending its beloved capital, and the enemy suffered innumerable casualties. Yet Steven wondered how they would fare when the enemy attacked from all sides and not just on the eastern front.

At dusk a fantastic new sight appeared in the eastern sky—the moon, so close that it seemed several times larger than its normal size. But the strangest thing of all was that the moon was blood red. Steven had seen red moons before during a new moon, but tonight the moon was completely full. *Another sign,* he thought as the bloody moon stared down on Israel, as if reflecting the horrible carnage that had occurred there that day.

The day after the destruction of the enemy's laser guns near Jerusalem, early in the morning, a UGOT coalition army of eight hundred thousand, attacking from the south, east, and west, made a surprise ground attack against Israeli forces in the southern Negev, overwhelming the defenders in two hours, and an air armada bombed transport planes, warplanes, troop ships, tanks, APCs, and ground personnel. Now the small number of survivors could do nothing except heed David Omert's call that all remaining troops should hurry to Jerusalem, if they had the power to do so.

Civilians in the region, those too young or too old to fight in the military, abandoned their cities and towns and sought refuge in the desert. Due to the lack of fuel, they forsook their vehicles and went on foot, carrying as much water, food, and supplies as possible because there was little to be found in the forbidden countryside. They knew it would be better to experience any kind of hardship—even death—than to fall into the hands of their vicious, implacable enemies. Some suggested they try to reach Jerusalem, but wiser heads convinced them it was too far, and they would become easy targets trudging in caravans along desert roads. Their only chance of survival was to hide and live off the land for as long as they could.

Around four in the morning, John, Paul, and eight other soldiers left the area and sped north through the Negev desert in a Wolf APC. The soldiers riding in the APC represented all the nations fighting against UGOT: two Americans, two Canadians, three British, two Israelis, and one Australian. They avoided the mains roads and bounced along precariously across the desert floor, at times following desert trails that led north.

At first they spotted hundreds of individual soldiers on foot heading in the same direction, but they had no more space in their vehicle and couldn't offer rides. Later they began to see many different types of military conveyances—trucks, jeeps, and an occasional APC, rushing northward. They also sighted enemy warplanes in the distance, flying low in search of adversaries, and often they heard the noise of explosions coming from far away.

Gerald Galloway, Lucienne Delisle, and Colton Aldridge were traveling south in their armored personnel carrier at the head of Gerald's army, supported by nearly a half million coalition troops. Behind them were two other APCs, the first occupied by Major General Pascal Laurent and his aides, and the second by General Konrad Drescher and his people. The road, which was only five miles from the sea, was very good, but their pace was slow, for such a massive army could only travel so fast. The president of UGOT felt perfectly safe surrounded by six armed guards in the vehicle and great armies behind him and to his left.

He felt like an emperor leading such a magnificent force to battle against the hated Jews. This had been his recurring dream for most of his life, and now it was all coming true; soon he would receive the great reward he so fully deserved. His mouth formed a sly smile when he saw Israeli civilians and an occasional enemy unit flee at the very sight of him. Not even his so-called master, the god of this world, could have achieved this level of glory and success.

Since the enemy had breached Israel's borders on all fronts, except Jerusalem, and devastated Israeli forces, the Jews were beginning to resort to guerilla warfare as their only recourse. Everyday citizens, including women and children and small military units, were secreting themselves in ravines, woods, basements, attics, empty buildings, underground caves and tunnels, mountain clefts, or any other place where they could hide. Sometimes they had guns, but most often they only had knives, tools, bows and arrows, Molotov cocktails, and other weapons they fashioned themselves.

Yet their greatest weapons were secrecy and rapid mobility.

And who did they attack? Any enemy soldier or unit they were sure they could overcome quickly and easily and then escape completely unseen. They were always on the lookout for Palestinians attempting to use the same tactics against them. History had shown that this type of warfare was very effective and could go on for years until the occupying armies became exhausted and finally abandoned their ambitions.

"Gerald, you're a stupid idiot," Lucienne hissed, her eyes blazing. "You used to have enough common sense to listen to me. But now you do any idiotic thing that enters your mind."

"Tsk, tsk, my dear. You must learn to control your emotions—like I do. Anger only causes people to make bad decisions."

Lucienne eyed him with scorn. "And so does fear and blindness. You're only leading this army southward because you believe some nutty, unconfirmed report that half a million American troops just landed at Ashdod Port."

"Well, they're no doubt trying to maintain their hold on the Gaza Strip and preparing a counter offensive to retake the southern Negev."

"There are no American troops!"

"You're wrong, dear heart. One of my men heard an Israeli officer use the word *Yank* while he was hanging from his cross. This was right after our Lebanon offensive. Two other soldiers told their officers that they had seen dead enemy soldiers who had American memorabilia in their pockets."

"All hearsay. So on the basis of such flimsy evidence, you lead our forces to Gaza instead of taking them to Jerusalem. That's where the real battle is. As long as Israel possesses Jerusalem and their precious temple, they will never consider themselves defeated."

"We'll get there soon enough, but first we must destroy this army that could attack us from the rear."

"There is no great army to attack us from the rear! Ask your personal prophet." She looked over at Colton.

"Well, Colton, what say you?" Gerald asked.

"The master revealed to me that there is no American army near Ashdod or Gaza," Colton said. "We should go immediately to Jerusalem where the two Jewish prophets are fighting our troops." Lucienne gazed at Gerald with triumph in her eyes.

"Your master told you that, huh?" Gerald asked.

"Yes, sir."

"Well, I have good information to the contrary. Maybe your master is leading you astray."

"He never has—"

"Enough!" Gerald shouted.

"Gerald," Lucienne countered, "did you even bother to consult with your favorite generals, Drescher and Laurent?"

"Of course. I usually do,"

"And what did they say?"

"They agree with me." The truth was that both generals thought Galloway was a fool to lead the troops southward on the basis of his weak evidence, bypassing communities that he should capture, but when they saw his crazy eyes and heard his impassioned voice, they thought it wiser not to contradict him.

Lucienne decided to take a different tack. "Listen, Gerald," she said in her most cajoling voice. "Why don't you radio down to our armies in the south? The ones in the Sinai near Gaza. You haven't contacted them for hours. Maybe they've already recaptured Gaza or at least can tell you about any Americans."

"I haven't contacted them because my radiomen can't get through. They always get nothing but static, as if the transmissions are being blocked."

"Well, tell them to keep trying!" Lucienne thumped back into her seat and said no more.

Gerald remained silent for a full minute but finally said, "Okay, I promise you we'll go to Jerusalem—as soon as we defeat the American army near Gaza." Somehow, Gerald figured that would appease her, but Lucienne rolled her eyes and refused to even look at him.

❦

The friendly young couple drove Daniel, Jarrad, and Ruth to a military checkpoint on the outskirts of Haifa and then set out on back roads for Jerusalem. By that time, Gerald's army had already passed by. Because of Gerald's haste to reach Gaza, he had refused to delay long enough to attack the three brigades of Israeli troops guarding the city, which was especially surprising since Haifa was Israel's third largest metropolis, after Jerusalem and Tel Aviv. However, the defenders of Haifa were still on alert because they had receive reports that other UGOT armies were moving down from Lebanon and might attempt the capture of the city.

"How long do you expect to be in Haifa?" the guard said in English as he examined their military ID cards.

"Not long," Jarrad replied. "We're here to check on one of our comrades who was wounded on the Lebanon border a few weeks ago."

"Better not stay long. We're expecting an attack at any time. Half the city has already evacuated."

"Attack? From which direction?" Daniel asked.

"The scuttlebutt says there's an army moving this way from Lebanon and another from Syria. Our commanders could order us out at any minute."

"Where to?" Ruth asked.

"Don't know for sure. Probably Jerusalem. Omert's asked all military personnel to gather there."

"Will they warn us before the attack?" Jarrad asked.

"Yeah. You'll hear three siren blasts in a row, repeated every thirty seconds. That will mean get out now."

They left the checkpoint and walked a few blocks into the city. After signaling a half dozen speeding taxis, they finally caught one. Daniel didn't know where they had taken Rachel, so he asked the man to drive them to the biggest hospital in Haifa. Before long, they arrived at Rambam hospital, the largest medical center in northern Israel.

Daniel feared the worst when he approached the information desk and asked the receptionist for the room number of Rachel Salant. What if Rachel wasn't here or the woman told him that she had died from the stabbing? He was immensely relieved when she said that the patient was in room 530 on the fifth floor, but she declined to answer when he asked about the patient's condition. Daniel requested a doctor to look at Ruth's leg, and was told that Ruth should wait in the reception area for a nurse to come for her. While Daniel rode the elevator up to the fifth floor, Jarrad stayed in the waiting room with Ruth.

Rachel was napping when Daniel entered her room. She looked wonderful, and he stood at the head of her bed for ten minutes admiring her beauty as her long dark hair spread over most of her face. Several nurses came and went, their eyes watching him all the time they were in the room, obviously admiring the tall, handsome soldier with the golden hair. Finally, Rachel's eyes opened and she saw him. A smile quickly transformed her face and her eyes shone.

"There's my hero," she said tenderly. "I was so worried you be hurt or killed perhaps, but now you are here."

"Nothing could kill me as long as I had the hope of seeing you again." Since no one else was in the room at the moment, he stole a few furtive kisses on her lips, her forehead, and her cheeks.

They spent the next half hour catching up on everything that had happened to them in the past few days, especially the details of Rachel's treatment. She had been brought into the hospital six weeks earlier and had been rushed immediately into surgery because the enemy's knife had punctured one of her kidneys. At the same time, they began giving her blood. During the first ten days, they weren't sure if she would live or die, but finally she began to recover and then all she needed was antibiotics, the usual fluids, and lots of rest.

At last Daniel said, "When are you getting out of here?"

"They said I be going tomorrow at eleven, but I should be taking it easy for several months until I am being better."

"Okay. I'm going to try to get some transportation, and I'll come for you tomorrow. We'll drive to Jerusalem, if we can."

Great tears filled Rachel's eyes. "Oh, yes. I heard Israel losing war and President Omert is wanting all fighting peoples to be going to Jerusalem."

"They just told me the same thing at the checkpoint. What I don't understand is why UGOT hasn't tried to capture Haifa already."

She looked at him with big serious eyes. "Daniel, I am not knowing that. But here they telling me all peoples in Haifa preparing to leave this city at the first sign of UGOT attacking. They saying over half of peoples have left Haifa now."

Daniel kissed her again several times and turned to leave.

"Private Christopher!" she called sharply. He stopped dead in his tracks and wheeled to face her. She grinned and said, "I be loving you forever, I think."

"And me you," he said, his heart full of joy. After kissing her again, he hurried from the room.

Daniel went down to the main lobby and saw Jarrad waiting.

"What's up?" Jarrad said.

"Rachel's okay. Recovering fast. They're releasing her tomorrow morning. What about Ruth?"

"The doctor dressed her wound but wants to keep her overnight for observation."

"Good. Now we need to find some transportation. Do you have any money?"

"Oh, about twelve hundred shekels."

Daniel checked his wallet. "I've got a thousand." He did a quick calculation. "That's only about five hundred and fifty dollars. Can't buy much with that."

"Well, we'll have to try. Maybe we'll get lucky."

They hailed another taxi and drove to three used car dealers, but every dealer had abandoned his lot and locked the keys in safes. After paying the taxi driver, they set out on foot. They saw hundreds of cars parked along every street but at first didn't think to look inside any of them. Finally, Daniel started looking through car windows, and within ten minutes he saw a dozen parked cars with the keys still in the ignition.

"They're abandoning the cars for some reason," Daniel said. "How do they expect to reach Jerusalem without transportation?"

"My guess is they're not going to Jerusalem," Jarrad replied. "Probably heading for the nearby countryside to hide out. Remember, Omert only asked for military personnel to go to Jerusalem. These people may think they'll have a better chance of surviving if they stay clear of the capital. That's where most of the fighting will be."

"You're probably right. Okay, we'll just have to appropriate one of these vehicles. For the sake of national security, of course."

After choosing a crew cab pickup truck, they peeled away from the curb in search of a grocery store still in operation. That night they slept fitfully in the truck, which they parked on the outskirts of the city.

Chapter 13

After traveling north for half the night, John and Paul spotted them at dawn, coming from the west, a line of fighting vehicles moving fast and kicking up clouds of dust. They carried long-barreled machine guns visible above their open beds, manned by a single gunner. The brothers and their eight passengers had traveled over a hundred and fifty miles from Eilat, driving their Wolf APC mostly over the desert floor but following isolated trails when they offered themselves. They were on the border of the Negev and Judean deserts, only two miles south of Arad, a small Israeli city sixty-nine miles south of Jerusalem. So far, they had succeeded in avoiding enemy patrols, but now they figured they had been seen.

"What should we do?" Paul shouted to the others.

"Stop a minute," John said. "Maybe they haven't seen us."

Paul slammed on the brakes, bringing the vehicle to a sudden stop. "Fat chance of that. We're as visible as a bald guy in a barbershop."

They searched the desert around them, trying to locate a defensive position. At last, a soldier sitting in the back yelled, "Over there." He pointed to the southeast at what looked like some hill formations. "Looks like a bunch of ridges."

"Let's try it," John said. "I don't see anything better."

Paul turned off the trail and drove across the desert toward the ridges. "Have you contacted Steven yet?" he shouted.

"Not in the last fifteen minutes."

"Try again."

Paul drove the Wolf across the sand and gravel terrain as fast as he could. The vehicle swayed back and forth precariously, and John was afraid they'd tip over. Five other vehicles, four pickups and a small bus, followed them as best they could, having more trouble on the unstable ground and falling behind gradually. The others had been following the big APC for fifty miles, apparently figuring they were safer doing so.

John tried the radio again but couldn't even talk into the speaker, so wild was the shaking. He gave up and looked back to see if the enemy was following. His heart sank when he saw the distant line of vehicles turn off the main road and head in their direction, but he knew those lighter machines would have as much trouble moving across country as the five friendlies following them.

At last they drove in and out of a ravine and then climbed a moderate grade forty feet up onto one of the nearest ridges, which had a flat crest about thirty feet wide before it dropped steeply on the other side, sixty feet down into another ravine. Situated at the front and back side of the crest were dozen of huge boulders, a few as large as a car. John was surprised to see such a good defensive position in this area, and he relaxed a bit. Paul turned the APC around and parked it behind a boulder about ten feet long and five feet high. The soldiers exited the vehicle and took positions among the boulders. A minute later, the other vehicles reached the top of the ridge, all except the bus, which got stuck halfway up. The fifteen passengers jumped out of the bus and scrambled up the rest of the way to join the others.

John watched the enemy through binoculars for a minute and then said, "Yep, they've seen us all right, and they're coming fast. Looks like ten GAZ Tigr units." The Tigr was a Russian-made, light-armored vehicle with a machine gun on the top. It could carry up to ten troops. "Get ready men. I know they've got us outgunned, but Russian soldiers, if that's who they are, have a reputation for being pretty stupid. Besides, they have another serious disadvantage: they only have us outnumbered two to one." John tried the radio again.

The enemy approached to within two hundred yards of the ravine and stopped. All the occupants poured out, except the machine gunners, and took cover behind the vehicles or outcroppings of rock. They did nothing at first, and John figured their leaders were trying to decide how to proceed against an enemy that had such a good position. At that moment, he heard Steven's voice on the radio. He answered and quickly described their predicament and their location.

After disconnecting, he walked over to Paul. "I just talked to Steven." Paul nodded and waited for more. "He said he'd do all he could to get us some help, but he couldn't promise he'd succeed. Jerusalem is under heavy siege."

"I understand," Paul said with resignation. "I guess we're on our own."

"We'll be okay. We've got a good defensive position here." John looked through the binoculars again. "Wait! They're on the move. Half of them are heading south, and the others are drawing closer. My guess is they're trying to get some men behind this ridge and trap us in a cross fire."

The remaining five Tigrs stopped only a hundred yards from the rising slope. At that point, the enemy soldiers exited their vehicles, took cover, and opened fire.

Since John was a major and the highest ranking officer, he took control. "Stay low, men. Don't give them a target." Suddenly an idea came to him, and he decided to act on it. Keeping low, he left Paul and went from man to man and gave each of them quick instructions.

The enemy laid down a blistering barrage of gunfire, and bullets sprayed all around the defenders, tearing up the ground and smacking the boulders with such force that fragments of rock flew in all directions. The men had to protect their faces and eyes in any way they could. When there was a brief lull in the attack, they would rise and take one or two rapid shots and then duck down again.

Paul moved closer to his brother, his eyes bright with excitement. "I have a suggestion. If they charge the ridge, we could push some of these boulders down onto them without them being able to hit us."

"Humm, that's not a bad idea, but first I'd like to try something else. If my plan doesn't work, we may need to go that route."

"What's your plan?" Paul asked.

"I want to entice them to waste their ammunition. That's what I just told the other men."

Paul shot him a sly grin. "You want us all to stand up in a line and wave at them like beauty queens in a Fourth of July parade so they can take potshots at us?"

"Funny, Paul," John snapped. "No, I intend to be a bit more subtle than that."

"Whew! That's a relief," Paul replied with a smirk. "What are we going to do about their men coming around behind us?"

There was a break in hostile gunfire, and Paul rose and took a shot, dropping low immediately afterward.

John checked the five men watching the back side of the ridge and saw they weren't firing at all yet. "The slope on that side is long and steep. They won't be able to get their Tigrs up it, and if they charge on foot, they won't be able to fire and still climb. We'd have plenty of time to mow them down."

"I guess you're right about that," Paul said. "Man, I hope Steven can convince David Omert to send a jet fighter from Jerusalem."

"Me too. But for now we have to depend on ourselves."

As soon as there was a break in the assault, the defenders popped into view briefly as they moved to different positions. At their new positions, they aimed at the enemy carefully and fired short bursts, purposely trying to provoke the opposing force to renew their gunfire. They succeeded in killing one hostile and wounding two others, but so far none of the defenders on the ridge had been struck seriously, except for receiving painful lacerations from flying pieces of rock.

Half an hour after the fighting had begun, the men on the back side of the ridge began to take fire, and John moved twenty more men to that position. Their job was to return fire, but only sporadically. The same scenario continued for four more hours, and still no help arrived from the north.

Around noon, the enemy fire stopped abruptly. John watched them for fifteen minutes and still no gunfire. They were so close that he didn't need binoculars. He and Paul and several of the others discussed the unusual situation for a while, with many possible reasons being raised.

"Are they going to wait and starve us out?" asked a young second lieutenant.

"Hah! I doubt that," said an Aussie lieutenant. "We probably have as much food and water as they do."

"Maybe they're waiting for air support," suggested Paul. "I intercepted one report that seemed to indicate the Gaza Strip has changed hands again. This time it's UGOT's Russian allies who have taken control. If that's true, it would mean their nearest air base is in Gaza, which is only about eighty miles from here. Wouldn't take a jet hardly any time to get here."

"Doesn't seem to reflect Russian mentality—waiting for help, I mean," retorted an older captain. "They know they have us outgunned. In such a case, it would be humiliating for them to ask for help."

"Look! I think they're getting ready to rush us," said a private.

"I agree," said the older captain. "Probably trying to decide whether to use the Tigrs or do it on foot."

John shrugged. "At any rate, we're not going to wait for them to decide what happens. I want all of you to get ready for a charge."

"But that would be suicide!" complained the Aussie, his eyes full of fear. "Maybe those creeps don't know what to do and are simply waiting for us to do something stupid."

John gave him sharp look, and the man's mouth snapped shut. "Not all the way to their position. This maneuver is just part of the original plan. We'll leave two guys on the back of the ridge and some on the front side to give covering fire, and the rest of us will charge down the slope. We'll move as fast as possible without firing, and when we reach the bottom, we'll drop to the ground and open up on them. Then when I yell 'back,' we'll tear up the slope as the guys at the top cover us. Do any of you have a problem with that?" No one said a word, but the Aussie looked at John as if he were crazy.

John caught sight of a Canadian sergeant who had just come from guarding the back of the ridge. "Sergeant Heudier, what are the Russians doing on the back side?"

"Same as on this side. We've only fired fifty or so rounds at them, and they look kind of bored, hardly taking cover at all. Their leader seems to be talking on his radio all the time. If you want my opinion, I believe they're wondering if we're about out of ammo."

"That's what I want them to believe. All right, this operation calls for volunteers. Raise your hand if you are willing to join me and Paul in the charge." Paul's eyes bulged, and he swallowed hard at having been volunteered for such a perilous operation by his own brother. Thirty-three hands shot into the air. "Good! That leaves about twenty men to cover us. You guys who remain here, I want you to concentrate your fire on the machine gunners. Stop firing the second we get back here. Okay now, I want the volunteers to spread out and move close to the front of the ridge. Stay behind cover until I give the word." John checked the enemy one last time, paused a few seconds, and then shouted, "Charge!"

It took them about six seconds to reach the bottom of the slope. The

Russians were so surprised by the abrupt charge that they didn't fire a shot. The only shooting came from the top of the ridge, and it caused the enemy to scatter for better cover and the machine gunners to drop down into their vehicles. As soon as the volunteers had descended the ridge, they fell to the ground and opened up on the enemy. Surprisingly, they were able to hit a half dozen of their targets.

Thirty seconds after they had begun firing, John shouted "back," and the men sprang to their feet and dug for the top, most of them making the ascent in less than ten seconds. The only "casualty" was one man who slipped on the sand and sprained his ankle.

At that point, the Russians made a determined charge of their own, and the machine gunners shot hundreds of rounds up the hill to cover them. But these attackers had farther to go, a hundred yards before they were able to reach the base of the incline, and the defenders dropped eighteen of them just as they started the climb. The remaining Russians broke their charge and retreated to safety. However, even then they continued to fire at every movement or shadow they saw on the rise.

The Russian soldiers on the back side of the ridge had apparently received the same attack signal, and forty of them began to struggle up the steep grade while their machine gunners poured streams of .50 caliber bullets over their heads at the enemy above. But most of their rounds did more damage to the rock formations than to their targets. They even launched grenades, but many of them exploded against the boulders or bounced off and detonated in the midst of their own men. The hostile gunfire continued another fifteen minutes and then slackened until only an occasional shot was fired. In all the gunfire, only one defender was killed and six others received flesh wounds from ricocheting bullets.

It was a little past two in the afternoon when John heard the sound of engines revving up. He waited a minute, wondering what they were up to now. He looked around his boulder and saw ten enemy vehicles racing away across the desert.

"Looks like your plan worked," Paul said. "They seem to have run out of ammo. Or patience."

"Yes, I believe you're right," John replied. "All this shows the folly of attacking an enemy who's established in a good defensive position, unless you have overwhelming superiority."

"By the way, where's that jet fighter Steve promised?"

John shrugged. "He didn't promise anything, but I'll have to talk to him about that when we reach Jerusalem. For now, we'll just try to let him know we're okay."

As Daniel and Jarrad were walking through the hospital lobby, they heard the first three blasts from the sirens. Abruptly, everyone in the room stopped what they were doing and scattered, some to offices, most to exits. The two Americans hurried to the stairs and ran up five flights. When they reached room 530, they found Rachel and Ruth sitting on the bed, their faces pale.

"We got here just in time," Daniel exclaimed, panting hard. The sirens sounded again, encouraging them to hurry. "Wait here," he told the women. "We'll get a couple of wheelchairs."

"But I don't need a—" Ruth said as the men left the room. "I can walk with crutches."

"They need to move us faster than that," Rachel said.

After two more siren soundings, the men rushed back into the room, pushing two wheelchairs. They lifted the women onto them and sped away toward the elevators, almost tipping the chairs over in their haste. When they reached the lobby, it was empty except for several other patients being wheeled toward the exits. They went through the doors, raced their charges across the parking lot to their requisitioned pickup, put the women into the rear passenger compartment, and drove away.

As the sirens continued their warning, they drove out of the city and turned south-southeast toward Jerusalem. They had gone no more than ten miles on a main road when they saw a barricade ahead.

"Who are they?" Daniel said as he slowed the truck.

"I don't know," Jarrad replied, "but it doesn't look good."

"They're Palestinians!" Ruth exclaimed. "They'll kill us if we stop."

"We must be turning around!" cried Rachel.

"No way," Daniel replied. He looked at Jarrad and saw him nod. "Okay, hold on, everyone." He gunned the truck. Within the two hundred yards separating them from the barricade, the powerful truck reached seventy miles an hour. With relief, Daniel saw that the barrier seemed to be made of wood and resembled a fence with horizontal slats. There were a dozen

Arabs in front of the roadblock, wielding knives, bats, and rifles, and some standing behind the obstruction.

Just before he slammed into the barrier, the Arabs scattered to the sides of the road, not having time to make an attack. The powerful truck went through the fence without slowing down or swerving in the slightest. However, as they passed, one Palestinian threw a Molotov cocktail at them, which exploded in a burst of flames in the bed of the truck, but the fire was quickly extinguished by the rushing wind. After Daniel had driven another mile, Ruth asked him to stop.

"That's not the only barricade we'll run into," Ruth said. "There are probably Palestinians and UGOT patrols all over this region. Next time we may not be so lucky."

"I agree," Jarrad said. "What do you suggest, Ruth?"

"Probably the best thing would be to ditch this truck and go on foot. We're too visible on the roads and in this truck. On foot we could slowly work our way cross-country to Jerusalem and hide more easily."

"But you're both recovering from serious injuries," Daniel said. "You could never walk that far. It's got to be almost a hundred miles."

Ruth smiled at Daniel's concern. "I know, but I have a plan. A good one I think."

"What is it?" Jarrad asked.

"Well, I was born in this area. In Baruch Village. It's a tiny Jewish settlement a little over three miles from here. Nazareth is only six or seven miles farther on. Last I heard, there were only four hundred people living in Baruch, but we'd have to go cross-country to reach it."

"Maybe it's been taken over by enemy patrols or Palestinians," Jarrad said.

"I truly hope you're wrong," Ruth said sadly. She paused a moment to compose herself. "Yes, I suppose that is possible, but I'm not suggesting we go directly to Baruch. When I was a girl, I used to play in the countryside near Baruch, and one day I found a hidden grotto quite by accident. The tiny entrance is impossible to see unless you know it's there. After you go past the entryway, you crawl through a narrow tunnel for about ten feet. Then the tunnel opens onto a cave as large as a living room. I spent many happy hours there playing house. I even dragged several small pieces of abandoned furniture into the cave, and I stocked it with dozens of candles and boxes of matches. I'll bet they're still where I hid them."

"So you're suggesting we hide there until you two have recovered enough to travel."

"Maybe a lot longer if we have to," Ruth said.

"Where do we get food?" Daniel asked.

"Well, you boys will just have to beg it from Jews in the area or steal it from Palestinians."

"I believe we can do that," Jarrad said with a big grin.

"I think it's a wonderful idea," Rachel said.

That decision made, they turned off the road and made for the area of Baruch, stopping a mile from the village and hiding the truck as best they could.

Not only did Gerald Galloway lead his armies past Haifa, but he also bypassed Tel Aviv, the second largest city in Israel, which was guarded by six brigades. Instead, he pushed on toward Ashdod, convinced that a great American army had recently landed there.

Seeing Gerald's continued bullheadedness, Lucienne scowled at him frequently. "You're making a huge mistake, Gerald. You worry about an imaginary American army while you disregard two known Israeli armies at Haifa and Tel Aviv. When you discover there are no American armies in the south, and then head to Jerusalem, what do you think the brigades we avoided are going to do?" She didn't wait for him to answer. "Like I said before, they'll strike us from the rear."

"No, they'll stay where they are to defend those two cities."

"Not at all. Jerusalem is at the center of this war. They'll drive on to Jerusalem with all their supplies, and we'll have to contend with them there."

Gerald paused a moment, wondering if she was right. Should he ask his supposedly unerring master? No, that personage was an ignorant fool and wasn't worth consulting. He, Gerald Galloway, was much wiser than any master, or any opinionated woman for that matter. From the bottom of his soul, he knew he was right. His mind told him so, and his heart too. This was much more than a hunch. He had to follow his conscience and his own convictions and ignore all the presumptuous opinions to the contrary. After he smashed the troublesome Americans, he'd double back and annihilate the armies guarding the northern cities if he had to.

And so Galloway continued southward in spite of the admonitions of his mistress, the dire warnings of his prophet, and the unspoken opinions of the generals he had chosen to guide him.

After ten hours of travel, when they had almost reached the vicinity of Ashdod shortly before dusk, he saw a military jeep speeding up the road toward them. The jeep slammed to a stop and a Russian colonel got out and walked up to their APC. Gerald laboriously climbed out of his vehicle and shook hands with him.

"President Galloway, it's so good to meet you for the first time. I've seen many photos of you, but I've never had the pleasure of meeting you in person. I'm Colonel Anatoli Krupin, at your service," he said, pounding his right boot suddenly into the ground and standing at attention.

Gerald looked at him with bored eyes and gave a little smirk. "I assure you, the pleasure is all mine, Colonel Krupin. I assume you're here to ask my support against the Americans."

Krupin's eyes shot sideways and his eyebrows formed a pyramid. "Americans? What Americans?"

"The ones who landed at Ashdod last night or the day before. A half million of them."

"In the last two days we recaptured Gaza and gained control over southern Israel, including the Negev, but I haven't seen any American armies in this whole region."

"You must be mistaken."

"No, sir, I'm sure that if they had landed, we would know. Right now we're preparing to head northeast to reinforce the other UGOT armies poised to take Jerusalem."

Gerald tried hard to control his anger and frustration. "How did you know I was moving south with a large army? There's almost no radio communication."

"I know. The Israelis are using radio interference devices. We knew you were coming because of the runners."

"Runners?"

"Yes, sir. Several soldiers on motorcycles arrived early this afternoon and told us you were on the way. I thought you wanted to join forces with us to move against Jerusalem."

Chapter 14

In late afternoon, the small caravan of vehicles was only ten miles from Jerusalem and was moving cautiously slow. John knew the city was under siege and feared they might run into enemy troops. He slowed down even more as he rounded a hill because he couldn't see ahead. Then he stopped dead, sure he had seen a military vehicle. He told the others to sit tight and got out of the APC. After climbing the hill to get a better look, he saw about twenty vehicles with soldiers milling around. Soon he was joined by Paul.

"Who are they?" Paul asked.

John lowered his binoculars. "They look like Israelis, but I'm not sure." He handed the glasses to Paul. "Tell me what you think."

Paul scanned the company for over a minute. "Yeah, they're Israeli all right. I see their blue and white flag with the Star of David in the center. Focus on the tank to the extreme right."

John took the glasses and studied the area mentioned by Paul. "You're right. Come on, let's go."

They returned to the caravan and proceeded ahead at a low speed. Paul volunteered to sit on the front of their APC and wave a white flag to make sure they weren't mistaken for the enemy. The Israeli troop spotted them right away, and a delegation of thirty soldiers left the company to check them out. When they were fifty yards apart, John stopped again. Paul slid from the APC and hurried ahead to greet them. They talked for a while and then shook hands. Paul waved John forward.

When they reached the Israeli company, the motley group of tired retreaters poured from their vehicles and rushed up to shake hands with the new troops. They immediately began to share experiences as if they were old friends, and soon they were kidding and laughing at jokes, and yet their merriment was not as carefree as it would have been under different circumstances.

Fortunately, most of the Israelis spoke enough English that they had little trouble understanding one another.

The colonel in charge of the company walked up to John and shook his hand. "Good day, Major, we're certainly pleased to see you," he said in perfect British English. "I'm Colonel Ruben Eidelman."

"I'm Major John Christopher. Believe me, we're very glad to see you too."

"Had a rough time of it, eh?"

"Maybe I'll get a chance to tell you some day."

"We've had a lot of men come in from the Negev. Many of them hailing from America, Canada, the United Kingdom, and Australia. You people are the only ones who have offered to help us in our darkest hour."

"Well, as I see it, we're all brothers in the same cause."

"Indeed! Right you are, Major Christopher. Are you related to Colonel Steven Christopher?"

"Yes, he's my brother."

"Good man that. I understand President Omert values his counsel and keeps him close."

"We're on our way to see him now, but we don't know how to enter the city safely because of the siege."

"At present, most of the fighting is taking place on the eastern side of the city. However, the enemy is converging their forces and will soon approach Jerusalem in greater numbers. In a couple of days it will be suicidal to attempt an entry on any boundary. Actually, this company and many others like us have a twofold responsibility. We're assigned to monitor the enemy's progress and to welcome all military personnel who want to enter the city and offer their help."

John admired the colonel's almost clinical—and highly understated—view of their perilous situation. He sensed that behind that impassive mask was a courageous heart.

"So, Major, all you need to do is lead your group around to the west and soon you'll find an Israeli checkpoint that will grant you entry. You could enter from the south, but for some reason those checkpoints have been flooded with Jewish refugees coming from nations to the south and east. President Omert seems to feel they can provided us with special intel and is allowing a limited number of them to enter the city. Well now, I must leave this place and check on another area. Good luck. I hope you find your brother."

"Thank you, and may God be with you."

At that the colonel smiled, his eyes piercing John's. Then he turned and ordered his troops to mount up.

John's caravan drove around the city to the western boundary and turned east. As they drew closer, the travelers expressed surprise at the series of Israeli defensive barriers. When they finally reached a checkpoint, the guards examined their credentials carefully. The officer in charge took special note of the brothers' names and told them President Omert wanted to see them as soon as possible. Omert had given instructions to all the officers in charge of checkpoints to be on the lookout for troops arriving from the Negev, especially the Christophers. If any officer spotted them, he was charged with leading them directly to his fortified compound.

Twenty minutes later, John and Paul walked into the compound's small dining room occupied by a dozen people. John was struck by the subdued tones of their conversations and the grim looks on their faces. They seemed like people who had lost all hope. Only a few glanced in their direction, but then he saw familiar faces moving toward him: Steven, Mary, and Ruther, who came and embraced them with happy smiles.

Unexpectedly, their ears were struck by the frightening noise of machine guns and cannons coming from the region east of the city. It increased in intensity until its source seemed only a few blocks away, shaking the walls of the compound.

"Whew! It's like a horrifying dream!" said John.

"Yes, it is," Steven replied somberly. "It goes on like this night and day, and frequently you hear artillery fire and missiles exploding into targets. Every time that happens, you know some unfortunate souls have lost their lives." He paused and stared at his brothers as if seeing them for the first time. "I'm so grateful you made it here safely."

"Well, we almost didn't," Paul said. "We were hoping President Omert would send a jet fighter to rescue us."

"It didn't get there? I told the president about your predicament, and he said he'd try to send help right away."

At that moment, David Omert was approaching and overheard Steven's words. "I did send an F16 to rescue you. It didn't arrive?"

"No, we saw no sign of it," John replied.

"The only explanation I can think of is that the enemy shot it down," David said. "At this time they have thirty warplanes to our one, and we're losing pilots and jets every day. Also, communications are so unreliable, we seldom get timely reports. I'll double-check with the air chief to see if that plane returned." Later, David would learn that the plane had been shot down by an enemy warplane. "But tell me, how did you escape the Russian patrol?"

Paul gave him a summary of the action, and everyone was impressed. "I blame it all on John," Paul said. "It was his plan, and it worked like a charm." He paused a moment before adding, "Any word from the boys."

Steven and Mary shook their heads, deep shadows filling their eyes. "No," Steven said, "we haven't heard a word." He hesitated a little and then said, "I'm sure the Lord will protect them."

After a long silence, David looked at his watch and said, "Why don't we go into the conference room next door. In a few minutes I'm having a meeting with some of my advisers."

"Um, as visitors to your country, we don't have a right to join in the discussion," John said.

"Oh no, you people have sacrificed everything to help us, and we welcome your counsel."

The Americans seemed pleased with that answer and followed David. As they walked into the conference room, Steven saw that a group of officers and ministers had already taken seats around a long table that bore several bowls of assorted nuts. A minute later, General Michael Jamison and Colonels Mosheh Lazar and Yaakov Raphan entered and took seats.

"Welcome, friends and colleagues," David said. "I'm grateful to all of you for your service and dedication. I realize that our nation is in grave peril, but I'm certain we'll triumph in the end. I assure you of that with all my heart, and therefore, I ask you to continue the struggle with hope and courage. Our people have suffered untold trials and horrors for hundreds of years, and we've always survived and even prospered. I know God will not forsake us now." He paused for a full minute, obviously struggling to control his feelings. Several Israelis wiped tears from their eyes.

"Okay," David continued. "We still expect two more people, but my aides have been having trouble locating them. They never remain in one place more than a short time."

They heard a tremendous detonation as a missile struck a building not far away. The entire compound shook so violently it seemed as if it would collapse. Everyone ducked instinctively and held on to the table with clenched fists.

"Man! That was close!" Chaim exclaimed.

"Yes, it was," David said, still grasping the table. After waiting a couple of minutes, he said, "Where was I?"

"I think you were talking about the two prophets," said Yeshaya Chorney, chief of the General Staff for the IDF.

David nodded. "Some of you may still not believe it, but I can give you proof that those two prophets have greatly frustrated UGOT's forces many times. If it had not been for them, Israel would no longer exist. The most obvious proof is UGOT's ten new laser batteries that were destroyed in just a few seconds. That was clearly an act of God. Colonel and Mrs. Christopher attested to me that in their observation bunker the two prophets prayed for God's help moments before the miracle took place. I'm certain they'll work even greater wonders in the coming days."

"I didn't believe it at first, but now I'm also convinced that God does miracles through them," said Elazar Adelstein, chief of the air force. This was astonishing coming from a man who had always prided himself on being nonreligious. However, others still looked skeptical.

"Thank you, General," David replied. "I'd also like to report that we're keeping our twenty checkpoints open as long as possible. We have hundreds of stragglers coming in every hour, and we certainly need them."

"Military personnel, aren't they?" asked one of the war ministers.

"Yes, nearly all of them. I'm also allowing entrance to certain nonmilitary people who can aid in the war effort or have specific information we can use. And we're accepting offers of weapons, supplies, medicines, water, and food. Fortunately, we're getting a flood of it in spite of the shortages. I've been touched at the people's love for Jerusalem and the holy temple. For your information, we're keeping most of those supplies in hidden, fortified places to provide for the future needs of the soldiers and the citizens of Jerusalem."

"How long can we keep our city inspection stations open, Mr. President?" asked Beth Moskal, an Israeli colonel from Galilee.

"We're monitoring the matter carefully. In the districts outside the capital, the enemy has torn up the roads and bridges, appropriated most of our food and water stores, and seriously damaged our infrastructure. UGOT has done these things on purpose, but by doing so, it has radically delayed its own troop movements. So, to answer your question, Beth, I'd say we can keep city checkpoints open at least another two days. Are there any other questions?" No one had any.

"Okay, there's another matter I need to mention. We're still getting dozens of Jewish refugees from other lands as far away as the Far East. This has perplexed me for several reasons. I don't know how they've been able to travel such great distances under the most hazardous and menacing conditions in world history. Also, it amazes me how they manage to slip through UGOT's lines when getting caught would mean instant death. And finally, I don't understand why they would want to jump into this appalling hornet's nest in the first place."

Mosheh Lazar, a leader of the Ten Tribes, raised his hand, and David recognized him. "What answers have the refugees given you?"

"They tell me it's just as dangerous in other countries as it is here. Since so many nations sent the majority of their troops here, at UGOT's behest, the neighbors who remained in those regions—or who sent only token forces—became emboldened and attacked their traditional enemies with all the troops they could muster. For example, when China brought three quarters of its armed forces here, Japan took advantage of that and invaded China. The result is, all the nations of the earth, with few exceptions, are engaged in destructive warfare. So what we have now—for the first time, really—is a true world war.

"As for how they slipped through enemy lines, the answer is by any subterfuge they could invent. And believe me, they invented a lot of them. When I ask them why they took the risk in the first place, they answer that Israel is the only hope they have and the only hope the world has."

General Michael Jamison looked somewhat agitated. "What I'd like to know is why those nations that were set upon by their neighbors didn't contact their forces here and ask them to return to rescue them?"

"Mainly because communications are nearly impossible these days, especially over long distances. The only reason we know about those conditions is because Jewish refugees from those lands have been courageous enough to make the journey here. Besides, even if their troops here got word of the struggles taking place back home, think how difficult it would be for them to return in time to do any good."

Right then the two prophets entered the room. David, Beth Moskal, Elazar Adelstein, and all the Americans stood to show their respect. Soon the others began to rise, one at a time.

"Welcome!" David exclaimed. "Please sit down." Jacan and Ephrem sat next to each other near the middle of the table, and the others took their seats also.

"I see my people found you," David said.

"Actually no," Ephrem said. "The Spirit told us to come." Jacan's head bobbed slightly.

"Do you mean the angel?" David asked.

"No, the Spirit. Sometimes it's the angel and at other times it's the Spirit. We can tell the difference in their voices. The angel speaks in a light tenor voice, while the Spirit's voice is deeper and slower."

"Interesting," David said. "How long can you stay with us?"

"Only a few minutes," said Jacan. "The Spirit has given us a special work to do somewhere else in Jerusalem. We must be there within an hour."

"Do any of you have questions for them?" asked David.

Chaim Yehoshua stood to indicate he had a question. "Brethren, I have a very serious question to ask you." Both prophets nodded, and everyone got the impression they already knew what the question would be.

"Please ask, Brother Yehoshua," said Ephrem.

Chaim paused for a moment and then said, "Will Israel win this war?"

The two prophets looked at each other, and by some subtle movement known only by very close friends, Ephrem told his companion that he should answer.

"No, we will lose the war," Jacan said. This curt answer brought gasps and groans from many in the room.

Chaim waited until they had regained their composure. "But will Israel survive as a nation?"

This time it was Ephrem who answered. "Yes. After much bloodshed and agony, Israel will survive. Yet it will not be Israel that defeats the armies of the Evil One, but the Messiah himself, as we have testified many times, and the time of his coming is upon us. Now we must go, for we have other work to do."

"What about your safety?" David asked. "There are bands of Palestinians in Jerusalem waging war against Israelis, especially civilians, and I'm concerned they'll attack you."

"God will protect us, until our time," Jacan said.

"Would you object if I sent a squad of soldiers to escort you?"

Jacan smiled at David's worried face. "Not at all."

"Chaim, would you please arrange for that?"

Chaim nodded and followed the prophets from the room.

No one in the room said a word at first, but soon there was an animated discussion, some challenging the prophets' predictions, others defending them. Yet Steven knew that every word they had spoken would soon come true. As the group finished their debate and rose to leave, another series of explosions were heard nearby.

Several days later, near the middle of September, Gerald Galloway finally reached the western borders of Jerusalem, near the village of Zova, with several large armies. With him at his new headquarters were Lucienne, Colton, and his two generals, Drescher and Laurent. They were talking about their allies' attacks against the eastern quadrant of Jerusalem during the past week.

"Six days ago they moved in their new hundred kilowatt lasers," said Drescher. "But just as they fired them, all ten lasers shorted out."

"Shorted out!" exclaimed Gerald. "How did that happened?"

"It's a mystery to everyone."

"The Jewish prophets!" cried Colton. "It has to be their work!"

Both Drescher and Laurent frowned and shook their heads. They had always decried mystical explanations. But Gerald was convinced.

"Colton, we need to get you into Jerusalem somehow," Gerald said. "As soon as possible. You need to face them and defeat them, using your miraculous powers."

Colton beamed. "Yes, I'll kill both of them. But first I must get into Jerusalem."

Lucienne gave Gerald an ironic grin. "Whatever happened to your precious group of assassins who were supposed to do that job?"

"Who?"

"Forgotten already? You know, Taban Nahas, the Hezbollah terrorist.

The monster you were so proud of and who charged you a fortune to murder the Jewish prophets."

"Oh, him. A traitor. He and his men disappeared a week ago with all the money I gave him. Since then, I realized Nahas would never have succeeded in getting into Jerusalem."

Lucienne rolled her eyes but said nothing else, reluctant to provoke Gerald further.

Gerald turned back to Colton. "Don't worry. We'll find a way to get you into the city. Now back to the lasers. In spite of the fact they were destroyed, our allies have the numbers and firepower to break through the enemy front. Why haven't they done so?"

"The main reason seems to be that the stupid generals in charge have little knowledge of battle tactics," Laurent said. Drescher nodded in agreement.

"Explain what you mean," Gerald said.

"After the destruction of the lasers, they led their attack with infantry, followed by armored brigades. Yes, the infantry had air backup and artillery support, but that wasn't enough. They should have moved their tanks in first, followed closely by infantry. The result was, their infantry were mowed down by the thousands, like sitting ducks, in spite of their protective vests."

"I see," Gerald replied. "Okay, Generals, I want you to communicate with the commanders of our allies in the eastern sector and instruct them in tactics."

"The problem is," Drescher said, "the war we have now is a lot like the trench warfare of World War I. Your commanders have no training in that type of fighting."

"Well, what do you suggest we do now?"

General Laurent cleared his throat and use his red scarf to wipe his eyes that were smarting from all the fumes and smoke in the air. "We now have two separate fronts. The enemy still has a sizable force on the boundaries of the Plain of Jezreel, sixty miles north of here. And then we have the Jerusalem war. My question is, do you want to pursue these two fronts at the same time, or take them on one by one?" The Plain of Jezreel was also called the Plain of Esdraelon, and the collective community of Megiddo overlooked the plain. Har-Megiddo was a Hebrew word meaning Mount or Hill of Megiddo and was probably the source of the Greek word Armageddon.

"How many troops do we have in the Jezreel area?"

"Thirty times as many as the Israelis," said Laurent.

"Good. Still, I don't understand where all those Israeli troops came from."

Laurent pursed his lips tightly to prevent his mouth from smiling. "It seems they came from the nine brigades that were defending Haifa and Tel Aviv, the forces we bypassed."

Lucienne laughed out loud and said triumphantly, "I told you we should have wiped them out when we had the chance!"

"Yes, you did, but you were dead wrong when you said they would end up attacking us from the rear near Jerusalem. Anyhow, that's all water under the bridge. Let's pursue both engagements at the same time. Now, I would like suggestions on how to capture Jerusalem."

"I think we should try poison gas," Drescher said. "That way, we might be able to gain an early victory and save the lives of thousands of our troops. I understand our allies have about a thousand gas cylinders available. It will only take them two hours at the most to set them up in the right places."

"That's a monstrous way to wage war!" Lucienne declared angrily. "We simply can't do it!"

"Killing is killing," Gerald said. "What difference does it make how you do it?"

"You can't—"

"Let me decide that!" Gerald shrieked. He paused to catch his breath. "How much of the population could we kill with the gas?"

"It depends on the type of gas and the wind patterns," said Drescher. "I know the gas we have is very lethal. It might kill most of the inhabitants of the city, if we're lucky."

"Would this action put us in danger here?"

"Very doubtful. The gas will completely dissipate before it reaches our troops."

"Then we'll use the gas," Gerald said calmly, as if he was ordering pizza.

"But it's a war crime!" Lucienne lamented.

Gerald glowered at her. "All war is a war crime."

"There *is* one problem with gas," Laurent said. "You need a favorable wind, moving in the right direction. In this case, blowing from the east toward the west. Right now, the rain has stopped and there is virtually no wind at all."

"I can fix that," Colton said, his face red with excitement. "Give me the word, and I'll soon have the wind blowing in the right direction. Just an ordinary little miracle."

"You can do that?" Gerald asked. Colton nodded. "Are you certain?" Colton smiled and nodded again. "All right, do it as soon as you can. In the meantime, Generals, contact our allies and tell them to place the cylinders at once. When they're ready, I want them to send me word."

"You realize there are Palestinians, Armenians, Christians, and other ethnic groups living in Jerusalem, not just Jews, don't you, Gerald?" Lucienne said.

"Hah! I guess they would call that collateral damage. Anyway, I have no qualms about sending a few Palestinians on their journey to the Arab paradise."

"With your permission, I'll leave now," Colton said. "Two of my fellow prophets just joined us this morning, and I want them to assist me in this sacred undertaking. We'll try to find a nearby hill that provides a view of the city."

Gerald summoned an aide and ordered him to send a small detachment of soldiers with Colton to ensure his safety.

After Colton had left, General Laurent turned to Gerald and gazed at him with narrowed eyes. "President Galloway, may I ask you a question?"

"Of course. Proceed."

"What plans do you have for the world when we exterminate the Jews and all the other religious fanatics?"

"What do you mean?"

"Well, when you conquer the world, what kind of government, what kind of society, do you intend to create? How will you control the destinies of billions of people? What great projects do you have in mind for making the earth a paradise?"

Gerald was completely stymied by such strange questions, for he had never given those things a second thought. He started to answer, then stopped in confusion. After a full minute, he said, "I'll figure that out when the time comes." Then he dismissed the generals without another word.

Later, Drescher and Laurent discussed the matter over glasses of wine in Laurent's camp tent.

"You know, Drescher," Laurent said, "all conquerors are the same. They often plan their victories with great astuteness, but they never make serious provisions for what they will do when peace finally arrives."

"I've noticed that too in my studies of military history. Hitler and Napoleon were perfect examples of that bizarre weakness."

An hour later, Colton Aldridge stood on a hill several hundred yards from Gerald's headquarters. With him were Santiago and Dedrick, two antiprophets who had performed many great miracles for UGOT in the past. They looked around and saw—as far as the eye could see—fires, tents, milling soldiers, and every imaginable type of war-waging machine known to mankind.

Then they turned toward the east and saw battle-torn Jerusalem in the throes of a siege. They saw the flash of laser beams and heard the distance sound of gunfire and the boom of explosions that never seemed to end. Most of the blasts took place in the sky above the city as missiles, rockets, and warplanes were struck by defensive weapons used by both sides in the conflict. It reminded Colton of a gigantic display of fireworks, but the bursts were far brighter and made the earth and atmosphere shudder for miles around.

After the three men spent a few minutes talking about what they should do, they knelt on the earth, facing east. They had decided Colton would be their voice. "Oh mighty Master," exclaimed Colton in a voice filled with passion. "Let the wicked suffer for their great sin of rejecting the earth-healing doctrines and practices of UGOT and for rejecting the inevitable advent of our marvelous one-world order. We ask thee to send a strong wind from the east to the west across the rebellious city before us. This I ask in thy holy name, amen." The other prophets repeated amen loudly.

Almost immediately, a breeze picked up and began to blow steadily from east to west. Pleased with themselves, the miracle workers sat on the ground and waited patiently. Thus it is that Satan can use his false prophets to perform mighty miracles to further his wicked designs.

❧

Jacan and Ephrem stood on the crest of the Mount of Olives looking east at the hosts of UGOT's forces. They didn't know why the Spirit had summoned them to this sacred spot. Maybe it was for some fresh revelation or assignment. Before long, they saw in the distance, about a mile away, a great cloud boiling toward them. It was at least seven miles wide and was flowing quickly. Perhaps a new and stronger rainstorm was bearing down on them. No, the white cloud had a strange greenish tint and was moving far too close to the ground, actually touching the grass and bushes as it swept along.

"*This is a cloud of evil,*" said the Spirit's deep, penetrating voice. "*It will bring death to your brothers and sisters in Jerusalem. Ask the Lord to reverse the winds to save your people and to punish the evil ones who have created it.*"

Without hesitation, Jacan raised his voice and asked God to reverse the winds. When he had finished, Ephrem repeated the same supplication with a fervent voice.

As quickly as the wind had arisen and blown westward, it reversed its direction, swirling in powerful eddies. Soon the deathly cloud turned and rolled toward Jordan, slithering over UGOT's armies, asphyxiating every person in its path. Only a few who had worn gas masks when they fired the poisonous canisters escaped death. After five or six miles, the gas began to dissipate, leaving distant troops untouched, but within that six-mile radius, over three hundred thousand men died a horrible death.

As the prophets started to descend the hill, the Spirit spoke to them again, saying, "*Return to the compound. There you will find one who has authority to baptize you and to endow you with priesthood power.*"

The prophets were astonished, and Ephrem said aloud, "But Lord, you have already done mighty works at our request. What is that final power you said we needed?"

"*The Lord has granted your requests because of your faith and obedience. He has given you a special dispensation of power. You have done all God has required of you, but now you must receive baptism and a permanent endowment of power after the holy order of the Son of God in order to be acceptable to him, and you must receive it from one who is authorized by the Lord.*"

"Holy Spirit, you spoke of the Son of God," Jacan said, his voice trembling. "Tell us, please, who is this Son of God you speak of?" In the Jewish religion, there was only one God—Jehovah—and he did not have a son.

"*He ministered unto your ancestors in the meridian of time and died on the cross to save all mankind.*"

"Do you mean Jesus of Nazareth?"

"*Yes. Go now and do as the Lord requires.*"

The prophets descended the hill, numbed to the bone and unable to speak, for they realized that the rabbis had falsely taught the Jews that Jesus was a false prophet, and worse, their ancestors had crucified the Messiah, the Holy One of Israel.

Chapter 15

Two Israeli officers stood on the Mount of Olives near the prophets when the strange cloud appeared and began to rush toward them. They saw the prophets drop to their knees and heard their prayer. Like most of the inhabitants of Jerusalem, they knew who the prophets were and expected something wonderful to happen.

After the cloud reversed its course and bore down on the enemy troops, the officers descended the hill and raced toward the president's compound. They didn't know what the cloud was, but they figured its appearance must be significant. On the way to their destination, they overheard people discussing the strange new phenomenon, some declaring they had learned that the greenish white vapor was poisonous and had killed enemy troops. The officers were amazed that this news had spread so quickly.

When they reached David Omert's compound, they were escorted into the president's private office, where they reported what they had seen and heard. David thanked them and summoned his guests, friends, and several leading commanders. They met a short time later in the conference room, and David reviewed what the two officers had told him.

"That's just further proof that the Lord is on our side," Chaim Yehoshua declared.

"I believe the prophets defend us every day in ways we don't even know," said General Jamison, who had just returned from leading a patrol to observe the movements of the enemy army amassing on the western front.

"I agree," said Steven Christopher. "I'm also convinced that UGOT's armies will never capture Jerusalem as long as we have their protection." He knew from his research of last days events that the prophets would eventually be overcome and killed. That was a necessary happening preparatory to the coming of the Messiah. He stared into David's eyes and realized that he too understood the same thing.

Mosheh Lazar stood and stretched his six foot six frame and then sat down. "Sorry, I just got a twinge in my lower back . . . I was going to say that this poison gas thing proves what we already knew—Gerald Galloway has no respect for human life. Maybe he'll try biological weapons next."

"If he tries that, our prophets will turn it to his disadvantage also," said Mary Christopher.

David smiled at the Americans' use of "we" and "our" in their comments. He knew it was because they personally shared and identified with Israel's suffering and its current dilemma. After they had discussed Galloway's character and possible tactics for a while, David said, "What did you learn on your patrol, General Jamison?"

"From what I've seen of his preparations, I believe Galloway will attack very soon with all he's got."

"How soon in your estimation?" asked Brigadier General Danny Fischer.

"It's possible he may order the offensive today, but at least within the next two or three days."

The fifteen people present eyed one another with shocked looks and pale faces. At that moment, Yaakov Raphan rushed into the room, out of breath. He had been on patrol with a small troop of men to study the northern border of the city. Yaakov was Mosheh's friend and colleague and had been one of the primary leaders of the first group of the Ten Tribes to arrive in Zion.

"Good! You're here, Yaakov," said David. "Let's ask Yaakov the same question."

"What question?" Yaakov said.

"When do you think UGOT will begin their offensive on our other perimeters?"

"It could happen anytime now."

At the end of the meeting, the Israeli commanders left the room, but David asked Chaim and his American friends to stay for a few moments.

"Steven, I read the Book of Mormon you gave me a few days ago. Chaim read it too. We believe it's the word of God and gives us the answers we've been seeking for years. I know you are a member of the

Church of Jesus Christ of Latter-day Saints, but I'm not sure about the rest of you."

"All of us are members," Steven answered, not really surprised that the inspired Jewish leaders had somehow found time to read the Book of Mormon since he'd given them copies of it.

"I see," David said. "Well, in the Book of Mormon it talks about the holy order of the Son of God. This holy order is also called the high priesthood. It's in the Book of Alma, I believe. It seems that those who are obedient to God are given this high priesthood. Is that priesthood in your church?"

"Yes, it's called the Melchizedek Priesthood."

"Do you need that priesthood to receive the highest blessings of God in the hereafter?"

"Yes. It's given to worthy men. Women don't receive the priesthood but share in the same blessings."

David looked a little anxious. "How can I get that priesthood?"

"You can become a member of the Church through baptism and later receive an ordinance giving you the Melchizedek Priesthood."

David sighed with relief. "Can you do all that for Chaim and me?"

Steven was pleased and excited. He had worried that convincing David that he needed baptism would be the hardest part of his calling, but David had been prepared by the Lord. "Of course. The president of the Church gave me the authority to do that. Before we left Zion."

"Are you saying he knew I would ask?"

"Well, he is a prophet, after all. When do you want to proceed?"

"Today. We have very little time before the Christ comes. The Lord has spoken to my heart and told me that we should seek you out. He also said we would need priesthood power to receive the Messiah and escort him to the holy temple."

All at once, the shepherd prophets entered the room. Without greeting anyone, Jacan blurted out, "The Spirit sent us here. He said that Jesus Christ is the Messiah and that we must be baptized into his Church and receive the holy priesthood. He also said someone here has the right to do those things for us."

David gestured toward Steven. "Yes, here he is—Steven Christopher." At that moment, Jacan and Ephrem remembered the vision they had received showing them Steven's face.

"Can he do it all right now?"

David turned to Steven. "Well, Steven?"

"All we need is a pool of water."

"There's a fountain two blocks away," Chaim declared.

Everyone in the room left the compound and rushed to the fountain, followed by an armed escort. When they reached the fountain, Steven was surprised to see that the water was almost three feet deep. Without hesitation he proceeded to baptize the four men by immersion: David, Chaim, Jacan, and Ephrem, in that order. Then he laid his hands on their heads and endowed them with the Melchizedek Priesthood. The new members of God's kingdom rejoiced openly as they walked back to the compound. Steven assured them that their family members would also be baptized at the first opportunity.

"I warned you, Gerald," Lucienne said snidely. "I knew using poison gas would backfire." She turned toward Colton Aldridge. "I'd like to strangle you, Mr. Prophet. It seems to me that their prophets are stronger than you and your so-called miracle workers. Or maybe their master is stronger than yours." Colton gazed back at her with hatred in his eyes.

Gerald glared at Lucienne. She had been a major thorn in his side ever since he had decided to bypass Haifa and lead his army south. She certainly didn't look beautiful or desirable with her tongue wagging all the time, bugging him with her contrary opinions. And he didn't feel any better about Colton. Maybe he could do without either of them.

"I'm not pleased, Colton, not pleased at all. You promised me results."

"I gave you results, but it was your idea to use something as dangerous and uncertain as poison gas. How could I know their prophets would be ready to counter my glorious miracle? I told you before, I need to face those two prophets in person, and then we'll see who overcomes who."

Two hours later, in the late afternoon, Gerald learned from Generals Drescher and Laurent that his forces in the Plain of Esdraelon had surrounded the Israeli army in that region and that it was only a matter of hours before they would achieve a complete victory. Flushed with the joy of that good news, Gerald ordered a full-scale attack against Jerusalem on all fronts.

The struggle for the control of Jerusalem was not over quickly as Gerald had imagined it would be. Seven months later, near the middle of April, the war was still raging on. Most of that time, both sides had been suffering from agonizing scenes of death and destruction, but before long, they saw frightening new specters: drought, famine, and disease. Even in the north, on the Plain of Esdraelon, the Jewish troops were still dug in and resisting UGOT's forces in spite of all odds.

When the shortages and illnesses began to occur among the invaders, Colton and his workers of magic held back complete disaster by performing surprising miracles. They frequently conjured evil spirits and their master to produce rain, filling the dry river beds of Israel with water, and to grow plants for food. Several times they duplicated God's gift of manna to the ancient wandering tribes of Israel. They even prevented the spread of some deadly diseases, caused by thousands of rotting corpses, for which they could not dig graves fast enough.

Colton and his helpers had tried several times to infiltrate the capital, but each time their attempts had failed.

In Jerusalem, the two prophets did similar miracles in the name of God, and if they had not done so, the capital would have fallen after only a few weeks.

The struggle was not only between men, but also between the powers of good and evil. Yet it could not go on forever, and all the combatants, even the men of evil, sensed that the end was drawing near.

And once again the blood-red moon appeared above the horizon at nighttime, several nights in a row. When the Jews of Israel saw that strange spectacle in the heavens, nearly all of them interpreted it as an evil omen, and throughout the land voices of lamentation rose to the heavens. They feared that God had once again turned his back on them and that their marvelous dream of achieving a permanent nation—a sacred home—of joy and freedom after centuries of wandering and persecution in foreign lands was destined to die forever.

Both religious and secular Jews joined their voices in crying out to God, asking him why he had forsaken them. Their forefathers had suffered and died to bring about their long-awaited miracle, the only free democratic republic in the entire Middle East. No other people had been able to accomplish it, but now it seemed to them that their race would perish and disappear from the annals of history and that this entire region would be doomed to be governed forever by crazed, fanatical monsters wearing long "holy" robes and flowing white beards, who ruled the people by strict, soul-destroying laws, supposedly according to the will of Allah.

It was in April that Gerald Galloway finally humbled himself enough to ask for help from the god of this world. He had to pray, on his knees, for half an hour before he got a response. His master had apparently decided to make him suffer and grovel for a while.

At last, the spirit being suddenly appeared and descended from the ceiling in a blaze of glory. Gerald recognized his bright, handsome countenance and his smile of supreme self-assurance.

"Having problems, Gerald?" the bright angel said with a tiny smirk on his face.

"Many problems, almighty Master. With all our weapons and all our strategies and all our manpower, we still can't capture the capital of the Jews."

"I have noticed that, my lowly servant. Actually, you shouldn't be so depressed. You have accomplished a great deal. You have conquered almost all of Israel and killed millions of your enemies. All you lack is Jerusalem and Esdraelon. Yes, you have used many excellent resources and tactics, but now you must proceed in a different manner."

"A different manner?"

"Yes. By using a tiny bit of brainpower."

"Brainpower?"

"Let me help you, my poor servant. Your main problems are fear and ignorance. You fear those two so-called prophets, and you overestimate the resources of your enemy. The prophets and David Omert are the Jews' main sources of hope and courage. When you kill them, you kill their will to fight. I'll give you a clue: their deaths can be brought about by a few well placed-bullets. At the same time, you are ignorant concerning the supplies available to the Jews. They are almost out of food and ammunition."

"I'm still not sure what to do."

Lucas Nigel scowled at Gerald's ignorance, but then his smile broadened abruptly. "You have tens of thousands of tanks. Line them up around the periphery of the city. The Jews do not have enough firepower left to destroy many of them, and the very sight of the tanks will strike terror in their hearts. But before you attack with the tanks, drop thousands of paratroopers into the city just behind their front lines. Concentrate them in two or three specific locations. Your instructions to those troops should be to attack the defenders' front lines from behind, especially the reinforced bunkers. Then order the tanks in. All you need to do is penetrate into the city at one or two points, and soon Jerusalem will be yours."

"As for the two prophets, let your miracle workers track them down as soon as you breach their defensive lines. They are under my guidance and will know what to do."

"What about the Israelis in the rest of the country? There must still be nearly two million of them."

Lucas's fierce eyes bore straight through Gerald. "You mean, how do you deal with their guerilla warfare?"

"Yes."

"You sweep them up like dust on a dirty floor and toss them into trash bins."

At those words, Lucas rose quickly and disappeared through the ceiling.

The next day, Gerald put his master's instructions into operation. The paratroopers were dropped behind the city's front lines and severely weakened Jerusalem's defenses in several spots, and UGOT's tanks penetrated the city in three places, all on the western borders. As the tanks roared through the streets of the city, heading east, they fired machine guns and cannons, decimating thousands of Jews, Palestinians, and Israeli troops. Following the tanks came streams of enemy troops, quickly filling the streets as they advanced throughout the city. The Jews fled in terror, seeking any safe place they could find.

However, even now, the battle for the capture of Jerusalem was not accomplished easily. Nearly a million citizens and troops made a prompt recovery from the initial shock and began to resist UGOT's forces entering from the west. Bloody battles swept through that section of the city, and the defenders fought bravely for control of every foot of their precious capital.

Later that same day, a military courier, who had been flown in from London on a series of special flights, arrived at Gerald's headquarters. Gerald greeted him with a warm smile.

"You have something for me?" Gerald said.

"Yes, Mr. President. I have a parcel for you." Gerald looked at the large envelope and was delighted when he read the sender's label: Doctor Lewis Adler, Genealogical Researchers, Inc. He laid the envelope on his camp table among a pile of other documents. The courier also handed Gerald a smaller envelope containing a bill.

"Why has this taken so long to get to me?" Gerald grumbled. "I ordered this report a year ago, and Adler said it would take less than four months to reach me."

"I'm not certain, sir. I believe Mr. Adler had some trouble finding your whereabouts. And then there was a problem delivering it because of all the bad weather and the fighting everywhere."

Gerald opened the smaller envelope, wrote out a check for the amount on the bill, handed the check to the courier with a big tip, and dismissed him without another word. He thought about looking at the results immediately but then decided not to. That pleasure should be saved until after the current conflict was resolved and he had time to savor the exciting revelations that the documents surely contained.

When David Omert learned that the city defenses had been breached on the western front, he summoned his family, friends, and key government officials to his compound, asking the Americans and the prophets to gather in the dining room area. The American friends included Steven, Mary, John, and Paul Christopher. The complex had walls six feet thick, reinforced with hundreds of bars of steel, and it had room and emergency rations for about two hundred people. A short time later, some five hundred Israeli soldiers moved in and took up positions in the immediate neighborhood, while another fifty manned dozens of vertical slits in the walls of the compound.

At about one o'clock, the occupants of the compound heard the roar of motors and heavy clanging. "Tanks!" several people shouted at once. It was an advance thrust of tanks, which had preceded the other columns in hopes of killing Israel's leader. Soon the clanging stopped, and one man called out, "They're getting ready to fire the big guns." But then they heard swishing sounds, followed immediately by explosions.

"What is that, David?" Mary Christopher said with apprehension.

"Anti-tank RPGs."

"RPGs?"

"Rocket-propelled grenades." As he spoke, the rat-a-tat of machine guns broke the brief silence, accompanied by the loud crackle of gunfire. "That's probably our guys, defending the compound."

One of the defenders darted into the dining area and yelled, "Our guys blasted some enemy tanks. Now the tanks are blocking most of the roads leading here."

"Good," David said. "Maybe that'll give us some extra time."

The firefight continued the rest of the day and into the night. The following day, early in the morning, there was a short pause in hostilities, and then it began again, continuing that day and the next. David couldn't get any news of what was happening in the rest of the city, but he knew the end was fast approaching.

Two days after Jerusalem's defenses had been breached, Colton Aldridge thought it relatively safe to enter the city, and he did so early in the morning under the protection of four soldiers, members of an elite squad of fighters. He had asked his fellow prophet, Santiago, to go with him as spiritual support, and he had also procured the services of an Israeli interpreter who was familiar with the city. This man had rejected the Jewish religion, fought against the policies of the new ruler, and prided himself on being an enlightened, secular Jew. Their goal was to find and murder the two prophets who had caused UGOT so much misery.

They searched for two hours, but without obtaining a clue concerning the whereabouts of their targets. At last, they questioned a Palestinian who gave them a valuable lead after demanding a small reward, not of money but of food. He told Colton that he had seen the Jewish prophets enter President Omert's private compound ten blocks away. Colton had to give him more food to obtain directions to the compound.

When the seven men approached within four blocks of the compound, they had to stop because the fighting was so fierce that they dared not come closer. They waited an hour, but still the battle continued. Then Colton got a brilliant idea.

He turned to the leader of the elite squad and said, "Let me use your radio." He took the radio and called Galloway's headquarters. Gerald answered, and Colton told him where he was and what he wanted. Gerald assured Colton he would act on his request. "Now all we have to do is wait," Colton declared to his companions, pleased with his cleverness.

Within fifteen minutes, UGOT's troops began to pull away from the area, and the gunfire fell silent in the immediate vicinity. Colton was surprised to see the defending soldiers abandon the area almost at once and head west, seemingly in an effort to pursue the enemy. After he and the others observed the compound for another half hour, watching for anyone leaving, a stream of people finally exited the building. Most of the soldiers among them also moved off to the west, but the civilians headed east, guarded by a squad of soldiers.

But where were the prophets? Colton was furious when they didn't appear, but he steeled himself to wait longer. A few minutes later, he saw them. Jacan and Ephrem left the building and walked up a street toward the north, and Colton and his party followed them. Ten minutes later, Colton spotted the prophets entering a bazaar whose booths and stands were empty. By the time Colton had drawn within a hundred feet of his victims, a small crowd had already surrounded them in the small public square.

Colton stopped short and turned to his followers. "There they are. In that crowd."

"Looks like they're healing some kid," Santiago said. "Maybe we should wait until they're done. Too many people around them."

"No, we must act now while we have the chance."

"Colton, you've never told me exactly what you plan to do."

"Our powers versus theirs."

Colton walked forward, close to the buildings girdling the square, followed by the others. When he was within forty feet, he stepped away from a wall partially hiding him and faced the crowd surrounding the prophets.

"Your end has come!" Colton shouted. Many in the crowd turned to see who had called out. In doing so, they moved partly to the side, exposing UGOT's hated tormentors. "Your end has come!" he repeated. "Today you will behold the power of the master." Jacan and Ephrem regarded him with utmost calm, without the slightest sign of fear.

Santiago was the only one who could hear Colton murmur his next words. "Oh holy Master, let the fire of thy indignation spring forth from the tips of my fingers." He held both hands high, his fingers pointed at the prophets. He waited . . . and waited, yet nothing happened. He looked and saw the patient smiles of the men he yearned to incinerate. He repeated the same words and the same gesture, expecting flames to spring from his fingers and engulf his enemies, but still nothing happened.

Feeling abandoned by his guiding angel, Colton turned in a rage and snatched a rifle from the grip of a soldier standing a few feet away. His eyes almost completely blinded by tears, he fired on the prophets, ripping holes in their bodies and cutting down half of those standing close by. When he saw the prophets lying on the square in spreading pools of blood, he gloried in his success, shouting, "I've won. I've won," over and over. And as he expressed his joy, he cast his weapon away.

Then, all at once, a Jewish mob swooped down upon the seven assassins from all directions, bludgeoning them with clubs and stones. One old Jew swept up a rifle from the street and methodically shot rounds into the four soldiers. Colton lay on the stones of the square, senseless and bleeding. A few minutes later, he came to and tried to rise, but his battered body would not respond. Soon he heard another rush around him and another battle taking place. He didn't understand what was happening and fell unconscious again. What he didn't realize was that a band of Palestinians, a hundred strong, had overwhelmed the Israelis, killing most of them.

When the Palestinians checked the dead bodies, they recognized the two Jewish prophets and their joy was indescribable. At last the two men who had blasphemed Allah and had caused them so much anguish were dead. They kicked the corpses, reviled them, spit on them, and cursed them with eternal punishment. Let them lie in the streets of Jerusalem until their bodies rotted away and turned into dust. It would show the Israelis, and all men, what happens to infidels who thwart the designs of the great Allah.

Colton awoke once more and felt a sharp pain in his back. Turning his head upwards, he saw a small child jabbing a pointed stick into his spine. The child grinned as he poked and poked and poked. Tiring of the game, he left, and another child, almost a teenager, took up the task, stabbing him in the neck over and over with a fork. Colton prayed to his master for deliverance, but his glorious lord had already abandoned him. Before he died, the great false prophet lay there for two days, serving as a pincushion to nearly every Arab child who passed by.

The news of the death of the two prophets swept the city like wildfire, and the laments among the Jews was widespread and excruciating. Most declared in agony that all hope for Israel was lost, and now they faced nothing but destruction. Yet in spite of this terrible calamity, there was still something inside most Israeli hearts that propelled them into continuing the struggle, even without any hope of success.

⁂

David Omert, Chaim Yehoshua, and the Christophers had made their way to the temple with the help of armed guards. Now they sat together in the vestibule of that temple, discussing the news that had spread rapidly throughout the capital—the death of the prophets. Yet for some strange reason, in this sacred place, all the terrible sounds of war faded and seemed remote.

"The prophets knew what was going to happen to them, didn't they, David?" said John Christopher.

"Absolutely. Jacan whispered their secret to me before we left the compound. He said the Spirit had spoken to them, declaring that their mission was over and that soon the Lord would take them to himself. He said they were especially happy because the Spirit had told them the Lord was pleased with them. Jacan also said that recently they had added to their prophecy concerning the Messiah, telling the people the Messiah would come before the great war was over."

"David, is that why you brought us to this part of the city?" Mary asked. "You knew the time was near, and you wanted us to witness everything."

"That's true for the most part. But also, I knew UGOT's forces would destroy the compound within a day or two. Here we will be safer until the time comes. Not only because the Temple Mount is the most fortified and protected area in the city, but also because I knew that no power on earth could destroy the temple. Soon many others will join us, people who have a deep conviction regarding the purpose and sanctity of the temple. All we need to do is wait a few days."

"Don't you need to direct defense efforts?" asked Steven.

"Oh, I have a radio in case officers and officials need to contact me. They know the proper code. Essentially, however, there's little more I can do. The city is lost, and now everything is in the hands of the Savior."

"I've seen a lot of horror, pain, and death," Mary said, "yet in spite of that, my heart rejoices at the thought of what will soon take place."

David looked around at them with tenderness in his eyes. "Yes, those events will be earthshaking and will transform the world we know, both literally and morally. Transform it for the better."

"I only wish our sons, William and Daniel, were here." After saying that, Mary looked at her brothers-in-law, John and Paul, and remembered their sons. "And also our precious nephews, Cory, Michael, and Matthew. We don't even know if they are still alive." Her voice caught on the words, and she swallowed hard to maintain her composure. Steven put an arm around her.

"Well, I have good news for all of you," David said. "Ephrem told me just before we left the compound that Daniel is alive and well. He's been hiding out with some friends in the countryside some fifteen to twenty miles east of Haifa. And that's not all. This morning I checked on the progress of the battle on the Plain of Esdraelon and learned at the same time that the other four, William, Cory, Michael, and Matthew, are still alive and fighting UGOT's forces in the same theater. It's a very dangerous battle, but I have faith that soon the Lord himself will resolve it in our favor."

Steven felt immense relief at those assurances and saw the same relief on the faces of Mary and his brothers.

"Thank you for that," Paul said. "It makes me feel a lot better, and I'm sure all the Christophers here feel the same way. By the way, one of the friends hiding with Daniel wouldn't be Jarrad Babcock, would it?"

"Yes, I believe Ephrem did mention someone by that name." Paul gave a big sigh of relief.

⁂

During the first day after the death of the prophets, there were five massive earthquakes—tearing up streets and leveling buildings, monuments, and retaining walls—as if nature was protesting injustice. Millions of tons of bricks, stones, and cinder blocks fell upon weapon-carrying Arabs and foreign troops, killing thousands of them. But in spite of those calamities, the conquerors rejoiced and paid no heed to the damage, interpreting the quakes as divine approval of their great triumph. After three and a half days, the bodies of the two prophets still lay in the streets of Jerusalem, ridiculed and mocked by those they had frustrated.

Then in the afternoon of the fourth day, a loud voice was heard by all, loud enough to shake the earth. The celebrating crowds in the vicinity of the bazaar stopped their merriment all of a sudden, looking around for the source of the sound. The voice came again and the people looked upward, for it seemed to come from the sky above their heads.

This time they could distinguish the words of the voice clearly because the crowd was silent. "Come to me, my sons, for your reward awaits you."

At that point, the two prophets stood on their feet, their bodies restored in perfect form. They looked up and soon rose quickly into the heavens until they disappeared from sight. Seeing this miracle, the crowd fell to the earth weeping and wailing and gnashing their teeth. News of this wonder spread rapidly throughout the city, striking terror into the hearts of many.

UGOT's armies swept across the capital, driving the inhabitants eastward and killing almost seven hundred thousand of them in the process. At the same time, they breached the city's defenses on the northern and southern perimeters of the city, gradually forcing the three hundred thousand survivors into a bottleneck.

Around noon on the day after the prophets had been taken into heaven, the enemy forces began to storm the Temple Mount and its environs. Thousands of desperate people who had sought shelter in that area poured into the Kidron Valley between the Temple Mount and the Mount of Olives. They fled pell-mell into the valley, crying in terror and calling on God for help. Among the rushing throngs were David Omert and his family and friends, including the Christophers.

Yet there seemed to be no escape, except to the territory east of the Mount of Olives, where enemy forces had recently been wiped out by the great cloud of poisonous vapor and by Israeli artillery and laser fire. To make matters worse, the enemy was beginning to swarm into the northern and southern ends of the Kidron Valley, also called the Valley of Jehoshaphat, in an effort to block that route of escape. Indeed, it seemed that it would take a miracle to save the surviving Jewish hordes now, but only a few knew that the greatest day of wonders had finally arrived.

PART TWO

Behold, I come as a thief

(Revelation 16:15)

Chapter 16

❦

At the moment of utmost peril, a blinding light burst forth in the east, flashing instantly to the earth, and in that light, the Messiah appeared, descending to the Mount of Olives as he shouted mysterious words that reverberated across the surface of the planet. As those words echoed in every valley and mountain in Israel, they pierced the hearts and minds of the millions of people who had stopped to witness this great wonder. Then, suddenly, the earth began to shake, and the trembling gradually increased until it became so intense that it threw the inhabitants of the world to the ground.

As the people hugged the ground in terror, the earthquake became more and more violent, until every person felt as though this would be his last day alive. In reality, the quaking was much greater outside the boundaries of Israel, to the point that there were gigantic upheavals and cataclysms on every continent of the planet. The boundaries between the continental plates were broken up, and the great landmasses began to shift, moving closer and closer to one another. The process started with the first huge jolt and would persist for years, involving continual recurrent earthquakes, until one day the landmasses would form one great continent.

Most of the buildings and structures throughout the world crumbled to the ground, except those in New America and some in Jerusalem. And yet, the Jerusalem temple remained straight and firm. The great quake also split the Mount of Olives into two parts, the northern section moving north and the southern portion moving south. The result was a wide valley between the two sections. After that happened, the earthquakes suddenly stopped—but only temporarily. When the citizens of Jerusalem saw this great breach, they rose from the earth and rushed into the new gap and on to safety in the land to the east.

As David Omert, Chaim, and their American friends passed into the divide, they looked up and saw the Messiah standing upon the southern portion of the mount.

"Let's climb up to see him," David cried out.

The others agreed, and they began to ascend the hill, full of excitement. Steven glanced back and saw hundreds of Israelis following them. He surmised that many in the crowd had seen them start the climb and had decided to do the same. Ten minutes later, they drew near the Messiah, and he turned toward them with a kindly smile on his face.

"Ah, my faithful friends have come to see me," said the Messiah. He looked behind them at the crowd coming up the hill. "Followed by others, I see. All to fulfill the words of the scriptures . . ." He gazed at David for a moment, and then said, "Blessed are you, my servant, David, for you have believed in me without miracles, and you have done all I required of you. Blessed also is your loyal friend, Chaim Yehoshua." Next, he turned to Steven and Mary. "And you, Steven and Mary, I am proud of you for your obedience to the Father's words and for your courage in coming to this dangerous land."

At that point, the first Jewish survivors arrived and dropped down on their knees twenty feet away from the Anointed One, bowing their heads in reverence. Steven Christopher thought that they must truly be amazed that the Messiah was far more powerful and so much closer to divinity than any of them had ever imagined or been taught by Jewish traditions and the words of the rabbis. At last, one Jewish teenager dared to raise his head, and when he did, his eyes fastened on the marks in the hands and feet of the Messiah.

"Dear Master," the boy called, his eyes incredulous. "What are those scars I see in your hands and feet?"

The Messiah smiled at him benevolently. "These scars are from the wounds that I received in the house of my friends. I am he who was lifted up. I am Jesus Christ that was crucified. I am the Son of God."

Every person on the mount heard him clearly, and those words penetrated to the core of their beings. Then the Jews began to weep and lament uncontrollably, for they realized that their ancestors had crucified the long-awaited Messiah, and they themselves had ridiculed, denied, and persecuted the Christ, his teachings, and his followers.

"Now, my brothers and sisters," the Lord continued, "it is time for you to repent and strive for the remainder of your days to establish my kingdom and preach my word to your nation and to the world."

Jesus remained with them on the mount for another fifteen minutes and then commanded them to join their fellows in the lands beyond the Mount of Olives. He warned them that soon he would call down the judgments of God upon the wicked of Gog's armies. Reluctantly, the Jews, David, Chaim, Steven, and Mary descended the hill and joined the refugees traveling east.

When they had departed, Jesus turned toward Jerusalem, raised his arms high, and cried, "Oh my Father, I ask you to send fire and brimstone upon the wicked of this army that sought to destroy my people. Curse them with plagues of flies, maggots, and diseases that shall devour their flesh and dissolve their bones, for the appointed time of their judgment has come."

A short time later, great black clouds began to rush across the heavens from the west, covering the sun and darkening the entire region. Thousands of bolts of lightning struck the earth, accompanied by hail weighing as much as large stones. Soon the city and the entire nation of Israel were battered by bright beams of fire and by brimstone. The greatest miracle was that the destroying fire, the hail, the pestilence, and the intermittent earthquakes punished the wicked but spared the innocent. Within one hour, God destroyed over eighty percent of the invading armies.

On the Plain of Esdraelon also, the judgments of God fell upon the wicked of Gog's armies, destroying eighty-five percent of the evil combatants, only a few minutes before they were about to overrun and annihilate the surviving Israeli army.

Gerald Galloway and Lucienne Delisle heard and saw the destruction from a nearby hilltop. That's when Gerald knew his so-called master had failed him and that he was being punished by the real God, who was the true God Almighty. All his hopes and dreams had been destroyed in one hour, but he didn't feel sorry for what he had done, and he had no intention of weeping and asking for forgiveness. The only thing he really couldn't understand was why he and Lucienne had not been struck with disease or bolts of lightning, for he had witnessed thousands of his troops dying all around him, yet he and his mistress had not been touched. With stunned resignation, he led Lucienne to his headquarters and poured them a drink of fine wine.

"Gerald, I told you so many times," Lucienne said as she curled her long legs up on a comfortable couch.

At that moment, the earth shook violently, and they held on to the nearest support until it was over thirty seconds later.

"Like I said, I told you so. I gave you good advice dozens of times and you arrogantly rejected them out of hand. If you had listened to me, we would have won this war years ago." Her words infuriated him. Would she never stop with her all her prattle, her endless lies and accusations? "Most of all, Gerald, you won't get the fabulous reward you expected for murdering the world's Jews."

"What reward are you talking about?" he growled. "To rule the world without the interference of religious fanatics?"

"Yes, that of course. But the great one you treasure just as much, probably even more." He gazed at her quizzically. "Oh, Gerald, don't be so obtuse. Did you think you could keep your marvelous little secret from me, your lover?"

He continued to stare at her, uncomprehending. "What secret?"

"The one you always mumble about in the middle of the night when you're dreaming. I'm amazed that you don't realize I know everything about you. To me you're an open book. Anyway, you had this weird belief that your god would give you immortality—eternal life—here on earth when you had finally reached your goal of annihilating the Jews." Noticing the brown folder on the table, she retrieved it and sat down again. Gerald was so stunned by her revelation that he couldn't move or think clearly for a full minute. Then he heard her snickering.

After shaking his head, trying to clear his mind, he focused on her mouth and said, "What are you laughing about?"

Her tittering continued, and her eyes were wet with tears. After a few moments she controlled herself enough to say, "There's certainly no doubt that you're of noble birth, Gerald Galloway."

Seeing the documents in her hands, he lurched to his feet and seized them, glaring at her with hatred. He dropped back into his chair and examined the first page, which was a summary of the folder's contents. At the top of the sheet he read these words in bold: "99.98% probability of accuracy." As Lucienne's giggling persisted even louder, he read the results on the next line: "10% Germanic heritage, 5% French heritage, 85% Jewish heritage." Those last words stunned him, but he went on reading, looking for an explanation. The third line said, "Sixth generation parent, Aaron Goldberg, occupation farmer, legally changed his name to Aaron Galloway in . . ." He looked up and gazed blankly out the doorway of his camp tent, numb from shock.

"Do you hear laughter, Gerald?" Lucienne said snidely. "All this time I've been sleeping with a lousy Jew."

With calm determination, Gerald reached inside his coat and pulled out a small pistol, aimed it at Lucienne's startled face, and pulled the trigger, blowing away her jaw and the lower part of her face. After rocking backward against the couch, she fell forward onto the floor, bleeding profusely. "You'll never say another word to me again," he murmured, putting the gun back into his coat. He sat there for ten minutes as if paralyzed, watching her blood spread over his bright new carpet.

Then he started to think. *I must do something quickly. If the Jews find me, they'll tear me to pieces.* He couldn't bear the thought of shooting himself. What if his hand jerked at the last instant and he was only wounded? Think of the excruciating pain and the chance of becoming a vegetable. He might even lie there for hours in agony before he died.

Then suddenly, he knew what he had to do. He took a necklace from underneath his shirt and grabbed the small ampoule attached to it. He hesitated for over a minute, reluctant to damage his marvelous brain and end such a remarkable life. He closed his eyes, and vivid, unwanted memories of his past life shot through his mind like a horror film on fast forward: the wife he had cheated on so many times, the children and grandchildren he had neglected and betrayed, the thousands of people he had intimidated, the millions of Jews and Christians he had murdered, and so many other unspeakable acts.

Do it now, he thought. *The doctor said the suffering would only last a few seconds.* Finally, he put the ampoule into the back of his mouth and bit down on the glass vessel, releasing the potassium cyanide into his throat. Almost instantly, his brain exploded with pain, and he fell forward into the pool of Lucienne's congealing blood, his body convulsed by seizures.

The pain was terrible, his fear unbelievable. He struggled for breath but couldn't get air. He was so dizzy that the room spun around in a violent whirl, and his head hurt so bad that he thought it would burst.

It didn't stop anytime soon, but went on and on as if it would continue forever, but at last, ten minutes after ingesting the poison, the pain disappeared suddenly as he dropped into a coma. Fifteen minutes later his heart stopped beating.

⁓✻⁓

Shortly after Galloway's suicide, the heavenly destruction ceased, and the surviving inhabitants of Jerusalem began to return from the territory east of the capital. As they entered the Valley of Jehoshaphat, they saw the Messiah sitting on a great stone, looking toward them. The rumor that he was Jesus Christ had circulated quickly among the population, but only a small number had seen his scars and heard his testimony.

As a result, the multitude approached him with great trepidation. He stood as they slowly surrounded him, looking at his bare hands and feet. A few ventured close and reached toward him tentatively as if they wanted to touch him but were afraid. Yet when they saw him smile, they did touch him and felt the scars in his hands.

Many of them had seen him descend from heaven in a beam of blazing fire and had seen him split the mountain in half to create a passageway for their escape. All of them had felt the mighty quake as he touched the mount, and now in this valley they could see his glorious countenance and the exquisite beauty of his body. All these wonders compelled them to conclude that their Messiah was a divine being, and not just a great mortal prophet as all the rabbis had claimed throughout the ages.

That shocking revelation alone should have been enough to refute everything they had learned about the nature of God, for their religion had taught them that there was only one unique God who had no offspring, either mortal or divine.

The astonishment of this huge crowd became even greater when they saw the scars in his hands and feet, and they wondered about the rumors they had heard that the Messiah claimed to be Jesus Christ, the Son of God. Still, how could he be the Son of God? Their religion claimed that God had no son, and that since there was no Fall, there was no need for a savior to be crucified upon a cross for the redemption of mankind. And yet the proof to the contrary stood before them.

One tall Jewish soldier, with a gaping wound in his shoulder, stepped up to Jesus and said, "Great Messiah, are you truly Jesus Christ, who died on the cross? Are you the Son of God?"

"Yes, I am he." Jesus reached out and touched the man's shoulder, and instantly it was healed.

Others who surged forward from the back asked the same questions and received the same answer, and Jesus healed the injuries that many had suffered.

Before long, David, Chaim, Steven, and Mary appeared before him after working their way through the crowd. Steven thought the Lord looked just as he had at Adam-ondi-Ahman: young, tall, dark brown hair and beard, blue robe gathered at the waist with a white sash, exalted appearance. The only difference was that he wore no sandals and his feet were bare.

"I am glad you are here, David," said the Lord. "We must go and dedicate the temple."

"I'll be happy to lead you there," David replied.

The Lord threw him a little grin. "You think I don't know the way?"

"Oh! Of course you do."

The small group started off for the Temple Mount not far away. A mob of people followed them, every person straining to get a closer look at the Messiah. Jesus made a short detour to walk through the Garden of Gethsemane but seemed sad that it looked so different now. Steven watched him move across the rough terrain on bare feet, but the sharp rocks and undergrowth didn't seem to bother him or damage his feet. Instead, Steven got the impression that the Lord glided over the ground in such a way that his feet hardly seemed to touch it.

Finally, they reached the Golden Gate, the middle eastern entrance in the Old City Walls of Jerusalem. Just in front of the huge gate was a metal fence, and the gate itself had been sealed off in the sixteenth century by the Ottoman sultan, Suleiman the Magnificent. Legend had it that Suleiman had blocked the gate to prevent the Messiah from entering. To Steven Christopher, that was a perfect example of the ignorance the world had at that time as to the real identity of the Messiah.

"Do you want my men to break out the stones that seal the gate?" David asked.

"No, that would take too long, and we have very little time," Jesus said. "I'll take care of it." He raised his right hand and a fiery beam shot from it, disintegrating the metal fence and the stones blocking the gate.

"Yes, that is better!" David said, his mouth half open.

At Jesus's request, David told the crowd that only a small number of them could enter the area immediately surrounding the temple, for the number of people that area could accommodate was limited. The majority would have to wait outside. Jesus led the two Jewish leaders and the Americans onto the temple grounds. Looking around at the smaller crowd entering the grounds, Jesus pointed to three other Jews, who were obviously rabbis, and beckoned them forward. He told David he wanted them to be witnesses of the solemn ceremony he was about to perform. Next, Jesus escorted his select group into the temple itself.

As the small band of people stood around the Lord, he offered a prayer to his Father, and in his prayer he accepted the temple and dedicated it for the ordinances of the Melchizedek Priesthood. No longer would the Jewish temple be used for the ancient rituals of burnt offerings and sacrifices. No longer was there any need for the people to make sacrifices to typify the future sacrifice of God, for Christ had already made that sacrifice during his mortal sojourn upon the earth, and now he had come to his people, requiring a broken heart and a contrite spirit and obedience to the gospel law.

After this dedication, Jesus offered a prayer for the people of Israel that they might find peace and joy, and open their hearts to receive his ministers and accept his gospel. He gave David Omert the special commission to see that these things were carried out.

After they had walked out onto the courtyard of the temple, the throng grew silent in order to hear every word of the Messiah. Jesus looked around at the crowd and finally turned to the same group of witnesses he had escorted into the temple. "Now I must leave you and return to my Father," he said. "Soon I will return, in a day that you know not, to bring great judgment to the people of the earth, to accomplish the first resurrection of the latter days, and to usher in the great Millennium." At those words, he rose into the heavens in a shaft of light and disappeared from view. The crowd watched him go with cries of disappointment and tears in their eyes.

David Omert led his small party to his home in Jerusalem, hoping it had not been destroyed by bombs or earthquakes. He was especially worried about his family, for they had become separated as thousands of Israelis rushed blindly across the Kidron Valley to escape the enemy. At last he found his house in a neighborhood partially reduced to rubble. To his great relief, Edra, his wife, rushed out of the building and hugged him with tears of joy. David could see that their home had suffered a significant amount of damage. Heisa, Chaim's wife, was also there, but she had been seriously injured by falling debris. Fortunately, an American nurse had appeared from nowhere and had given her medical treatment, although the nurse had no antibiotics.

After the men kissed and embraced their wives, Chaim stayed by Heisa's bedside as David and Steven began to clear the home of wreckage. An hour later, as nighttime approached, John and Paul Christopher surprised everyone by popping their heads into a front window whose pane had been shattered. David gestured for them to enter, and Steven and Mary laughed as they hurried up to hug them.

The men joined forces to continue the cleanup while Mary and Edra prepared a quick, sparse meal. They had nothing but crackers with peanut butter and a little fruit juice. As they ate the food in Heisa's bedroom, sitting on chairs near the bed, they discussed the day's events by the light of an oil lamp.

"Did you all see the Lord?" David asked the others.

"Paul and I did," said John, "but it was from a distance. We tried to climb the mount, but there were too many people in the way. By the time we got halfway up the hill, the people came rushing down, and we were pretty much swept down the hill and into the valley."

"Heisa and I didn't even make it out of the city," Edra said. "Too much fighting going on, and Palestinians everywhere looking for Jews instead of escaping the city. We decided to work our way back here and hope for the best. Later however, we heard lots of people running back into the city, talking about the Messiah. Some of them said the Messiah declared to everyone that he was Jesus Christ, the Son of God. Of course, thanks to what David and Chaim had taught us many years ago, we already knew that."

"Were they glad or angry?" asked Steven.

"Some seemed happy while others were ranting. A few said they refused to believe it was the Messiah and especially that it was Jesus Christ. They were mostly orthodox Jews."

"So they saw the light and the appearance of the divine being?" asked David.

"Probably most of them. How could they miss it? We even saw it from here, and the earthquake hit at the same moment."

"Did you hear any of the religious Jews say who they thought descended upon the mount?" Paul asked.

"Yes. Some said it was a mighty angel, and others thought it was God himself."

David frowned with displeasure. "Obviously those people weren't near Christ when he showed the people his hands and feet and declared he was Christ, the Son of God."

"Hopefully, they'll come around eventually," Steven said. "It has to be immensely hard for them. To admit that the divine visitor was Jesus Christ is tantamount to saying their ancestors crucified the Messiah."

Paul shrugged his shoulders. "I don't get it. Why do they think God commanded the ancient Israelites to offer up all those burnt offerings and sacrifices? Their own version of the scriptures says God commanded sacrifices as early as the days of Cain and Abel."

David popped his last cracker into his mouth. "The original meaning of sacrifices become lost because of the sins and rebellions of the ancient Israelites. They lost the truth that the sacrifices were meant as a type or semblance of the future sacrifice of the Son of God for the redemption of mankind. The Lord wanted Israel to look forward to that great day and never forget it."

"What do the rabbis say today?" John asked. "What do they think the sacrifices were for?"

"They claim that sacrifices were primarily a means of bringing the people closer to God. In other words, sacrifices served the same purpose as praising God, giving thanks, and prayer. The ancient rabbis began to teach that sacrifices were only one way of obtaining forgiveness. The other ways were prayer, repentance, and doing good works."

"The ancient rabbis also taught the necessity of repentance and good works?" asked Paul.

"Yes," said David.

"Well, if the ancient Israelites could obtain forgiveness by the deeper and more personal means of repentance, prayer, and good works, why did they still need sacrifices?" Paul said.

David smiled, knowing Paul had asked the central question. "Like I said, the early Israelites lost the truth that sacrifices had a very special meaning, beyond the idea of repentance for personal infractions of the law. They lost the knowledge that the sacrificial lamb was a symbol of the Lord's infinite and willing sacrifice for the salvation of the world." David's explanation seemed convincing to everyone, and no one said anything for a while.

Mary walked over to the bed and checked Heisa, who had been listening to the conversation. "She looks a lot better. I changed her bandages before we ate, and the wounds seemed to be healing." Returning to her chair, Mary said, "I have a question about something that has been bothering me."

"What's that?" asked David.

"The Bible talks about a great river of water that will spring from the temple at Jerusalem and flow east and then south until it reaches the Dead Sea. Once there, those holy waters are supposed to 'heal' the Dead Sea. I assume that means the extremely salty water of the sea, which is really a lake, will be turned into fresh water. This is predicted to happen in the last days, but I saw no river flowing from the temple. So, I'm wondering what that scripture means."

"Yes, it's found in Ezekiel, chapter forty-seven," David replied. "I believe that prophecy is symbolic. The Dead Sea represents the blindness of latter-day Israel, and the temple represents the truth of God. The river is the word of God, which leaves the temple and enters the hearts of the people and enlightens them."

"So the whole thing isn't literal, but a metaphor?" Paul asked.

"That's what I believe. The only way the Dead Sea could literally become a body of fresh water is for a canal to be dug or a deep fissure to be created by natural phenomena to allow the Dead Sea waters to flow the seventy miles to the Gulf of Aqaba."

David noticed that Mary appeared to be satisfied with that answer, but again she raised her hand. David grinned at her wonderful curiosity. "Yes, Mary, another question?"

"Well, was this visit of Jesus the Second Coming? I thought that at the Second Coming he would come with the hosts of heaven to the whole world, and that the wicked of the earth would be burned."

"I think Steven should answer that one," David said. "He's better versed in gospel doctrine than I am."

Steven's stomach started to burn. This wasn't the first time Mary had put him on the spot about the Second Coming. "I don't have the perfect answer. All I can do is give my opinion."

"Shoot, brother," Paul said with a slight smirk.

"Well, in Christ's earlier visits, he restored truth, organized his kingdom, and blessed his people. However, one of the main purposes of what we call the Second Coming is to destroy the wicked. In the first stage of his Second Coming, which just took place, he punished the wicked armies of Gog who were seeking to destroy Israel. In the second stage, he'll destroy the rest of the earth's wicked."

John handed Steven a cracker and said, "Good summary, Steve. Since I agree with you, I'll give you my last cracker." Everyone laughed and seemed to accept Steven's review.

Afterwards, they discussed what Israel should do now that it had been freed from UGOT's armies. David felt that the remaining enemy forces would be so disheartened by their defeat and the death of most of their leaders, they would evacuate Palestine with their tails between their legs. Then Israel would be faced with the job of burying the dead, cleansing the war-torn land, and healing itself spiritually with God's help.

They had been hiding in Ruth Tishler's childhood grotto since the middle of September of the preceding year, over seven months. Both Rachel Salant and Ruth Tishler had fully recovered from their wounds. Nearly every night, as soon as the sun was down, Daniel and Jarrad had left the cave to procure food and water, always proceeding cautiously, freezing in place whenever they heard movement or saw silhouettes in the darkness—most likely UGOT soldiers or Palestinians in search of Israelis. The two men were armed but knew they needed to avoid detection or confrontation because the enemy could easily overwhelm and kill them quickly. Fortunately, when the moon appeared from behind the clouds from time to time, they could see well enough to make their way.

Daniel and Jarrad knew that the most likely places to find food and supplies were the many Israeli farms in the region. But by now, those farms had no doubt been occupied by the enemy after murdering the owners or driving them out. So the two Americans dropped to the ground some distance from each farm and crawled forward on their bellies, maneuvering toward the area of the barn.

Sometimes they found small quantities of fruits and vegetables stored in underground cellars, bags of oatmeal, or eggs in nearby chicken coops, but most often they found nothing. In that event, they approached the farmhouse itself, but after a few nights, they stopped doing that when they discovered the houses were of enemy troops, sometimes sleeping but more often playing cards as they drank themselves into a stupor.

However, in the last few days a series of earthquakes had begun to strike the entire region, and the refugees feared that their shelter might cave in on them, but each of the quakes had stopped a short time after they had started, doing no more than covering them with thick layers of dust. Luckily, the cave remained basically sound.

Then on the fourth day a quake struck that was so powerful it threw them to the ground and collapsed the wall at the rear of the cave, partly sealing off the main chamber and blocking a portion of the exit tunnel. They didn't realize it, but the first quakes had occurred at the death of the two prophets in Jerusalem, and the greater one hit when the Messiah descended to the Mount of Olives.

They worked hard and cleared the tunnel, hoping the worst was over. Daniel and Jarrad continued their foraging expeditions but returned empty-handed several nights in a row. They were shocked, however, when each night they discovered the grisly sight of at least a dozen dead Palestinians or soldiers dressed in strange uniforms. It was only by striking matches that they could more or less identify the corpses.

On returning to the grotto, they mentioned these terrible discoveries to Rachel and Ruth, but no one knew for sure what was going on. Jarrad thought that maybe an Israeli army had entered the area and was systematically decimating its enemies. Rachel suggested that perhaps a terrible plague had struck the region, visited upon the wicked by God himself. Seeing that the men had not been able to find food, Ruth told them that their only hope was for her to lead them to Baruch Village.

Jarrad eyed Ruth as if she were crazy. "You must be kidding. That town has to be packed with UGOT troops and Palestinians. They'd kill us on sight."

"Not necessarily. When I lived there, nearly all the Palestinians were Israeli citizens. They had some complaints about Israeli favortism, but they always said it would be much worse if they had to live under Palestinian rule or to live in an Arab country. They hated the intolerant Arab religious leaders who wanted to rule over them and force them to live by Shariah law."

"What's Shariah law?" Daniel asked.

"It's the strict Islamic law that governs the public and private lives of Muslims. Many of those Palestinians were good friends of my family and may give us food if they still live there."

"I still say it's too dangerous," Jarrad insisted. "Think of all the dead bodies out there."

"I be going with you," Rachel said. "I be starving to death and willing to be doing most anything to get something to eat."

"But you're weak from a lack of food," Daniel said, his lips tight. "I think you should stay here."

"I am being fine now. Besides, Ruth is being weak too and she is going with you." She set her jaw firmly and stared Daniel down, daring him to refuse.

"Well, I suppose it's okay if we can find someone who remembers Ruth," he replied.

Since they hadn't eaten for days, they decided they had no choice except to follow Ruth's suggestion. The following night, they set out for the village, and in the course of feeling their way around in the dark, they stumbled across decaying bodies every few minutes. They steered clear of them as best they could for fear of catching some lethal disease but still forged ahead, trying to find the village. The trip was especially unnerving since—strangely enough—they didn't spot a single active enemy patrol.

When Ruth was a small girl she had made the trip from the grotto to the town in about twenty minutes, but tonight it took almost three hours. It would have taken them even longer if Ruth had not recognized several familiar landmarks.

After they finally reached the town, Ruth led them behind a row of houses situated on the main road through town.

"Lights are on in most of these houses," Jarrad said. "That's got to be a good sign."

"Yes, it is," Ruth said, smiling. She stopped at the sixth house. "These people used to be good friends of ours, and I often played with their two little girls. Stay here, and I'll go around to the front and knock on the door. Don't wait for me if I'm gone more than half an hour."

As soon as she left, Jarrad said with tight lips, "Yeah, right. We're going to leave her here."

They waited for at least thirty-five minutes and were beginning to fret. "Let's go, Daniel," Jarrad said. "Rachel, you stay at the back corner of the house and cover our retreat if necessary."

"But I want to get in on the action," Rachel complained. "You're going to need my gun in this action."

"Sorry to pull rank on you, but that is my order," Jarrad replied firmly. "You'll help us more by covering our retreat." As a lieutenant, Jarrad outranked Rachel, who was only a sergeant.

Rachel scowled but nodded her compliance. She carried an M16 rifle and was an expert markswoman. She felt weak and trembly from a lack of food but still hoped she could shoot straight.

The men worked their way around to the front door. When they reached it, Jarred tapped fairly hard on the door with the butt of his rifle. The door flew open and two Palestinians—one extremely tall and muscular—stood facing them, their rifles pointed at their heads.

"Drop your guns. Hands up!" shouted the tall Arab. Daniel and Jarrad let their weapons slip to the ground and raised their hands. Without warning, two other Arabs appeared from each side of the doorway and forced them into the front room. Daniel saw Ruth tied to a chair at the back of the room with tape over her mouth. Her tear-stained eyes darted back and forth, signaling both fear and guilt.

"Now we have foreigners to torture along with the Jew," said the leader. "And in the name of mighty Allah, we will do it! You must be fools to think you could come here." In the corner of the room, Daniel saw three dead bodies—all Arabs—covered with blood. He suspected they were the Palestinian owners of the dwelling, an elderly couple and a middle-aged woman, no doubt executed by the intruders.

The Arabs forced their hostages onto a couch and began to congratulate each other for their good fortune. Then while one held his gun on the Americans, the others debated on how to make their prisoners suffer as much as possible.

The heated argument continued for quite some time, and the guard grew less vigilant, grinning in varying degrees as his comrades proposed a litany of creative methods of torture. Gradually, he focused more and more on the debate between his comrades, paying less attention to the captives on the couch. Finally, Jarrad sprang from his seat and seized the guard's weapon with such violence that he knocked the Arab to the floor. Then Jarrad swung the rifle toward the other three captors, who scattered in all directions in a desperate effort to reach their weapons. Jarrad wounded two of them with a burst of gunfire, while the third man scooped up his rifle and returned fire, hitting Jarrad in the stomach.

Daniel also leaped from the couch, charged the third Arab, picked him up bodily and slammed him against the wall, knocking him unconscious. The man who had been guarding them pulled a knife, jumped on Jarrad, who lay moaning on the floor, and stabbed him several times in the chest and shoulders. In spite of his wounds, Jarrad reached up with his right hand, seized the knife-wielding fist, turned the knife toward his attacker, and pushed the blade into the man's neck. The Arab died immediately. Rachel heard the sounds of battle but decided to remain where she was as Jarrad had instructed.

Meanwhile, the two wounded Arabs rushed Daniel as one, high on adrenalin or drugs, knocked him to the floor, and reached for their own knives to finish him off. At that point, Jarrad, bleeding profusely, rolled over in great pain, grabbed a rifle lying nearby and pumped several rounds into both of Daniel's attackers, killing them outright. That ended the battle.

Daniel hurried to Ruth and released her from her bonds with his knife. "Go, Ruth," he yelled. "I'll take care of Jarrad." As Ruth charged out the door, he went to Jarrad and started to throw him over his shoulder, but Jarrad demanded to stay on his feet. As they stumbled through the door, the Arab that Daniel had thrown against the wall regained consciousness, crawled to a rifle lying close to the people he had slaughtered earlier, shook his head several times as if trying to clear his head, struggled to his feet, and staggered toward the door in pursuit of the two Americans.

After leaving the building, the Arab saw the Americans forty yards off, one of them half dragging the other across the road. He drew a bead on them and hesitated as he tried to steady his aim. Suddenly, there was a blast, and he was hurled to the ground as Rachel's bullet hit him in the side of the head. When the other Palestinians, who were approaching from their homes, saw this, they turned and ran for cover. Rachel overtook Daniel and Jarrad and helped them disappear into the darkness.

They did escape, but Jarrad died on the way. The next morning, they buried him a hundred yards from the grotto. With tears in their eyes, each of the three survivors said a prayer, praising Jarrad for his heroism. Without his brave actions they all might have been killed. They decided they would leave for Jerusalem that very day.

Chapter 17

❦

There were still millions of enemy troops in the land of Israel, but they set out for their various countries immediately after their ignominious defeat and the death of their commanders. Most of them rejoiced openly when they heard that the great tyrant, Gerald Galloway, was dead and his oppressive worldwide government no longer existed. Moreover, all their invincible machines and instruments of war had been obliterated by heavenly balls of flaming fire, so they fled on foot, fearing that further judgments might overtake them at any time. Most of all, they feared the terrible plagues that had consumed the flesh of millions of their comrades.

When David and Chaim learned of Galloway's cowardly suicide, they were glad that he could no longer torture their people. From all the reports he had received, David surmised that the great War of Armageddon had resulted in the death of almost three hundred million human beings worldwide, with far more wounded or maimed.

Escorted by a troop of soldiers, David and Chaim toured the vicinity of the capital, and everywhere they looked, they saw rotting corpses. David knew that soon the bodies would become a national health hazard. Most of the cadavers were covered with maggots, and starving wild animals gorged themselves on the polluted flesh. He quickly commanded his troops, and even civilians, to begin burying the Israeli dead and burning the bodies of enemy troops. In two dozen sites, they made great piles of weapons and began disposing of them. The parts made of wood were burned, and those made of metal were melted down to form ingots. The disposal of the bodies took several months and that of the weapons even longer.

Earthquakes continued to strike, sometimes several times a day, often causing significant damage. After consulting the scriptures, Steven told David that he believed the quakes were mostly due to the movement of the continents drawing closer together. His belief was later confirmed when reports began to come in from Israeli scientists that showed New America was already several hundred miles closer to Europe and Africa than before. Many Christian scholars in Israel claimed that soon there would be only one great landmass and a single mighty ocean.

A short time later, Israeli scientists reported to President Omert that the length of the days and nights were gradually becoming shorter, and they reckoned that a full day was now only a little less than twenty-three hours long. They also noticed at night that the visible stars in the heavens were gradually forming new patterns, rendering invalid current astronomical charts. Both day and night, the people saw thousands of small particles enter the atmosphere from space, most of them disintegrating in bright flashes of light but some striking the earth. Fortunately, most of the strikes took place outside the borders of Israel.

Two weeks after Steven and Mary had been given refuge in David Omert's home, they went outside one morning and sat on a bench in front of the building. Steven opened his scriptures to a passage he had marked and said, "I found a scripture that might interest you. It's in Isaiah 13:13. The Lord says, 'Therefore I will shake the heavens, and the earth shall remove out of her place, in the wrath of the Lord of hosts, and in the day of his fierce anger.' This passage refers to the last days and may explain the geophysical changes we're seeing."

"Perhaps," Mary said, "but frankly, the whole thing scares me half to death."

"Well, it tells me that the next phase of the Second Coming is very close."

Mary put her head on his shoulder. "I know these happenings are supposed to be miraculous and wonderful, but for some reason, I still dread them."

Steven put his arms around her. "I know what you mean. The evidence seems to show that the earth has left its normal orbit and is traveling to a different place in the galaxy. At least the sun and the moon are still with us."

Mary pulled away from him. "A different place in the galaxy! What's causing it? We still feel the force of gravity and have air to breathe."

"I don't know what's causing it, but I feel that God is supporting us.

All these strange things seem to be progressing rapidly and yet we're still okay."

That night, while Mary and Steven cuddled in a makeshift bed they had set up in one of David's spare bedrooms, she told him about something she had been worried about for some time. "I wish I knew how William and Daniel were. How can we ever find them when chaos and disruption are everywhere? They could be dead, or lying somewhere hurt really bad, and we wouldn't even know it."

"I'm sure they're fine. Both of them are very resourceful. Do you want to leave Jerusalem tomorrow to search for them?"

"Yes, I do!" she said with excitement.

"Okay, tomorrow I'll tell David that we intend to do that. We'll see if he has any objections. Actually, it would also be a good time to begin our journey back to Zion. I feel it's important we return as soon as possible."

"But how can we? It's such a dangerous trip and—"

"We'll solve the problems as they come. I'm certain we won't be alone. There should be hundreds of Americans—perhaps thousands—already on their way back. Don't worry. We won't leave Israel unless our sons are with us."

Mary sighed and kissed him. "That makes me feel better. I love you, sweetheart."

The next day during a breakfast of oatmeal and rice milk, Steven looked up at David and said, "David, I need to ask your advice about something very important."

"Certainly, I'd be glad to help."

"Mary and I are very worried about our sons, and we know that John and Paul here are just as concerned about theirs. We'd like to find all of them. Didn't you tell us a couple of weeks ago that Ephrem said Daniel and Jarrad were still alive and in hiding in northern Israel?"

"Yes, that's what Ephrem told me."

"Did he say where in northern Israel?"

"No, but it's unlikely they're still in the same place. They may even be on their way here."

"That's true. And didn't you say you received reports indicating that William, Cory, and Matthew were fighting on the Plain of Esdraelon?"

"That's right. We now know that the Lord himself destroyed UGOT's forces there before they could completely overcome our troops, so their chances of being okay are very good. By the way, Steven, the Plain of Esdraelon is very close to where Daniel and Jarrad were reported to be. The two groups couldn't have been more than ten or fifteen miles away from each other. Do you want to travel to that area to find your sons?"

"Yes, we can't leave Israel without them."

"Of course not." David paused, then added, "So I take it you've decided to return to New America."

"We feel sad to leave Israel, but we all sense an urgent need to return home before the next series of events take place."

David stared at them intently for a while. "Of course. I understand how you must feel. When do you want to leave?"

"Today, if possible." Chaim and the two Jewish wives looked at them sadly but said nothing.

"All right," David replied. "Let me make arrangements. I'll find transportation, gather some supplies, and assign a troop of soldiers to accompany you."

"A troop!" Mary said. "That many?"

"It's still dangerous out there," Chaim said. "We haven't caught all the Palestinian guerillas."

"Only about forty or fifty men," David said. "I'll instruct them to escort you as far as necessary to ensure your safety. My guess is that large numbers of Americans will join you before you leave the borders of Israel. There's always safety in numbers. Even though it's late spring and the weather should be good, the climate has been changing radically, becoming more and more extreme. I guess it's a sign of the times."

"Indeed it is," Steven said as tears welled in his eyes. He hesitated, finding it hard to express himself. "I can't thank you enough. We're grateful for everything you've done for us."

David nodded. "You're more than welcome. After you find your children and Jarrad, go to Haifa. I'll arrange to have a plane ready to fly you and your group to your home in America. All you'll have to do is give the airport officials your name."

"Thank you again," Steven said, wiping away his tears. He looked at Mary and saw her face wet with tears.

David paused and looked down at his bowl, struggling to control his feelings. He cleared his throat and said, "It's . . . it's me who should thank you, and all your American boys, for your sacrifices in our behalf. And also your wonderful nursing corps." He couldn't say more for half a minute. Then he went on, "Oh, there's something else. I understand Daniel was traveling with one of our female soldiers. Her name is Rachel Salant, if I remember correctly. She might be a lead to help you find Daniel."

By two o'clock, David had made all the arrangements: ten vehicles, including two small transport trucks, a light APC, three pickups, and four cars; enough rations and supplies to last two weeks; and forty-two soldiers equipped with grenades and M16 rifles.

As Steven, Mary, John, and Paul said good-bye to their Israeli friends, David gave them suggestions on how to spot their children on the road as they traveled north, and he promised that if their boys turned up in Jerusalem, he'd send them on to Haifa as quickly as possible.

At last David turned to Steven and said, "By the way, I forgot to tell you something the Lord said."

"What's that?" Steven said, very curious.

"He said I shouldn't worry about trying to do temple ordinances or establishing his Church in Israel at this time. All I should do is testify to my people that he—Jesus Christ—is the Messiah, the Son of God, and the Savior of the world. He stated that some day soon he would send those who had the knowledge and authority to show Israel the way concerning the ordinances of the Melchizedek priesthood and the building of his kingdom here in this land. Those people would come from the American Zion."

Steven nodded and smiled. Just before they climbed into the vehicles provided by David, the Americans gave their Jewish friends one last hug, and the small caravan began to make its way north through the tortuous streets of the city.

The thousands of weary soldiers wended their way through the Taurus Mountains in southern Turkey through a pass called the Cilician Gates. After their terrible defeat in Israel and the destruction rained upon them from the heavens, the only thing they could do now was move blindly and uncertainly away from the devastation in hopes of finding a safe haven. So they directed their march northeast toward home, not knowing the best roads to follow.

Among them were men from many nations, including Spain, Portugal,

France, Italy, and Germany. All they had seen in Israel was death and horror as thousands of their comrades-in-arms had died all around them from lightning, hail, fiery stones, and body-consuming diseases.

They were bruised, battered, hungry, and soaked to the bone, for a torrential rain had been attacking them for an hour as if to punish them for their sins, and they had no protective coverings to ward off the onslaught.

Then it got worse.

Giant chunks of hail began to pummel them. For the first five minutes, the pieces of hail were small, but as they increased in size, some weighing eighty pounds or more, the men rushed to the sides of the road for any cover they could find, hiding under trees, ledges, road signs, and abandoned vehicles. But the hail seemed to seek them out, and when it found them, it was as if they had been struck by large-caliber bullets.

After fifteen minutes, the hail stopped, but it had taken its toll—a fifth of their number had been maimed or killed. The survivors trudged back onto the ravaged road and continued their way, still assailed by the rain. Finally, the road turned downwards, and the leaders saw a pleasant valley below, filled with bright sunlight. It was only two or three miles away. Ignoring the rain, they picked up their pace, hurrying toward this unexpected paradise.

As they continued on, their hearts full of hope now, they suddenly heard a great roar and a rush from both sides of the road. Millions of tons of mud rushed toward them like gigantic tidal waves and buried them instantly in a crushing tomb. The mudslide killed every man in the first half of the column. The mud-splattered survivors milled around angrily and debated for quite some time on what they should do. Many cursed God for their evil luck, for the only thing they could do was backtrack and find another way through the mountain range.

Millions of other ragtag armies met similar calamities as they retreated, striving to reach their homelands. But they weren't the only people experiencing disasters because across the globe God made his wrath felt against all nations. There were devastating earthquakes, violent rainstorms, hail, floods, mudslides, exploding volcanoes, great storm surges, tsunamis, tornadoes, thousands of celestial projectiles pounding the earth, and widespread plagues.

Mankind also contributed to the desolation, for everywhere there was rioting, looting, mayhem, wanton killings, destruction of property, immoral acts flaunted in public, the open mocking of God and of believers in God, attacks against authority, and every evil imaginable. Even the police and armed forces participated in these vile actions. However, in all these wicked nations, there were thousands of pockets of decent people who resisted the flood of evil and violence occurring around them. In order to survive, they found it necessary to join together in small groups for mutual protection in hidden safe places.

To a lesser degree, New Zion also suffered from natural disasters, which took the lives of many, yet the people in general remained steadfast in adversity and obedient to the laws of the gospel. The other nations that had sent troops to help Israel—the United Kingdom, Canada, and Australia—also felt the chastening hand of God, but nothing like the rest of the world. There were also rebellious people in those nations who tried to disrupt society, but they were controlled by the law and the decent citizens.

The Christophers had been traveling in a car for two days as a part of a small caravan heading north, and yet they had only covered fifty miles. Most of the highways and roads in Israel had been demolished by missiles and bombs, and at times they had to stop and find cover when they were fired upon by surviving bands of Palestinian guerillas. When that happened, their guards leaped from their vehicles and advanced on foot against the attackers, driving them off quickly. Luckily, they saw no UGOT forces, and they concluded that the remaining troops had already left the country.

Nevertheless, the trip was difficult for other reasons too. Everywhere they looked, as far as the eye could see, they beheld dead bodies covering the land like some grotesque, unnatural blanket. And thousands of burned-out vehicles of all kinds. Plumes of smoke rose in numerous places, and the travelers knew that each one represented a team of Israelis who were incinerating human and animal corpses. The only consolation they had received so far was the fifty-three other Americans who had joined their caravan, most of them soldiers but also a few nurses.

"How are we ever going to find our sons in all this terrible chaos?" Mary asked.

"I wish I knew," Steven said.

"We could spend weeks or months trying to find them," Paul added.

No one said anything for several minutes, but at last John spoke up. "Well, we know in general where both groups were supposed to be located, and we're making for that area now. I figure we have about twenty-five to thirty miles to go. From now on, why don't we look for Israeli soldiers, especially officers, and ask them if they might know our sons' whereabouts?"

"It's a long shot, but I can't think of anything better," Paul said.

"I think it's a wonderful idea, John," Mary said. "I've been praying and I'm sure the Lord will help us."

Within the next twenty miles, they stopped and questioned over thirty Israeli soldiers, but no one recognized the people in the photos they were shown. In spite of that dismaying disappointment, each of the Christophers affirmed several times they'd never leave Israel without finding their sons and Jarrad. They continued on, swaying back and forth on the pitted road, when they heard shouting. As Steven slowed the car, they searched around for the source of the clamor and finally caught sight of a half dozen soldiers stumbling toward them from the right side of the highway.

They didn't recognize any of them because of the soldiers' dirt-besmirched faces, disheveled hair, gaunt bodies, and tattered uniforms. By the time the soldiers reached the car, Steven had brought it to a complete stop. A familiar face poked inside the open front window. It was Daniel Christopher, alive and seemingly well. Behind him were Rachel, William, Cory, Michael, and twenty-year-old Matthew. The parents piled out of the vehicle, and they and their sons joyously spent several minutes hugging and kissing one another while Rachel stood off to the side.

"How did you all join up like this?" John asked.

"Well," William said, "when the boys and I were resting by the campfire and discussing the thousands of fireballs that fell from the sky and wiped out UGOT's forces, two beat-up soldiers wandered into camp and spied us. I was kind of shocked when one of the mangy fellows walked up and threw his arms around me with big tears in his eyes. It took me awhile to recognize my own little brother." He gestured toward Rachel. "The second grungy soldier turned out to be this beautiful young woman." The "boys" mentioned by William were Cory, Michael, and Matthew.

"Hey!" Paul exclaimed. "That's certainly a blessing for us. We thought it would take weeks to round you all up."

Steven looked at Rachel and motioned for her to draw closer. "And what is the name of the beautiful young woman?"

"This is my fiancée, Rachel Salant," Daniel declared proudly. "Actually, she's also my sergeant. We've been hiding out together for the last seven months." Daniel introduced his parents and uncles to Rachel.

"Where's Jarrad?" Paul asked. "I heard he was with you."

Daniel's face fell and he couldn't speak for a long moment. Finally, he explained what had happened, and everyone was stunned into silence. Paul looked devastated because Jarrad had been his best friend since they were teenagers. His only consolation was that Jarrad had saved his nephew's life and probably the lives of the two female soldiers. Steven put his arm around Paul and assured him that it wouldn't be long before he saw Jarrad again in the flesh.

"Daniel, you mentioned another girl in your story of the grotto," Mary said. "Ruth Tishler, if I remember. Where is she now?"

"She left us yesterday to join a platoon of Israeli soldiers," Rachel said, speaking with greater confidence now because Daniel had been giving her regular lessons in English.

They held up the entire caravan for another twenty minutes, catching up on all the events each of them had experienced since they had separated a year earlier. At the end of all this, Steven said, "We need to move out now. I'm sure you'll all be happy to know that David Omert has made arrangements for us to fly from Haifa to New America." The young people cheered and gave each other the high five.

After Mary made sure the emaciated youths were provided with all the food they could eat, Steven quickly found places for them in the other vehicles. After that, he walked to the front of the caravan and instructed the lead vehicle to head directly for Haifa.

One of the first things Steven did when they reached Haifa was to contact David Omert and obtain his permission to allow Rachel Salant to be released from duty with the IDF and travel with them to New America. David graciously gave Rachel the permission she sought.

The C-130J Super Hercules military transport plane flew eighty-two Americans from Haifa to the Dublin Airport and, after refueling, continued on to New York City. Fortunately, the plane had no problem flying this longer second stage because the movement of the continents had reduced the normal distance of thirty-two hundred miles by four hundred miles.

Steven assured Rachel that the president of Zion, Douglas Christopher, would give her special permission to become a legal citizen of New Zion. From New York, they traveled in trucks to various spots in New America.

Steven and Mary were grateful they had not met any serious difficulties or obstacles during the trip, and they rejoiced at finally being in the safety of their own home. Of course, it helped to be friends with the principal leaders of two nations. They spent the following week doing nothing but resting and recovering from the traumas of the last year. But during the fourth week of May, Steven resumed his duties as the governor of Missouri, and Mary set out to visit her friends in order to tell them the story of their experiences in Israel.

At this time also, Rachel Salant was baptized and a few days later, she and Daniel were married in the temple at Independence. Steven remembered a time when those newly baptized would have to wait a year before being sealed in the temple, but that rule had been for different times.

As the weeks passed, hundreds of Americans arrived from Israel, and one of them was Ruther Johnston. Ruther soon visited Steven and Mary and, after hugging them, reported that Mosheh Lazar and Yaakov Raphan had decided to stay in Israel to help rebuild the country.

Chapter 18

On Friday of the second week of June, Steven and Mary held a family reunion at their home, also inviting Andrea Warren, Andrea's family, and Ruther Johnston. Ruther had told Steven that after his experiences in Israel, he was thinking about joining the Church before it was too late. After all, he declared, he wasn't getting any younger. When they had finished dinner, they sat down in the living room to catch up on past experiences. Everyone was especially interested in the appearance of Christ on the Mount of Olives. Those who had not been present at that time wanted to know all the details, including every word that the Lord had spoken and what he looked like. However, the conversation soon turned to the future.

"I understand that the next time Jesus comes it will be to the whole world," Andrea said. She looked at Steven anxiously. "When do you think that will occur, Steve?"

"Well, like they say, no one knows the hour or the day. I asked the prophet the same thing yesterday, and that's the answer he gave me. He also told me that the Second Coming was fixed in time and had been chosen before the foundations of the earth were laid. Only the Father knows the exact time."

"Not even Jesus?" asked Rachel.

"No, only the Father."

Andrea frowned. "But don't the scriptures say the elect won't be deceived? I take that to mean that the righteous—or some of them—will have a general idea about when it will happen."

"What makes you think I might know? I don't consider myself righteous."

"Listen up, Steve," Ruther said with a touch of impatience. "Yuh might as well own up to them gifts the good Lord done gave yuh. You're a dern sight more prophetic than most people I knows."

"Yeah, big brother," Paul quipped. "You know we depend on you for such things."

Steven was amazed at Paul's statement because Paul had always insisted that he could figure things out, more or less, just as well as Steven.

"I think Jesus will come this summer," Mary declared boldly. "It's a strong feeling I have."

"What do you base that on?" John asked.

Mary paused, looked at Steven, and seeing his encouraging smile, went on. "Look, we know he comes shortly after his visit to Jerusalem and after the destruction of Gog's armies, and we know the world is 'ripe in iniquity' as the scriptures say. So everything is in place. Besides, something in my heart tells me it won't be long."

"I have the same feeling," said Tania Christopher, John's wife. "What do you think, Steve?"

"Well, I admit I've been having a pretty vivid dream lately. I don't know if it means anything or not."

"Describe it for us," said Maryann, Paul's wife.

Steven thought for a moment about how he could best describe his recurring dream. "I see an unbelievably bright light in the sky. Somehow I realize it's not the sun, but in the middle of that light, I see a strange phenomenon." He described the unusual thing as best he could. "I gaze at it for a while, and the light surrounding it doesn't hurt my eyes. Yet the air seems quite hot. Soon I glance at the scene around me and I see thousands of trees, very green and bearing fat golden fruit. That's it, the same dream every time."

"The hot air you describe shows it's summertime," said Mary. "Just as I thought."

"And the green trees bearing fruit suggest August," Andrea added. "Peaches and apricots usually get ripe in August."

"Okay," Steven said, "but what do you think the object in the light is?"

"In my opinion, it's the great sign that appears shortly before the coming of the Lord," Paul said.

John gave a quick nod. "That's what I was thinking." The others also said they agreed.

"I'm glad to hear you all say that because I too felt it was the grand sign Joseph Smith talked about. All the inhabitants of the earth will see the sign, but won't know what it means. Many will think it's a comet or a new planet. Its meaning will also be withheld from Satan, but the Lord's people will understand it when they see it."

The others said nothing for a while, pondering the import of Steven's dream. Finally, Paul broke the silence. "Whew! I guess that only gives me seven or eight weeks to repent." At that, everyone burst into laughter. Daniel quickly whispered into Rachel's ear, explaining Paul's brand of humor.

"Steve, may I ask you a question?" Andrea Warren said.

"Of course. I just hope I can answer it."

"Doesn't the resurrection happen at the time of Christ's Second Coming?"

"Yes."

"Well, I've heard about several resurrections. I'm confused. Weren't some people resurrected at Jesus's resurrection a few days after his crucifixion? Maybe you could summarize the whole thing for us."

Steven groaned a little. "Um, well, I guess I could try."

"Swell!" cried Tania Christopher. "And why don't you include what has happened and will happen to all people, both the wicked and the righteous?"

"Whew! That's much harder to do. Maybe John or Paul—"

"Please, Steve, I want to know too," Mary said with pleading eyes and a little pout.

"Okay! Well, uh, let's see now. Hmm, for the sake of simplicity, why don't I call the wicked people 'telestials,' the decent people 'terrestrials,' and the righteous 'celestials'?"

"Great! Go for it, Steve," Paul said. "I'll correct you when you make mistakes."

The corner of Steven's mouth twisted ironically. "See that you do. All right, let's take the fate of telestial people. When they die, they go to a special place in the spirit world called 'hell,' and they stay there until the end of the Millennium. At that time they're resurrected in what we call the 'second resurrection.' Of course, telestials who are alive at the Second Coming will be consumed by fire."

"I've heard that most of the population of the earth have been telestial people, from the time of Adam to our day," said Tania Christopher.

"Yes, some people are of that opinion, but it's probably impossible to prove. Now then, we turn to 'terrestrials.' When they die, they go to a place in the spirit world called 'spirit prison,' where attempts are made to teach them the gospel. They stay there until the beginning of the Millennium, at which time they're resurrected in what's called the 'afternoon of the first resurrection.' Terrestrials *still alive* at the Second Coming will be quickened and survive the day. They'll live on into the Millennium as quickened mortals.

"When celestial people die, they go to a domain in the spirit world called 'paradise,' where many are called to teach the gospel to those in the spirit prison. In the meridian of time, at the time of Christ's resurrection, all celestials who had died prior to that time were resurrected in what is called the 'first resurrection.' All celestials who lived and died after Christ's resurrection remain in paradise until the Second Coming when they too are resurrected and caught up to meet Jesus in the clouds. That is called the 'morning of the first resurrection,' so it's still a part of the first resurrection. Of course, all *living* celestials are quickened and are also caught up to meet Christ when he appears in the heavens. Later, they live on during the Millennium as quickened mortals. I guess that gives you a very general summary of what is supposed to happen."

"But what about resurrections during the Millennium?" asked Andrea Warren.

"Well, when terrestrial and celestial people reach the age of a hundred years, they will be changed—that is, they will die and be resurrected—in the 'twinkling of an eye.' It is said that they die, but they do not 'taste death.'"

"I think I'm beginning to understand," Daniel said. "But what about translated beings? What happens to them?"

"Oh, yes, translated people. They exist in mortal bodies, but those bodies have been changed or made semi-terrestrial to prolong their lives so they can perform special missions. At the time of Christ's resurrection, the people who had been translated *before* that time experienced an instant death followed by an immediate resurrection as celestial beings. That included the people of the City of Enoch, Elijah, Moses, Nephi, Alma, and many others.

"The people translated *after* Christ's resurrection, including John the Revelator and the three Nephites, will continue as translated beings until the Second Coming and then will die and be resurrected instantaneously with celestial bodies. All these people will descend from the heavens with Christ at the Second Coming."

"What about the sons of perdition?" asked Maryann Christopher.

"Well, they are even more evil than telestial people, but at the end of the Millennium they will receive resurrected bodies that are perfect and immortal. That's because Christ's eternal sacrifice completely reversed the universal death caused by Adam's transgression.

Of all the types of people I've mentioned, the sons of perdition will be relatively few in number and are the only ones who will be resurrected unto eternal damnation . . . Okay, that's all I have to say about it. Any further questions?"

"Yes, I have one," Daniel said. "But it's sort of off the subject. I've heard many people talk about the moon turning to blood before the coming of Christ to the world. If I remember correctly, there is one reference to the blood moon in the Old Testament, two in the New Testament, and several more in latter-day scriptures. I've also heard skeptics dispute the significance of the blood moon as a precursor to the coming of Christ. They say red moons are natural events and happen regularly and therefore people of faith are wrong to make it a religious omen. So, my question is, how can we answer such scoffers?"

Steven squirmed a little and looked at John. "I don't know much about red moons. Maybe John can answer that."

John grinned because these science-related questions were right down his alley. "Well, the skeptics who enjoy attacking Mormons and other Christians misrepresent the beliefs of religious people. People of faith don't say that when you see a series of red moons, you can be sure the Lord will appear shortly thereafter. Instead, they say that before Christ does come, red moons will precede and announce his appearance. The red moons may be the result of natural occurrences, as when there is a total eclipse, or they may occur because of volcanic eruptions or smoke and fumes from the fires of planetary wars. In other words, a red moon may mean nothing in a spiritual sense or it may be a sign. Do you understand what I'm saying?" Daniel nodded and several others said yes.

"Oh, by the way," John added. "I saw a number of blood moons when we were in Israel."

"Yes!" exclaimed Mary. "I did too." The others who had been in Israel agreed that such had been the case.

"Okay, thanks for the summary, John," Steven said. He looked at Mary. "Is it time for dessert yet, sweetheart?" Everyone laughed at Steven's abrupt change of subject.

During the last week in August, several Christopher families met at a local park for a picnic. Frequently their eyes searched the skies because all of them vividly remembered Steven's recurrent dream. However, today there were only a few white clouds and the sun shone bright. Being August, it was ninety-three degrees, but the heat was tempered by a pleasant breeze. The children went swimming for a couple of hours with their parents in the park pool, and later they gathered in a grassy area near some picnic tables and played various kinds of games. At twelve thirty, the women called everyone to the tables to enjoy potato salad, tuna sandwiches, chips, watermelon, and root beer. As they ate, there was chatter, happy laughter, storytelling, and the usual swatting of flies.

At fifteen minutes before two, one of Steven and Mary's grandchildren, the son of their oldest daughter, Jennifer, seized the chance to be heard during a lull in the talk. "What's that, grandpa?" asked the precocious six-year-old, pointing upward.

Steven looked up and saw a light forming in the eastern sky. It grew slowly larger and brighter, and within a few minutes it made the sun appear dim in comparison. The Christophers stared at it intently, spellbound and unable to speak. Surprisingly, for all its brightness, it didn't hurt their eyes. In the midst of the light, they saw the strange sign that Steven had described.

"Is that it, Steve?" Tania said at last, her lips quivering.

"Yes."

"So the time has come," said Maryann in a calm voice.

At that same moment, every person on earth, even those on the dark side of the globe, saw the light and the sign. Yet they had no idea what the light and sign were or what they meant, and there was a great deal of speculation, some declaring there must be a great comet or asteroid plunging downward in a planet-destroying fall to the earth. The fear of many knew no bounds because they realized that if such a great object struck the earth, it would destroy the planet and all life on it. Others claimed it was a new sun created by some unknown astronomical phenomenon and would probably benefit mankind.

However, in Zion most of the people understood almost immediately what the sign was, and they studied the sky anxiously, waiting for what would come next.

"Steve, how long do we have before the Savior comes?" Mary asked.

"The D&C 88:95 says that after the great sign there will be silence in heaven for a half hour before the face of the Lord is revealed. It's also referred to in the eighth chapter of the Book of Revelation. My guess is the half hour will not begin until this great light disappears."

Daniel looked perplexed. "But the half hour might be a very long time because, as I understand it, one day of the Lord's time is equal to a thousand years of our time."

"That refers to the time reckoning of the great planet Kolob, which is the planet nearest the

celestial globe of God. One day on Kolob is equal to a thousand years of our time. When God

created planet earth, he had not yet given Adam a new reckoning of time, so he measured creation time by Kolob time. In other words, when the Lord said he created the earth in six days and rested on the seventh, he meant that the earth took six thousand years to create, as compared to earth time today. However, when the scriptures talk about a lapse of a half hour before the Lord appears to the world at large, they are using normal earth time, not Kolob time."

"So you mean the half hour is exactly a half hour?" Tania asked.

"Absolutely. In D&C 130:4-5, Joseph Smith explains that God's time, angel's time, prophet's time, and man's time are reckoned according to the planet on which they reside." Steven checked his watch—two o'clock.

So the Christophers waited patiently, unaware of the absolute terror felt in the hearts of most of the earth's inhabitants.

An hour later, at three o'clock, the dazzling light faded until it disappeared, and all things on the earth seemed the same as before the light came. Except for a deathly silence on earth and in heaven—no whirlwinds, quakes, storms, human cries, or natural sounds of any kind. But a short time later, in other regions beyond Zion, the world's inhabitants gave a mighty shout of joy and relief. It was not a dangerous new planet or comet after all, and the terrible turmoil and disruption seemed to be over. Many others rejoiced, declaring that the "myth" regarding the end of the world had now been proven to be a lie.

Yet new events soon overtook the world. People on the dayside of the globe saw the sun lose its power, becoming so dim that the inhabitants had trouble seeing forty feet away, and those on the nightside saw the moon turn blood red. Seeing these wonders, they again cried out in anguish, running to and fro to find explanations, but finding nothing but terror everywhere they went. The noise of their weeping and screaming ascended high into heaven.

Steven looked at his watch, struggling to read the dial in the faint light. Three thirty.

Within a few seconds of Steven's reading, the veil between this world and the unseen world was torn asunder, and the sky from one end to the other was filled with a blinding light. By some miracle, the inhabitants of the entire planet saw the light at the same time, no matter where they were. But this light was different from the first light. It was so powerful that few could gaze upon it for more than a second without pain in their eyes.

As the bright light moved rapidly toward the earth, the people began to feel immense heat, gradually increasing in intensity. They hid inside houses, caves, holes, or any enclosure they could find. Many were in open fields and sought refuge under bridges or behind fences or rock formations.

However, people of terrestrial or celestial nature felt themselves invaded by some marvelous power which radically transformed their bodies and filled their being with warmth and joy. Only the Lord's people recognized this as the power of the Holy Ghost transfiguring their bodies and protecting them from destruction.

The increasing heat came mostly from one area of the sky—the region populated by resurrected beings and the hosts of heaven. The planet increased the speed of its rotation and the source of the fire—the divine beings—moved rapidly over the surface of the earth from the east to the west.

As the devouring fire drew closer, Steven and Mary felt nothing but the protective glow of the Spirit. Before long, they heard a great voice from above, which said, "Come forth from your graves, my righteous children, and ascend into the heavens to join with your brothers and sisters." They looked around and saw many graves open and disparate particles rise from the ground and then regenerate to form living creatures. Steven knew this was the morning of the first resurrection.

A short time later, Steven saw a multitude of living mortals and resurrected people being lifted upward by some immense power to a place high above the earth. As he watched, his view began to extend outward for vast distances and he beheld innumerable hosts of people rising from everywhere on the earth, their bodies burning with celestial fire, a fire that cleansed rather than consumed. Steven realized that both he and Mary had been lifted up and transformed in the same manner as the others.

Then Steven heard a familiar voice, which said, *"Those you see around you are the newly resurrected dead and also the righteous mortals who have been transfigured as Christ was on the mount. They are the righteous saints, living and dead."*

The unseen force carried them upward fifteen or twenty thousand feet into the heavens, but even at such great height, Steven felt secure and had no fear of falling. He saw above them a multitude of living individuals descending, and he knew they were divine beings coming to meet them. He turned his eyes toward the brightest portion of the sky, in the center of the throng, and he caught sight of a glorious person dressed in red garments. That's when he realized that the greatest source of the consuming fire was that personage, not the hosts accompanying him.

Steven pointed at the man in red and said to Mary, "It's Jesus."

"Yes, I know," she replied with a radiant smile.

After the two masses of people met in the air, they began to descend together toward the earth. As they slowly drew closer, Steven could see the western continent pass by and then they were over the great ocean. At that point, he realized that as the earth rotated—even faster now—from west to east, the multitude of celestial souls were also moving west as a single body. From some fifteen thousand feet up, he could see massive clouds rise off the boiling ocean waters and dissipate before they reached the heavenly throng.

Sometime later, the ocean gave way to a second landmass, and Steven—who was much closer to the earth now—saw myriads of people below covering broad regions of the earth. They were trying desperately to hide from the intense heat and light, and those who could find no protection covered their eyes with their arms or buried their faces in the ground.

Yet it was to no avail. The celestial fire quickly became a blazing inferno, incinerating every hiding place, even disintegrating solid rock, metal, and pulverizing the ground itself. The bodies of every wicked, telestial person melted or burst into flames and died almost instantly. Steven thought, *At least they're dying quickly.*

Surprisingly, some of the people were not consumed, although they too were struggling to escape the increased temperature. It suddenly occurred to Steven that they were people of terrestrial quality—those who had not reached a state of righteousness but were basically decent, law-abiding individuals. They had not been lifted up to meet the Savior, but somehow they had been transfigured by the power of God, and their bodies glowed with inner light.

Steven and Mary continued to gaze upon the earth, and the scene was unimaginable. The world was an enormous blazing inferno. The trees, lakes, mountains, seas, fields, human constructions, and the soil itself was on fire. Steven knew this was the second great cleansing of the earth. The first cleansing had been with water at the time of the all-encompassing flood, but this time, it was being cleansed by fire.

Then the view changed again. They were "flying" over Israel, and there they saw that every plant, structure, and human being that had survived the great war, except the evil enemies of the Jews, were being shielded by the power of God. The temple especially remained intact and was more splendid than ever before. Steven knew that not all the people in Israel had progressed to a terrestrial state, but God was giving them a special dispensation because they were the people of the covenant, and most of all because they were beginning as a nation to accept Jesus Christ as their Lord.

As time passed, they went over a second ocean and finally saw another continent below. Soon they beheld the marvelous temple of the New Jerusalem, shining with glorious colors, still standing firm and erect, and Steven knew they had been transported to Zion. They saw the green earth, graced with grass, trees, rivers, lakes, hills, and human structures, all glowing with the same miraculous light as the temple. After all, Zion had already transformed itself into a righteous nation and had achieved a measure of terrestrial transcendence.

As they studied the scene below, they saw dozens of human beings moving gracefully over shining streets as if they were looking for something, their bodies aglow. Steven surmised that they were resurrected beings, perhaps part of the throng that had descended with the Lord. He looked around frantically, searching the heavens, trying again to locate the Lord in red garments, but he was nowhere to be seen.

At that moment, another powerful earthquake struck, shaking the entire planet. Steven knew it was all part of the signs of the last days and was precipitating the joining of the continents.

Steven realized that what he had seen across the planet was the baptism of the earth with fire. It marked the end of the world—that is, the end of days, or the end of time—and the fall of spiritual Babylon. From this point on, there would be a new heaven and a new earth, and the earth would soon receive its paradisiacal glory. It was the commencement of the great Millennium.

PART THREE

A New Heaven and a New Earth

Chapter 19

A fter Christ's coming in glory to bring judgment to the wicked of the world, he descended a month later—as reckoned by earth time—to visit the people of New Jerusalem. With him came Michael and one hundred and forty-four thousand high priests, who had been ordained to the exalted state of gods in the celestial world. Of course, these exalted beings would always operate—and could only operate—under the direction and authority of the infinite and eternal Father.

As the Lord and his companions hovered a thousand feet above Independence, he called to the people in a penetrating voice, commanding them to gather to one central location a few miles south of the city. The people heard him clearly and could see him as if he were twenty feet away, and his soft, gentle voice pierced every heart. This visit had been prophesied centuries earlier when the scriptures declared that the Lord would visit his people on Mount Zion.

When the people had assembled at the chosen spot, the Lord descended to a hill two hundred feet high and began his message. He blessed them and said the Father was pleased with their faithfulness. Then he described the future growth of Zion, the major events that would take place during the Millennium, and their role in those events. The message lasted two hours but seemed like only a few minutes, and when it was finished, Jesus and the divine visitors walked out among the thousands of mortals and communed with them.

Three hours later, the people began to return to their homes, discussing every detail of the Lord's message. Steven and Mary spent another hour calling on friends and relatives, inviting some of them to visit in the early afternoon. Soon they reached their own home and immediately began to straighten the living room, feeling nothing but exhilaration from the morning's proceedings.

"You know, Steve," Mary said, "I could really get used to this nice new body."

"Hah! I hear you, sweetheart. I feel the same."

"Usually long meetings wear me out, but I don't feel the slightest bit tired. I especially enjoy looking at myself in the mirror again. I'm fifty-four years old, but after the quickening, I look twenty years younger. Maybe more."

"Oh, lots more, I assure you. I can't see a single wrinkle."

"I know! And I feel a lot stronger and more energetic. In fact, I'm bursting with energy. Yep, I sure like having a terrestrial figure—I mean, body."

"Me too. Before, I always got twinges in my knees whenever I went up stairs or knelt down, but now I don't seem to have a sign of arthritis. I feel almost like a kid again."

Mary looked at him but wasn't seeing him. "Um, if a terrestrial body is this good, I wonder what a celestial body would be like."

"I don't want to throw a logical monkey wrench into your musings, but you don't actually have a terrestrial body. Your mortal body has only been transformed or quickened, just like the earth itself. A real terrestrial body would be far more magnificent and capable."

"Oh, yeah, I guess you're right—technically. But why does everyone say we used to live in a telestial existence but now we have a terrestrial one? And after the Millennium, a celestial one?"

"It's just using comparisons as a teaching aide. Actually, you can't even begin to compare the mortal world of the past with an actual telestial existence. The telestial world will be vastly different and better. And this so-called terrestrial life is nothing compared to the future terrestrial kingdom."

"I guess you're right, but still, it's very nice."

Steven shot her a sly grin. "The thing I like best is knowing I'll never have to go to the doctor or hospital again. I'll never get sick or feel any real pain. And especially, I don't have to worry about getting old and decrepit and facing a gruesome, debilitating physical decline until I die, slowly and painfully."

"My gosh! The way you describe old age!"

"Well, sometimes that's the way it was."

"Listen, I don't want to talk about unpleasant things. Steve, do you believe that everyone on earth will receive the same blessings—not suffering pain, disease, or sorrow, and living until they're a hundred years old and then changing instantly?"

"People still have their free agency, and because of that, some will commit sin."

"Oh no! I thought everyone would obey the laws of the gospel, and that's why Satan will be bound during the Millennium."

"Most people will, and their children also. The knowledge of God and his Son will fill the whole earth, but in spite of that, some people won't accept that knowledge. Joseph Smith even said there'll be wicked men on earth during the Millennium—I assume that means wicked women too," he added with a knowing wink. "Joseph also said that the nations who don't come to Jerusalem to worship the true God will receive the judgments of the Lord, and if they persist in their rebellion, they will eventually be destroyed." Mary gave a deep sigh at the words "wicked" and "destroyed."

Steven added, "Brigham Young said not all the inhabitants of the earth will join the Church during the Millennium, for there'll be as many sects and parties during that time as before the Second Coming. At another time, President Young said that when Christ comes, the world will see who he really is, but that will not automatically make them Latter-day Saints, and they'll still have the freedom to be members of other religions. However, they won't be permitted to blaspheme God or deny Christ as the Son of God, because every knee shall bow and every tongue confess Christ's true nature. All these ideas are found in President Young's Journal of Discourses."

"Are there statements in the scriptures to support that idea of bad people living during the Millennium?"

"Yes. In Isaiah 65:20, the prophet talks about conditions during the Millennium and says, 'There shall be no more thence an infant of days, nor an old man that hath not filled his days: for the child shall die an hundred years old; but the sinner being an hundred years old shall be accursed.' Also, Zechariah 14:16-18 says that all heathen nations who don't come to Jerusalem to worship the God of Israel will be punished."

"That's very disappointing to me," Mary said sadly. "I always believed everyone would be righteous during the Millennium and the wicked would be removed from the earth before then."

"You know, I think the problem lies in the meaning of the words 'sinner' and 'the wicked.' These words will no longer refer to murderers, adulterers, thieves, and others we used to call 'wicked' in Old America. Instead, they'll refer to those who are living a terrestrial law—at least in the beginning. They were good enough to avoid the burning, but during the Millennium, they'll still have their old habits, such as the inability to reject false beliefs in order to accept the gospel of Christ. They'll still be engaged in the pursuit of wealth, self-advancement, criticizing others, jealousy, and selfishness. And since they have free agency, some will gradually corrupt themselves and descend to a lower level of morality."

"In other words," Mary observed, "their former faults and weaknesses become serious sins now that we live in a world where the standards have been raised and we have further light and knowledge."

"Exactly! That's what I was trying to say."

Mary frowned, her eyes perplexed. "Do you think the rebellious people will reap the benefits of good health and a quick, painless transformation to immortality when they reach the end of their lives?"

"Well, Isaiah seems to say that many sinners will live until they reach a hundred, but I don't see why they should automatically live that long or enjoy the fruits of a healthy, pain-free life. It just doesn't make sense. In any case, they certainly won't be changed from death to immortality in the twinkling of an eye. That's what Isaiah means when he says the sinner will be accursed at the end of his life."

"Do you think 'accursed' means they'll be sent to hell after they die?"

"No, I believe it means their old age will be debilitating and their death slow and maybe painful. After this life, they'll probably be sent to the spirit prison, not to hell. Of course, this stuff gets into the realm of personal opinion." Steven saw her face cloud over. "But don't be sad, Mary. Those people will be the exception, at least until the very end of the Millennium."

She paused, apparently trying to absorb that last comment. "Oh, right. You're referring to the final war."

"Exactly! During the very last period of the Millennium, probably the last fifty years or so, a great number of people will rebel once more against God because of their pride and lustful desires. That fact alone shows that such rebellion would always have been at least possible during the earlier portion of the thousand-year epoch."

Mary groaned. "We won't have to be a part of it, will we?"

"I don't know. If we remain faithful until we die, we'll be transformed into celestial beings. The great war of Gog and Magog will be waged by Satan and his evil spirits and wicked mortals against celestial beings and quickened mortals. Of course, the celestial beings can't be killed."

"But neither can evil spirits. So does that mean the conflict will only be a war of words and principles and not of weapons?"

"I really doubt it. That kind of war was already played out in the preexistent War in Heaven. Of course, people will compare and debate philosophies, but I believe there'll be direct physical conflict also. That's why God will end it by sending fire down from heaven to consume the wicked."

Mary sighed again. "Maybe Father in heaven will insist that all you men do the fighting."

Steven laughed. "I'm sure you won't even have to be there. When John comes, why don't you ask him about the existence of wicked people during the Millennium? He usually has interesting ideas."

"Okay, I'll do that."

Shortly after noon, the door opened, and several family members stuck their heads inside. "Come in, come in," said Steven. They streamed through the door, followed by Doug and Elizabeth Cartwright. Soon the room was filled with chatter and bubbling laughter.

"Where are Daniel and Rachel?" Mary asked.

"Daniel told me they'd be a little late," Paul explained.

A few minutes later, Daniel and Rachel arrived, followed by Ruther Johnston. Steven let them chat for a while longer and then said, "Well, what did you think about Christ's message on the hill this morning?"

"It was unbelievable!" exclaimed Tania Christopher. "When Jesus and Michael descended to the hillock, I had to cry. The Spirit was so strong." The others nodded, most with moist eyes.

"I'm not sure I understood all of the Lord's message," Rachel said.

"Maybe John could go through it for us," Steven suggested.

"Yes, John, please do," said Mary. They heard knocking, and Mary hurried to the door and let Andrea and her husband, Preston Moore, into the room.

Steven retrieved two chairs for them from the kitchen. "Glad you came when you did. John was about to give us a summary of the meeting today."

"All right, I'll try to summarize the main message as best I can," John said, "but I want you guys to fill in what I forget or correct me if I make mistakes. Well, let's see. Basically the Lord told us that we'll now live under a theocratic government. Since our citizens are currently about ninety percent members of the Church, most of the government leaders will be LDS. However, non-Mormons will be welcome to seek office."

Maryann Christopher raised her hand, and John nodded for her to go ahead. "I understand we'll still be under the Constitution and that the government will be organized in almost the same way as it was before Christ's coming."

"That's right," John replied. "Douglas will still be the president and Steven the governor of Missouri, and we'll continue to hold elections for offices. I've heard many people say that Christ will create a government similar to that under Moses in ancient times, and that's true but with some differences."

"How was Moses's government arranged?" Andrea asked.

"Well, at first Moses was trying to run the government by himself, acting as judge, lawgiver, and administrator. But then his father-in-law, Jethro, told him he was not acting wisely, for instead of doing all the work, he should allow the people to elect subordinate leaders. I'd say they ended up with a theocratic representative republic. Moses was not elected by the people but was chosen by God, and the laws were based on principles revealed to Moses by the Lord. The people elected over seventy-eight thousand leaders to govern a nation of more than three million people. Those leaders were organized on at least five levels and acted as judges and administrators. Nevertheless, Moses had the power to approve or reject the leaders elected on the upper levels."

"How will our government be different?" Andrea said.

"We'll have the same government as before, from local levels to the federal government, including the presidency. The political structures of our republic were divinely inspired to provide the greatest measure of freedom possible to vast populations of people, far more than three million. However, every citizen will be obliged to recognize Christ as the supreme king, lawgiver, and judge, who has the authority to approve or reject judges, leaders, and also the laws passed by legislative bodies. As Zion fills the earth, this government and Christ's authority must be accepted by all the peoples and nations of the earth. Christ won't remain on earth permanently during the Millennium but will visit from time to time."

"It'll be the most efficient and just government to have ever existed on the earth," Steven added. "We won't have to worry about evil laws, like Roe vs Wade, being approved by courts that betray the provisions of the Constitution to promote their own social agendas."

"Or presidents and congressmen buying votes by approving endless handouts to special interest groups," Paul noted.

"That's right," John said. "Christ will stop all attempts or movements toward evil, such as vote buying, lobbying, party politics, greedy politicians plundering the wealth of the people, exploitive businesses, and mass brainwashing of the people by duplicitous leaders and the media. Fortunately, we already did away with almost all of that in New Zion, and we established a righteous society like the City of Enoch, in which there were no rich or poor."

Maryann took Paul's hand, her face glowing with happiness. "So the kindness, service, and love we experienced everywhere in New Zion will continue and be even more complete and wonderful in the future?"

"Yes, I'm sure it will," Steven said. He noticed the bewildered look on Ruther's face. "Ruther, do you have a question?"

Ruther looked up in surprise. "Well, um, I guess I does. What did Jesus say about lost scriptures? I'm fearin' I didn't get the gist of that."

"I think I can answer that," Paul said. "In his message, the Lord explained that God revealed his gospel to many nations throughout history, but we only know about a relatively small number of those revelations. We have the Bible, the Book of Mormon, the Doctrine and Covenants, the Pearl of Great Price, and the scriptures the Ten Tribes brought with them, but his words to many other peoples have been lost or hidden from us. Still, all of them have been preserved somewhere by the power of God."

Steven saw Ruther's eyes bulge a little and realized that Paul's statement must be very hard for the old mountain man to swallow because all his life he had believed that the Bible alone was the only true and complete word of God.

"Yuh know," Ruther said, "I done read those stories the tribes brung with 'em, and I'll have ta admit they was purdy revealin' and convincin'. But what others are yuh talkin' about?"

"There are many we can't name," Paul replied, "but we do know about others—sealed parts of the Book of Mormon, Adam's Book of Remembrance, the writings of the ancient patriarchs, the prophecies of Enoch, most of the writings of an ancient people called the Jaredites, and others too numerous to mention."

"But tell me now," Ruther said, "how come yuh don't have them scriptures?"

"On that, I'm not completely sure," Paul said. "Steven?"

"Primarily for two reasons," Steven said. "Many scriptures have been lost through the neglect and sinfulness of record keepers. Others were withheld by God until the people became righteous enough to understand and accept them. In his talk this morning, the Lord promised that all the things we lack will soon be given to us."

"I hate to change the subject," Mary said, "but I wanted to ask John a question. Of course, any of you can jump in if you wish."

"What question?" John said.

Mary cleared her throat. "Before you arrived, Steven gave me references showing that there will be wicked people during the Millennium. I was surprised because I had always thought Satan would be bound at that time by the righteousness of the people, and so I used to believe no one would be wicked during the Millennium. Can you clear it up for me?"

John paused for a while, apparently organizing his thoughts. "Well, we know God has always given man his agency, and since that's true, people will use that freedom to do both good and bad. The more they choose good, the more freedom they'll gain, but the more they choose evil, the less freedom they'll end up with. It's always that way in any stage of existence—in the preexistence, in mortality, during the Millennium, and in the eternal worlds to come."

Rachel Christopher, so recently a member of the Church, looked shocked. "Do you mean there'll be sinners in heaven, in the celestial kingdom?"

"Definitely. You must remember that Lucifer and billions of his angels rebelled against God in the preexistence, during the War in Heaven. Wasn't that the ultimate wickedness? Of course, their ability to sin in other ways was greatly restricted by the circumstances. For example, spirits didn't possess physical bodies, so they couldn't commit murder or sexual sins, but they could lie, steal, cheat, and rebel against God. In the future celestial world, some of the inhabitants living there will be able to produce spirit children, and those children will have agency, and where agency exists, there too is the potential for sin."

"I've never thought of it that way before," said Preston Moore.

"Did I answer your question, Mary?" John asked.

"Yes. By adding your ideas to Steven's, I believe that I have a clearer understanding of the possibilities."

For several hours, they continued to discuss sin during the Millennium, the lost scriptures, and the great changes that had recently been wrought upon the hearts, minds, and bodies of Zion's citizens. They also marveled over the great increase of beneficial plant life all around them. None of the useful plants had been destroyed, but every noxious weed had been eradicated and showed no signs of reappearing. Even beautiful new plants, unknown before in Zion, had begun to blossom in radiant colors throughout the land.

A few days after the gathering in Steven's home, Steven, Mary, Douglas, and Elizabeth rushed on foot toward the temple a half mile away. They had been summoned by the Lord and wanted to make sure they weren't late, even though he had not mentioned a specific time. Nevertheless, their efforts to hurry were futile because at nearly every corner they were stopped by passersby and people working in their yards. Dozens of people, many they didn't know, greeted them with smiles and hugs and asked if they needed a ride or anything else.

"Wow!" Steven exclaimed. "People have always been thoughtful and friendly in Zion, but this is unreal. It must be your fault, Doug. It's what you get for being our famous president."

"Yeah right! I don't know any of these people, and I doubt many of them know me. You well know I try hard to keep a low profile. You don't see my mug on TV all the time like the presidents of Old America."

"You boys are silly," Elizabeth said. "It has nothing to do with being famous. These people are simply full of love and really care about others."

"That's right," Mary said. "They're behaving pretty much like they used to in New Zion. The only difference is they're doing it with a lot more joy and exuberance. It certainly helps to be free of want, pain, and physical impairments, and to know you'll never suffer disease and death in the usual sense."

"You're right, of course," Steven said. "Even in New Zion, the people greeted their friends and neighbors by their first names and were overjoyed at seeing one another's accomplishments, instead of being jealous and critical. They learned to look for the good in every person, without noticing faults. The same seems to be true even more now. Everyone strives to live the spirit of the gospel, not just the letter."

"Well said," Douglas replied, "but I think we should try a bit harder to get to the temple as soon as possible. We don't want to keep the master waiting."

They continued their short journey, trying to minimize the time spent greeting people. A quarter of a mile later, they were joined by President Wilford Benson, the prophet. Though he was eighty-four years old, he looked entirely different now from the way he did just before the beginning of the Millennium. His hair was still white, but his face had lost the old wrinkles and blemishes, and his step was strong and brisk. Before, his body had been weak and bent over and his legs crooked, but now he was as strong and straight as a forty-year-old. He greeted them with a cheery hello and embraced each of them in turn. Then he set off toward the temple at a pace the others found hard to match.

Finally, they reached the temple grounds and saw several beings standing near the entrance. Steven recognized the Lord and Michael but didn't know who the other two were, a man and a woman.

"Bless you for coming," said Jesus as the newcomers approached.

"Did we keep you waiting?" asked President Benson.

"Oh, no," Jesus replied. "We knew you'd be held up a little by the friendly people, and we had things to talk about. You all know Michael, of course?"

"Certainly," said Mary. "Adam-ondi-Ahman."

"Yes, indeed." Jesus gestured toward the woman and the other man. "This is Adam's wife, Eve, and this is Gabriel, whom you know as Noah."

The four celestial people warmly embraced the transfigured mortals, and Steven felt an increase in warmth and joy burn through his heart at each embrace.

"I asked you to come for several reasons," Jesus said. "Let's get right to the point." He looked at President Benson. "I want you to initiate the greatest missionary effort in the history of this planet, using all the resources at your command. I have chosen one hundred and forty-four thousand high priests from all over the earth, and they are now here in Zion. They will remain on earth to help organize and direct the activities of your missions. I want you to start your missionary efforts in Israel. In that land, you will establish my Church and commence the work of temple ordinances."

Steven noticed dark clouds beginning to form in the western sky.

"I also want you to expand genealogical research as never before. Establish libraries for this purpose in every city in this nation and in other nations. I will send you hundreds of thousands of beings from the spirit world to help you in this effort. Many of them will bring their own records and books of remembrance. You must tie together the lineage of the entire human race from the time of Adam until today." Steven was shocked because Zion already comprised five thousand cities, averaging a population of five thousand each. Of course, there were also thousands of smaller communities. The only really large cities were Independence and Salt Lake City, both having a population of about two hundred thousand.

The clouds grew darker in the west, and it began to sprinkle. At the same time, the sun shone bright in the other part of the sky. Yet Jesus continued to give instructions, and none of the celestial beings seemed the slightest bit concerned by the rain falling on them.

Suddenly the Lord paused and looked up, his face transfigured by a smile. In the western sky, a beautiful rainbow had formed. Mary looked up too and said, "Oh! I'm so grateful we still have the normal seasons. I love the rain and the snow and especially rainbows."

"I love them too," Jesus said, holding his hands out to feel the rain. "However, the Father sent this one to remind me of something. Soon we will have very special visitors."

As the Lord spoke those words, a light formed in the heavens and grew so radiant that most shadows disappeared on the earth. Steven stared at the center of the light, surprised that it didn't hurt his eyes. He supposed that his eyes had been transformed in some way to allow him to see more acutely without discomfort. Then the light concentrated around a central focal point and moved closer to the earth as a shining conduit that was broad as the boundaries of New Jerusalem.

Before long, Steven was able to make out people in the conduit, and they were approaching with amazing speed. He glanced down and made out the land of Zion far below him and getting farther away by the second.

Gazing around, he saw the same people who had been with him in front of the temple, including the Christ, and beyond them thousands of mortals ascending just as he was. *I'll never get used to this business of flying around miles above the earth*, he thought.

When they reached the body of shining beings, the heavenly hosts, hundreds of thousands of them, swarmed around the quickened mortals, smiling happily and embracing them just as beloved, long-separated family members would do. Steven was astounded that all of them acted as if they were interacting on solid ground, without the slightest regard for the fact that they were thousands of feet above the earth.

Then, after what seemed less than half an hour, the entire mass of people, divine and mortal, started moving toward the earth, and Steven nearly swallowed his tongue at the dizzying drop. It reminded him of the worst roller coaster ride he had ever been on. He tried hard to divert his mind from the experience, asking himself who this new crowd of celestials could be. But suddenly it hit him—the City of Enoch.

At last they alighted surprisingly softly on the temple grass and everywhere else in New Jerusalem, and Steven found himself once again in front of the temple. He was especially relieved to see his precious wife standing near him. Yet now another personage—a man of radiant appearance, short of stature, with long black hair—had joined the former group.

Michael grinned at Steven and said, "All this ascending and descending is kind of hard to get used to, isn't it, Steven?" Steven was still breathless, and Michael didn't wait for him to reply. "Do you know who this is?" He pointed to the new person.

"I, uh, don't know for sure, but I can guess." The short man stepped up and gave Steven a full-body hug so strong that he heard a vertebra in his back snap into place. Steven couldn't prevent the next thought from popping into his head. *Hey! This guy's better than a chiropractor.* "I think he might be the prophet Enoch."

"Right you are," Michael said. Enoch proceeded to embrace every person in the group, including Jesus and President Benson.

"Do you have something for me?" the Lord asked Enoch.

"Absolutely." Enoch shouldered out of what looked like a leather backpack, placed it on the grass, removed a very large book that was made up of parchment sheets bound together in a leather frame, and handed it to Jesus. Steven knew it was the famous lost Book of Enoch, and he was itching to get his hands on it. But what good would it do him, for he knew it was written in the Adamic language, a tongue he had no knowledge of whatsoever?

"You brought thirty copies of this book, Enoch?" Jesus asked.

"Yes, certain men who came with me have them nearby."

The Lord nodded and turned to Steven, handing him the book. "As a reward for your obedience, Steven, I lend this book to you in order that you might be one of the first mortals to read it."

"But I can't, Master, I don't know the Adamic language."

"Look at the book," the Lord said.

Steven opened the book and was struck by the tiny, perfectly formed words written across the first page, from left to right. He turned the page and saw that the back of it was also covered by beautiful small words. He turned back to the first page and read aloud, "Behold, when I reached the young age of sixty-five, the Lord appeared to me in all his glory and called upon me to preach repentance unto this wicked and perverse generation." Steven looked up in surprise. "Hey, this is written in English. I can read it."

"No," the Lord said. "It is written in the original tongue of the eternal Gods, the language spoken in infinite realms throughout the vast immensity of the universe."

"I'm reading the Adamic language!"

Jesus couldn't avoid smiling at Steven's consternation. "Of course, and you've been hearing it and speaking it for some time now. An hour ago, I removed a portion of the veil from the minds of you five mortals in order to allow you to remember your native tongue, the language you spoke for thousands of earth years in the celestial realm of the Father."

The father of the human race chuckled. "Now you see one of the main reasons why I told you at Adam-ondi-Ahman that I couldn't give you lessons in the Adamic language."

Steven shot Adam a grin. "I understand now. You were right."

"We will also give President Benson and President Cartwright a copy," Jesus said. "Brethren, be sure you make those copies available to your dear wives, or you will hear from me personally. All right, that concludes our meeting for today." The Lord smiled one last time, and all the celestial visitors suddenly disappeared as if they had stepped into another dimension.

As Mary, Steven, Elizabeth, and Douglas walked slowly back to their homes, which were only a block apart, they caught sight of a shining figure moving gracefully toward them. The personage was grinning broadly, and at first Steven feared it might be Lucas Nigel, striving once again to appear as an angel of light. But then he remembered that Lucas had pretty much been banned from the planet, at least for the foreseeable future.

At last, they could make out the features of the smiling being, and all of them recognized him at the same time—Jarrad Babcock, Paul's best friend, in a glorious new resurrected body.

"Hey, guys," Jarrad said. "At last, people I know."

"You're alive and well!" Mary exclaimed happily. Then she stopped herself. "Well, of course you're alive. Wow! All these recent changes and transfigurations have boggled my brain."

"Yep. Here I am in the flesh, so to speak. And believe me, very much alive! Still, I haven't yet learned to completely handle this suppression of glory stuff. I'm always afraid of frying someone." Then he guffawed at his own humor.

"How did you get here?" Steven asked. "And when?"

"I came with the Enoch crowd. Let me explain. When Christ came in glory to the world, I was resurrected with all the other celestials—man, am I grateful the Lord didn't condemn me for being such a smart-aleck joker. Then Michael sent me straightaway on a mission. To another world—don't ask me to locate it. Anyway, I was given the assignment to alert Enoch that he needed to organize his people and hie down here to earth. So that's what we did. I don't know how it happened, but I'm guessing it took all of three minutes to travel across the universe."

"Can I ask you a question?" Elizabeth said.

"You bet. Fire away, Liz."

"Well, I always had the idea that when the City of Enoch came, I'd see a huge landmass floating down from heaven, maybe as big as the Gulf of Mexico basin, supporting thousands of marvelous, golden buildings swarming with millions of divine beings."

"Yeah, I had that same idea before I actually got there and Enoch told me that the word *city* meant the citizens, not the land or buildings. Too wasteful and expensive to transport all that stuff is how he put it. Enoch gave me a tour of his city, and it was indeed spectacular. Still, I'd say it was about the size of the old Los Angeles County. Certainly not even close to the Gulf of Mexico." Jarrad fell into snickering, and the mortals burst into laughter at hearing him.

After they all finally controlled themselves, Steven said, "What are you doing wandering around alone like this, Jarrad?"

"I was looking for Paul's house, but things are so different, I didn't have any luck. I'm not omniscient, you know, at least not yet—I expect that to come in a month or two." More laughter from the mortals, and this time the immortal glared at them with mock sternness. After Steven had given him directions to Paul's home, they discussed what Jarrad had undergone in Israel, his untimely death, and his experiences at being resurrected.

Just before they separated, Jarrad said, "Well, I guess I'll go and track down Paul. By the way, I suggest you prepare for what's going to happen in the next few days."

Steven shifted the Book of Enoch from one hand to another. "What's that?"

"I'll tell you because I don't want you to be shocked. It's about the afternoon of the first resurrection. The terrestrials who have worked their way out of the spirit prison and those remaining there still will soon be released and united with their restored terrestrial bodies. They've been waiting ever since the days of Adam and are extremely anxious to move on to the next stage."

"Where will they go after they're resurrected?" Mary asked.

"Some will remain here for a time during the Millennium to help with genealogy and missionary work, but most will be—what's the word—deported to interim terrestrial worlds already prepared for them by God. Later, after the final judgment, they'll have to organize their own planets, with the help of celestials, for their permanent residences. Okay, take care now, I've got to go. Remember, I love you all and I assure you we'll see each other often in the future." Jarrad suddenly popped the side of his head with his hand. "Man! I almost forgot something very important."

"What?" Mary asked, surprised.

"There's somebody special waiting for you at your house. He traveled with me to the City of Enoch, and we left together when everyone got word that we needed to hie to earth. Somehow I lost track of him in all the excitement. As you can guess, moving across the universe in a few seconds can really boggle your brain."

"Jarrad, back to the point. Who's waiting at the house?" Steven asked.

"Well, I don't know if I should say. He wanted to surprise you. He'll kill me if—"

Mary stomped her foot impatiently. "Who is it, Jarrad?"

"I can only give you a hint. It's someone you love very much and lost several years ago. But now he's back. Okay, toot-a-loo, y'all."

The mortals watched in amazement as Jarrad flew down the street without even moving his legs.

"It's got to be Andrew," Steven announced.

They all rushed as quickly as possible to Mary and Steven's home, including Douglas and Elizabeth. Bursting through the front door, Steven saw his youngest son, Andrew Christopher, who was killed seven years ago in Zion's war with UGOT, grinning at them as he leaned against the kitchen door.

"Wow! You guys can sure make a racket when you're in a hurry. I heard you coming from two blocks away."

Steven laughed and said, "Nah. We're as quiet as church mice. It's the fault of your new super hearing."

At that they all rushed Andrew and overwhelmed him with hugs and kisses. This went on for about five minutes until Andrew looked just about kissed out.

"You look like you did just before you left us," Mary exclaimed. "Except now you're all bright and shiny." Andrew was twenty-five years old when he was killed and appeared to be the same age now. "You don't even have bullet holes in you anymore."

"Nope," Andrew said with a grin. The resurrection took care of that. I'm just surprised I ended up with a celestial body."

"But why?" Elizabeth asked. "You were always a noble soul. A bit mischievous sometimes"—she said with a wink—"but basically a good, obedient son."

"Sit down, everyone," Steven said. "We need to get reacquainted with Andrew and hear everything that has happened to him in the last seven years."

Andrew rose from the floor, flew across the room, and landed lightly onto the couch just like superman in the old movies. "And I want to hear about you guys. I understand from the celestial grapevine that you've had some harrowing experiences."

Chapter 20

❧

A few days later, during the first week of October, the citizens of Zion saw another miracle in the early afternoon. Unexpectedly, there was a mighty earthquake, and hundreds of thousands of graves were opened throughout the land of Zion, and disintegrated remains rose a few feet into the air and instantly reformed into beautiful terrestrial bodies, animated by happy spirits, who rejoiced at once more having tangible bodies, this time bodies that were strong and magnificent. These terrestrial bodies looked almost like celestial bodies, except not as glorious.

In the scriptures this was called the "afternoon of the first resurrection." Steven and Mary marveled over the infinite power of God that could produce such a miraculous event, and they knew this same scene was occurring all over the earth.

Most of the terrestrials shot upward in vivid shafts of light and disappeared into the heavens, but some remained and began to mingle with the celestials and mortals still walking the earth.

Of course, the celestial beings had to restrain a measure of their full glory. The expressions of joy and love between the various categories of beings was unbelievable and beyond anything the mortals had experienced before.

❧

In the following decades, Zion grew and prospered, extending its power and influence throughout the Western Hemisphere, and from there across the entire Western World. Hundreds of thousands of missionaries, led by the hundred and forty-four thousand sanctified high priests, were sent to all corners of the earth, spreading the gospel message and converting many.

There was a special effort to convert the people of Israel, and within one decade, nearly every Israeli accepted Jesus as the Son of God. They joined the Church in droves and build five new temples in a few short years, and in those temples, they no longer practiced the ancient rites of sacrifice but offered up the sacrifice of their hearts and received their endowments according to the gospel plan. David Omert still ruled as the head of the nation, and the rapid changes in Israel were largely the result of his untiring efforts to serve the Lord.

Steven and Mary served a three-year teaching mission in Israel and then were transferred to Japan, where they served another four years. Steven had the advantage of speaking Japanese fluently, and he and Mary helped to convert over two hundred of the people they taught.

At the same time, the Church launched the greatest genealogical research program in history. Nearly every church member participated, and those who reached an impasse received special help from genealogical experts from across the veil. As the result of this mighty effort, the LDS temples in all lands held nonstop sessions six days a week.

When Steven approached one hundred years old, he was still mentally bright and physically strong, and on his hundredth birthday, at three o'clock in the afternoon, he was changed to an immortal state in the twinkling of an eye. Although he was now a celestial being, he still lived with his beloved wife, engaging in the same activities as before.

A few years later, Mary too went through the same experience, and her emotional exaltation was far more expressive than her husband's. "Steve, look at me," she said with a huge grin on her face. They were in their backyard working in their garden. He looked up and saw her balancing a hundred-pound stone in her right hand, without the slightest sign of strain. "Pretty good for a hundred-year-old girl, eh?"

"Wow! You must be stronger than I am." Steven remembered dropping a fifty-pound rock on his foot three weeks earlier. He had felt the pressure as the rock hit him, but when he removed his shoe and looked, there was no damage at all, not even a scratch. Somehow he had felt the impact and could measure the exact amount of force applied to his foot, and yet he hadn't even felt a twinge of what he used to call pain.

Mary gave a big laugh. "Yep. Listen, my weak little husband, you better not mess with me now."

Steven rushed forward, took the stone from her grasp and heaved it twenty feet into the air and halfway across the backyard. Next he swept Mary up in his arms. "I'll mess with you if I want. You're still my wife, you know." He put her down and gave her his usual wet, sloppy kiss right on the mouth. Mary didn't resist one bit.

Most of Steven and Mary's friends were also resurrected with celestial bodies. Even Ruther Johnston, when he was eighty-five years old, finally renounced his Baptist beliefs and accepted the restored gospel, and his subsequent commitment to the Church and its teachings was absolute. When Steven asked him why he had made his decision, Ruther responded that he finally realized how genuinely unchristian it was to condemn other religions for not believing the way the Baptists did and how foolish it was to accept the inane belief of evangelical and born-again Christians that "true" believers would do little more in eternity than sing the praises of Jesus.

After about one hundred and fifty years, eighty percent of earth's population had heard and accepted the gospel and had been baptized into the Church of Jesus Christ of Latter-day Saints. Still, there were some who resisted, and when prominent national leaders balked, often the people did also. Even though they acknowledged the moral and political leadership of the Son of God, they refused to accept the gospel, pay religious homage to the Christ, and visit the center stakes of Zion in humility and faith. Most of the rebellious peoples were those formerly called the "heathen" nations.

By that time, the continents had joined into one great landmass that people called Pangaea, surrounded by a gigantic sea, which comprised all the former oceans and seas of the planet. The New Jerusalem and Old Jerusalem were now only thirty-two hundred miles apart, rather than over sixty-five hundred miles apart as they had been before the Second Coming. The main role of the New Jerusalem was to promulgate divinely inspired constitutional laws to the world, laws ratified and overseen by Christ himself, and the primary burden of Jerusalem was to teach gospel truths.

At the beginning of the third century of the Millennium, the Father finally decided to bring judgment against the rebellious. He summoned his Beloved

Son to appear before his celestial throne and told him to begin applying pressure upon the disobedient, at first little more than gentle persuasion. Since Jesus was one with the Father—of the same mind and heart—and in the "express image" of God's person, the Lord knew what to do.

After his visit to the Father, Christ returned to earth in a blink of the eye and commanded the elements to send forth little or no rain upon the recalcitrant nations. It didn't take long for the leaders of those nations to realize that something was seriously amiss, and they sent envoys to Jerusalem to beg Israeli leaders to share their abundant supplies of water, preferably by building concrete aqueducts or by running steel supply lines hundreds of miles to their countries.

The Israelis refused.

They explained to the envoys that the only way their nations could obtain water was to obey the Lord who created and provided water, and if they did, God would send them rain. Some of the rebellious leaders humbled themselves quickly and traveled to Old Jerusalem or New Jerusalem to kneel before the sacred temples and pay homage to Jehovah, who was none other than Jesus Christ, the Jewish Messiah. These leaders brought thousands of their citizens with them, and they all returned home quickly when they learned that rain was falling in their homelands. When all these people finally reached their destinations, they spread the word concerning the magnificent power of the God called Jesus Christ.

However, a few obstinate rulers still resisted and let their people suffer drought and famine. In the face of this terrible catastrophe, the people eventually rose up and eliminated those foolish leaders, some peacefully, some violently. Then they chose new rulers who were willing to travel regularly to Zion to worship the God of the earth.

Within two years, the number of those converted to the Church rose to over ninety percent of the total population, and the remaining ten percent expressed a sincere belief in Christ but declined to join his Church. For this, the Lord did not punish them but allowed them to choose for themselves. As a result, there were still dozens of Christian denominations on the earth during the rest of the Millennium.

From then on, the earth was peopled by a largely righteous population, and the land blossomed in every clime until the earth became as beautiful and fruitful as the Garden of Eden, and there was continual peace, prosperity, and cooperation among men.

In spite of that, there were a few who secretly resented and criticized the obedient and bided their time until they could push themselves into prominence and declare themselves to be the true rulers of the earth. They exemplified the almost universal desire in the hearts of all men and women—from the beginning of time—to be gods without earning that right. Most people recognized that they had that secret yearning for ultimate control over their own lives and the lives of others, and they resisted and suppressed that foolish desire, but some would always strive to assert themselves over others in every way they could.

Chapter 21

Toward the second half of the last century of the Millennium, fifty years before the scheduled end of the earth, a great secret society, a conspiracy of enormous wickedness, after the ancient order of Cain, gained power and influence among men. The seed had been there all along, hiding in the hearts of individuals lusting for wealth and power. Because of this hidden conspiracy, promoted by dynamic leaders, many men once again began to choose wickedness over righteousness.

The father of this malignant movement was Lucifer himself. He and his angels rejoiced to see their vile practices, false philosophies, and wicked inclinations rage in the hearts of men. The plague spread quickly across the earth like an all-encompassing, soul-destroying, deadly virus. Within thirty years, there were millions of these operators of evil, and they won the support of three quarters of the world's population.

This remarkable reversal of circumstances had many surprising effects. Since the entire earth had once again become corrupted by wicked men, all the terrestrial and celestial beings, unable to endure the wickedness, left the planet and sought refuge on heavenly spheres. And even the quickened mortals were affected—they returned to the state of ordinary mortals and consequently suffered disease, pain, and normal human deaths at the end of their lives. The earth itself returned to a "telestial" state and groaned within her bowels at the iniquity of mankind.

Soon, different parties of conspirators began to wage war against one another, striving to gain precedence, and after a decade of violent struggle, resulting in the slaughter of millions of people, the most powerful party, called the People's Liberation Consortium, gained the upper hand. Immediately, the Consortium murdered the leaders of all the competing parties, and then established a one-world, all-powerful, tyrannical government.

This government enslaved the entire population of the earth, appropriating most of the wealth, resources, and property of the people, and establishing thousands of abusive rules and regulations for citizens to live by. They set up elaborate spy networks, using sophisticated computers and video monitors in every home, public building, and street corner, and paying tens of thousands of citizen informants to report even the smallest infractions of the so-called "laws."

Where there was happiness and freedom before, now there was nothing but misery and slavery. Those who broke the laws or resisted or dared raise a voice of protest were summarily imprisoned or executed. This monstrous government was controlled by a club of twenty-five wicked oligarchs, who chose a new "president" every two years by secret ballot. The current president was called Gog of Enith.

When the Consortium gained ultimate power, the decent people of the earth fled to the countryside, seeking safety in small groups in the wildest regions of the planet. They lived almost like animals, barely eking out an existence on roots, shrubs, insects, and occasional game animals. Of course, most of these people were Christians of many denominations, including Mormons. The Consortium pursued these tiny communities with a vengeance, for they were the last threat to their universal power, and it succeeded in destroying thousands of them.

Finally, the righteous holdouts, under the guidance of five surviving apostles, organized an underground network of fighters, who used guerilla tactics to frustrate and defeat hundreds of small battle groups dispatched by the military generals of the Consortium. As the brave rebels wiped out one enemy detachment after another, they increased their knowledge of guerilla warfare and their supplies of food, weapons, and ammunition.

Then in the last few months of the Millennium, the Consortium formed six mighty armies comprised of over four million troops each. These forces were called Magog. Their orders were to march across the land in six different directions, using all types of new weapons and war machines, and to exterminate the religious "fanatics" once and for all.

The apostles learned of Consortium plans and sent out word to all their people everywhere to gather quickly to one place ten miles south of Jerusalem. Surprisingly, the Consortium had not razed the city or the temple, but they used all the holy temples as shrines to honor Satan. The decent people of the earth set out immediately for the designated place, wearing the same red garments chosen by the Consortium to identify their slaves. It took several months for some of them to reach their destination, but they had faith in God and the inspiration of their leaders to strengthen them.

It seemed like a foolish plan to gather the saints and other decent people to a single location, for surely they would not be able to defend themselves. Since their numbers were few and their weapons inferior, they would not be capable of resisting the combined might of the Consortium. Now all of them would be together in one place, easily available for destruction by vastly superior forces. When the Consortium realized where the dissidents were assembling, it ordered all its troops to redirect their march toward Jerusalem for the final showdown.

The enemy moved in and gradually surrounded the Christian forces, and their proud, evil leader, a warrior of many great victories, waited a few days before giving the order to attack, desiring to intimidate and strike fear in the hearts of the "lawbreakers." Then on the fourth day, he commanded his men to move forward from all positions and to annihilate their victims in one final, definitive battle.

However, when the evil army began their advance and opened fire with millions of weapons, they saw an astonishing phenomenon. Covering the dissident forces was a colossal, protective dome of energy, sparkling with blue and green colors. The attackers could see their targets inside the dome, but their bullets, shells, bombs, and lasers could not pierce the impenetrable force field shielding their prey.

Then something even more remarkable happened. A gleaming light began to form high in the heavens above them, and the intensity of that light was much greater in a small area at the center. Millions of soldiers gazed at the brightness in consternation, partly covering their eyes with any object at hand. Even those wearing sunglasses had to limit the time they spent looking at the radiance. But soon they could see several personages grouped closely together, descending rapidly toward them.

Soon the ten extraterrestrial entities stopped their descent and formed a circle, each of them facing a different part of the evil army. Next, they raised their hands and pointed at the Consortium forces, and from the tips of their fingers, blue flames erupted, flashing downward like megabolts of lightning, disintegrating the attackers' bodies and machines of war. The celestial beings moved their hands slowly back and forth until Satan's army was reduced to ashes.

The "angels" who had destroyed Gog's army were Michael, Gabriel, and other resurrected beings. At the same time, thousands of other celestials had appeared in many lands throughout the earth and had incinerated the leaders and adherents of the Consortium and every other evil person on the planet. During this destruction, the families of the righteous army were protected by the powers of heaven. Their work finished, all the divine visitors vanished into the heavens, and the great energy dome dissipated.

Thus ended the second War of Gog and Magog.

Soon other wondrous events took place. A few hours after the destruction of the wicked, the remaining righteous people of the earth were transformed instantaneously from mortals to immortals and were drawn upward to meet their maker. After that, there was silence on earth for the space of two hours.

Then the second resurrection began, and billions of the dead arose in telestial bodies. Some of these people had been waiting in the spirit world since the time of Adam. These immortal bodies also were perfect and would never endure disease, pain, suffering, or death, but their brilliance and glory could not be compared to celestial or terrestrial bodies. These telestial people were also taken up into the heavens and placed somewhere that no man knows.

Finally, the second stage of the second resurrection occurred. This time, the number of people involved was far less. These were the sons and daughters of perdition. They received tangible, perfect, immortal bodies, but those bodies were devoid of light. This was the resurrection of damnation. These children of perdition were also lifted from the earth and placed in a special, temporary realm a few light years away from the earth.

At that point, a great fire descended from heaven, and the earth went through a second cleansing by fire. The heat of this burning was so great that it completely changed the earth, both inside its bowels and on its surface. As a result, the earth was transformed into a celestial planet, a massive Urim and Thummim, like a sea of glass and fire, to be peopled eventually by the righteous men and women who had lived there in mortality.

All the resurrected beings, no matter what their ultimate reward might be, would soon face Jesus Christ in the Final Judgment. At that time, they would be granted the right to inhabit the kind of worlds they merited by the degree of righteousness or unrighteousness they exhibited on the earth.

Already, the inhabitants of the earth had experienced two judgments. When they died, they were sent either to paradise, spirit prison, or hell, which are three different realms or communities found in the spirit world. That was their first judgment. Their second occurred when they were resurrected, for when they saw the type of bodies they received, they knew what their final state would be.

In spite of those two judgments, all men and women had to go through the great last judgment, when the books recording their deeds would be opened. At that time, they would have to kneel, confess their sins, and swear allegiance and obedience to the Son of Man. Only the sons and daughters of perdition would refuse to do so and thus would be cast into outer darkness, also called the lake of fire and brimstone. There they would rule over their former master—Lucifer.

They had gathered in Steven Christopher's "mansion"—nearly every family member and friend of Steven and Mary with three generations of relatives. The three Christopher boys—Andrew, Patrick, and Raymond—who had been killed in New Zion's war with UGOT, were there. Invited also was Ruther Johnston, who was now entirely spruced up in shining new clothes but still sported his proverbial beard. Ruther had not met a suitable wife during his earth life, but as soon as he was resurrected in his fantastic new celestial body, looking like he was twenty-five, dozens of unattached females had pursued him. Then at last he had chosen one of them, and the Lord promised Ruther that he himself would take time out from his busy schedule to seal the two sweethearts for all time and eternity.

Sixty-five people in one huge, exquisitely decorated family room. Yes, some of their more distant friends and relatives hadn't quite made it and were waiting on other planets, mostly temporary terrestrial globes, to stand before the great judgment bar of the Son of God.

Steven's mansion was also located on a temporary planet, which was already incredibly magnificent despite the fact that it was only a temporary "holding place" for celestials awaiting judgment. Everyone on this planet was busily engaged in designing lesson plans to teach other celestial beings all the wisdom and knowledge they had gained during their lives on earth.

Moreover, since the veil had been lifted, they could also benefit from the vast knowledge they had acquired for thousands of years in the preexistence. And their students were also their teachers in many other subjects at the same time, including history, physics, mathematics, chemistry, religion, celestial mechanics, astronomy, human physiology, genetics, logic, ethics, computer science, foreign languages, and dozens of other disciplines.

It was infinitely easier now for them to learn those subjects because their minds functioned at optimum levels, with lightning speed, without the dulling impediment of mortal bodies, and their memories were perfect. In spite of the vastly increased abilities of the students, the teachers were instructed to start with the basics and gradually increase the difficulty of the lessons over time. Experienced celestial beings, who had already mastered all the knowledge that was to be taught, wandered through the organized classrooms, gently and patiently correcting errors and misconceptions.

It would take the newbies a hundred earth years or more to master all the information and skills, and then they could move on to the deeper and more complex material, far beyond the greatest advancements of their former mortal world.

When they finally acquired enough knowledge, they would assist the designers and builders of other planets, and they themselves would help the Lord create new worlds to function as the homes of people working out their salvation with the help of the Spirit. Some day in eternity, they would be in charge of their own creations, but always under the guidance and authority of the Father and the Son.

"Steve," Mary said, "how long will the judgment take? How long do we have to wait? There must be at least a hundred billion people who need judgment."

"Maybe far more if the judgment involves the people of other worlds," Steven replied. Mary groaned loudly, and Steven couldn't keep back a laugh. "But don't worry, the judgment of righteous people is a time of glory and triumph, not one of condemnation. For the most part, the righteous will judge themselves."

"I know, but the waiting! Will the celestial people be judged first?"

"I have no idea. Listen, there'll be thousands of priesthood leaders called to judge also. That should hurry things up."

"Oh, good! I hope their wives get in on the act. Sometimes men don't have very good judgment." She gave a deep sigh while Steven stifled another laugh.

"Don't worry. I'm sure the wives will make their opinions count and rein in their husbands when they get out of line. Besides, if there's any doubt at all as to the fairness of a judgment, the case will move up to a higher authority. Ultimately, it'll be the Lord who will settle the hard cases. Remember, the Father has given all judgment to his beloved Son."

"But the waiting! The earth has already been prepared for us, so why don't we go there and do our thing while we're waiting? After all, the earth will be our final celestial home."

"Once again, I don't know. I'm not running the show."

"You know, Steve, in spite of all my increased faculties, I guess I still haven't completely mastered the moral quality of patience."

"Well, the moral qualities like patience and kindness will be the hardest things to master, but we'll have to learn them eventually if we want to be like the Father."

Mary kissed him tenderly with divine tears flowing down perfect cheeks. "You know, sweetheart, I'm glad I chose you back on earth in the little city of Provo. I can't think of anyone else I'd rather spend eternity with."

THE END

Kenneth R. Tarr taught French language and literature at Brigham Young University for fourteen years, and French and Spanish for three years at Snow College. He received a master's degree in French and Spanish at Brigham Young in 1965, and a doctorate in French at Kansas University in 1973, with a minor in medieval history.

Kenneth was born and raised in southern California and has been a member of the LDS church all his life, serving in many capacities. He and his wife, Kathy, have been married fifty-two years and have eight children and twenty-eight grandchildren. Currently they live in Utah where they operate an herb store. Kenneth enjoys writing, reading, exercising, doing repairs, and listening to good music.

End of the World is Kenneth's fourth and final novel in *The Last Days* series. The author welcomes questions and comments. You can contact him at krtarr015@gmail.com.